MW00882870

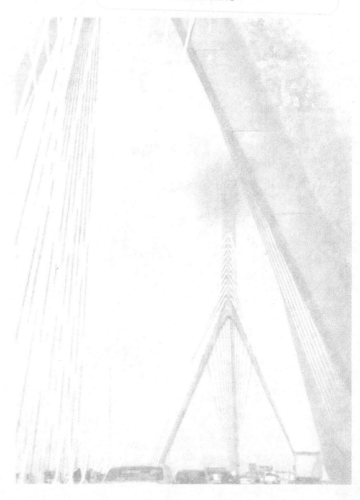

2272 40075

ALSO BY BEN MONOPOLI

The Cranberry Hush: A Novel

FORTY-SEVEN

The Painting
of Porcupine City
a novel

Ben Monopoli

For Chris

*

"Clearly the story is true even though invented...."

—Clarice Lispector, *The Hour of the Star*

The Painting
of Porcupine City

PART
ONE

The Maker of Arrows

THE PAINTING OF PORCUPINE CITY

Now the new guy held

out his hand. On top of his natural olivish complexion was a blast of neon green that went from the tips of his close-cut nails, over the first joints and fuzz of hairs to the second joints, finally fading to a mist along the back of his hand. His olive skin continued over his wrist and up underneath the sleeve of his neatly-ironed shirt. The paint might've made another person look grubby but this guy was cute enough to get away with it. Wavy, unruly hair, dark as a typewriter ribbon. Green eyes that made you want to put the pedal to the metal.

My heart went pitter-patter. "Welcome aboard," I told him, jumping up to shake the neon hand he was offering, my chair spinning behind me. *Welcome aboard* had somehow become my standard greeting for new coworkers—turnover was high at Cook Medical Publishing—and over the years it'd taken on a more and more piratey tone. I was only a few new people away from adding a *Yaarrrr*. "I'm Fletcher Bradford."

He told me his name was Mateo Amaral. He had a nice smile—or probably would if he were truly smiling; his face was pasted with that overwhelmed grin you typically see on these introductory tours. He also wore a tie, and this broke my heart a little, struck me as precious. *Awh. A tie.* New people always wore ties or power pantsuits their first day, probably expecting/hoping the job they showed up for was as glamorous as it sounded in the interview. *You poor stud*, I thought, me in my khakis and iron-scorched button-down. *You poor fuck-stallion with the weird painty hand.*

"Nice to meet you," he told me. His handshake was mediocre but his skin was surprisingly cool, with none of that typical first-day clamminess — mysteriously confident, as though the limp grip was all act. After pumping a couple times his painty hand released mine and returned to his pocket.

At the request of his tour-guide (i.e., the head I.T. guy, his supervisor) I made brief chatter about my own job, about the office in general, blah blah, while the new guy glanced around my cube looking uninterested. Then they left my cube to move on to the next — and as they left I amended my appraisal of New Guy's hair and eyes to include his killer ass. That ass and those pants were perhaps the most successful pairing since Lennon and McCartney.

I sat back down (the chair was practically still rotating, that's how brief that first encounter was) already nursing the seeds of an office crush.

That was a few days ago, and during that time the new guy wiped off the grin, ditched the tie, and otherwise blended into the maze of cubes with a skillfulness rarely seen at Cook, and which I found intriguing but ultimately disappointing. You hope for shirtless back-flips down the hallway, and what you get, if you're lucky, is a glimpse of him around the bend of a corner once or twice a day. He seemed not to talk to anyone except when it directly involved work, he arrived very early (or so I heard, not exactly being an early riser myself), and, on the Friday of his first week, I learned that he took his lunch standing in the doorway of the break room. Just standing there, as though he were afraid to enter a space with only one exit.

I wondered what color his hand would be today. Each day the color changed. Sliding past him to get at the fridge, I stole a glance. Purple. And today it went all the way to his knuckles, leaving across the back of his hand a drip that seemed to illustrate a tendon. The sloppiness was so odd in contrast to his clothes, which looked Banana Republic all the way. They were sharp and new, the pants as crisp as the shirt—you could slice open your finger on the creases of his shirtsleeves. Even without the tie he looked too dressed up for Cook. And yet, this guy who somehow got through the morning without catching a wrinkle apparently couldn't be bothered to wash his hands. It was like he was two different people.

I smirked. Yes, I wanted both of him. Preferably at the same time. It was good to have a crush at work—made the day pass quicker—but it was rare. The execs who did the hiring usually had lousy taste.

"Hi," I said.

"Hey."

He was an inch or so shorter than me, slim but not skinny. His hair hung in loose waves against his collar and against his eyebrows, the kind of hair you have to restrain yourself from grabbing to twirl with your fingers. The kind you want to find strands of on your pillow.

I opened the freezer and took out a box of Eggos with my name on it (literally), dropped two frozen discs into the toaster and pushed them down. I imagined grabbing the sink hose and soaking his hair and that crisp shirt—he probably had the perfect amount of chest hair under there. Instead I looked up at the TV suspended from the ceiling in the corner. ESPN was on but the volume was muted.

"Like baseball?" I asked.

"More of a soccer guy."

"Me too," I said, though I didn't add that it was because the guys in soccer are better looking.

When the TV faded to black right before a commercial I could see him in the reflection. He looked out of place in the harsh fluorescent light. In this light his face looked somehow naked, too vulnerable and exposed, his eyes not quite nervous, but alert. His eyebrows were thick and dark, the same color as his hair and his longish sideburns. It was the kind of face that needed a make-up of shadows to really come alive. To pop. New Guy was a night owl, I could tell.

The toaster popped-up my waffles and I squirted syrup across them and sat down at the little round table in the center of the room.

I thought I saw him glance at my brunch, but I wasn't sure, but I said anyway, by way of explanation (and small talk), "I never get up early enough for breakfast."

He nodded and took a bite of his sandwich, which looked like turkey or chicken. An open Tupperware sat on the counter by his elbow.

"Friday at last," I said, trying again at conversation. "Any big plans for the weekend? Weather looks to be a total scorcher."

He was still standing in the doorway and it was making me uncomfortable. His shoulder was against the wall, his legs were crossed casually at the ankles—the heel of his shiny wing-tips was on the hallway carpet, the toe on the lunch-room tile. He lifted his sandwich to his mouth and took another bite. Yes, purple today. Yesterday they'd been red, looking alarmingly like he'd been bleeding. Red yesterday, purple today—whatever New Guy did in the space between work hours, I guessed last night he did it with blue. Wednesday I hadn't seen him at all, but Tuesday they'd been orange. And then, of course, the famous neon green of his first day. He was a walking art project.

"No? No plans?"

"Huh? Oh. Not really, nope." He looked from the TV to me and back again. I decided he was either lying or playing coy. "Just, you know, being breezy."

"Breezy." I repeated it to see if there was meaning in the sound. "You mean like blowing on the breeze?"

"Sure," he said, with an ambiguous curve of the mouth that you might call a smirk if you were feeling generous. He had an accent, too, slight and nearly lost amid the intrigue of his hand, but undeniable nonetheless. South American, maybe. Venezuela or one of those. It could even be some kind of Mediterranean. Sicily? I'd already perused a map for country names, but the zilch I could glean from an accent and a simple outline of national borders wasn't the point. It wasn't about geography, it was an imagination exercise. I was building his character. I had a lot of free time at work.

"Blowin' on the *breeeeze*," I warbled, as though it were a chorus to an indie rock song. I looked up at the TV for a minute. Chewed some waffle. Looked over at him and nodded at one of the empty chairs. "Sit down if you want." I wished he would because frankly he was making me nervous standing there.

"S'OK," he said, but it was, judging by the quick shrug of his shoulders, a no. He continued to lean in the doorway eating his sandwich, watching the muted TV. When he was done he clapped crumbs off his painty hands, wiped his mouth with a napkin, squeezed the cover back onto his Tupperware, and turned around. As he was leaving he said, "Enjoy your breakfast." It sounded like *brefess* — like how kids say it.

As I watched him go I felt my face pop like a spring with pent-up curiosity.

Nothing had happened and yet when he left the lights seemed harsher, the air staler, as though his presence had charged the atmosphere, made it seem less like work and more like possibility. But any office crush of mine would have to do better than possibility. I wanted action.

So nice of you to ask, I thought, filling in for him. *Actually I'm hanging out with a friend this weekend. But I'd gladly blow him off if you'd rather spend it with* me.

I scraped up the last bit of syrup and licked the fork, watching the silent TV.

What was with the finger paints? Did it have anything to—

"Fletcher— Oop, didn't mean to startle you." It was Janice, my boss, knockers straining the fabric of a powder-blue blouse. Her cheeks were flushed. At lunch, weather permitting, she sat in the parking lot sunning herself like a blond-haired iguana. "Can you have chapter twenty-three of *HMOs* copyedited by the end of today? Author wants a final review."

"Sure."

She smiled, disappeared.

After rinsing my plate I went back to my desk. No sign of New Guy for the rest of the day. And then (a mixed-blessing this week) it was the weekend.

The blazing-hot morning

made the T a stuffy nightmare. Too many passengers were crammed on, sweaty and cursing the feeble a.c. Arms stuck off the handrail in front of my seat like branches ending in melting people. An old guy standing in the stairwell held a paper bag of groceries with the silver rim of a can pushing its way through the bottom. A BU jock had skin the color of cocoa; his friend sported shiny blond-haired legs curtained with swooshy basketball shorts. A sleeping baby's face screamed with heat-rash.

"*Woooh*," breathed the oldster through a waxy mustache. He hiked up his groceries in his thin, papery arms. I would've offered him my seat but no way were either of us getting around the rotund woman sitting beside me.

I stopped looking at everyone, abandoning even the jock's cocoa legs. I watched out the scratched window while the T jack-rabbited along the aboveground Green Line track. Outside pedestrians were moseying. Cars idled in late morning traffic, the air drunk over their hot hoods. The T car rounded a bend in the track and sun lashed my face. I squinted and turned away. The plastic seat vibrated beneath me. The rotund woman shifted, knocking my elbow with hers and leaving in her wake the cool evaporation of transferred sweat. I shuddered and looked down at my shoes. A bead of sweat made its slick, ticklish way down the bridge of my nose and plopped onto the backpack that lay on the floor between my feet. The backpack contained two days worth of supplies for avoiding my apartment on Cara and Jamar's anniversary weekend. My roommate Cara's boyfriend was something like seven feet tall and the apartment was crowded enough with just Cara and me. That and they were still all lovey-dovey, even after six or whatever years. Most of the time it didn't bother me—they were cute together, and I should add that Jamar was my best friend—but every once in a while when the kisses and the *honeys* start flying a guy needs to get away, especially a single guy like me. It was an open question, though, whether I was going to Alex's because they bothered me, or whether they bothered me because all I had was Alex.

I stretched up the bottom of my t-shirt and smeared it across my face, conscious that I was revealing what I considered a decent stomach and hoping the BU jocks would notice. I'd accept from them either appreciation or desire.

I smoothed out my shirt, leaving it like a Shroud of Turin in sweat. Looking up again, I noticed a guy on the other side of the T car, sitting and looking out the graffiti-streaked window. Soon I would notice his hair, which looked as though a few months ago it'd been a short mohawk, and how the divot between his pecs was a darker gray than the rest of his t-shirt. But what I noticed before all of that was his hand creep across the thigh of his holey jeans, just past the pocket, and press against the spiky outline of keys beneath the thin denim. It was only a touch—then he withdrew his hand and crossed his arms against his chest. He did all this without taking his eyes from the window.

To the fat lady beside me I almost said, *Did you see...?* I exhaled a mix of laughter and exhilaration. The guy had been checking for his keys, I was sure of it. Checking to make sure that in the hubbub of the train they hadn't fallen through a hole in his pocket or been stealthily stolen. I licked my lips and felt a smile there. The *keys*. I even knew what the guy had been thinking immediately before and after he touched them—*Are they still there? Whew, yes, they're still there*—and that felt overwhelming and good, as though he were a character bursting fully formed into my mind, as though I'd known him forever. Funny I couldn't place his name.

The guy rubbed his finger under his nose and turned away from the window, leaned forward, clasped his hands between his knees.

I gathered up the straps of my backpack; at the next stop I planned to go say hi. I would say "Crowded today, huh?" and the rest would be history.

The train was jerking to a stop now. People began shifting

around and a girl wearing headphones stepped between me and the key-touching guy. There was a whine of brakes and the *ding-ding* of the doors, and just as the doors folded open, the oldster's soup can fully penetrated the brown paper bag and fell—not soup at all but *canned spinach*—onto the exposed toe of the young mom holding the heat-rashed infant. Mom screeched, and then baby was screeching, and the BU jocks jumped up to save the day, and when I looked back from all this the key-touching guy was gone.

I spotted him through the window. The guy I'd seen touch his keys was already half a block out of my life. I stood up to chase after him, but when I realized I'd literally have to climb over the woman beside me, I sat back down. Before the train pulled away I saw him touch his back pocket—feeling now, I knew, for his wallet. Just to make sure. My lungs felt heavy with wonder and loss and I slid lower into my seat.

Ironic that the stainless steel

button on Alex's intercom should look like a funhouse mirror and I should be so miserable to press it. I did, finally, and said, "I'm here. You there?"

Thirty seconds passed and then a static crackle and "—ey stud."

"Buzz me in, will you? I need some a.c. ASAP." Extreme heat tended to make me abbreviate.

"Hold," said the voice on the other end, snippily; but that was Alex, in all his Alexy snippiness. "—uzzer's broken."

I sighed and dropped my backpack on the step beside a terra cotta flower pot sprouting a few withered carnations from cracked dirt. I hopped from foot to foot, repulsed by the squish of my socks, but kind of liking it too. A hot breeze swooshed down the street and cooked the trees, scorched the grass. I gasped.

The door opened.

"Welcome," said Alex, "to my humble abode."

"Thanks." I picked up my bag. "You wish it was yours."

"A boy can dream," he said demurely. He was wearing cargo shorts and a white beater that clung translucently to his freckled skin.

I reached out and pinched the shoulder strip between my finger and thumb. "I don't like the look of this," I said, letting it snap back.

His eyes betrayed a zing of hurt. And then: "Oh—you mean I'm sweaty. Yes! It's hot, Fletch. In case you haven't *not*iced."

"Hot out here, OK. But why is it hot in *there*? Alex?"

"Don't you worry, there are fans."

"Fans? Come on. You told me air conditioning. It's almost 100."

"There *was* air conditioning. That was incident number one." His yellow hair clung wet to his forehead and ears and framed his shiny pink cheeks. "Coming in?"

"I guess."

We climbed the circular stairs to the third floor slowly, the railing slick under my palm. Gross gross gross, and it only got hotter as we went up. Alex's flip-flops banged against the green carpet. I watched his ankles and his calves and the backs of his legs and felt inclined to reach out and grab one—either to feel him up or bring him crashing down. I wasn't sure which. We had a weird history.

While we were climbing Alex told me the story of two days earlier, when, in facilitating the removal of a "creepy spider web"—his words—from the outside of the bedroom window, the air conditioner, all 12,000 BTUs of it, tumbled three stories and landed in a child's vegetable garden, sending a chum of zucchini and watermelon spurting onto the sidewalk.

I wiped my forehead and plucked my shirt. In a.c. I might've laughed. "You're lucky no one was killed, Alex."

"Believe me, I realize." His flip-flops were driving me fucking nuts. "The squishing sound— It took me like an hour before I could bring myself to even look out the window."

"And how long were the owners gone when incident number one struck?"

"Like barely a few hours." He stifled a giggle. "Oh god, they'll kill me. Gah, they'll *murder* me!"

"Best house-sitter ever. How many incidents have there been?"

"Two."

"What was the second one?"

"Kitchen fire. Minor. Really more like one-point-five."

The stairs ended. Alex pushed open the door and the apartment revealed itself in a steamy yawn that smelled of hotdogs and cologne.

"Nice?" he said, stepping inside and twirling around, a princess in his turret.

"It'll do." I dropped my backpack, walked across the parquet floor and the living room's white rug. Big bright windows leaked in sun like toxic radiation. I drew the vertical blinds, giving the room a sepia tint. "Whew." I sank into the cushions of a sticky leather couch. "No a.c., this is gonna be tricky." I kicked off my sneakers, peeled off my socks and rolled up the legs of my jeans. I put my feet up on the glass coffee table; gray misty spots spread out from my heels. "Maybe we should get a hotel."

Alex was still standing near the door, watching me. Finally he stepped out of his flip-flops and glided into the living room.

"Oh it's not that bad, for god's sake, Fletch." He crashed next to me on the couch in a puff of hot breeze. "And won't be, once we get you out of those clothes. Ha!" He looked away.

"Alex, Alex, Alex."

The flirting was 20 percent titillating and 80 percent boring. But this was how it had always been between us. My job was to supply the aloof innuendo: the casual removal of clothing, spontaneous references to my dick, hugs that lingered just enough. Alex provided the steady stream of double entendres he could never bring himself to commit to, always adding a goofy laugh to lend plausible deniability.

I yawned, reached down and scratched an itch and smoothed the hair on my shin.

"Well thank you for coming to keep me company," he said. "More so because I can tell you're already *miserable*."

I put my hand on his leg. "I'm not miserable. I'm sorry.

I'm just hot. You know how I get."

He was looking at my hand. "It's OK." After a second he said, "So Cara and Jamar are going to be screwing all weekend, huh?"

"Their anniversary."

"Steamy weather for it."

"Yeah, well. How about us, Alex? What do you have planned for us to do this weekend?" I set it up for him, knowing he'd bite.

"Do?" he said, getting it ready. "You mean besides each other? Ha!"

There it was. I patted his knee and stood up. "Yes, honey, besides each other. Got anything to drink?" I stepped over him and looked for the kitchen. It was all black and white tile and stainless steel appliances. "Where'd you find these people, anyway?"

"An ad," he said, padding into the kitchen. Our bare feet were leaving footprints on the tile. "Drinks— You mean like booze-wise?"

"In due time." I opened the fridge, looked around, pulled out a Brita pitcher. There were glasses drying in a rack by the sink. I filled one with water.

Alex grabbed a glass. "Fill me up? Heh."

We stood sipping, looking at each other over the rims of the glasses. I thought, *OK, this is us drinking water*, which made me think of a movie my neighbor and I made in her backyard when we were seven, said movie consisting solely of us standing in front of the camera eating slice after slice of Wonder bread. (Small evidence that although I'm not the best writer in the world my skills at narrative have improved over time.)

"So what do you really have planned for us?" I asked. "Anything on the agenda?"

"I do need to get some photos developed."

"Oh." Wow, this was going to be an exciting weekend! "There's a CVS right down the street."

"I tried there. Would you believe they don't develop film there anymore? We need to go to a specialty store. Which is fine. These are important."

"What are they of?" I put down the glass and wiped my lips with the back of my hand.

"Nuh-uh," he said, shaking his head, mouth full of water. He swallowed. "You'll see soon enough."

The Wonder bread movie had ended when we ran out of bread. Here the water was gone and no one was saying *cut*. I felt a bead of sweat go down my ribs and I twitched.

It rained briefly and then

the sun came out again and made the sidewalks steam. Gray air moved in through the apartment's open windows and I retreated to the bathroom for a shower, more for sanity than sanitation.

I set the water cool and got naked. Then I fished in a bag of my toiletries and pulled out my toothbrush. This whole situation was kind of lame and I sighed at myself in the mirror, watching my lips grow foamy with toothpaste. I spat.

Being in a strange bathroom was making me horny, though, too—I'd been in tons of strange bathrooms, usually for a quick clean-up before I split—but the water was cold and that cooled it. When it didn't feel as cold anymore I turned the knob colder. When I was used to that I turned it even colder. And when I was numb, I got out.

"My nipples are like drill-bits," I announced upon stepping out of the bathroom, dressed in shorts and a fresh yellow t-shirt. "If you need any cavities filled, now's the time." I laughed. Feeling was coming back into my toes. In a moment I'd be sweating again but for now I felt OK. "Alex? Hello?"

The apartment was quiet save for the humming thump of an inkjet sloughing pages. I dropped my towel over the doorknob and went over to the printer. Was it a ransom note? A suicide letter? I examined a page. None of the above—it was a map. An awfully big one.

I put the pages back in the tray and stood with my hands in my pockets in front of the living room window, looking past the rattling blinds. I could see a strip of sidewalk, along which a woman was pushing a baby stroller, one of those rich ones with the three big wheels. A corgi tethered to the stroller by a red leash was trying to go in another direction. I watched them and wondered where the key-touching guy lived. Had he been heading home or somewhere else when he got off the T? A boyfriend's house, a girlfriend's house, a job, a hook-up? Finally I turned and called, "Alex!"

After a little searching I found him on his hands and knees in the bedroom, waist-deep in a closet, butt wagging around like a gopher's.

"So!" I shouted from the doorway, leaning against the wall with my arms crossed. "Where are we headed?" His ass lurched and he backed out of the closet.

"God, Fletch, don't sneak *up* on me like that!" He crawled over to a cream-colored rug and sat down hard, looking like he was recovering from a case of the vapors, like a chick out of Dickens.

"What are you looking for in there, anyway?"

"Walking shoes. I'm *shopping*." He fanned his face.

"You're wearing their clothes? That's gross."

"Why's it gross? Both these guys wear my size. Why would I *not*?"

"A gay couple lives here?"

"Fletcher!" His eyes bugged and his jaw fell slack. The forced drama annoyed me even more. *Plunk plunk*, these drops of annoyance were like water torture. "Do you think I'd sleep in a *breeder* bed?"

The word made me cringe, was one of my least favorites. This was like being in battle. "Well did you find any shoes?"

He stood up shoeless, his task forgotten, and put his hand on the bed in a way that can only be called a caress. "They get in this bed—they're both gorgeous, of course—*naked*—and they do beautiful things to each other. Oh god. *Oooh* god." He fanned his face some more and rolled up his eyeballs.

I rolled my own to keep from giving him the satisfaction of turning me on. But maybe he was, a little.

He flung himself face-first onto the bed amidst a billow of sheets and waved his arms like he was making a snow angel.

For no reason I was aware of I jumped barefoot onto the

bed and started hopping around him, holding out my elbow in position to jackhammer him.

"Eeny meeny miney—" I began.

He rolled onto his back. "Fletcher, what're you—? *Hey!*" He flung one hand over his face and the other over his stomach.

"Homo!" And I dropped—

But I landed harmlessly beside him, elbow bashing only mattress, and bounced off the bed to my feet. On my way to the hall I stopped at a bureau and picked up a framed photo for a better look. They *were* both hot. I put it down.

"So where's that map go?" I said, and I left the room before receiving an answer.

Alex insisted on walking.

He offered as reasons (a) the "relaxing breeze" that had sprung up and (b) his need for exercise, but I suspected it was because he wanted to use the giant map he'd printed. For all the time I'd known him Alex had a weird fixation with maps and cartography that ran counter to everything else I knew about him. His favorite website (after Manhunt) was Google Earth. "If you use a map," he once told me, "everything is a treasure hunt." It was sort of endearing. Until today.

The map he'd printed took us, after an hour of twists and turns down vaguely suburban streets, along a flat, straight highway that gave the impression of rural Nebraska. Every so often a car or truck would blow a wake of hot sand against our legs. I could barely believe this was happening to me. The dust was on my face, was salty when I licked my lips, was gritty when I wiped sweat off my forehead. I needed another shower and I was barely dry from the last one.

"I guess I'm not clear on why we're going all the way out here. There *must* be some place you can mail the film."

He patted the messenger bag thumping at his hip. "They could get lost in the mail. I don't want to take any *risks*."

"And amazingly we're back to the part where I ask you what's in the pictures."

"Heh. Soon." He gave the map a look after shuffling some

pages. "We go under this bridge," he said, pointing, as if there were any other way to go.

"You need a pith helmet," I told him.

I was grateful for the shade under the graffiti-covered overpass and slowed down to make it last. On the concrete among the typical tags and spraypainted anarchy (someone wanted to FUCK THE POLICE) was another Fact, as I'd come to think of them. The Facts were all over Boston—on bridges, in alleys, sometimes on the sides of post office trucks. Affirmations of obvious things, and almost always grammatical nightmares. This one said THIS IS WAY in tall colorful letters on a street that receded into a fictional distance; as the street receded and narrowed it became the shoes of a portly yellow man in a too-small blue business suit, wiping his stylized brow.

"What do you make of these?"

"The pictures?" Alex said. "Ugly. All those yellow people with their creepy eyes. And they're *every*where. They need to find that guy and lock him up."

"I think I like them."

"Let's push on. We're almost there."

"*Push on?* You definitely need a pith helmet."

As we walked I dragged a finger along the white and blue word WAY. Despite the grammar I did like them, though I often imagined going around with a red marker and filling in the missing words. THIS IS *THE* WAY.

We came out the other side of the overpass and our heads bent under the slamming sun, as though the rays had weight. Far in the distance, much like the Fact, the highway tapered to street. A switching traffic light wobbled there like a mirage. That was a long way away, though—if it was even real.

I was browsing the Canons

and I thought I heard the clerk tell Alex "tomorrow." Then I definitely heard Alex say it back.

"You've got to be kidding," I mumbled. After that walk, *tomorrow* was the last word I wanted to hear. My balls were rubbed raw, my shirt was soaked, my feet probably had cherry-sized blisters. I wanted this errand done. I put down the camera.

"We can just wait for those," I told the clerk.

But the clerk said that the photo guy was out sick, that tomorrow was the earliest they could do.

"You only have one photo guy? This is a camera store."

The clerk shrugged. "Everything's digital now."

"Tomorrow's OK," Alex said. He didn't seem nearly annoyed enough for my taste, so I glared, and he said, "Well, Fletch, what *else* do we have to *do*?" Then he guffawed—ha!— and started fumbling with his bag.

We left the disposable camera

with the clerk—though when the moment came Alex seemed weirdly reluctant to hand it over; just what was on that fucking film anyway?—and stepped into the dreary glow of the Watertown Mall. Muzak wafted from the walls. People milled around carrying bags. A cluster of tween girls giggled over something on a phone.

"Why do you even need pictures developed?" I said. "Don't you have a digital camera?"

"It was a party favor. From that wedding I went to. We were supposed to take pictures and leave it but I snatched it."

"Oh. Can we at least take a cab back? Now that we know it's like 600 miles. I'll pay for it."

"We can do that." He smiled. "And tomorrow too." In a goofy burst of camaraderie he attempted to thread his fingers through mine, but I kept mine stiff and it didn't take.

On the ride back to his place I thought about the key-touching guy. I wondered what his name was. I wondered whether his mohawk was really overgrown, and if he would Bic down the sides again—or whether his hair was cut that way in a Newbury Street salon to mimic a style without committing to its full effect. If the latter, was he some kind of poser or did he have a straight-laced job and was trying to get away with as much as he could?

What bothered me more than anything was that I'd never know. It was highly likely that I'd never see him again, that the moment we shared when he touched his keys was a single, isolated event.

The cab stopped in front of Alex's sublet and my daydreams poofed into clouds of hot air.

Outside it grew dark

and inside lights were turned on sparingly to avoid adding to the heat. We played Scrabble in the living room in the quiet and the dim light waiting until it was late enough to go out.

When I asked if we should try to round up some people Alex said, "Let's just go out dancing ourselves. It'll be like a date—ha!"

We took a cab downtown

and dropped in on one of our usual places. The lights and the *oomp oomp oomp* were welcoming enough, familiar enough, but the last dozen or two-dozen or hundred times we'd come here I'd been feeling bored. I danced with Alex for a while and then suddenly Alex was dancing with someone else, a tall shirtless beanpole with bangs like a sheepdog. I took that opportunity to slip outside, which over the last hundred times had become my territory.

Once upon a time I was all about the bump-and-grind, the sparkling shirtlessness, because it was a sure-fire way to get a dance-floor make-out session, and usually to meet someone to spend the night with. Eventually I learned the stories were better outside. Outside is where the characters were. The lonely guys who'd gotten separated from (or ditched by) their friends. The guys who were getting burned by other guys inside. The guys who came outside for a smoke. Inside the guys were sweaty and delirious but outside they were angsty and ready to leave. And they might as well leave with me.

I breathed in humid night air tinged with exhaust. Street lamps and neon signs covered the street in a fetid, hazy light. The music faded as the door closed behind me. I checked that my phone was on for Alex, slid it back in my pocket, and looked up to check things out.

There were a few options but most of them were already having intimate relations with their phones. One guy was alone, fiddling with the sleeve buckle of a leather jacket it was way too hot to be wearing; I didn't like the look of him. I walked over toward the only other non-chatting guy, a guy leaning with his hip against a *Phoenix* box. Cute, nice arms, t-shirt that wasn't trying too hard. He was smoking and staring intently at something across the street. I sat down on the curb four or five feet away from him.

"I was hoping it'd be cooler out here," I said, "but man, this weather." Say what you will, but the weather is a good start on anybody.

"Yeah." He looked down at me when I looked up. There was a twitch across his brow that might've signaled recognition, but since he didn't look familiar to me I was pretty sure he was deciding I was cute. "It's murder."

"Is it supposed to be this hot in May?" I plucked at my shirt. "I don't think it is. Maybe that's why our friend over there still has his jacket on."

"Global warming, man. The world's on fire." He flicked his cigarette butt into the gutter, gave a little tug on the thighs of his jeans before sitting down—he was wearing those slip-on Vans and (I noticed) no socks. I'm not one of those guys who's into feet but I am, like a Victorian-era gawker, a sucker for ankles. "Fletcher, right?"

OK, I wasn't expecting him to know my name. I deflected with stagecraft. "Doth my reputation precede me?"

He laughed, a nice laugh. If he lived nearby we could go to his place and get jiggy and I could be back before Alex was done dancing with the beanpole.

"Not exactly," he said. "I guess you don't remember?" He gave me a moment to remember and then filled me in when I clearly didn't. "We hooked up a year or so ago. Not here, at the other place." He gestured vaguely down the street and then knocked another cigarette out of the pack, put it to his lips. "Smoke?"

"Nah, thanks, I quit. Sorry, I guess I don't remember."

"S'OK. I wore glasses then."

"Ah."

"We went to your place. Third floor? Little red-haired chick for a roommate? Typewriter in your bedroom." The details—he wasn't making this up—made me feel like a total fuckhead.

"Yeah. Hmm. That's me."

Cupping his hand, he transferred the glow from a match to the end of his cigarette. "I waited to see if you'd call. Then I mentioned you to my buddy and found out you didn't call him either."

"Oh."

"Yeah." He was quiet a minute. "You here with friends?"

"One," I said, happy to change the subject. "You?"

"Me and the ex are trying to do the let's-hang-out-as-friends thing. Totally awkward. I needed a smoke or five."

"I hear friendships with exes are tricky waters to navigate."

"Only hear?"

"Well. Let's just say you and your buddy aren't the only guys I've never called back. —Excuse me a second." My phone was buzzing. A text. Alex, with multiple question marks, wanted to know where I was. Before I finished typing a reply, he came strutting up the sidewalk.

"There you are," he said. "I've been looking for you."

"Found me."

"Can we leave?"

"Already? I was talking to—my friend here." The one whose name I still could not remember.

Alex nodded to the guy and said to me, "If it's OK I'd really like to leave."

"What happened?"

"I'll tell you in the cab, OK?" He turned to the guy. "I'm sorry to interrupt. Can you give him your number or something and you guys can pick this up later?"

The guy gave a little shrug. "It's probably already in his phone."

Alex looked at me and raised his eyebrows and went to grab a cab.

"So. Have a nice night," I said to the guy. "I hope things smooth out with your ex."

"Yeah."

"Hey," I said, turning back, "how was it last year? With me. Fond memories?"

"I'm not plucking flower petals for you or anything." He breathed out some smoke. "Fond enough."

To the cabbie I gave

my own address, and then Alex corrected me by providing the address of his sublet.

"Oh," I said, "yeah, that's right." Only then did I realize how flustered my encounter with the Forgotten Trick had left me.

"Sorry I cock-blocked you," Alex told me quietly. "I wouldn't have done it if I wasn't in the middle of a nightmare."

"You didn't. It was *my* nightmare. He says I slept with him a year ago but I don't even remember him."

"Maybe he's lying."

"No. He described my bedroom."

"Oh. Well that's embarrassing. For him, I mean. He must've been totally forgettable in bed."

"Yeah. Maybe. So what was your nightmare?"

"I saw this guy Jimmy in there and bolted."

"That's all? Who's Jimmy?"

"Oh it's this whole big thing. Remember that wedding I went to a couple of weeks ago?"

"The wedding with the camera?"

"Mm. There was this guy there, we were at the same table. Hit it off."

"Jimmy."

He nodded. "Gorgeous. Funny."

"You didn't tell me about this."

"We spent the night together. Me and Wedding Jimmy. The night and the whole next day. Largely in his bed. He was so good and it felt so good and he was *nice* too. I was like in shock."

"Wow. So what happened?"

"Nothing. At the end when we had to go home I was like, *When can I see you again?* and he was all, *Actually, I kind of have a boyfriend.* Can you believe it? So tragically cliché." He knocked his head against the window and sighed.

"I'm sorry."

"Why? Are *you* his boyfriend?"

"Hah."

"But thanks."

"So then what's with the photos?"

"I don't know. Mementos."

"Of you and him?"

He shrugged.

"X-rated?"

"No. PG-13. Well, we're gay, so R."

"You waited a month to have them developed?"

"I guess I wasn't ready. Or I wanted an audience. I probably shouldn't even pick them up."

"No, you should see them. They've gained a mythic quality in your mind. You'll see them and you'll see he's just a dude, you know? Like all the others."

I put my elbows on

the window sill and looked down at the shadowy street. *Fond enough.* The words still stung. I thought of the key-touching guy and searched my mind to make sure I'd never been with *him* before. I was sure I hadn't, but there must've been a reason I was still thinking about him. No way should I be harping on a random guy over some three-second quote-unquote *moment.* He touched his keys. Big whoop. As if that meant anything. It felt like it did, though. It felt like I knew him, more than guys I'd actually been with. I lay back down on the couch and adjusted the pillow and fixed the sheet—it kept sliding off the leather.

Fond enough. Fuck.

Alex came out of the bathroom and made an obvious detour into the living room. He stood for a moment near the end of the couch. "Do you want to watch a movie or something," he said, "or are you ready to sleep?"

"I could watch a movie. I might fall asleep though."

"They have a TV in there. Come to the bed with me."

He turned and left. No guffaw this time, not even a smirk, just the pat of footsteps as he went to the bedroom. I thought that was about right, and it was OK. At least I would still remember Alex a year from now.

I slid off the couch and grabbed my pillow. I was wearing only my underwear and didn't bother putting my t-shirt back on.

"I'll try to find something decent to watch," I heard him say as I went down the hall. In the bedroom he was nosing around in a bookcase of DVDs.

"I don't understand owning movies," I said. "Who wants to watch a movie more than once?"

I dropped my pillow against a wood headboard carved into the shapes of fruit—apples, bananas, a pineapple. Strange for a bedroom. It was the kind of design you'd expect in a kitchen, on a carnival-glass lampshade or a set of ceramic canisters. The bedspread was rolled down to the foot of the bed and it pulled itself onto the floor when I lifted the sheet.

"Anything good?" I said, fitting the pillow behind me to keep the fruit from jabbing my kidneys. I pulled the sheet up around my waist.

Alex held out a disc I couldn't see in the dark. "How about this? It's some silly British gay movie. You seen it?"

"No."

"OK." He loaded the disc and came around and got into bed. "Where's the—? Fletcher! You're sitting on it!" He tugged the remote out from under me.

The little flatscreen on the bureau lit up and music ushered in the opening titles. Outside on the street an ambulance went by, and then a Dopplered burst of hip-hop. A few minutes into the movie Alex slid closer and put his cheek against my shoulder. "You're boney," he said, poking my bicep. I felt with deadpan amusement the first twinge of what would soon be a dutiful erection.

This was going to happen and it was going to be fine.

For the first half of the movie the characters struggled with their sexualities in a way I couldn't relate to. I'd never come out of the closet because I'd never exactly been in one — when I started going boy-crazy at age twelve I made sure everyone knew it. But the characters' plunge into the sack halfway through the movie was plenty familiar.

Alex had his hand on my thigh and up to this point I assumed it was there in cinematic anticipation — the way he would sometimes grab my arm during horror movies. Then we seemed to notice at the same time that I had a tent on my lap.

"Uh," I said.

"Oh," he said. "Ha."

He gave the sheet a playful tug, almost teasing, but it was enough to move the sheet aside. My dick stood protruding through the flap in my boxers.

"Oh," he said again.

There was a chance now for conversation and we chose not to use it. No double entendres, no guffaws, no commentary of any kind. Just a slow, unimpassioned entwining.

Unlike with the dudes on TV, no strategic shadows concealed anything and it felt funny (i.e., weird) to see my pal Alex doing this. Funny (odd) to have his dick in my hand and his too-smooth chest against my mouth. Kissing was another thing that was funny (awkward) and we stopped after a brief try and never did it again — funny (curious) how it's never awkward with strangers. And funny (humorous) when we couldn't get my boner to bend back through the hole in my boxers, and decided just to leave them on. Despite all the funny it was fine. Alex's skin was surprisingly cool and his body, though I'd never been with him this way before, was familiar. This had a weight. Not a great weight, but a weight. I certainly knew when it was nothing.

The whites of his eyes glowed red and blue in the alternating flicker of the TV. British accents filled the background. Upset parents, intolerant classmates. Sometimes there was music. Alex looked up at me.

"You're so beautiful, Fletch."

I winced and began to wonder how fine this actually was. I was ready to go for a quick finish after that when Alex, lying on his back, banged his hand into the nightstand drawer and withdrew a box of Trojans.

"Fletcher, will you?"

I hadn't really expected that and I wondered if doing it would have the awkwardness of kissing, times a hundred. But it's not a request you turn down if someone asks and you've already gone this far. I unrolled the condom down to the flaps of my boxers (with boxers and condom on was I technically even naked anymore? There was some relief in that) and added a dollop of lube from a little bottle Alex waved at me.

He threw his legs over my shoulders. "Hurry, Fletcher. I need this."

"I'm hurrying, I'm hurrying. Jesus."

"Do it," he said, and he was annoying me again. I put my thumb against his lips to keep him from talking anymore, and pressed inside.

I held still until his face cued me to start moving. I could go on autopilot now. After a minute he squirmed out from under me and motioned for me to lay on my back. Then he climbed on top and put me back in, riding my hips. My boxers clung briefly to his butt each time he rose up. I watched him reach out and place his hands on the headboard in seemingly strategic positions against a pineapple and what looked like a pear. Their placement there seemed to bring new contentment to his face.

"What are you doing?" I said, looking up through his arms.

"They—hold this—headboard—like this. When they're—making love. Their—hands go here."

"How do you know? *Ow!*" I put my hands under his ass to slow him down and to keep my dick from cracking. My erection was saying sayonara.

He looked down and frowned. "C'mon—they do."

What a relief to hear this, especially after that stuff about me being beautiful. He wasn't really fucking me at all, he was fucking the couple—the couple whose kitchen he cooked in and whose TV he watched, whose shoes he wore, whose towels he used, whose headboard he clenched when he came.

Afterward I had no desire

to share the bed with him and thought about sneaking back to the couch, but that was risking more drama than I wanted to deal with in the humid air at 3:00 a.m. Alex lay on his side, naked still but with the sheet over him, politely allowing some space between us.

"Did you know that would happen?" It seemed about the least flirtatious thing he'd ever said.

I said I'd had a feeling it would.

"Did you—like it?"

"It was nice, Alex," I supplied. "Thank you."

"It was a long time coming."

"A lot of years, yeah."

He sighed. "Do you ever imagine what it would be like if we were—" But he stopped when he must've noticed I was looking out the window, barely hearing him. "Well. We have a ways to go yet before we get that desperate." He pulled the sheet up farther and fluffed his pillow.

A few minutes later his breath was rumbling steadily through his open mouth. I kicked off my half of the sheet and lay spread-eagle on the bed, allowing maximum area of my skin to touch the air. The fan chugged back and forth but the air it blew felt like dragon breath. My back and the backs of my legs and my heels and my shoulders were sticky against the damp sheet. My boxers clung like those lead aprons you have to wear when getting an X-ray. I went into my memory and imagined the morning had gone differently, that I'd been able to talk to the key-touching guy instead of losing him in the hubbub of the fucking canned spinach. I imagined going home with him instead of coming to Alex's.

I imagined the key-touching guy had a.c.

I awoke like a zombie,

stiff from tossing, damp from sweating, poisoned from the whirring fan's dragon breath. I stumbled into the bathroom, passing the stainless-steel kitchen where Alex was cooking waffles just by bringing them out of the freezer into the fucking air.

The cool shower softened my mood, though, and the memory of the hours I lay sweating beside the snoring, nude Alex began to recede like a polluted tide. With it went my sense of time. Hard to believe I had spent only one night with him, been here only one day. It could've been a lifetime. Because here was Alex's underwear on the floor by my feet. Here were our toothbrushes side by side on the sink. All the hallmarks of a domesticity I stopped wanting long ago.

I sighed and examined my shaven cheeks for patches missed. Then I got dressed, put stuff in my hair, dropped my towel over the bar on the wall, and opened the bathroom door. The air smelled of burning waffles.

The photos were handed over

in a blue envelope by a middle-aged woman whose nametag said Sherri. Alex paid with a leopard-print credit card and turned toward the exit with his fingers creeping up to his mouth to hide a grin.

"Now that I have them I'm glad you made me get them."

"Maybe you should look at them before you decide that."

"Because if nothing else, it's a deposit for the spank bank, you know?"

"True."

He whirled around, holding out the envelope. "You look first. I can't do it. I can't do it!"

I took the envelope and slapped it against my palm. "Let's go sit down."

We parked ourselves on a bench near the food court and Alex clasped his hands between his knees. I tore the sticker and pulled out the glossy three-by-fives.

"Wedding cake. Bride. Bride and groom kissing. Bride and

groom dancing." I handed them to him one by one, five pictures like that. Boring. But at the sixth I knew instantly what the fuss was about. The sixth showed a blue-eyed jock in a tie, mugging for the camera with his cheek pressed against Alex's. During the fraction of a second it took me to complete a double-take something very small but powerful shriveled inside me. "Your Jimmy was Jimmy *Perino?* From Shuster?"

"Yeah." His eyes narrowed. "You *know* him?"

"Well yeah."

"Did you—?" The obvious question: did I fuck him.

"No, but I *wanted* to, all through college. Jimmy Perino was like my all-time biggest missed opportunity. I thought he was straight. Everyone said he was straight!"

A grin tore across Alex's face like some kind of injury. "Apparently he came out late. Like senior year."

"..." I handed him the photo and pretended to watch someone loaded with shopping bags tug at the mall's glass door. "So Wedding Jimmy was Jimmy Perino. You had sex with Jimmy Perino."

"The proof's in the pudding. Here, let me see."

He took the remaining photos and flipped through, and yes, here was one clearly after the reception. Their heads were on big white pillows, their faces were flushed, their shoulders were bare.

I took the photo and looked it over. I wished there was more to see. Jimmy: he had thick shoulders, killer biceps—classic, like a roofer, just like I'd imagined when I'd imagined him shirtless. And I'd imagined him a whole lot more than shirtless. I was desperate to know everything but to give Alex nothing. I dialed down my envy, cleared my throat. "So. It was good?"

"It was so good, Fletch. It was the sweetest and craziest sex of my life. The things he does! It's like he's trying to make up for lost time."

"Better than me?" I said. Jimmy Perino. It was impossible. It was *unfair.*

Alex blushed a little. "Nobody's better than you."

I could tell he was lying but I smiled and smiling softened

my mood. "Jimmy Perino," I mused. "Wow." I handed the photos back to him. "These are art. You could frame these."

"I'm glad you're here to see them with me. And not just because I like making you jealous—I had no idea you were that into him, I promise. Why didn't you ever say anything?"

"I don't like going around harping on straight guys."

"But not all straight guys are really straight." He laughed. "Anyway, your envy's a bonus. It's pretty rare that *you're* jealous of *my* sex life."

In a weird way, I was touched.

We looked through the remaining photos. There were a half-dozen more photos of that same shot, as though they wanted to be sure to get it, in various conditions of blur. One photo of lampshade, and one of knee.

Alex sighed. "That's all I have left of the bastard. His fucking *knee.*"

I still couldn't get it

through my skull, and if not for the photo evidence I wouldn't have believed it at all. Not for a second. That my silly, guffawing pal Alex had been with Jimmy Perino. And recently. If only I'd known last night that my dick was sharing the same space inside Alex that Jimmy Perino's once occupied.

When we got back to the apartment we had sex again, on the couch, with the photos spread out like a buffet on the coffee table. We'd been looking at them and then it just happened. It was better than the first time, more exciting—but more awkward afterward.

We lay on the sticky leather couch, him wearing only his shirt, me with my pants still snared around one foot. We looked at each other knowing we'd both have rather been with Jimmy. That we hadn't been fucking each other at all, but the photos. I looked up, away from him. The ceiling sported decorative swirls of plaster that were flaking in places like white scabs.

Finally he peeled himself off the couch, stood up, held out his hand for the condom, which I slipped off and gave him. He invited me into the shower.

"You can go first," I told him. Showering together wasn't a step I wanted to take. "Don't hurry."

"Ah," he said, and shut the bathroom door behind him. The water cranked on. I think he knew I'd be gone when he got out.

On the sidewalk I was feeling damp, slightly guilty, and more than a little like having to pee, but otherwise free. I hiked up my backpack, regretting having to leave my toiletries behind. Sometimes you just want to get out. The whole walk to the T, I waited for a call or a text asking where I had gone, but neither one ever came.

Alex knew me.

The smell of spaghetti sauce

rode heavy on the humidity in my apartment. I dropped my backpack against the TV table. The stereo was playing Guster and colored sunlight from some of the crystal doodads Cara kept on the window sills danced across the scratched hardwood floor. The windows were open and the breeze fluttered the pages of the Junot Díaz book I'd left on the sill.

"Something smells yummy," I said, breathing hard from the heat and the three flights of stairs. I pried off my shoes and sat down on the coffee table to get rid of my socks.

In the kitchen Jamar stood in front of the stove, stirring a bubbling, boiling pot. He was wearing only his boxers, red and white striped that made him look even more like an All-American Boy than usual. He had a nice chest but I'd stolen enough furtive glances of it when we met years ago to make it old news by now.

"Hey Bradford," he said. He had a toothy smile he used often. We were roommates in college, our freshman and sophomore years. Somehow from the paperwork on our room assignment he gleaned that my name was Bradford Fletcher. It stuck.

I leaned in beside him to investigate the stove action. Pasta. In another pan sauce bubbled like magma. A pop flicked boiling tomato puree at me.

"Ow, shit."

"Watch out."

"You're making spaghetti. In your underwear. Hey, and you got a haircut."

"Cara did it this morning." He rubbed the back of his close-cropped head. "Is it even? This feels like a nick here but Cara says it's fine."

"You think she'd tell you?" I stood on my toes to examine his head. Jamar claimed he was six-four, but he was bashful about his height, so the truth was more likely six-six or six-seven. I once tried to measure him in his sleep but the tape ran out at his knee. "I don't see any nicks." I settled back on my heels and picked a spoon off the stove. "You look like a scary black man now, though."

"Go away, homo."

"Heh."

"And it's not spaghetti, it's rigatoni. Give." He snatched the spoon from me. There's a unique way that a straight black guy and a gay white guy can understand each other, and Jamar and I had it all worked out.

"Spaghetti, rigatoni. The question is, why are you making all this? We're not having people over, are we?"

"It's for Cara."

"*All* of this? She's not preggo, is she?"

"Don't even—" He swooshed me away. I went along with it and danced backward but the truth is I would've been swooshed even if I tried to stand my ground, push-ups be damned. "I'm so a double-rubber guy. Don't even think that, Bradford. It's bad luck."

"What is?" Cara came out of her bedroom, hair done up in a starfish beach towel. A couple of reddish swirls hung out, dark and shiny from water. She had on jogging shorts and a gray t-shirt. She slipped her arms around Jamar's bare middle, looking like she might be going to give him the Heimlich, and put her cheek against his ribs. She was short and looked short next to almost anyone, but it was striking next to Jamar. I couldn't imagine what their sex was like, mechanics-wise. "Do you like his hair, Fletch?"

"It's very short. I miss the dredlets."

Jamar said, "It's very hot out."

"Never base haircuts on weather. And you copied me." I rubbed my own short hair.

"Oh, it's all part of my plan to create a duplicate Fletcher," Cara said. "One who'll actually marry me."

Jamar dripped a blob of sauce on the stove and was reaching for a paper towel when I wiped my finger through it and put it in my mouth. "Mmm." I looked at Cara and said, "I've told you a hundred times I'll marry you, Car. I just won't play with your girly parts."

Jamar smirked.

"Mmhm," she said. She tucked her hair back up under the towel. "Speaking of, how was your weekend with Alex? We've been taking bets on whether you guys finally boned."

"Ew, what makes you think we boned when we've never boned before?"

"I don't know," she said, "the sleepover, the sultry weather. Plus you haven't been going out as much lately. We figured you'd have a jizz overload or something."

Had I been going out less often? I guess I had, now that she mentioned it. "Well, you're right," I said. "We boned."

"I win!" Jamar pumped his fist.

"Twice, actually. I'm just not sure he knew it was me."

"Huh?"

"He's got this weird fantasy thing about the couple he's house-sitting for. Some kind of domesticity fetish or something. You know Alex. I think he was playing a game of replace-the-face in his head while we were doing it."

"You should try taking him on a date some time," Jamar said.

"Yeah. Right, Jamar. Sure. Me and Alex. *Wooooo.*"

He smirked. "All I'm saying is, maybe it's time you start looking for a guy to settle down with. That's all I'm saying."

"OK, happily-ever-after is my cue to bail," I said. "You," I said to Cara, "would you mind giving him a pinch on that fine black ass of his, for me?"

"Gladly."

"Not while I'm cook— *Yipe!*"

"Hey," she said to me, "since you're home, how would you feel about this pot-luck I have to go to?"

"What kind of pot-luck?" I said suspiciously. "Is this a Big Brothers thing?"

"Yeah, a work thing."

"Isn't that his job?" I pointed to Jamar.

"I'm going car shopping with the Robot," he said.

"Your brother got his license?"

"Yeah."

"Nice."

"Please Fletcher?" Cara said. She pressed her hands together. "There'll be at least one cute guy there."

"Oh, I'm not falling for that. What you really mean is cute like seven-year-old orphan cutie patootie cute."

"No, I mean cute like late-twentysomething chemistry teacher cute."

"Hey, chemistry!" Jamar said.

"No more guys," I told her. "My pelvis is still sore from Alex riding on me."

"You can try *talking* to a guy, Bradford," Jamar said.

Cara snorted. The timer started dinging. Jamar twirled the strainer and emptied the pasta over the sink, steaming the already moist air.

"Oh all right," I said. "Just let me take a freaking shower first."

"You're a life-saver. You can carry the spaghetti."

"It's rigatoni," said Jamar.

I hoped this one cute

guy at the pot luck, this teacher of chemistry Cara had promised, would turn out to be the key-touching guy—but this guy never touched his keys, and he wasn't even that cute. I didn't try talking to him, not even about the weather. Instead I stuffed my face with various desserts and clung to Cara like a shadow.

"Jimmy Perino?" she said, forking onion chunks away from the otherwise edible potato salad on her paper plate.

"Can you believe it? Alex, of all people, with Jimmy

Perino. It's a stake through my heart. The only consolation is that they're not together anymore. If they were actually dating I'd die."

A pair of Little Brothers ran past us carrying what looked like a giant inflatable grasshopper, while their Bigs tagged along with plates of half-eaten food.

"I guess I vaguely remember a Jimmy Perino," Cara said finally. "Blondish? Oafish?"

"He's hardly oafish. You'd remember him if you saw him. How were you not paying more attention back then?"

"I was with Jamar!"

"Whatever."

"Poor you. Your favorite frenemy was fu — being naughty with your dream guy."

"He's not my dream guy. He was my dream lay."

"I repeat, poor you. The world is just passing you by, isn't it?"

I raised my hand and spoke as with a sock puppet: "Blah blah."

"How about that new guy at your office?"

"Mateo. I'm working on that."

"Work harder. He sounds foxy." She held out her plate; she'd given up on the potato salad. "Go get me one of those cupcakes, cupcake."

Monday was cooler but the

office a.c. was still waging war with last week's heat, unaware that the weather gods called a truce. I sat shivering at my desk, curled practically fetal in my chair, left hand tucked under right armpit for warmth, eyeballing the filing cabinet. In one of the drawers was a frumpy but toasty sweater (green wool, zipper-up) specifically for use on days when the a.c. was on hyperdrive — but it was way too Mr. Rogers to risk being seen in now. I wanted to have an extra spring in my step in case I ran into Mateo. No telling when a chance encounter might occur. The sweater would stay in the drawer.

Another day, another dollar, another dude to watch out for.

So far today there were no chance encounters to rival that lunchroom encounter of last Friday, and it was 11:00 already. I was getting impatient to know what color his hand was today. I'd already been on two beverage runs and one bathroom run and had scored not even a *glimpse*.

I gazed at the clock and sighed. The end of the morning — when lunch was so close yet so far away — always passed slow.

A stack of manila folders sat on my otherwise pretty blank desk (I never felt the need to decorate), each one a chapter in some book about the health-care industry, *HMOs And You*. Last week when I was making the book's copyright page I'd permitted myself to test *Homos And You*, a much more interesting title (one that would no doubt sell better, too). This I changed to *Homos Heart You* before returning it to its true title, saving, and submitting it to the art department, which consisted exclusively of an overworked woman named Sonia, two cubes away.

"Check your in-folder, Sonia," I'd called out.

"Checking it, Fletcher," she'd called back through the padded walls.

Aside from my soda-machine chats with the talkative Babette from customer service, that was as stimulating as conversation usually got at work. I blamed the ugly fluorescent lights, which made everyone here look like blue zombies. Everyone except for New Guy, who somehow seemed immune. If this were a movie New Guy would be the lone survivor of a zombified wasteland, out of whose miracle blood a vaccine could be formulated to save the world.

New Guy, who I hadn't seen yet today.

I looked for a little while at the crumpled accordion of manila folders on my desk before pulling off the top folder and opening the corresponding file on my computer. The book was supposed to be getting finalized for print. This was my favorite part of an otherwise pretty boring job. Setting the type, making it permanent. What I saw the reader would see. It was reasonably satisfying, which is to say that when I was doing it I only had to check my personal email every fifteen minutes instead of every five.

I worked for a while, still stopping every few minutes to rub warmth into my hands and then, why not, to check my email, which I kept discreet at the bottom left corner of the screen. A new one from Cara asked whether I'd seen New Guy yet. Reluctant to let her down, I got up and took another walk, this time detouring all the way to the I.T. cubes, as far from both the soda machines and the bathrooms as it was possible to get without leaving the building. When I spotted him I felt like a jungle explorer glimpsing a rare Amazonian feline.

He was slouched in his chair, his back to me as I strolled nonchalantly/creepily past his cube. His left hand was on the keyboard but unmoving. His right, the one that changed colors, was folded in front of him, blocked from my view by the chair and his crisp-shirted torso. He looked asleep. On his screen was a scary-looking program we didn't use in my department. Was it that boring?

I refilled my coffee near the soda machine, then went the same long way back, hoping for a better view I could exaggerate into a fun reply for Cara—but he was in the same position as before.

After I told Cara all this (employing rare frowny-faces in my email), she suggested I manufacture an encounter and we ran through a few scenarios before settling on one. At noon I placed my mouse on the floor, put my heel on it and, clearing my voice loudly, stomped down.

The casing cracked edge to edge across the top and one of the buttons sprung up like the hood of a crashed car. *Way* too much. No one would believe this was accidental. I picked it up, wondering what to do. There was another, older mouse in one of my drawers—I could try for more authentic damage on that one or, maybe better yet, cut my losses and use it as a replacement.

But that hair. Those eyes!

I picked up the phone and left a voicemail for I.T. detailing my hardware issue. There was a fifty-fifty chance a new mouse would be delivered by New Guy. I'm not much of a gambler but I could live with those odds.

With a broken mouse there was nothing I could do while I

waited, so I pretended to look through folders and let my mind wander. Mostly it wandered to and over and around and into Jimmy Perino. Then someone was in my cube.

It wasn't New Guy, though, it was Bassett. My heart sank, my libido got whiplash. Larry Bassett was only in his late thirties but acted like he was seventy-five—even styled his hair in a comb-over he didn't need. Tall and gaunt with a weary plainness, he reminded me of someone from a Philip K. Dick novel. No mysterious green-eyed hottie by any stretch. And before he got around to any maintenance or anything, Bassett always spent ten minutes talking about his most recent knee surgery and maybe even modeling the scars.

Holding the new mouse in his hand, still in its carton, he told me about how on Sunday when he was leaving for church he'd slipped on pea-stones someone had scattered on his front stoop. He'd nearly gone sprawling into the hydrangeas.

"That's really terrible, Larry," I said. "You need to be more careful."

"It's the neighborhood kids again," Bassett said. He made a motion as though to approach my computer—installation seemed imminent!—but then he backed off and leaned against the filing cabinet. He sighed. "Two weekends ago they rammed a stick into my garage door's pulley-chain thing, you know the thing that hoists up the door? They're setting traps."

The neighborhood kids were always making life hell for Bassett, but as far as I knew he had no kids of his own. Wondering if those facts were related, I nodded politely, delivering appropriate cues of sympathy and surprise. Just as Bassett was trailing off, New Guy appeared around the edge of my cube. His blue-fingered fist was raised in an aborted knock. Blue.

"Oh, Larry," he said, "you beat me to this one."

I nodded at him. He lifted his chin at me.

"Ah, thank god," Bassett said. "You can do this. You're half my age. You're at your peak. I'm in steady decline, about to hit bottom. Install this man a mouse, will you?" He pushed the new mouse against New Guy's stomach and withdrew from the cube. I could hear him groaning through the maze of cubicles as he retreated to his own.

"I think he's twice his age," New Guy said. I guessed it was a joke but he wasn't smiling. "Did you order a mouse? You left a voicemail about a broken mouse? — You're Fletcher, right?"

The first two questions were odd given that Bassett had been in my cube and already dished out the instructions — but maybe New Guy liked to go by the book. The one about my name, though, that was a hope apocalypse. Did he really not know my *name?*

"Um. Yes. I'm Fletcher. I called. Just one is fine. I'm not ambidextrous." I grinned. I'd tricked New Guy into coming but I didn't know what to do now that he was here — here among all these mice, under this garish lighting where I never look my best. "I can install it myself, if you want. You probably have other things — "

"It's my job," he said. "Yikes, what'd you do to this guy?"

He picked the mouse up off the desk to examine the carnage — this gave me an opportunity to slide my focus from the mouse to his knuckles. The way the paint faded along the back of his hand was indicative of spraypaint. It looked precisely as though he'd been holding something small to paint it, and his hand caught the residual spray. Maybe he was a modeler.

"I — stepped on it," I said.

He raised a dark eyebrow. "You walk around on your desk?"

"It fell on the floor."

"No." He held the plug-end of the cord against the back of my computer and let the mouse dangle over the edge of the desk. "It's not long enough to fall on the floor." The mouse swung gently like a pendulum. "See?"

"Oh. It unplugged and then fell on the floor."

His green eyes drilled straight into mine, somewhat mocking, totally hypnotizing. "I think you broke this on purpose."

My cheek twitched. I felt it. " — Why would I do that?"

"I don't know. You like hearing about Larry's neighbors?"

"Oh. Haha. I sure do. But no. It came unplugged. And I stepped on it. A series of unfortunate events."

"Quite a series. OK. Well. Blue or black?"

"Sorry?"

"They're different colors," he said. I was looking at the fingers. "Blue? Or black?"

"Oh, the mouse, sure. Blue's fine. Whichever."

He shrugged. He put the black mouse on the filing cabinet and tore open the blue one.

I leaned forward in my chair, clasped my hands between my knees. "Cooler out today."

"I guess. Need to get in here a sec."

"Sure." I scooted my chair over to give him access to the computer. Then he was right there, leaning over my desk, fighting with the mouse plug. His belt was scuffed brown leather and sat low on his hips. His crisp shirt was tucked-in neatly, making his torso look long and lean, a swimmer's body. I felt my eyes roll up. I was tripping on hotness.

"You should dust back here," he said, un-entwining himself from the cables in the back and then straightening up and giving a quick upward tug on his belt. "OK, let me test it." He put the back of his hand—*3, 2, 1 contact!*—against my shoulder to push me away from the monitor. The touch was of dubious necessity, which I hoped boded well for the likelihood of future sexual relations. As he wiggled the mouse we watched the cursor scoot across the screen. Little did he know he was inches away from maximizing an email entirely about him. "OK. All set."

"Thank you."

"It's what they pay me big bucks for," he said sarcastically. He collected the other new mouse. The empty box he held over the wastebasket. "Can I toss this?"

"Sure." I reached for the box just as he let go—it dropped past my hand into the bucket. I recovered quickly and extended my hand. He shook it awkwardly. "Thanks."

"No problem," he said.

"Oh—the old mouse. Should I throw it away?"

"Sure, it's broken."

"I — didn't know if we recycle them or something."

"No."

"OK. Thanks Mateo." I liked how his name felt on my tongue.

"No problem," he said again.

I turned back to my computer, surprised and intrigued that I'd felt so intimidated by him, and continued the email to Cara. In my re-telling Mateo had a special smile for me at the end of our encounter. Its absence from real life was a little annoying.

Babette, from customer service,

had my ear good. I didn't mind because the day and its interminable afternoon were finally over. Today the subject was Babette's sixteen-year-old daughter, who she suspected might be gay — Babette called it *of the lesbianic persuasion*. I'm not great at advice but at work I was apparently the go-to guy for all things homosexual, so I did the best I could.

"You probably shouldn't ask her about it outright," I said, taking a big bag of shredded papers from her to carry out to the recycling. "You don't want to rush her before she's ready." We went through the doors and the soupy, late-afternoon air instantly made me feel damp. "Just drop some hints, plant a seed about how it'd be no biggie if she is."

"But *if* she is," Babette said, "I worry about, you know, prejudice and things."

I shifted my messenger bag away from my back, where it was pressing my shirt against damp skin. "If a person has support at home, um, I think she'll be able to handle anything that —"

The conversation spilled off my brain like an upset Scrabble board. In the parking lot Mateo was leaning into the open hood of his car, one hand holding it up as he peered in.

Babette followed my gaze, shielding her eyes with some mail. "Looks like Matthew is having trouble over there."

"Mateo," I corrected. It was too good a name to ever get wrong. He was rubbing his chin now. What we had here, ladies and gentlemen, was a hottie in distress. "Guess I better

THE PAINTING OF PORCUPINE CITY

go see if he needs any help or anything."

"He's gorgeous but he smells," she said in a whisper, this time using the mail to shield her lips. "Have you noticed? As though he goes running around before coming to work. You know what I mean? Can't be his clothes—he's the most well-dressed one here. So I think that boy might need a lesson in soap."

"I don't know, I've never been one to complain about man-smell."

She laughed. "Maybe not when they look like him. Hmm, maybe I'll introduce him to Lily, turn her straight lickety-split!" We both laughed. "In the meantime, get that boy into a bath," she said, putting her hand on my arm. Then she giggled and her boobs bounced around. "I'm sorry, I didn't mean to imply...."

I batted my eyelashes. "Babette, what kind of vixen do you take me for, anyway?"

"Scan-da-lous!" she said. "Thank you for your advice. Here, let me take that back." She reached for the bag of shreddings. "Go be his knight in shining khakis."

I started walking in Mateo's direction, slowly to limit sweat production. I tugged out some wrinkles the messenger bag strap was making in my shirt, moved the strap down so it accentuated my pecs.

He dropped the hood closed and slumped onto the bumper in a pose resembling the Thinker. When I approached from around a minivan he stood up. The cuffs of his shirtsleeves were unbuttoned and turned up around his wrists. Too well dressed to be straight. Too un-groomed—because Babette was right, he did smell like he'd been running around—to be gay.

"Hey."

"Fletcher."

"Some car trouble?" I said, thinking: *This time he remembered my name.* I raised a hand to block the sun from my eyes.

"Doesn't want to start. I know fuck-all about cars, alas."

"But I thought you were the I.T. guy!" I said, laughing at

my own joke, but his non-reaction made me realize it made no sense. I crossed my arms. "Well, does it make any noise when you turn the key?"

"I'm supposed to turn the key?" he said. And I was astonished to witness, for the first time in the six days of our vague acquaintance, a genuine smile. "Sorry, no, I know that much. I'm just kidding."

I laughed again. Maybe too much, too loud. I checked myself, shifted from foot to foot, hooked a thumb under the strap across my chest. Why was I being such a dork?

"When I first tried there was a—" He made some whirring and ticking sounds. "But now there's nothing."

"Sounds like it could be the battery?"

"That's what I was thinking. I've been letting it sit for a half-hour or so, but it didn't do any good."

"No, that's not going to help." I looked around. My car was ten or so spaces away. "I wish I could jump you but I have no cables," I said, thinking: *I wish I could just plain jump you.* "Open it up?"

"It's OK, you don't have to."

"I don't mind."

"OK." He went around and pulled the latch inside and then splayed his blue fingers against the hood of the gray Civic, lifting it. It was kind of a shitty car, but that boded well for gayness: Mateo spent his money on clothes and not cars. I pointed to the stick and he stood it up.

"I don't know," I said. "Nothing looks crazy broken, but I'm no expert. Battery looks kind of old though. This thingy here is pretty corroded."

"It's probably kind of old," he said with finality, as though it were a death sentence rather than a diagnosis. "Well, thanks for the look. Have a nice night." He started to reach for the stick.

I laughed. "You think I'm just going to leave you stuck here?"

"I'm not exactly stuck, since I have to be right back here in like—fourteen hours."

"Uh, yeah, but I imagine you'd want to go home and

shower." Poor choice of words, Fletcher. "And sleep, of course," I amended quickly. "Let the dog out. Watch TV." I stopped.

If he took offense he didn't show it—I figured he probably couldn't smell himself, and the paint on his hand was such a fixture he'd probably forgotten it was there. "Yes, that would be nice," he said.

I jingled my keys in my pocket, wondering if that meant he had a dog. "Well there's an AutoZone down that way a ways." I pointed to some trees but I meant past them. "I could give you a ride."

"You don't mind?"

"No, it's cool."

"Thanks. So should we write down this battery stuff or what? Want to be sure I get the right kind."

"I could take a photo with my phone."

"Let's just bring the whole thing with us," he said, jiggling the cord.

He sat in the passenger

seat with the battery on his lap. His fingers were blackened with car grease, on top of the blue. He looked diseased, a refugee from a medieval plague. But there was something articulate and sexy about his hands, too, even beyond the mystery of their ever-changing color.

He seemed oblivious to the grease on his hands as well as the grease that was surely getting on his pants, which were nice enough to be described as *slacks*. I reluctantly put a mark in the straightboy column. Someone who put money into his clothes wouldn't be so careless about dirtying them up. Probably this guy had a girlfriend who managed his wardrobe. It made sense, actually. A disappointing amount of sense.

His cheeks were shining with sweat and a few licks of hair around his sideburns clung to his skin as though dipped in wax. His smell, while noticeable in the office, was all but gone now, and I realized I never would've noticed it at all outside the sterile, filtered, perpetually-chilly office air. It was the smell of life, of living, of activity. It was foreign at work but fit perfectly outside it.

"So how do you like the job so far?" I asked.

"It's OK. Pays the bills."

"Where did you work before this?"

"At my last job." He smiled. Man, his teeth were white. Then he looked out the window for a while, drumming his fingers on the battery. "Speaking of which, how much for a new battery, do you think?"

I didn't know. "Like fifty maybe?"

"Huh. Figured more."

The ride was over in

five minutes even though I stopped at yellow lights. I wanted more time but it was unlikely I could've gotten anything more out of Mr. Zipped Lips if I'd had an interrogation lamp. I wanted to find a hook, some little quirk or peccadillo upon which to hang the hat of a connection, but so far he was giving me nothing.

He insisted on dragging the old battery into the store with us. I was hoping to roam the aisles looking for the batteries, to prolong the errand, but he showed his crapped-out battery to the first salesperson we saw. We picked out a new one that matched. Carrying them both, one on top of the other, made his shoulders look amazing.

At the cashier he pointed at the display—$57.45—and said to me, "You were close." He slid his debit card through the machine in a way that was cute or clumsy or even a little precious—but not quite a hook. And then we were back in my car.

"So do you have lunch with Megan and Candace a lot?" I asked.

"From work?"

"Yeah. I— I saw you coming in from lunch today, with them."

"Oh. No, I haven't ever had lunch with them. I was in the parking lot playing with the car. Just crossed paths with them on the way in."

"Oh. OK."

"Why?"

"No reason." Again I stopped for a yellow light. This time he seemed to notice but didn't say anything. "So then your battery died during lunch?"

"Since this morning."

"Oh." But that didn't make sense. "Since this morning? How did it die this morning?" I pulled into the parking lot and stopped alongside the gray Civic.

"Must've left the radio on last night or something."

Then how did he drive it to work? Before I could ask, he said, "Will you show me how to put it in?"

At this I tingled. I'm not one to boast but I'd been asked that before. "Sure."

"I mean install the battery."

" — I know what you meant."

I got out of the car and before I turned around I nursed the *What-was-that-about?* look I could feel plastered on my face, savoring it there for a second or two before pulling on a mask of indifference. When I turned around he'd set the new battery on the asphalt and was poking his fingers through the plastic wrap.

"Hand me your keys," I said, "I'll pop the hood."

He fished in his pocket and extended his hand. In addition to two car keys, his office key, and what looked like a house key, there was a blue Swiss Army knife and a tiny LED flashlight. All these things rode together on an orange carabiner. Sadly the keychain offered no clues about his identity. No hooks. I unlocked the car door, hoping the inside would be more interesting, would yield more clues, would feature a pride sticker or an *Out* magazine. But there was nothing of note except for a phone charger in the dash, the CD of a band with a Portuguese name wedged between the seats, and an open can of Red Bull in one of the cupholders. A few empty coat hangers hanging from the ceiling handle in the back clicked against the window. The only interesting thing about the inside was that all the backseat seatbelts were tucked out of sight. That was weird. Didn't he ever drive friends around? I pulled the hood release and shut the door.

He'd lifted the hood and was extending the pole. I picked up the old battery from the back of my car and went around to the back of his Civic. I put the key in the lock, and turned it, and his trunk sprang up, and like a big amazed fish I was snagged on the mother of all hooks.

"Wow."

Built into his trunk were four plywood shelves, cut through with maybe two-dozen holes and padded at the bottom with egg-crate foam. Almost every hole was home to a can of spraypaint, one of every color in the rainbow and then some. A black backpack sat in the middle. A hooded sweatshirt, black with a sparkling coating of the surrounding colors, hung over one of the shelves; another was balled up farther back. An open box for a three-pack of Polaroid film was lodged at the side.

And then there was a sharp elbow in my ribs and I was pushed and the old battery clattered to the ground, barely missing my toes.

"Don't look in there!" he yelled, and he slammed shut the trunk hard enough to make the antenna on the hood swish to and fro like the tail of a nervous cat.

I held up my hands. "I'm sorry! Jesus! I was just putting the batt—"

"It's none of your fucking business!"

I saw a fist forming at his side and for a second I thought he was going to slug me. Instead he raised it and pushed it against my sternum, like a very slow-motion punch, dimpling the vertical stripes of my button-down shirt. He left it there for two or three seconds while he glared at me with almost iridescent green eyes that made my brain hit the Moon. When he took his hand away there was a smear of black grease shaped like knuckles. The shirt was ruined. I understood that was the point.

He pulled the keys from the lock and went around to the front of the car. With his forearm he brushed his hair away from his face but it flopped right back into his eyes. He stood looking at the engine. I watched, heart pounding. My back ran with sweat but my mouth felt dry. Though I'd been searching for clues, I still had no reason to believe this guy was gay, but I felt certain that if I was never able to be with him, even for a moment, in some way more significant than this, that my life would always have a hole in it. That I would die incomplete.

"So you're a graffiti painter, then," I said, bending down to pick up the old battery. There were yellow shards of plastic casing on the asphalt. "It's not exactly a mobile meth lab, you know."

"A painter," he said, as though the word were an insult. "I'm a *writer*."

"You're a writer? *I'm* a writer."

"What do you write?"

"Stories. Books. A book. Fiction."

"Fiction. *Pfft*. That's not writing."

"What do you write?"

"I write the truth."

"Fiction is true. It doesn't have to factual to be true."

"Says you. Have you been published?"

"As a matter of fact I have. My novel sold over 65,000 copies."

"All to your mom."

"My mom didn't even know about it. The question is, have *you* been published?"

"I'm published everywhere." He waved his arms. "Find me a bridge I haven't published on."

"The Zakim." Boston's most glamorous landmark bridge.

He frowned and squinted, sharpening his green-eyed glare into knives that seemed to want to slice and dice me. Clearly I'd hit a nerve. He returned his attention to the car and said, "Never mind."

I imagined myself grabbing a fistful of his carefully-ironed shirt, yanking him close and kissing him hard enough to split his lips against my teeth. "One week," I told him instead, holding up a finger. "I give you one week to paint on the Zakim Bridge." I started walking around to my car.

He looked up. "Or *what?*"

"Or—I don't know—I'm a better writer than you." I

sighed. "Can you handle the rest here?"

He glanced over at the battery and looked like he wasn't sure he could handle it, but he said yes, and he added a terse thank-you.

"I'm sorry I looked in your trunk."

"Do me a favor and pretend you didn't."

I got in my car and started it up, reached over and unrolled the passenger window. "For what it's worth, I don't have a problem with it. I think it's kind of pretty."

"Right."

"And by the way, you ruined my fucking shirt!"

A graffiti artist!

A graffiti artist ruined my shirt! I drove home with all the windows down despite the heat, the wind in my mouth carrying the taste of elation, wearing the knuckle-smear on my chest like some kind of superhero emblem.

Thak thak thak thak thak.

My typewriter keys slammed laboriously over a sheet of paper, making it inky but only inky. They seemed to be doing it independently of anything my fingers were making them do. I was too distracted. My mind kept playing back Mateo's weird, awesome request for me to show him how to *put it in*, and the way he'd clumsily re-phrased. Clearly he was aware of the double entendre. The nerves in my skin couldn't stop recalling the angry, wonderful push of his knuckles. *Oh, why the hell not*, I thought, popping open my belt. I started beating off with the shirt spread out on my bed, knuckles of my left hand pressed against the greasy smear Mateo left beside the buttons.

And in my head a stream of images: his hair eyes accent *slacks* arms shoulders *Will you show me how to put it in?* mouse mice 3-2-1 contact. Oh yes. A graffiti artist. Oh. *Yes.*

A few minutes later and a few ounces lighter, I sat back down at my desk. *Thak thak thak.* Relieved (for the moment) of my little obsession, I felt every boring keystroke. Lately I knew it was time to quit when I'd slid so far down in my chair that my head was practically on the seat. Writing was gut-wrenching but I couldn't stop, not even when my mind was elsewhere, not even when I had nothing to write. Sometimes it made me feel like a cutter.

Thak thak thak.

I sat up when I heard the front door open and close and the swish of a grocery bag, and soon the nose of Cara nudged into the space of my cracked-open door.

"Smello," she said.

I laughed. "You may enter."

She pushed open the door. "I'm home."

"I see. Was that groceries?"

"I went to the farmer's market in Copley."

"Nice. Cukes?"

"Several. Have some."

"Yum. Where's Jamar tonight?"

"Working now. He'll be here. Hey, I'm disappointed your broken-mouse encounter with Sexy New Guy wasn't more interesting. How could he not resist *ravishing* you?"

"No. After work it got a *lot* more interesting."

"Oh? Another encounter?"

"Such that he was in my car."

"You screwed him in your *car?* Fletcher!"

"No. I wish. No. But lo, he layeth his hand upon my breast." I reached for the shirt, held it up.

"What happened to your *shirt?*" She came closer to inspect it. "Are those—knuckles?"

"I'll tell in vivid detail. Would you cut me up a cucumber?"

"In exchange for the story, yes. Let me change my clothes first."

We sat on the couch in the living room with a plate of raw veggies, passing the salt shaker back and forth while I regaled her with the tale of The New Guy & The Old Battery, followed by an ecstatic episode of What Was In His Trunk. Her face registered appropriate shades of intrigue and surprise—but I think most of it was for show; she was playing along. Usually my stories had more, shall we say, *simmer* than this. I'm sure she wondered what all the fuss was about when the story had its two main characters parting ways in a parking lot. I hadn't even kissed him. Maybe I was wondering the same thing.

"So he's a graffiti painter." She salted a cucumber slice.

"Apparently."

"That explains the fingers."

"Yup."

"Mysterious."

"I mean obviously he was some kind of artist, but he's not exactly watching Bob Ross episodes and painting happy little trees in his bedroom, knowI'msayin'?"

"He's a criminal," she said.

And I repeated it, loving the word. "Yeah. He's a criminal."

At a little after 11:00

the following morning I received an email from one mateo_amaral@cookmed.com. The subject line said *Lunch?* but there was nothing in the body of the message except for his default office signature.

Mateo Amaral / I.T. Assistant / Cook Medical Publishing, Inc.

I leaned back in my chair and said, "Hm." If *he* was contacting *me* I could afford to take my time responding. *I suppose, you gorgeous shirt-wrecker, I could be bothered to have lunch with you.* I opened an email window and fired off the gossip to Cara. We analyzed his intentions over a dozen email back-and-forths.

Cara: "So do you think this lunch is a *date?*"

Me: "I don't know. His invitation was literally one word."

Cara: "To me the single word implies a nervousness or a bashfulness that shows you have rendered him speechless... which clearly hints that his intentions are romantic. Thus: date."

Me: "That's one way to look at it."

Cara: "Do you even remember how to have a date?"

Me: "I think I can figure it out, biatch."

Cara: "So he hasn't responded back to you?"

My mouth dropped open. I'd been so busy analyzing that I'd forgotten to actually reply. The original message was now an hour old.

Sorry to keep you waiting, I slammed out, breathless, afraid the invitation had expired. *Lunch would be cool. How about 12:30?*

I sent it and scrambled to the restroom to check my hair.

A few minutes past 12:30

there was a knock on the wall of my cube and Mateo said, "Hey."

"Oh. Hi." I closed a few windows—one containing some final words of encouragement from Cara, who was acting like I'd really never done this before—and spun around to face him.

"How's the new mouse working out for you?" he said.

"Clicks like a champ. Thanks."

"Staying connected OK this time?"

"Yeah. Guess you put it in there pretty tight." I watched his face. Nothing.

"Yeah. Hey, want to eat outside?"

"Sure, I just need to grab my sandwich from the fridge."

We detoured silently to the break room and I smelled his smell, and then we emerged into the sunny outside and I couldn't smell it anymore. He looked awesome in the sun, which went against my original instinct that he'd look best at night amid shadows.

I followed him to the curb at the edge of the parking lot and we sat down there in the shade with our sandwiches. His pant legs went up enough to reveal a few inches of blue-and-white argyle socks and a half-inch of fuzzy, olive-skinned shin.

"Busy today?" I said.

"A little."

"Me too."

We ate for a while in what would've been silence if not for a pair of birds squawking on the roof, and I was starting to wonder why he bothered asking me to lunch.

"How's the car?" I said. "Get the battery in OK?"

"Yeah. Started right up. So I guess that's what it was."

"I guess so."

He finished half of his sandwich and started in on the other half. "That's kind of why I asked you to lunch, actually, because—"

"—Oh?"

"—Because I wanted you to know I feel— Well, it wasn't cool. What happened yesterday."

I paused mid-chew. Peanut butter gathered in my cheek. "What wasn't cool?"

He crossed his arms over his knees, his sandwich dangling from fingers that today were orange. He looked off into the corner of the parking lot. "When you saw what you saw in my car. That just wasn't cool."

I forced the glob down my throat. "I told you I was sorry."

"Yeah. I know."

"What more do you want me to say?"

"Nothing. Just know that I'm pissed off about it."

I laughed—not the appropriate thing to do, given how serious he looked, but I couldn't help it. "Did we stumble into a therapy session or something? Would you like me to air my grievances too?"

"If you want." He took a big bite of sandwich, tilted a water bottle to his lips, looked at me expectantly.

"Never mind."

"See, you still have whatever secrets you have, Fletcher. Me, I don't have mine anymore. Because of what happened. And I don't like how that feels. Understand?"

I looked at his hand and then down at the sand on the pavement between my shoes. "I guess so."

He gave his shirt collar a tug. "This is my secret identity, right? It's for show. It's not who I am. When I've got a can in my hand, that's who I am. That's the real Mateo. It's not your fault that you figured me out. I know you weren't snooping. It wasn't on purpose. Accidents happen. But all the same I've lost something and I wanted you to know it."

"Maybe you should look at it not as losing something, but as sharing something," I said. OK, it was a direct quote from my novel, and maybe that's tacky, but it totally applied.

"Well I wouldn't have chosen to share it."

"Then I'm sorry," I said, meaning it a little more this time, but only a little.

"S'OK." He popped the last bite of crust into his mouth and washed it down with the rest of his water. He put the empty bottle on the curb and placed his hands flat on the sidewalk behind us, stretched his legs out over the hot asphalt. I looked out at the parking lot, where the sun glinted off bumpers and hubcaps, took another bite of sandwich and decided not to push this conversation any further. I'd been with weird guys but this guy was really weird. The question was whether he was prohibitively weird.

He shifted his butt on the curb, drew up his legs and rested his forearms on his knees. He looked up in the sky and shielded his eyes and watched some birds fly by. He grabbed a twig and broke it into a few pieces and flicked them onto the ground one by one. I watched all this, eating slowly.

"So nice out, I hate to go back inside," he said at last.

"Yeah."

Back at my desk I

banged out a long, frustrated email to Cara and she responded with one surprising word:

"Hot."

That night I made burritos

and when Jamar showed up Cara and I dumped some of the rice and beans out of ours so there'd be enough left for him to make one. When we were done and rinsing the plates I told them I was going to go do some writing.

In my room I opened the closet and looked at the shirt with Mateo's fist-print, which hung from a hanger at the front. I thought of our weird lunch, caught myself sighing, and felt silly. This all was uncharacteristic, a little too *Brokeback* for comfort. *Relax, Fletcher*, I told myself. *All you want is to bang the guy. It's familiar territory. What's unfamiliar is only that you haven't done it already.* I held my fist against the knuckle mark, matching the shape against my skin.

I imagined Mateo's greasy fist gripping my —

Gah, chill out! It was way too hot out to get worked up. At my desk I looked at the paper rolled through my typewriter. I'd written only two sentences on this page — the beginning of a short story much less interesting than Mateo. He permeated my thoughts. The way he had his sleeves turned up. The way he licked mustard off his lips. That heavenly inch of fuzzy shin. Those eyes.

Thak thak thak.

I'd slid into the usual position, staring at the inky paper, mind adrift, not-quite-absentmindedly rubbing a boner against the underside of my desk drawer.

I put my hands on my face and stalked around my room. The luminescent thermometer strip on the side of my fish tank indicated the water was running a six-degree fever. A trio of neons hovered huffing and puffing near the surface. They looked like how I felt. I went to the kitchen and got some ice and dropped four cubes into the water. A fifth cube I pressed against my forehead. Water ran down my nose and cheeks and I licked it off my lips. Then I fell back on my bed. I flat-out needed to get laid. It was the only way to clear my head.

I didn't have the energy to arrange a hook-up from scratch, and I hadn't heard from Alex since bailing on him last weekend — but there were other options. I got my phone and texted a number in my Favorites. An old standby.

How're you feeling tonight?

Five minutes passed. Empty minutes that years ago would've made me feel like a sucker, like a desperate horndog hanging on the other guy's whims. But experience taught me how exhilarating it is to be the receiver of such messages. I was doing him a favor.

A response came: *Have a raid at 10 but can fit u in b4 then.*

A short delay and then: *so 2 speak. ;-)*

A knock on my door. "Thanks for the food, Bradford. I'm heading out."

"Later Jamar."

I worked my thumbs: *See you in 20?*

The *OK* set me in motion. I pulled my shirt up over my nose to make sure my pits were decent, cleared myself for take-off, and went to brush my teeth. I pushed my wallet into my pocket and grabbed my keys off the kitchen table. Cara was stretched out on the couch with a journal open on scribbly pages and a pen wagging between her fingers like a joint. She slid her head over the arm of the couch and looked at me upside down.

"You leaving too?" she said. "You're supposed to be writing."

"I did write. A text." I grinned.

"A booty call?"

"Perhaps. What are *you* writing? Journalizing?"

"My manifestos," she said.

"When are you going to let me read them?"

"Never. You don't let me read your stuff anymore."

"I haven't written anything worth reading."

"Whatever. Write me a story and maybe I'll let you read a few pages of mine."

"That hardly seems fair."

"Take it or leave it." She looked me over, still upside down. "You going out with Sexy New Guy?"

"If only. No. A consolation prize."

"Not the Warcraft kid again, I hope."

I laughed.

"Fletcher!"

"Don't look at me like that. He's convenient!"

"You *use* him."

"How am I using him? He gets to get lucky without even leaving his apartment!"

"Ugh. Be safe."

"Always." I leaned down and kissed her upside-down forehead; her hair against my chin made me think of a bearded hipster I used to date named Scotch Tape. "Jamar went home?"

"Staying at his place tonight. He ran out of clothes here."

"If you're lonely I guess I could stay and chill...."

She looked at me and then up at the clock. "I'll see you in an hour, Fletch." As I was closing the door behind me I heard her mumble, her voice doing the equivalent of an eye-roll, "You and your Warcraft kid."

My Warcraft kid was a

college junior named Mike Stepp, who lived in a studio apartment in the Back Bay with a turtle named Agamemnon and a huge-ass computer (two monitors, tower the size of an armoire) that seemed to wrap around Mike like some kind of life-sustaining medical equipment. Although the padded captain's chair in front of said computer bore a permanent imprint of his ass, it was a good ass attached to a nice body, and Mike was cute all around. Tallish and lean, shaggy brown hair he was always swinging away from his blue eyes. And, most important in this kind of relationship, chill.

We met online a year ago, went out a few times, stayed in a bunch of times. I liked him. It'd been years since I expected anything to go anywhere, though, so I was hardly surprised when I felt him start to wiggle.

"Dating is so much work," he told me one night when we were standing outside his apartment after splitting a pizza in Harvard Square. He pursed his lips and swung his hair away from his eyes with a flick of his head. "Not that you aren't cool."

I smiled. I hadn't thought we were dating. Cute that he had.

"Between school work and work and my dailies," he went on. "You know." He looked apologetic.

"Busy schedule."

"Yeah.... So."

"So I'm getting the heave-ho."

He shrugged.

"No problem. It happens. So I'll see you around." I shoved my hands in my pockets and turned down the stairs. Once upon a time this all would've made me sad, would've felt like another false start, another loss. Now I was already thinking about who I could call.

"Well, I was wondering, though," Mike continued, leaning against the chipped black railing, "we get along well enough. Maybe we can still hang out every once in a while? Not dating exactly, but...."

I turned on the sidewalk and looked up. "Friends?"

"Sure, but more like...."

I smirked when I realized he was angling for what, in my opinion, we already had. Kiddo was looking for benefits. "Pals?" I teased, making him earn it.

"Oh, I don't know!" He looked down at his shoes with an exasperated smile.

"Oh oh *oh*," I said, rolling my finger in the air. I started back up the stairs. "You want us to be sex buddies!"

He gulped and grinned. "That's as good a word as any, I suppose." His eyes started to cross as I got closer.

"High five!" In a jocky, yeah-dude kind of way I smacked my hand against his. I could tell he was practically blowing his load.

"So you'd, uh, be cool with that?" he said.

"I'm open to whatever."

"Sweet." A giant grin.

"So text me, we'll work it out."

"Yup. OK." He licked his suddenly dried-out lips. "Would you, maybe, uh, care to step upstairs and take this arrangement for a bit of a — test flight?"

"Haha. Well." I wanted to, of course (little Mike wasn't the only one practically blowing it), but now was the time to establish things, to seize the upper hand. "I can't tonight. I really have to be getting home and — help Cara — with — groceries."

"Oh. That sucks."

"I know."

He swallowed hard and gaped a little, the corners of his lips dry and his eyes big. Jeez, the poor kid. I felt for him. I wondered if it was really necessary to be the first person to reject the other. Experience taught me it was. It was a power-grab, sure, but it had a way of making things easier down the road. It was a good precedent to have rejected; it was a good fact to have in your pocket. "Text me soon, though," I said. "We'll get together."

I waved and he waved and I walked up the street, feeling his eyes on me until I turned the corner. He was obviously going to scramble upstairs and rub one out ASAP, which probably meant the call wouldn't come tomorrow. I expected to hear from him on the second or third day. It was the second.

Knowing what I knew now — that Mike was a gamer but not a player of games — I would've gone for it that first night. There was no tug-of-war in our arrangement. No power trips. That's why I'd kept it going for so long. It was convenient when I was too lazy to get anything else started. For the first few months the arrangement was a novelty for Mike and he called me a lot, and I, even when I didn't really need it, got a kick out of obliging. But as with most things the novelty did wear off, and the booty-call aspect wore off almost completely. At this point we tended to hang out, get dinner, go shopping, whatever, and then fall into the sack almost as an afterthought. Over the last six months it had practically turned into dating. It was averaging once or twice a month at the moment.

I texted: *I'm parking.*

When I got to the front of his building I buzzed and he buzzed me in. The building smelled of Pine-Sol and old carpets. I went up the stairs — four flights in an old brownstone lit by funky chandeliers — and arrived panting at his door. I was regular enough to let myself in. The apartment was cool, almost cold. He had a big, rumbling a.c. to offset the heat his monster computer churned out.

"Yo," I said, shutting the door behind me. It was sticky in the jamb and a practiced bump with my shoulder closed it. I turned the lock. I was in a tiny kitchen that opened into the main part of the studio. I left my shoes near the door.

"Hey Fletcher," Mike said from around the corner. "Just give me a sec here."

I noted the mac and cheese clinging to a pan on the stove and I noted the dishes in the sink. I walked barefoot into the main room. It was long and narrow and if not for the fancy old marble fireplace (nonworking, I presumed, and in which

Agamemnon's twenty-gallon tank was wedged) and the ornate crown molding, the studio would've looked like a boxcar. If I spread my arms I could almost touch both walls at once. Jamar could easily have touched both walls at once. The rear of the studio was a loft, raised up like a deck, and beneath it, with his desk pushed against the back of the loft ladder, was Mike's computer and Mike, happy together, two peas in a studio.

He looked over the top of one of the monitors and smiled. His hair was pretty long but he'd clearly taken my advice and splurged on a good haircut. "What can I do you for?" he said.

"For free. Hey, your hair looks smokin'."

"Thanks. I tried that place on Newbury." He gave me a little smile before lowering his eyes to a monitor. "Find good parking?"

"Decent." I leaned against the ladder.

"We haven't done this like this in a while."

"I know. I kind of need it. Stressed."

"Uh-oh."

"Nothing major. Writer's block. The heat. Deadly combination."

"Ah." He looked at one screen, then the other, then back at me. "Sorry I have to rush it."

"No worries. Shall I go up?"

He looked at the other screen intently for a moment, typed something, and then looked up again, flicking his hair in a way that made my dick stir. "Yes. I'll be up in two shakes of a troll's horn."

I climbed the creaking ladder. I could feel on my toes the heat rising off the computer. Against the top rung I scraped the soles of my feet to rid them of the sand and tiny pebbles tracked in on shoes. Mike's futon mattress lay on the floor up here — there wasn't the clearance for an actual bed.

"Whew, hotter up here," I said, balling up my t-shirt.

"I know, sorry." He was coming up the ladder now, more and more of the body I'd come for staggering into view. "Heat rises."

"Must be a bitch to sleep in."

"Lucky we don't plan on sleeping." He said it sultry and we laughed and got undressed in a tangle.

Mike hadn't been with very

many guys before me but I wouldn't ever have guessed. He could've authored a series of instructional textbooks about the things he could do with his mouth. I lifted my head off his pillow and looked at the top of his head bobbing near my belly and fell back again and said, "Insane."

When we were done I

scooted to the edge of the mattress and reached for my shorts. Mike wiped at the jersey sheet with a hand-towel in quick little wax-on wax-off circles.

For the same reason I kept fish—to give a guy something to talk about while he was putting his pants back on—I sometimes wished Mike would hoist Agamemnon's tank up into the loft, to quietly scritch around on his rocks while we shagged and then be a post-coital conversation topic.

"Hey," Mike said after moments of silence, "thank you for the birthday card."

"No problem."

"It was funny." He balled up the towel and tossed it over the edge of the loft. It hit the floor with a thump.

"I saw in my news feed it was coming up. Do anything fun?"

"Went for dinner and a movie with my friend Jen. Came home and leveled some of my alts." He dropped onto his belly and reached across the mattress to grab his glasses off the loft floor. "Pleasant evening."

"No boys?"

"No boys, alas."

"Heh." I lifted myself up as far as space allowed before I would bonk my head on the ceiling, and zipped my fly. "OK, I'm gonna bounce."

"Thanks for coming, it was fun. Heh, *thanks for coming.*"

I reached across the mattress and gave a tug on his foot.

"Later. Have fun with your raid."

I went down the ladder.

Winding down the staircase—less than ten minutes after ejaculation—it was clear the hook-up, while good, was a failure. Because even while Mike was showing off I'd been imagining splotches of paint on his fingers. Only when I paused on the second floor to check for keys and wallet and phone, and the key-touching guy burst like a newsflash into my imagination, did Mateo leave my mind.

I wanted a shower but Cara was in the bathroom—I could tell by the water sounds that she was shaving her legs. I went to my room. Opened my closet door and had a look at the unwearable but hardly ruined shirt. Switched on my typewriter, started to roll in a clean sheet of paper, stopped, switched it off. Swiveled around in my chair. Climbed into bed. Slept.

At a time indeterminate

the ceiling turned blue and my desk started humming. I slapped my hand at the phone, held it some distance away from my face, squinting.

Im in bed, said a text from Alex.

Well I'm sleeping, I replied, ignoring his implied dot-dot-dot.

With jimmy, came the reply.

That sure woke me up the rest of the way. I wanted to ask how-how-how but seeming in any way interested would give Alex a win. *You're texting me while you're in bed with someone? Isn't that rude of you?*

Hes out now hes doing pushups naked, his muscles making me religious.

I remembered telling Cara that if they ever got back together I'd die, and it felt like that, like an icepick in my gut. I leaned up on my elbow and that wasn't comfortable so I sat up and that wasn't comfortable either.

I typed out *Congrats!* and threw the phone on my bed. It slid under the covers and made the sheet glow with the next line of Alex's gloating. But the light only illuminated how empty my own bed was.

My Perino angst kept me

up most of the night but withered at Cook when I saw Mateo and his colorful fingers. They were yellow today, a mustardy yellow that betrayed a muted rainbow of underlying colors. It looked as though he'd been messy with the sandwich he was now holding up to his mouth.

Just as I was heading to the lunchroom to make waffles I'd received another email from mateo_amaral@cookmed.com, this time with the subject line *Re: Re: Lunch?* and once again with nothing in the body of the message except my earlier frantic reply. That meant he saved our original correspondence in his inbox. Maybe he just didn't delete it. But maybe he *saved* it. A shiver of excitement rattled through me, an excitement that felt depressingly novel.

I sent an unpunctuated *OK* without offering details, and went to make my waffles. Then, with steaming plate in hand, I detoured to meet him at the I.T. cubes—an experiment in just showing up.

"Brunch again?" he said. He was fiddling inside an open computer but he left it and gathered up his sandwich and a bottle of water.

"Why not? I like brunch."

"Want to go outside?"

"OK."

The sun was blinding but he looked cute with his eyes squinted. He had on light gray pants and a pale blue button-down sheer enough to show the sleeves of his undershirt.

He started to sit down on the curb in the same place as before, but a picnic table was open and I started walking toward that instead. I was tired of looking at the side of his face; I wanted to sit across from him for once.

"How's your day going?" I said, rubbing a plastic knife back and forth across my waffles.

"OK." He took a bite of sandwich. "Kind of slow actually. Everything's running smoothly today."

"I've been pretty busy. I bet when it's busy for us it's slow for you. Like I bet people spend their idle time bitching about dead pixels and stuff."

"Haha. Yeah, probably."

"What do you do when it's slow?"

"Just sit at my desk." He hunched forward, positioning his hand on the table as though it were guiding a mouse. He closed his eyes and let his jaw hang slack. I was happy to have my attention called to his lips.

"You sleep?" I said, amused.

"No no no. Doze."

"I think I've seen you dozing, actually."

"Uh-oh. Have you?"

"You need those glasses with the painted-on eyeballs," I said.

He wiped a blob of mustard off his lip and I absentmindedly touched my own lip. We both seemed to notice.

"Haha, yeah, I do need those," he said. "Then I'll get a blanket with a shirt and pants painted on it, so I can hold it up to me like so."

"Randy needs that. I caught him looking at porn once."

"You wouldn't believe the X-rated shit I've seen on people's computers."

"This was pretty X-rated. Well, a very heavy R."

"Which one's Randy?"

"Reddish hair. Fancies sweater vests. Sits a few cubes down from me. Across from the mailboxes."

"Doesn't that guy Bob sit there?"

"No, the other one. In the corner. Last I knew he had a picture of Russian nesting dolls for his desktop wallpaper."

"OK, yeah yeah. Seriously? You caught him—you know?" He made a quick motion with his fist, the image of which my brain immediately archived into permanent file for lots of later recollection.

"God no. No no no. I had to ask him something and when I turned into his cube I got a facefull of this—uh."

"What was it?"

"This naked chick in a cowboy hat squatting over the head of a bear-skin rug."

"Oh god. And at work. So wrong." He shook his head,

smiling.

"He saw me and he starts clicking exasperatedly to minimize the window. Notice I say *minimize*, not *close*. He wanted to come back to it later."

"Haha. So he saw you?"

"Yes. Then I had to ask my question and interact with him for like three minutes."

"Raunchy."

"Randy."

"Haha."

A breeze whiffed my sandwich bag across the table and he grabbed it and I put my water bottle on it to hold it.

"Thanks for asking me to lunch," I said.

"Yup."

"I was afraid you were going to yell at me again."

"I didn't yell at you!"

"I know."

In the parking lot Bassett eased himself into his rusty Geo Metro and drove away. Mateo looked around. Outside the main entrance, Babette and Megan were sharing a smoke, but they were safely out of earshot.

He leaned forward the way a person does at a small table on a good date and whispered, "I'm going to paint on the Zakim tonight."

I leaned forward too. Until now there'd been no discussion at all of his extracurricular activities — I'd sort of assumed they were off limits. "You are?"

"You said you'd give me a week, right? Clock's ticking."

"Well I wouldn't want you to get arrested or anything. It's pretty visible, isn't it?" In fact, Boston's famous cable-stayed bridge (a) had about a million lights shining on it, (b) was a ten-lane highway, and (c) was featured regularly as the live video backdrop on at least two local channels' nightly news.

"That's why I need a lookout," he said.

Part of me wanted to take that as a joke. The rest prayed he was serious.

"What do you think? Interested?" Slowly he raised his arm and blew a ladybug off his sleeve.

I knew from the first moment I saw him that I'd never turn down anything this guy asked of me. Still, I took my time answering. After a slow sip of water I said, "I guess I could be up for an adventure."

He laughed.

"What would I have to do?"

"All you have to do," he said, leaning forward again, green eyes twinkling, "is just be a lookout. Right? And tell me if anyone's coming."

"It's a highway. Aren't there going to be tons of people coming?"

"Not cars. I'm talking about people who can Taser us."

Taser us? "I can do lookout, sure. Do you think we'll have to run? Have you ever been chased?"

"I get chased all the time." He took a bite of sandwich. "But never been caught." He knocked his fist on the wood tabletop and concealed a modest grin with chewing.

"What would happen if you were? What happens for writing graffiti? Do you get a ticket?"

"A ticket? No. I wish. It's the slammer."

"The slammer?"

"Jail."

"I know what the slammer is."

"Few weeks ago this writer, Melissa Something, I forget— she goes by Pell Mel— Have you seen her stuff?"

"I don't think so."

"You have. Anyway, Pell Mel got put away for six months for tagging a wall near the Back Bay T."

"Six months?"

"Six months in jail for tagging Back Bay Station." He shook his head.

"Yikes."

"She's good, it's a big loss for the city."

"I bet she won't be doing graffiti anymore."

He laughed. "She will. Bet she tags something on her way home from jail. Once a writer always a writer."

"Is that why you go out?"

"I guess. I do what I can to minimize the risk. Try to keep

my face covered, watch out for security cameras. That kind of stuff."

"So that's why you need a lookout to paint on the Zakim."

"Yup. Still interested?"

"Sure."

"Hold on." He pulled his phone from his pocket and spent a minute poking at it while I wondered what he was doing. Then he handed it to me. "Full disclosure," he said. "Go ahead and read that."

"*Massachusetts General Laws,*" I read off the little screen, "*Chapter 266, Section 126A: Whoever intentionally, willfully and maliciously or wantonly, paints the real or personal property of another including but not limited to a wall—*"

"Check."

"*Fence—*"

"Check."

"*Building—*"

"Check." He was smiling.

"*Sign—*"

"Check."

"*Rock—*"

"Check."

"*Monument—*"

"Check."

"*Or tablet—* What's a tablet?"

"Don't know. Whatever it is, I've probably painted on it."

"So you've really been around the block, then?"

"I get around. Keep reading. Best part's coming."

I continued: "*...Shall be punished by imprisonment in a state prison for a term of not more than three years or by imprisonment in a house of correction for not more than two years or by a fine of not more than $1,500 or both imprisonment and fine, and shall also be required to pay for the removal or obliteration of such painting....* Mateo, they really don't like graffiti artists, do they?"

"Admittedly it's an acquired taste." He smiled, taking back his phone. "So with that out of the way, are you coming?"

"The other day you were all pissed off that I knew. Now

you want me to come with you. What changed your mind?"

He shrugged. "You know, so you might as well see. Are you coming?"

"Of course."

"OK." Screwing the cap on his water bottle he added, "Then I'll see you tonight."

Cara and Jamar were spilled

across the couch watching some or other crime procedural when I came out of my bedroom. After looking around for my keys in the kitchen I paused beside the couch. Jamar offered up a bag of popcorn.

"No thanks. I'm heading out."

Cara rolled her eyes.

"Date?" Jamar said.

"Something like that." Really I had no idea what it was and had no idea how to prepare for it. So I was wearing my hook-up underwear and my comfortable sneakers. "Don't wait up."

"We never do."

"You're not getting any younger, you know, Bradford," Jamar warned.

I took the Green Line inbound. The subway map on the wall of the T was for me like notches on a bedpost. Practically every stop on this line (and plenty of stops on the other lines) represented a hook-up. One for Steve, one for John, one for Johnny, one for Jon (I'd been with more variations of the name John than I could remember). It was like having my sex-life flash before my eyes.

I got off at Copley (Mike's stop), walked to Back Bay and caught the Orange Line to Forest Hills. Forest Hills was a blank spot. I met a guy at nearby Green Street once, and I really worked Ruggles, near Northeastern University, for a while, but nothing at Forest Hills yet. Would that change tonight?

The fact that Mateo asked me to meet him at Forest Hills was a decent indication that it *was* going to change. The Zakim was at the opposite end of the city. To get there I would've continued inbound on the Green Line and not transferred. But he told me to meet him at Forest Hills. Maybe we were going to drive there.

Or maybe he had other plans.

The T pulled into the station and the operator announced that this was the *last and final stop*; mentally I dragged a red line through half of that phrase. The escalator was out of service so I took the stairs to the aboveground part of the station and looked around. It was surprisingly busy at this hour—a cop stood drumming his fingers against the side of the information kiosk, people bustled around, some loitered. I looked around. The shops—a donut place and a florist—were closed, metal gates rolled down over their fronts. Leaning against the florist shop gate was Mateo. He was playing with his phone. My breath caught in my throat. He was wearing a black sleeveless hoodie—his arms were bare and his inner forearms, both of them, were tattooed with blocks of some kind. The sweatshirt's open zipper revealed a white beater underneath. His jeans and sneakers were paint-misted. A backpack lay on the floor by his feet. His hair was pushed up away from his face with a black plastic hair band of the type worn by ten-year-old girls and South American soccer stars. He looked like the second coming.

Suddenly those green eyes were fixed on me but he didn't smile. He stepped away from the wall and stretched his arms.

I said hi.

"You came." He held out his hand and I shook it. I was surprised by his grip—there was a lot more in it now, a strength and confidence missing (or simply omitted) at work. I remembered what he'd said about his secret identity, how he was the real Mateo at night. I wondered what I was getting myself into.

"Of course I came." We stood facing each other, a stand-off. I wanted to suck his lips. "I—like your tattoos," I said, giving a nod at his arm. The patterns started an inch or two before his wrists and stopped in the middle of his biceps.

"Oh, yeah. Thanks." He raised his right arm and turned the forearm veiny-side up, gave it a little shake (I wondered if it was to shake off my gaze), and lowered it. "It's Boston."

"That's cool." I almost asked to see it again. "The skyline? From what angle?"

"Looking from Cambridge. From Memorial Drive." He raised his arm again and turned it over quick and put it down, more just to refer to it than to offer it for further inspection. "It's a little outdated now. They keep building. So."

"What's the other arm? Different angle?"

He raised his left arm. "No. This side's São Paulo."

"California?"

He smirked and I felt like a total dipshit. "No. Brazil. Where my family's from." He pronounced it like he was from there too. *Bra-ZEE-oo.*

"Oh. Cool. Yeah. I wondered."

"Boston and São Paulo." He dropped his arms to his sides.

"That's cool." No more talk of geography, I decided, eager to change the subject to one that made me sound less ignorant. I wondered if that was even possible with him. For as worldly as I thought I was, he seemed so much bigger. "So when do we...?"

"Start?"

"Yeah."

"Come on."

He led me out of the station, down a long flight of stairs and into the parking lot. The air was moist and I felt hot already. I plucked at my shirt and hoped the heat would make him shed his sweatshirt soon.

The smell of brick-oven pizza from a restaurant across the street caught my nostrils and I breathed it in.

"I saw the Zakim on TV tonight," I said. "You know how they use it as the backdrop on the news?"

"Oh yeah." He laughed.

"I say it's too clean!" I pumped my fist like a revolutionary.

He laughed again, this time like how you laugh at a kid who plans to lasso the Moon. "It *is* too clean."

"Then why are we here and not there? Are we driving?"

"Fletcher, we're not really doing the Zakim."

" — We're not?" I found myself disappointed but I'd be OK with a change of plans if they involved seeing those tattoos up close.

"Not tonight, anyway."

"Tomorrow?"

He turned and socked me playfully in the arm. "Tomorrow. Man, you're crazy. No. The Zakim's what we call a heaven spot. The best of all places. But it's a dream. A dream. It would be su-i-cide."

"Then why did you say we were going to?"

"Wanted to see if you'd go, I guess."

"So you know I'd go. What do you think about *that?*"

"Like I said, you're crazy. Louco." I shrugged and he added, "But that's good."

"Oh."

"You have to be, a little bit, to do this stuff."

"OK."

"Want to try something smaller?"

Before I had a chance to respond he gestured for me to follow.

He led me down Hyde

Park Avenue for a mile or more, blue TV light flickering in the windows of three-deckers we passed. Then we dipped down a side street, and at the dead end we climbed over a chain-link fence. Mateo went over it a lot easier than I did but I didn't embarrass myself. From there we entered the woods. He was silent but he picked his way among the bushes and branches carefully enough to imply a sense of direction. I realized I hadn't ever stopped to think about whether I trusted this guy. That just wasn't something that came up in the fluorescent-lit halls of our cubicle maze. And rarely was it something I thought about on dates. I'd never had a date in the woods.

Really, Mateo could be planning to kill me, could turn and plunge a knife into my belly at any moment and no one would ever be the wiser. Could drop me into a pit and seal it over with rotting plywood like in *Silence of the Lambs*. Could kidnap me and bring me to a den of Brazilian drug lords, hold me for a ransom Cara and Jamar could never pay. But I figured he probably wouldn't. And if he did, well, he was cute — and I could forgive practically anything of the cute.

I smirked at the thought, and tried to focus. I focused on the sounds of the woods, on the chirp of city crickets, on the softening traffic noises, on the steady huff-huff of our breath. Most of all I enjoyed the sound of the twigs crackling underfoot. I was almost never in the woods. I marveled that there could even be this much woods in the city.

"How much farther?" I said, feeling sweat slide down my back.

"Not far." He lifted a low branch over his head and held it until I could grab it. His bare arms looked ghostly in the dark. "Ever heard of Clarice Lispector?" he said.

"No, who's that?" His gang leader?

"A Brazilian writer. A novelist. I was thinking about what you said, about something not having to be factual to be true. It reminded me. One of her books has a line like that, something like, *This story, although invented, is true.*"

"Cool."

"Had to read it in high school. *Hour of the Star.* Worth picking up if you can find a translation. It's super short. You could read it on your lunch."

He stopped suddenly and I almost bumped into him, then regretted not seizing the chance. We were standing against a chain-link fence looking down into a concrete canyon through which, at the bottom, fifteen or twenty feet down, ran two sets of train tracks.

He pointed. "See that wall down there? It's just begging to be painted on. Don't you think?"

I laughed. "How do we get down there?"

I wondered if he had some kind of rope ladder set up and once again worried about embarrassing myself. But he bumped the back of his hand against my arm and said, "Down here." He led me down some leaf-covered concrete steps I hadn't even noticed were there, and he pushed open a door that had appeared to be locked. The city seemed willing to permit him access to whatever parts of it he wanted, all its secret places. The stairwell emptied out alongside the tracks.

"Oh."

"Don't trip," he said.

"Is there a third rail here?"

"Nah, this is the regular train, not the T."

We walked across the tracks and I marveled at the thickness of the rails and at the huge width of this space, this canyon for trains. When you're on a train the concrete walls are only ever a few feet beyond the windows, but standing on the track, well, haha, you could drive a train through here.

"So this is safe?" I wondered aloud, looking around, looking up at the fence where we'd been standing moments earlier. In the dark among the shadows it seemed impossibly high up. We were trapped down here, vulnerable. If some sneaky woods-dweller were to shut that door behind us, how far would we have to walk before we found another one unlocked? And would we be able to get there before a train came blasting along?

"Safe how?" he said.

"Safe from trains, I guess?" But I also meant safe from cops, rabid hobos, graffiti gangs....

"Well, the commuter rail you can hear a half-mile away," he said. "It's that high-speed Acela you have to watch out for. Those things are silent!"

"Those are the ones that track-repair guys are always getting creamed by."

"That's why you do your research. Know the schedules. Know them like your phone number. And always be aware of the time." He pulled out his phone. "I've got the Amtrak and MBTA websites bookmarked." He grinned. "We have some time." He shrugged off his backpack and kneeled down with it on the ground in front of the concrete wall. Water marks covered the concrete like roots, and creamsicle-colored sodium lights bulged every twenty feet along the wall, throwing pools of orange light at the darkness. From the backpack Mateo pulled a pair of latex gloves and held them up to me. "You'll probably want to use these."

I took them. They didn't seem new, exactly, but they were

free of paint—like an aging condom in a hopeful high schooler's wallet. "You don't? Isn't this type of paint pretty toxic?" I snapped them on.

"I'm used to it."

"Shame shame," I said, thinking *No glove no love.*

"Haha."

"I noticed your hand right when I met you. It doesn't help your secret identity much."

"Can't be 100 percent. I figure people figure I build models or something."

He stood up, slipped one spraycan into the pocket of his hoodie. The other he shook, the pea inside clacking—a familiar sound to me even though I'd used spraypaint only once before in my life, to paint a bike. He held out the can.

I took it. Shook it again. "I have no idea what to write."

"Start with your Social Security number."

"Ha."

A grin. His teeth stood out white. "Just throw up a quick tag."

"A tag."

"A signature. Your name."

"Hmm. I'm not about to paint my name on here."

"I don't mean your *real* name, silly," he said. "A nickname. An apelido." He took the other can from his pocket, uncapped it, shook it. His fingers seemed to know the can by heart. He didn't examine the valve to make sure it was pointing the right way, as I'd already done at least twice. He made a quick arc on the wall, then another. I watched. "Where'd you get your real name, anyway? Fletcher."

"My grandfather." I shook the can some more, getting ready, psyching myself up. My heart was beating fast.

"Was he an arrow maker?"

"An arrow maker? No, he worked in a factory that made—telephone wire, I think."

"Huh." He was outlining interconnected bubble-letters but I couldn't make out what they were or what they spelled. The pungent smell of paint made my nose itch.

"In middle-school I got *Fletcher the felcher* a lot."

"Felcher? I don't know what that is." He stepped back to examine his work and then started making more outlines beneath the ones he'd already made. There was no room for error here, I saw — no eraser at the end of the can, no backspace key. In that way it was like using a typewriter. His arm moved with certainty.

"Felcher. Like felching? A verb. To felch."

"To felch. I don't know."

"I'm not about to explain what it is."

"Why not?"

"It's mind-bogglingly gross."

He stopped painting and looked at me. I'd been right after all about his face coming alive at night. His green eyes seemed to glow like a cat's in the orange light. "Now you really need to tell me."

"It's when someone—" I felt my face get hot. "No, I'm not telling you. Google it. Use your phone. Go ahead." I shook the can some more.

"Never mind Google. What's to felch?"

"I'm really not comfortable."

"OK, OK, jeez."

He continued his outlining, then stopped and rummaged in his backpack amongst cans of paint, every once in a while holding one up in the light, which bent shadows around his eyes like a moving mask. He was a criminal, I realized, at least according to the cops. He was a wanted man. Yet he'd brought me here, showed me this, revealed his secret identity.

"OK, so to felch," I said. "It's when you ejaculate in someone's rectum and then — ingest your own semen out of their — rectum."

He gritted his teeth and said, "Oh, I've done that."

I stared in silence.

"I'm kidding! I don't even know why I said that. I'm kidding." He looked at me earnestly. "You believe me I'm kidding, right?"

"I believe you."

"We need to forget about that shit. That is some sick shit. *Fletcher the felcher* is not a good tag for the arrow maker."

"Arrow Maker. That doesn't sound like a very unique name."

"Arrow Maker." He said it a couple of times, testing it. "Hmm. Well Michael's not a unique name either, and he's an angel, right?"

For a second I thought he was talking about my Michael, but he meant God's.

"Are you saying I'm an angel?" I said, and instantly regretted it. Perhaps I was assuming too much here.

He looked at his work in progress and dragged his arm across his forehead again. "Just saying Arrow Maker is OK for a name."

I looked at the blank wall and shook the can again. "Arrow Maker. How about just Arrow. Or Arrowman."

"Sounds good to me." He made a gesture of moving the can across the concrete. "Go."

"I'm nervous."

"Nervous?" He shook his head and his tongue zipped over his lips. "Half hour ago you were ready to do the Zakim Bridge!"

I smiled. I pressed the valve and the spray came out hard, started dripping down the concrete. "Uh. Shit."

"Hold it farther away," he said, coming closer, sneakers crunching twigs. He took hold of the base of the can, directing my hand. "Here."

I sprayed a little. He moved his hand on top of mine, put his pointer finger on top of mine on top of the valve. "You want to move it while you spray, you know? Ever do calligraphy? With a fountain pen?"

I could smell him and he smelled like fabric softener and — what had he eaten? pancakes? — maple syrup.

"In high school, I guess. Art class."

"Remember how if you let the pen sit on the paper it would bleed? You needed to keep it moving. Same here." His finger on top of mine pressed the valve. My heart was pounding and I hated the presence of the glove separating us. He guided my hand and soon we'd produced three lines, a capital single-line A, dripping blue at the bottom legs and across the middle. "You want to make an outline first," he said. We went around the A again to make it bubble. "Looks good so far. Then you fill it in. Then you can do whatever shit you like to it, you know?"

He let me go on my own and moved back to his work in progress, rummaged in his backpack for a new color. He popped the cap off with a flick of his thumb and put it in his pocket.

And I remembered, as he was painting, that the clacking of the aerosol can pea was the same sound as the clacking of my typewriter keys.

With the low light and his heavy stylization, I couldn't read what he'd written—but then a six popped out. And a one. It was a date. Below the date, nudging the letters, was an apple.

"What's the apple?"

"Cherry. I haven't done the stem yet."

"A cherry. And numbers." I thought of a slot machine.

Suddenly his phone started chiming. We both looked down at his pants. "Gotta go, Arrowman." He capped his can and dropped it in the backpack.

"Train?"

"Acela."

We ran across the tracks and retreated to the stairwell and waited there like Jesse Jameses for the train.

When it finally blew past—it was four minutes late and as sneaky as Mateo had said—it sucked my breath from my lungs. Leaves whisked up around us. Mateo's hair and the strings of his hoodie swirled around his head but his face was all smile. When the tracks were clear and the night was quiet again we returned to our work.

We painted for another twenty

minutes and then went back across the tracks and up the stairs, Mateo carefully shutting the door behind us. We sat amid the grass and brush at the edge of the woods, knees against the vine-laced fence, to watch a second train go past.

The lights on the train sent stars skittering across the wet paint of our work.

Beside my drippy, embarrassing ARROWMAN, the R's of which were bent into arrows, was a remarkably three-dimensional cherry frozen in the middle of an explosion. Its stem was spinning in a vortex that seemed to be spewing forth a date, the numbers of which were highlighted in red that looked sticky and somehow even sweet. The numbers were today's date. Or yesterday's, now that it was past midnight.

"I get it," I said, feeling my cheeks heat up.

"The date upon which Fletcher Bradford popped his graffiti cherry."

I laughed while thrilling at the innuendo. "It looks incredible."

"Thanks. You know, usually this is a no-no," he said. "Sticking around."

"Because you can get caught?"

He nodded. "Usually I take a quick look, snap a photo, and scram. Usually you don't want to linger around any longer than that."

"But this is safe here?"

"It's pretty safe here. Nobody comes here. There's not really anyone to see it."

"Won't people on the train see it?"

"A blur, if that. So nobody bothers to paint here." He pointed to our graffiti. "Those'll run for a while."

"You mean drip?"

He shook his head, smirking. "Before it gets painted over or blasted off. More visible the location, shorter the run."

"Ah."

"All those squares and rectangles of gray paint you see on walls and stuff—the ones that look like Tetris blocks—that's where the city painted over people's work."

"Is it? That sucks. I've always wondered what those are."

We were quiet for a while. He pointed up and we watched a pair of squeaking bats dive at bugs in the air.

"A kid named Jeremy popped my real cherry," I said. "I'm gay, by the way." It felt funny to say it only now. Usually it was one of the first things I said.

He was poking a twig into a hole in his sneaker. He looked over and in the shadows his face revealed nothing. "Yep. You are."

"You knew?"

"Let's just say I know you were checking out the junk in my trunk long before you ever saw my car."

I was glad for the darkness but still I looked down, flooded in the incredible novelty of bashfulness. "I thought I was more discreet than that."

"You probably are. I was paying attention."

"You were, huh?"

"Maybe I was."

"Maybe you were?"

I felt my collar bones flush. I wanted to ask outright, get confirmation, put an end to the ambiguity. But on the other hand I was enjoying it too much to end it. With anybody else we would've screwed by now and I'd be home already, staring up at the ceiling, laboring over blank sheets of paper or watching my fish swim around.

"They didn't really know what that word meant, did they?" he said. "In middle school, I mean."

"Felcher? I doubt it. They just thought it was a funny word."

He nodded. "In Portuguese, arrow is flecha. It's more obvious from the Portuguese why a person who makes arrows is called a fletcher."

"That's true. You've stumbled onto one of my secret interests. I'm kind of an etymology nerd."

"I like words too."

I pulled my legs out of Indian-style, sat up on my knees and wiped dry leaves off my jeans. "We should probably get going, right?"

"Really should've been gone before the paint dried," he replied. "This was a bad example of how this is done. But I guess your first time is always clumsy." He reached for his backpack and from within it he pulled a paint-smeared Polaroid camera. He stood up, steadied his elbows on the rail of the fence, and pointed the camera into the train canyon. He took two photos of our work, held one out to me. "Here," he said, "put that in your black book."

I took the photo from him. It was developing slowly, but so far I liked what I saw.

I thought/hoped, when Mateo

offered to drive me home, that it was a bit of clever maneuvering on his part to get me to his place. Once there, there'd be some reason why he had to go inside—for his car keys, for a drink of water. It wouldn't be polite to leave me standing on the sidewalk, so he'd ask me to come in, and I would. Then there'd be some reason to go to his bedroom—his keys were there, he needed to change his shoes, check his email, whatever. The bed would be there and I'd sit down and then he'd sit down and before long we'd be in it together. That's how it worked. That's how I was used to it working.

There were other ways it could work, though, too. He could drive me home with the goal of wrangling his way into my bedroom, into my bed. This was the scenario that seemed more and more likely as the others, one by one, didn't pan out.

So, standing on the sidewalk outside my place, one foot still in his Civic, I helped it along: I invited him in to watch TV.

"Nah, thanks though," he said. It was a remarkably casual decline, the decline of someone who believes he's only turning down television. Giant mark in the straightboy column. "I'm gonna get home. See you at work tomorrow?"

"Cool." I was disappointed but not dismayed. I'd done this enough to know when someone wanted out of there, and I didn't get that sense from him. I just didn't get any sense from him. "It was fun."

"Yeah. Oh—hey, you've got the photo, right?"

"Right here." I patted my front pocket. Then I closed the door and watched the car take off down the street.

"Weird," I said out loud.

I went inside. I thought about waking Cara. I thought about beating off. But I ended up just going to sleep. I must've had the Polaroid in my hand when I lay down, because when I woke up the next morning I found it under my pillow.

Street art became synonymous

with Mateo Amaral, even all the stuff that obviously wasn't his. All demanded a moment of my attention—could *that* be his?—and reminded me of the wall by the tracks outside Jamaica Plain. I realized how ubiquitous graffiti was, and considered for the first time that every line was put there by someone with a story, and that every block of gray paint covered a story up.

On the columns of bridges, on the backs of trailer trucks, on newspaper dispensers and billboards and telephone poles and on the sides of stores. I saw it from my car, driving to work. I saw it from the T. I saw it running errands. Every time I saw it I thought of his colored fingers.

"You're really crushing on that guy from work, aren't you?" Cara said one night when I must've been staring too googly into the distance beyond the TV. "I think you're in love. You have the glow."

"I'm definitely not in love," I said. "Puh-*lease*."

"You're at least smitten."

"I may be smitten."

"You going out painting again?"

"I hope so."

"What's he like in bed?"

"I don't know. We haven't done anything."

"Nothing?! How does he kiss?"

"We haven't kissed."

"Are you still not sure he's even gay?"

"Haha. Nope. Not even sure."

"Why don't you *ask?* You can end the speculation any time you want."

"I don't want to end it."

She sighed. "Does he have roommates? Sometimes you can infer by the roommate."

"I don't know if he does. I don't think so. He rents a place in JP."

"Does he live with his parents? You said he's from Brazil."

"I don't think *he's* from Brazil. His parents are. Or were."

"Wow, you know almost nothing about this boy, do you?"

"Not much, no."

"No wonder you're in love."

A week after the first

night, he asked me, in a whisper in my cubicle, to go out a second time (though it was clear from his hand that he was going out every other night by himself, or at any rate without me). This time he suggested Brighton, which was closer to my home turf than his. I wondered if there was significance to that as we climbed into a fenced-in area surrounding construction on a small bridge. A clean new concrete wall stood in front of us. He seemed to know it would be here. I wondered if there was some kind of graffiti newsletter that advertised these ideal places.

I tried to be bolder this time. I turned down the gloves he offered and started painting while he was still picking through his colors.

After we'd been painting for a minute he stepped back and surveyed his work, shaking the clacking can. In tall letters with long, flowing serifs, stood DEDINHOS in black, brown and yellow.

"Those colors remind me of sunflowers," I said.

"Nice!"

"Is that your tag?" I tried to be nonchalant about asking, and continued painting. I was still trying to get the arrows right on my first R and was using way too much paint to do it—I kept lengthening and widening the arrows to subsume drips.

"Yeah. That's me."

I was surprised and delighted to finally know his tag. It was his identifier, could link him to everything he'd done around the city, however much that was, and until now I figured he didn't want me to know about everything he did. The way he carefully guarded his secrets, I wasn't going to risk taking another one from him. Here was proof that I only needed to be patient.

"I'm trying to think where I've seen it around," I said. "You paint all the time so I must've seen it around, right?"

"I'm sure you have."

"It's Portuguese?"

"Yup."

"What's it mean?"

"Fingers," he said with a smirk. "Little Fingers."

"Little fingers like your pinkies?" Why did that seem to warrant a mark in the homo column? "That's gangsta."

"Not little like small, really. Little like—endearing?"

"You mean little like *widdle*?"

He laughed. "My cousin Vinicius—" he said it *Vih-NEE-cee-us* "—gave it to me when we first started painting. I've always been messy." He held up his hand and grinned. "Vini called me Dedos and that became Dedinhos." And this he said like *DEH-jin-YOS*. "The rest is history."

"That's pretty cute. How old were you when you started?"

"Hmm. Around thirteen."

"Wow."

"I'll tell you about it sometime. Come on, let's find someplace else."

"But I'm still working on my R's."

"You and your R's."

"How do you know about

all these places?" I asked, figuring there couldn't really be a newsletter. "Do you have some kind of sixth sense for good places?"

"I keep my eyes open." He smirked. "Also you can read up online. Other writers make note of choice spots."

Ah, so there *was* a sort of newsletter.

On the brick wall of a narrow alley near Kenmore Square he'd produced a big green rectangle; this he outlined in white, making it look like a highway sign. When he began adding words to the sign, I wondered whether this was going to be another tag of his or something. But when the words PORCUPINE and CITY gained enough definition to be legible, my cheeks started getting hot.

"Oh man," I said, distracted enough to drag a stray blast of paint across a door. "You know my book?"

He stopped and wiped his forearm across his face, smearing a coil of hair straight across his cheek until it popped off and re-coiled like a spring. "Sorry? Your book?"

"You found my book. *Porcupine City.*"

"Oh, that's *your* book?"

"Haha. Yes. How'd you find it?"

"The interwebs." He turned back to the green sign. Beneath the first words he added 0 MILES.

"You were stalking me?"

"Hardly. You've seen my writing so I wanted to see yours. Fair's fair, right?"

"Oh man. You didn't read it too, did you?"

"Maybe."

"Maybe?"

"Maybe yes."

"You're ambiguous."

"It was good. I liked it."

"You read the whole thing?"

"It's only 200 pages."

"208."

"See?"

"Now I'm embarrassed."

"Why embarrassed? I said it was good."

"It's just so — ugh."

OK, so *Porcupine City* began

as my senior writing project at Shuster College, largely the thing that separated my BFA from a plain old BA. It almost kept me from graduating, though. Not because I didn't do the project, but because I did nothing but the project. A few halting, resentful paragraphs about the romantic tribulations of a guy named Bradley exploded in length and depth that scared me and exhilarated me and for months filled my days and nights with an unrelenting *tap tap* of laptop keys. Other classes and papers and projects faded into the background. Friends faded too. Jamar, when he claimed to notice dark circles growing under my eyes, tried to stage a one-man intervention.

"This story is killing you, Bradford," he told me, half serious.

Practically snarling, I hunched closer to my laptop.

Like Sauron forging the One Ring, into the book I poured my rage, my agony, my frustration with all mankind—all boykind. *Porcupine City* represented a decade's worth of malice. Bradley was a thinly veiled version of me, of course, and the small army of antagonists were all the guys I'd been with up to that point—all guys from college. Being out at age twelve had made for a lonely adolescence. In high school even the kids I knew were gay wouldn't admit it to me or probably even to themselves yet. They didn't want anything to do with me. And when I got to college and finally, finally found guys to go out with, one by one they'd blown me off, said there was someone else, said they weren't feeling it. These guys I'd been desperate to meet since age twelve were walking away just because they weren't *feeling* it.

That anger poured onto page after page and the book boiled and bubbled like a cauldron of angst, one I kept stirring for months while Jamar grew increasingly fearful for my health. When it came time to turn it in it was no longer a school assignment but my reason for living.

It was also, by the due date, very unfinished. I cobbled together a patchwork version of the best parts, turned it in, and got back to work. I passed and I graduated, but my diploma interested me far less than the sheets of paper sliding off my printer day by day—my sheets of revenge.

Eleven months I toiled on the first draft of that bitch and for another six I polished and, realizing how much aimless ranting I'd done, cut it down by 200 pages. Then I wrote another hundred pages and cut most of that down too. I knew being finished would feel like a death, something I'd mourn and feel empty about, so even after the book was done I kept polishing for another six months.

"You really should try to get that thing published," Cara told me. We were living together by then and she'd had plenty of time to witness firsthand the obsession Jamar had told her about. "If only so you can just stop *tinkering* with it."

Because finality (I thought of it in some way as burial) was a better reason for publishing than any other I could think of, I wrote to a handful of LGBT publishers whose names were featured on the spines of some of the novels I owned. *Why not*, I thought, when I sent out my queries. *Why not*, I thought, when a few of them asked for the manuscript. *Why not*, I thought, when one of them wanted to talk.

I read the galleys not sure I liked this story of mine. And when they sent me a few complimentary copies I flipped through the first few pages of it sure that I didn't. Publishing had been meant to be a burial, yet here was the corpse, neatly bound with a cover emblazoned with a stock photo of two shirtless twinks.

"How could you not like your own book?" Mateo asked.

The book was so angry. So *me*. It was like looking in the mirror and seeing someone I didn't like. It gave me the shivers.

I did some soul searching. With the book in print, all I could revise was myself. I tried celibacy. I got really horny. After eight months I gave in. I remember looking up at the random guy who ended that eight-month experiment for me, and thinking he was perfect. Perfect because all I wanted from him was this. I wasn't looking for a boyfriend anymore—it'd been eight months and all I wanted was to get laid. All I wanted was the thing this guy was happiest and most able to give me. It was a eureka, an epiphany—I actually started crying. The guy stopped quick when he saw the tears—he thought he was hurting me. After we finished I thanked him and moved on. And kept moving on. Practically every guy is the perfect guy the first night, so why ever bother with a second?

My publisher was still waiting for the follow-up to *Porcupine City*. Had been for years. I was waiting too. The problem with one-night stands was that there wasn't much of a story there.

I told Mateo a version

of that story, leaving out the details of my sexual epiphany for a variety of reasons. But he seemed to get the jist.

"I think you should be proud of your book," he told me. "Even if it represents a person you'd rather not believe you were. For one thing it captures a moment in time—what you wrote was true at the time, and that's important. But mostly, it changed you. Made you into a person you probably like better. One who's certainly happier. And that's the best we can hope for from art, you know? That it changes you for the better. That it lights up the world a little bit."

I could tell I was staring at him, could feel moisture drying on my hanging lip.

"What?" he said.

"Nothing. Just, I think that's the first time you've ever spoken a full paragraph."

He smirked. "Anyway, if anything I ever write on a building changes a person as much as your book changed you, and probably at least a few people who've read it, it'll all be worthwhile." He raised his can and made an arc. *Fffssshhht.* "I'm not sure I understand the title, though," he went on.

"Hah. Yeah. A *major* editing mistake. I accidentally cut out the part that explained it. Porcupine City. City of pricks. Get it? I seemed to meet them all."

"Oh. OK. *City of pricks.* That's good. Heh."

"Thanks."

"I've gotta say, though, I think you were too hard on old Beantown."

"Hard?"

"For example, the part right after the MIT guy with the blue hair breaks up with you. You're walking through Copley. It's the part where you overhear tourists saying how pretty the city is. And you realize they think it's pretty because they're always looking up. At the statues and buildings and things. And they don't see the bullshit going on at ground level. One of them doesn't even realize he just stepped on some passed-out homeless guy's coat."

"Yeah, and I just about die."

"It just about kills you. But you blame the city for that. There's like ten pages where you basically just bash everything about the city."

"Well I was pissed off. When you're pissed off in the city it feels like the city is out to get you, or conspiring to keep you unhappy or whatever. The ground-level grunge was tainting my mood."

"I've never felt lonely in the city," he said wistfully, as though realizing it.

"I wouldn't say I was lonely."

"I've always been happy just walking around."

"Well you're lucky."

"I'll admit it can be a little grungy in places," he said. "But that's why we're here. It just needs a fresh coat of paint."

Alex came with me

to Newbury Comics so I could grab something for Cara's birthday. It was the first time I'd seen him since our sweaty weekend together, but there was no mention of our "activities" (funny how when it came to sex with Alex I felt the need for euphemisms). He had plenty to say about his and Jimmy's activities, though. In a way it was torture but if I hadn't wanted to hear it I wouldn't have invited him along.

Alex gave me the details: Apparently Perino saw him that night at the club (around the time I was not remembering the guy with the slip-on Vans) and Perino couldn't stop thinking about him afterward. Seriously. So it was Perino who got back in touch with Alex, via friend request, a few days later. That just about killed me. Perino, now homeless after being dumped by the guy he cheated on to have wedding sex with Alex, had all but moved into Alex's sublet. I was sure the relationship wouldn't survive the remainder of Alex's short sub-lease, but he was acting like it was a forever thing.

He spun a rack of novelty buttons and touched one shaped like a basketball. "Did you know Jimmy is *athletic?*" he mused, reminded of his jock loverboy even by mass-produced trinkets. "I had no idea he was."

"He was on the soccer team in college."

"*Really?*" he cooed. "He's on this neighborhood basketball team, too. With all these *straightboys*."

"Amazing."

"You should come to one of his games. You can sit with me. I won't mind if you oogle him a little. It'll be fun."

"I don't know." Hearing about Jimmy secondhand was one thing; watching him run around in swooshy shorts was quite another. I might not survive it.

I picked out a couple of CDs for Cara and after dropping Alex off I stopped for a cake. The cake spent some time crammed in Mike's tiny fridge while he helped me work out my Perino tension in his loft.

The work day was almost

over. I was zoned out at my desk with my headphones on, waiting for the last two hours to tick by. If you keep moving windows and folders around it gives the impression of doing work. I rubbed my eyes. I still had a bit of a hangover from Cara's birthday rager last night. Suddenly Mateo was beside me and I was awake. He was like a jolt of Brazilian coffee.

"Oh—hey," I said, tugging out my headphones. "You caught me dozing."

"That's *my* trick." He helped himself to a pen from my desk and wrote on a Post-It. His fingers were yellow today. He peeled off the note and stuck it to the bottom right corner of my monitor. "That's where I live. Meet me at midnight. We have business in Charlestown."

"Tonight? I can't tonight. I—have a date."

He straightened up just noticeably and his radiance dimmed by a watt. At least I thought it looked that way. "Ah. Who's the guy?"

"No one. This guy Mike."

"OK. Well." He touched the Post-It. "For future reference, then, right? We'll do it another time."

"Sure. I'm free pretty much any time."

He nodded. He stood on his toes and peered over the wall of my cube. "Think Larry's looking for me."

"Hey, can I get your cell number or something too?"

"Sure," he said, then: "Didn't I give it to you already?"

"No, we've been kind of old-fashioned."

"Right. Well here." He plucked the Post-It back and added his digits under the address — small letters and numbers in clumsy penmanship that looked nothing like the grandiose fonts of his graffiti.

"For future reference," he said again, reattaching it to my screen. "Have fun with Mike."

I watched him go, then rolled my chair across my cube, grabbed my messenger bag. I took out my phone, rolled back to the desk, and programmed in his number.

Later in the evening, after I canceled on Mike, I used the number to tell Mateo I was on my way.

Not all the houses on

his street had their porch lights on so it was hard to read some of the numbers. The wrinkled Post-It on the passenger seat said 35. When I was in that range I kept an eye out for the gray Civic with the new battery. After a minute I spotted it parked on the street. The car was familiar in a way that tickled me. I'd been under the hood and, more importantly, in the trunk. If not for that accidental discovery I would be in bed with Mike right now. Mateo better make it worth it.

I idled beside the Civic, leaning to the passenger window to peer at house numbers. None of these houses looked familiar, even though Mateo and I walked up this street the first night we went out. Had I been that spaced-out that night? Or — not spaced-out, but rather, singularly focused? Yes, probably.

There was an empty space behind his car but it was small and I didn't want to try squeezing in. The last thing I needed was to ding his bumper.

It was OK just to wait. The street was quiet and I could stay where I was for now. The number of the closest house was — OK, good — 35. It was red brick with white shutters, tall and narrow. Three floors, or two and an attic with windows. I craned my neck to see up, wondering if he lived at the top.

The little front yard, with its short walkway and stone

steps leading to a small porch with iron rails, was filled with carefully-tended flower beds and two bushes bursting with yellow forsythia.

Mateo's house. The home of Dedinhos. I had no memory of it, even though he almost certainly pointed it out when we were walking to his car. But of course whenever he pointed at something my eyes rarely went beyond the tip of his finger.

I was about to text him when the front door opened, and then the screen door, and Mateo lifted his chin at me while he shut both doors quietly behind him. He came down the steps and tried to get in the car. I scrambled to unlock the door.

"Nice house," I said as he got in.

He reached around and dropped his clinking backpack on the backseat. He was wearing a sleeveless gray hoodie and long black shorts, with tall black socks pulled up so that between shorts and socks there was only an inch or two of skin visible. It struck me as a tad silly in a way that made him less intimidating.

"Thanks."

"Which window's yours?"

"Third floor. Attic is done over. I rent it."

"Yeah."

"It's fine. Between work and—nighttime stuff, I'm not here much."

"Yeah. Who lives below?"

"A woman and her daughter." He yanked his seatbelt across his chest and buckled it, fingers coming magnificently close to my thigh. "Oh—you can start driving."

"I don't know where we're going."

"I'll show you."

In the passenger seat he was even quieter than he'd been elsewhere, seeming totally unlike the person who was expounding on art philosophy the week before. He looked out the window mostly, directing me at intersections wth flips of his finger. Although he was still doing the navigating, this was the first time I wasn't just along for the ride. Tonight, significantly or not, I *was* the ride. It altered our dynamic just enough to make me giddy. It was as close to equals as we'd been. We were becoming partners in crime. Literally. The only thing that seemed likely about having me drive was that he planned it that way. To bring me in.

He'd said we had business

in Charlestown, and that's where he led me. When he told me to park I pulled into a space between two white sedans.

When I got out of the car I spotted right away the glowing obelisk of the Bunker Hill Monument beyond the roofline of a row of houses. I wondered if that was part of our business in Charlestown. The Navy Yard was nearby too, though I wasn't sure where. We weren't going to paint on the U.S.S. Constitution, were we? That would make tagging the Zakim Bridge look like child's play.

Not Old Ironsides, and not Bunker Hill—Mateo had something simpler in mind. A house on a street with houses so close together they looked like one long building. A house at the end of the row, made semi-private by a big leafy tree and a curve in the street. It was under construction heavy enough to warrant an entire temporary façade, complete with a wide, garage-like door—a façade of the type seen on coming-soon stores in malls. Blank plywood begged for paint.

Although the street was sleepy it was much more out in the open than anything we'd done so far, and not until Mateo clapped a can into my hand did I realize I was shivering.

The element of possibly being caught made it more authentic, though—that was obvious just from watching Mateo. He was going a lot faster than he had before, and he kept glancing side to side to make sure the coast was still clear. He dashed out a quick, gorgeous mural of the Bunker Hill Monument. Although he seemed barely to be paying attention to his work, I sensed that he was in tune with everything, perfectly harmonized with the city around him, one eye on his wall and the other on everything else. Since this felt so serious I tried to put an extra something in my ARROWMAN to push it from simple tag to decoration, if not quite art.

When we were done he snapped some pictures with his Polaroid and we were walking. Not toward my car, really, just strolling away in that *Whatever do you mean, officer?* kind of way. Whenever we left a scene after painting it always took me a long time to lose that charged-up, fight-or-flight feeling I had when the paint was streaming. But it seemed to melt off him immediately. He could be standing ten feet from a finished piece and appear as though he had nothing to do with it. In the beginning I thought this was him being cocky; only later would I understand it was because painting made him feel no guilt.

"When you do pictures instead

of tags," I said as we walked, not to break our silence—which wasn't an uncomfortable one—but because I wanted to hear his voice again and the subtle stresses of its Portuguese tint, "you don't sign them as Dedinhos or anything."

"No."

"So how will people know they're yours?"

"Hmm. Why do they need to know?"

"I don't know. So you get credit?"

He laughed. "Why would I want credit? I work hard to avoid getting credit. Credit means cuffs, Arrowman." He shifted his backpack and the cans clinked inside.

"I don't mean credit to Mateo Amaral. I mean, like, so Dedinhos gets credit. So people will know all your stuff is done by one guy. So then you could make a smudge on a trashcan or something with a marker and people would say, *Ooh, that's his.*" I wiggled my fingers and made that heavenly chorus sound, *aaaooouuh.*

He laughed again and looked at me. "Why?"

"I don't know, so— If we didn't know Michelangelo painted the Mona Lisa—"

"Arrowman. Leonardo!"

"Sorry—Leonardo. I always got the Ninja Turtles mixed up too. I mean if we didn't know Leonardo Da Vinci painted the Mona Lisa, it would be getting passed around at yard sales rather than worshiped at the Louvre."

"Maybe. I like to believe it'd still be in the Louvre even if it was anonymous."

"But the name assigns value."

"Monetary value. Not artistic value. The two things are completely separate. I'm only interested in one."

We walked for a while in silence. The idea of a graffiti artist who didn't want credit seemed to go against all of what little I knew about graffiti artists—artists whose art *was* their name.

"When I was putting out *Porcupine City*," I said, "I thought a lot about using a pen name."

"Heh. A novelist's tag."

"Yeah."

"Why?"

"I'm not sure. I think it was a reluctance to be truly associated with it."

"A gay thing?"

"No. No, I couldn't give a shit about that. I've been out since puberty. It just goes back to me realizing on the precipice of publication that I didn't like my main character. And he was so obviously me."

"I don't think so. I mean, if you say he's you, then he's you. You would know. But I don't think he's *obviously* you."

"Well, that's cool I guess."

"The main character was with a lot of guys."

"Yeah. A lot of villains."

"So you've been with a lot of guys too, then?"

"Some would think it's a lot. Some would think it's hardly any."

"How many?"

I wondered why he was asking, why he cared. I wondered what I wanted to tell him, since I felt no obligation to tell the truth. And I wondered whether I even *knew* the number. How many other guys, besides the one with the slip-on Vans, had I forgotten?

"It doesn't matter. I look at the number different now. It makes me happy now," I told him, telling myself too. "It makes me feel like I have a little something with each one of them. The guy I had plans with tonight? Mike. He's a nice guy, you know? That's all that matters."

"You sleep with him?" He turned to look at me with those green eyes.

Out of the blue I felt very embarrassed. It wasn't anything to do with his tone, which had no particular emphasis, and his eyes weren't judgmental. I just felt embarrassed. And I wasn't used to feeling that way.

"I mean I *have* slept with him. But it's not like we do it every time."

I wanted to change the subject, swing myself out of this position where I suddenly felt vulnerable. I wanted to turn the tables. I almost asked him how many girls/guys/people he'd slept with, but I hesitated long enough to regroup and to realize I didn't want to ask that question. Especially since I was more and more sure he was straight. Asking it would forfeit the mystery. And without this mystery between us, we had... what, exactly? Spraypaint? A mutual employer?

"Is the Navy Yard over there?" I asked instead.

"Right down there," he said, pointing.

"We're not going to— Are we?"

I half expected him to run into the entranceway and somersault over the gate. But he smirked and kept walking. If we were going to tag Old Ironsides it was going to be on another night.

We just walked. I didn't care where we were going, but I wanted to put some distance behind the sex talk. I asked him if he'd ever been to Honduras.

"Honduras," he said. "Nope. Why?"

"No reason. My mom lives there. She's always asking me to visit and I always avoid it. I have this recurring nightmare about forgetting English—forgetting *language*—and I think being surrounded by Spanish would basically be the same thing. I don't know Spanish."

"Your mom lives in Honduras? Why?"

"She's an agricultural anthropologist."

"Uh. Cool." He laughed. "I'll pretend I know what that is."

"There's this tree there called the noni tree. Ever hear of it? It makes this fruit that's pretty nasty tasting but has about a million pounds of antioxidants in every ounce. Like a pomegranate mixed with Godzilla."

"Haha. No, can't say I've heard of a noni tree."

"She's trying to show the people who live in this particular area of Honduras how to cultivate it so they can sell the fruit to health-food yuppies in America and get rich."

"Cool. But you say it tastes nasty?"

"It won't make your eyes water or anything, but it's not pleasant."

"You have some?"

"She sends me boxes of it from time to time. The juice. But I'm like never sick, so make of that what you will. You'll have to come over some time and try it."

"Maybe I will."

"Maybe you will?"

"Maybe I will."

The night air grew humid

and I thought it might rain, but really it was just the wind changing direction and blowing ocean air in from the Harbor. It felt steamy. Mateo's bare arms glistened when we walked under streetlights, and when we passed the neon signs of shuttered storefronts the moisture on his skin caught the colored light and made it look like he was glowing.

I stole glances, stepped wide around potholes in the sidewalk and slowly up curbs to let him get a half-step ahead of me as we walked, just far enough so I could freely take in the sight of his glowing arms and tall black socks. And then he would turn and slow down to let me catch up. His backpack clinked and every so often he'd dip into some nook or cranny and write DEDINHOS. Little Fingers. I had no idea where we were going.

When he stood up after

markering a hand on a mailbox he saw me rubbing my calves and he asked if I was tired.

"No way. Just breaking myself in."

He laughed.

"Where are we going to, anyway?"

"I don't know," he said, clicking the cap back onto the marker. "I was just following you."

"But *I* was following *you*."

"Hah. Then we're fucked."

"My car's way back that way. You seemed like you had someplace in mind. More business?"

"No. Guess I just like to walk. I like how the city sounds at night. Why, you have somewhere to be? Mike waiting for ya?"

"No. No one's waiting."

We passed a group of college kids on their way home from somewhere, probably a bar. Among them it felt more special to be with Mateo. Our reason for being out at this time of night was so much more secret and cooler than theirs. I thumbed the can in my pocket and smiled.

"How about your parents?" I asked Mateo when their voices had faded down the street. "Any noni trees in their lives?"

"Mine? They're in Brazil."

"You mentioned. There's a weird John Updike novel by that name, by the way."

"..."

"So what are they doing in Brazil?"

"Living. They're Brazilian."

"Oh. Yeah, of course. Ha. But you're American?"

He nodded. "Just like *you*."

He announced this similarity with enough of a *something* in his voice to send a charge through me. As though this point of commonality made him see me entirely anew. But I could tell he was playing.

"You were born here, I mean."

"Yup. My parents got married and moved here. To Framingham, Massachusetts. Their only child was born — that's yours truly. They got here just in time."

"You mean they moved here to have you?"

"Yeah."

"How come?"

"Land of the free, etc.? I don't know. Wasn't great there.

Military dictatorships and what-not. Economy was fucked. My mom used to tell about how inflation was so bad, buying groceries she'd try to run ahead of the guy with the sticker-gun to grab the stuff before he jacked up the prices."

"Wow."

"It's beautiful too, though, some of it. The kind of beautiful it's hard to know what to do with sometimes."

"I bet."

"But my mom was intent on having an American baby."

"An American baby," I mused. Up to that point I'd rarely considered that there were any other kind.

"My mom was in love with America," he said. "Still is, though it's a more mature, bittersweet love now, I think. Not the school-girl crush it started out as." We came to an intersection with a car going through too fast. He put his arm out to keep me from stepping off the curb—it was unnecessary but I liked his glowing skin so close to me. "She wants to be an astronaut," he said as we crossed.

"An astronaut? Your mom?"

"Believe it. When I was a kid she wouldn't shut up about astronauts. Told me a million times about how when she was a girl she watched Neil Armstrong walk on the Moon. All the people in her neighborhood gathered around this TV in someone's house. The Americans were walking on the fucking Moon, she'd say! Well she wouldn't say fucking, but it was that kind of excitement. She'd say, *the Americans are walking on the Moon. They're crazy and amazing. They have left the Earth and they're walking on the Moon.*" He did his mother's voice in an accent much thicker than his own. It made me smile. "So she wanted to be an astronaut too. But that wasn't possible because Brazil had no space program. The road to the Moon went straight through America. But still. She was a nurse, training to be a nurse. Not exactly the right résumé, you know? So the next best thing was to be the mother of an astronaut. To get postcards from the Moon."

"One small step for Mateo," I whispered, "one giant leap for the Brazilian people."

"She used to even use it as a threat, right? Like other

parents use the Tooth Fairy or something. Be good or the Tooth Fairy won't come. With my mom it was like, Finish your homework or you'll never get to the Moon, filhinho."

I smiled. I was doing a lot of smiling tonight.

"I don't know how much that was really figuring into her insistence that they come here to have me. Probably more than she'd let on. Somehow she got my dad to agree. And they moved."

"Why Framingham, though? That's so random."

"Why anywhere? They must've had some connection there."

"So you were born."

"Haha. Yes."

"Did they buy you tons of like rocket-ship baby clothes and stuff?"

"Oh yeah. What they couldn't afford, my mom made."

"I need to see pictures of that someday."

"Haha. There are plenty."

He went quiet. I didn't want him to stop talking. "Did you go back to Brazil a lot to visit and stuff when you were a kid?" I wondered how he'd caught the touch of accent.

"We couldn't ever go, no."

"Never?"

"My parents were illegal quickly. Overstayed their visas. Immigration is hard, you know? It's not all drive up to Ellis Island any more, if it ever really was."

"Oh." Immigration. Military dictatorships. This was so far outside my experience. It made me feel ashamed, though I'm not sure why.

"We went back for good when I was about ten."

"What happened when you were ten?"

"..."

"I mean why'd you go back?"

"My pai.... Hmm. My father had an affair with my landlady."

"Yikes. Wait, the landlady you have now?"

He nodded.

"You all lived in that house?"

"No no no. Guess it's kind of a long story."

I wanted to hear it. I looked at him expectantly.

He pushed his hair back behind his ear. "Makes me kind of squeamish to tell it," he said finally.

"Oh." I felt stupid. "Of course. Yeah. I would imagine it would. Sorry. I can get kind of nosey."

We were crossing the Charlestown Bridge on its pedestrian walkway, an expanse of holey metal grating that offered a vertigo-inducing view of the ink-dark river far beneath our shoes. From this bridge we had a killer view of its much grander neighbor, the Zakim. The multi-lane, cable-stayed bridge hanging between two forked obelisks (like two massive, upside-down Y's) was decked out tonight in purple and blue light. Through the week its colors rotated like the colors on Mateo's fingers.

We stopped to look at it, and after a minute of silence Mateo sighed and said, "Someday, Arrowman. Someday."

"You'll paint on it?"

"Someday. Yes."

We watched the traffic move across it for a few minutes and then started walking again, over the bridge and on into the North End, where all the little Italian restaurants were closed for the night. Then he said, "You tell the story."

"What story?"

"About why we moved to São Paulo. About my dad."

I looked at him, confused. "I don't—know that story."

"I read your book," he said matter-of-factly. "You can craft a romantic scene."

"But—that's fiction. I don't know what happened to your family."

"Well, what do you and Clarice Lispector say? Doesn't have to be factual to be true, right? Did you mean that?"

"Huh. Yeah. Sure I did." I paused. "Do you think of it as a romance, though? I mean, wasn't this pretty hard for your family?"

"It was what it was. I try to think of it in the best possible light. Try to make it worth what came after. That's *when* I think about it, which is rare. But you brought it up. So you tell it. It's

OK if you don't know the exact details about my life. You can fill in the blanks with what feels true."

I felt something in my chest, the fluttering of a tenderness I rarely felt outside of fleeting moments in various beds.

"OK," I said. "I'll tell it. I need a little background, though. How's the story start?"

"My landlady Marjorie worked at a middle school. As an art teacher. She works at a high school now, but back then she worked at the middle school, I think. And across the street from the middle school was an old-folks home. My dad was a groundskeeper there. I know that for sure."

"Do you not know much about it?"

"Not much. I was ten. It's never really been discussed except in bits and pieces. That's why your telling is as good as mine."

"OK." Like an old film it began flickering through my mind, complete with the smudges and soft lighting of old memories. It did nothing to quell the feeling in my chest. "She used to see him working across the street?"

"I guess."

"When she took the kids out to recess and stuff?"

"Probably, yeah."

I nodded, felt my lips scrunch up like some kind of fortune teller, one who was reading the past instead of the future. "I picture her standing like at the corner of the playground, with her back to the nursing home. Every once in a while she'd look over to check for the man who took care of the grass and flowers and stuff."

Already I was unsure of the tone. I felt weird. This was a story of adultery that apparently almost ripped Mateo's family apart. Ripped them at least from their adopted country. And I was going on about flowers?

"She'd be standing there," I went on, "kids screaming and crashing into each other—maybe she'd have a whistle around her neck or something—but feeling a million miles away from the kids and the playground, and instead connected by an invisible thread to the man across the street, listening so intently for his sounds, sounds of rakes and shovels and hoes

OK if you don't know the exact details about my life. You can fill in the blanks with what feels true."

and sounds of him breathing and the sound of him dragging the back of his hand against his forehead, separating all that from the kids.... Do you think she'd go out during lunch to get things from her car, things she left on purpose so she'd have a reason to go out?"

"Yeah."

"Do you think she'd like walk slow, glance across the street? Like on certain days of the week when he'd be mowing the lawn. He'd be shirtless and the sun would glint off his shoulders—"

"Fletcher, this is my *father*. And he's at work, he's not going to be shirtless at work."

"Sorry. Well."

"Hmm. You were doing fine until the shirtless."

I was quiet a minute before going on. "During the day, between classes, she'd manufacture reasons to go out to her car, to see if she could spot him. This man in the sun with his floppy hair— Did he have floppy hair like yours?"

"Haha. No. Short. He went baldy pretty early." He rubbed his own thick hair. "I think I'm safe."

I nodded and rejected the detail and kept his father's hair long in my mind. "She thought he was beautiful. It made her happy to see him, walking back and forth across the lawn of the nursing home, his arms loaded with sticks or pruned branches, with watering cans and sometimes riding the green and yellow tractor. She thought he was beautiful. Especially against the backdrop of the nursing home, you know? You think of places like that as so kind of sterile and lifeless and sad and boring. As so stagnant. The only change, really, is people leaving and new people coming but it's all the same. And against that, here was this man. And he was sweaty and he smelled, but he smelled like life, you know? Of doing things and being places. And his hands and fingers were always stained with—with soil."

I paused, thought: *Reel it in.* My heart was going like mad.

"And although she didn't even know his name, she felt like she knew him and the name was just something she couldn't quite place. Just a missing piece where everything else about him fit so nicely. She felt like he could be hers, and in some way already was. Sometimes that made her feel silly, because, really, what did she know about this man? Nothing at all. Nothing. But she'd been lonely for a long time, and, uh— Maybe I'm getting off track here."

"No, Arrowman, that's right." He looked at me with a delighted surprise that made my heart thump harder and made me uncomfortable, too. We seemed to be bonding and that was exciting. But what exactly were we bonding over? "Her husband left right after their daughter was born."

"OK." I thought for a minute before continuing. I'd gone about as far as I could without co-opting our own story (or at least my illusion of it), because I didn't have a lot of personal experience with, shall we say, *courtship* to draw from. The characters in this tale were going to have to meet soon. But how? My mind swung to car trouble but it couldn't be car trouble. Car trouble was ours.

He looked at me. "Stuck?"

"Just thinking." I paused. "One day when he was mowing the lawn and she was walking to her car feeling like she'd explode if she didn't talk to him soon, she heard a *thwunk* and a crash and she spun around, for an instant thinking: gunshot. Then there was silence as the mower motor stopped, and then the man was crossing the street onto the school grounds. She'd forgotten about the noise and was convinced he was on his way to talk to her, finally. She was walking before she made any decision to go to him. Her mind was on nothing more than the wish that she'd had time to check her lipstick. The man was kneeling in the grass by the sign, the kind of sign you can stick letters on to alert passersby of parent-teacher conferences and stuff."

"I've painted on a lot of those kinds of signs."

"She arrived at the sign as the man was standing up, brushing grass off his knees. He wore blue Dickies and his workboots were green from walking behind the mower. His waist was thin, his shirt tucked in neatly. A patch above the pocket had the name of the nursing home, and his name—"

"Renaldo."

"Renaldo Amaral. She turned the name in her mouth. His face was nervous—but up close like this it took her breath away. Those eyes." I looked at Mateo. "They were green-green and made all the grass around him look gray in comparison. Then she looked at the sign and couldn't see what was wrong. *It was an accident,* the man said. His accent was striking—not the Spanish she'd probably rather prejudicially been expecting. Something else. It was then that she noticed the glass in the grass. *I hit a rock with the mower!,* the man said. *Well,* she said, *you do such a wonderful job over there.* The man looked at her with a surprised smile, with green eyes and smooth lips, and said, *Over there, but what about over here!* And they laughed."

I was silent for a minute. I wanted to end it here.

"Go on," he said.

"You sure?"

"Hmm. I guess you have the idea."

Somewhere in the Financial District

now, near Post Office Square. Closer to dawn than to midnight. We lay on our stomachs beside a Dumpster in an alley, arms cushioning our chests on the cobble ground, looking across the street down into another alley between Starbucks and KaBloom. We'd leapt to the ground too suddenly for me to consider the grossness of it. I hoped there were no rats. Mateo put a finger to his lips, grinning. "*Ssshh.*"

I nodded. My heart was thumping against the stone. This was the first time we'd seen another writer. We'd been quick to hide and so far he hadn't seen us.

"Let's see if I know who it is," Mateo whispered. The guy had on a baggy t-shirt and shorts with pockets that bulged conspicuously in the shape of cans. "Be cool to see somebody I know of."

"Have you met others?"

He nodded. "I keep to myself. Most are more social. There's different philosophies."

"Hey," I said, "do you know who writes those Facts?"

"Facts?"

"The ones that are all over. The ones that say obvious things like *sky is blue* or whatever. You've seen them."

"I know them, sure. No, I don't know. No one knows, but rumor has it it's some oldster who's been at this shit since we were in diapers."

"Cool."

The guy across the street pulled out a can and aimed it at the wall. Before spraying he glanced around, looking much more cautious than Mateo did when Mateo was doing the same thing.

"Maybe this is the guy who writes the Facts," Mateo said. "Let's see what he does."

I nodded, but even I could tell this guy was too nervous to be the guy.

He put paint to the wall, a big arc that after a few strokes became a C. He made a few more and spelled out CATHODE. He wrote the same thing twice more in different styles, one of which covered part of my still-wet ARROWMAN.

"Hey, he's painting on my tag."

"He's a toy or he'd know better. That shit's frowned upon."

"It is? What's a toy?"

"A newbie. Or a poser. This one's probably a poser. Doesn't even know what he wants to write. Look." The guy had written FUCK YOU. "Bet he works at the KaBloom," Mateo said. "Flower boy. Yeah, he definitely works there. Or worked. See how angry he is? Graffiti should never be about vendetta."

"Am I a toy?"

"Technically. But a newbie toy, not a poser toy. *Ssshh.*"

"What are you?"

"*Sshh.*" He held out his finger to shut me up. "Let's say a knight. Some might say a king but I'm modest. Wait—"

And then suddenly there were lights, and in one second Mateo had his backpack in one hand and the hood of my hoodie in the other and we were running, out of the alley and down. For the first time in my life I was running from cops. Or more likely rent-a-cops, but it was exhilarating to think they were cops. While you're actually being chased it hardly matters by whom. A singular thought pounds in your brain: don't get caught. *Don't get caught.* Whether the chaser wants to tag you It or slap you into cuffs, the feeling's the same: *Don't. get. caught.*

"Go go go!" Mateo was almost laughing, loving this.

Our sneakers clapped on the sidewalk and we pulled the strings of our hoods tight to hide our faces, just in case. Down and through another alley, across the park in Post Office Square, kicking up mulch, shrubs whacking our arms. And then we were in the street, a brighter street, skidding out of our speed, breathing heavy, acting casual, wiping our faces. *No wonder you smell like adventure at work*, I thought. "You spend every night doing this, don't you?"

He smiled an out-of-breath smile. "But that's enough for tonight. We've been all over!" He stepped toward me face to face, close enough to stop my breath and silence my mind. I could feel his breath on my eyelashes and on my lips. I was sure he was going to kiss me. Instead he gently tugged the ends of my hoodie strings. "We'll get your car tomorrow. OK? Come home with me?" I nodded, heart pounding even harder. We caught a cab.

This is how it really

happened: The nursing home in Mateo's mind and in my story was not, I now understand, a nursing home but a senior center owned and operated by the Catholic Church. And the middle school across the street wasn't a middle school but a day-care center/preschool also run by the Church. On one side of the street people were raised up; on the other side they were sent off; and a half-mile down the road was the church were they were tended to for the years in between. One maintenance staff managed all three properties.

Marjorie had indeed noticed Renaldo for the first time outside of the senior center, so one afternoon when he came into her classroom to gather the trash, it felt to her like a follow-up meeting. Familiarity had been growing within her, whether he knew it or not.

The affair, the actual consummation of the affair, that I

had been reluctant to narrate to Mateo, ran through my mind as I watched out the window of the cab while he sat silently beside me, clutching his backpack on the floor between his knees. All the possibilities of it. The fact that for Marjorie it had worked out.

Marjorie had been pushy with Renaldo, she knew. He was quiet, shy, did not wear a wedding ring (she checked and delighted in his bare knuckle). She began waiting for him at the end of each day, sometimes staying late to wait, long after the toddlers were picked up by their parents. When he arrived she thought it was with more eagerness than collecting trash ought to warrant. After several weeks of this, when she knew his name, when she knew well all the ordinary things they small-talked about, in front of a long corkboard onto which were push-pinned three-dozen construction-paper hands decked out as turkeys (because it happened in November, not at all the summer), she kissed him.

It had the taste of an affair, his lips against hers, a forbiddenness that made her heart sink even as it pressed closer to his. But she couldn't decide what kind of affair. Was it adultery? He hadn't ever mentioned another woman. Or was it simply the affair of a groundskeeper and a preschool teacher behind closed Catholic doors? Or was it the affair of a Brazilian immigrant and a frumpy New Englander named Marjorie Miller? She didn't want to know and the ambiguity offered permission.

As she kissed him the trash bag fell out of Renaldo's callused hands and colorful balls of crumpled construction paper rolled out like confetti across the floor.

She closed the classroom door with one hand while holding his neck with the other. He slid his palm down her shivering belly, inside the waist of her corduroy skirt, and she let her body open like a flower to his gardener's hands.

When Mateo brought me into

his house, if I'd had any brainwaves to spare, I would've thought it funny — funny strange — to be in the home of the woman whose life I was narrating earlier that night. I had from time to time in my so-called writing career imagined my characters springing to Pinocchio-like life and existing in the real world, but now that it was basically happening I should've found it freaky.

Should have, but didn't. Because although I was in her house Marjorie was now the furthest thing from my mind. Everything about everything was Mateo. The water glass he held to his lips, the glass he gave to me. The one painty hand he splayed against the kitchen cupboard when he leaned down to untie his shoes.

Finally he interrupted long minutes of silence with two words: "Bedtime. Ready?"

We crept up the stairs

with our shoes in our hands and Mateo opened his bedroom door carefully to keep it from squeaking. He shut it behind us, revealing a big poster of the Zakim Bridge tacked to the back of the door. His room smelled a little musty and a little like cologne and a little like slept-in sheets. It was big and shadowy with sloping ceilings and three dormer windows standing blue against the low, dark wall. The room lit up suddenly and he withdrew his hand from a switch on a lamp on his desk—I saw that it was actually an old door lying across two metal filing cabinets. An open laptop sat on top, its screen dark. The walls were blank save for a cluster of off-kilter photos of people who must've been his family (a bald man who must've been Renaldo, a blond boy who looked out of place), and a framed poster of a fully-graffitied train in a city that was perhaps South American. Was that São Paulo? The poster was above the bed. Below the poster and above the pillows was a crucifix hanging from a nail—it cast a long shadow across the wall. I looked from the shadow to the rumpled sheets. My mouth was dry; the cool water he'd given me downstairs had been powerless to moisten it. Never since the beginning had being in a guy's room felt like this. And never since the beginning had I been so uncertain about what was going to happen. Now Mateo was pulling his shirt over his head and I thought, *This **is** going to happen.* In the low light

I looked for additional tattoos on his chest but apart from a burst of chest hair between his pectorals his skin was clear.

"Whatcha looking at?"

"Nothing." I lowered my eyes and smiled. I started unzipping my hoodie.

"My cousin did them for me." He folded his shirt over the back of a chair and started unbuttoning his shorts.

"Your tattoos? Yeah, you told me."

"Oh. Guess I forgot." He pulled off his tall black socks, one, the other, hopping a little. He wore a thin black band encircling one ankle.

"I remember." I laughed, stepping out of my pants. I folded them and set them on top of my sneakers, straightened my boxers on my waist. "Vinicius, right?"

"The one and only. Took a couple sessions and I had to be pretty drunk every time. I'm afraid of needles." A grin. He hopped barefoot, all shadows and skin, across the room in boxers of plain white, or maybe yellow, it was hard to tell in the reading-lamp light. He lifted the striped blankets and rolled into bed. The mattress squeaked. There was no headboard.

"Should I turn off the light?" I said, standing in my underwear near the door-desk. He watched what must've been my silhouette against the little lamp for a second before saying yes. I flipped the switch and his skin turned from orange to dark blue in the weak light from the windows. I felt my way to the bed. My fingers found the edge of the blanket and followed it up as I slid my bare feet across stiff carpet. It took this to remind me that I had not, in fact, memorized the route from a guy's bedroom door to a guy's bed. My hand went from blanket to sheet. I stopped. This couldn't have felt more different from the other week with Alex, or the other day with Mike. Maybe because I still wasn't sure what was about to happen. The fact that I would now have to make a conscious decision to get in bed with Mateo, as opposed to grabbing a blanket and crashing on the floor—which seemed equally plausible here in the dark—made the room explode in starbursts advertising newness and quality. I slid my foot another few inches on the carpet until my toe connected with what felt like a plastic stacker.

Maybe in Brazilian culture sleep was not as married to sex as it was in America. Maybe we were just going to sleep. Maybe anything. Maybe everything. I stood by the bed, the mattress against my bare knees, looking at him.

He was lying on his side watching me. At last he smirked. He lifted his arm open wide. "Come here, Arrowman."

I full-on guffawed. Of course. Of course. I got into bed and his arm closed tight around me.

"Bull's-eye," said Mateo.

Our lips met with no delay.

There was no mystery here anymore, at last, thank god. There was also no angst in his movements, no floodgates opening or anything like that, no grand, life-altering relief—nothing to suggest he'd never done this before. There was just warm, welcoming spit. I tried to match the gentle darts of his tongue, to keep pace, in the moments when I wasn't marveling at how smooth were his lips and tongue, how soft and sweet like some kind of gummy, translucent candy.

No, there was nothing to suggest he'd never done this before, and everything to suggest this was just how he did things. Surprise wrapped in surprise.

He pushed back the blanket and slid on top of me without ever taking his lips off mine. I could feel him hard against me. I ran my hands over his body. New Guy, Mateo, Dedinhos. His skin was in some places baby-smooth and in others—I moved my hand up the inside of his thigh—coarsely hairy. His torso was soft, especially near his hips, as though still, at age twenty-five-ish, he hadn't entirely shed his baby fat. The smooth electricity of his body against mine energized my every cell.

He was strong. He pinned me, let me go, pinned me again. I tasted the sweet saltiness of his skyline tattoos. São Paulo on my tongue.

Kneeling in the dark to rid him of his underwear there was a spark as the cotton tugged across his pubic hair, and the area around his pelvis lit up briefly in a flash, and after glimpsing it, no way could I leave it, so I filled my mouth with it, and felt his hands seize the back of my head, and heard Mateo laugh.

Afterward when we were done

and the windows glowed pink he crawled naked to the end of the bed, reached down and heaved the blankets up off the floor. I sat up, looked dizzily around, touched my lips, yawned. I reached to the floor too, for what I thought was my underwear, but it was a t-shirt. I reached around, dragging my fingers along the carpet, found my boxers and put them on.

"Do you have to use the bathroom?" he said.

"Oh — no, I was just gonna, you know, get going."

He stopped fixing the blankets. "Really? It's 4:30 in the morning."

I dithered. "Yeah — "

"How come?"

Because that's what happens afterward. "I was going to let you get some sleep."

He shook folds out of the blanket. "You should stay if you want."

"I don't have any clothes, though. For work tomorrow."

"Arrowman, there's no work tomorrow. It's Saturday." He reached out and gave a tug on my boxers. "Go to sleep."

I looked at the bed. He had it mostly re-made. The sheets were straightened, the pillows fluffed. He'd prepared it for something I had little practice at.

I looked at the lightening windows, at my clothes stacked on top of my shoes across the room, at his tattoos, at his hair, which was goofily, vulnerably messed.

"I'm not a prick," he said, patting the sheet. "If that's what you're worried about. I don't come from your Porcupine City. I'm more like — pizza. Even better the second day." He smirked.

God he was cute. "Like pizza, huh?"

"Like pizza with noni fruit on it. Good for you."

"OK." I pulled back the covers. "I guess I can't resist a man with a good simile."

"I think you mean metaphor," he said, sliding over. "Oops, no underwear allowed."

I sighed as though getting naked again was such a bother, and then, laughing, maneuvered under the covers and let my boxers fall to the floor. He was lying on his back. I lay on my stomach beside him. He curled his fingers around my elbow, rubbing it with his thumb. It felt odd to be touched now that the sex was over.

"I mean simile," I told him. "A metaphor would be you saying you *were* a pizza. You said you were *like* a pizza. Similes use *like*."

"Ah. That's what I get for trying to be all smart." He yawned.

"I'm tired too."

"Can't believe you were going to bail on the after-party."

At first I wasn't sure what he meant, then I realized he meant *this*.

"I can't believe you never told me you like guys, Mateo."

He lifted his head off the pillow and stared. "Sure I told you," he said, with a tonal concession to the fact that he hadn't. "OK, but a little mystery is good for the soul."

"Yeah."

I guess I should've seen it. I should've known. But in my world guys normally didn't operate like this, with this kind of slowness, this kind of reserve. Normally there was no mystery. In my world guys were out, loud. You went to a place where gay guys go, you found one, you went home with him. This was so different. And special. Was it special because it was different? Or different because it was special?

"Well," he said, "now you know, in living color."

"It was a heck of a way to tell me. Rubbing yourself all over me like that."

He laughed. "You liked it."

"I loved it. But it was fun, not knowing."

He smirked. "Now that you know, are you not interested anymore?"

"Maybe I'm interested."

"Maybe you are?"

"Maybe I am."

As the sun lit up

the bedroom we lay on our backs, pointing out shapes in the plaster swirls on the ceiling. His boxers, which in the dark I thought were white or yellow, were in fact pink. The blankets were rolled down into hills that elevated our feet. There was something nice about his feet; they looked solid and sturdy, good for a quick getaway. I absentmindedly fitted his black leather ankle band in between my toes. My feet were usually good for a getaway too. I could barely believe I was still here, still in this bed now that the sun was up. I wondered if he used his parents' story to keep me around. Did he know I couldn't let a narrative drop in the middle? There was still so much more I wanted to hear.

"Do you know how long your father and Marjorie were — together?"

"I always see that one as a horse with an elephant trunk," he said, pointing up at one of the plaster swirls.

"Why not just an elephant?"

"Too svelte. — I can't imagine it was very long. Maybe only days. Maybe only once. My father makes mistakes like anyone but he's not a deceptive man. Can't imagine he kept it from my mother for long."

"Oh." I felt surprised to be disappointed that the romance — Mateo had given me permission to think of it as a romance — had been so short-lived.

"And after the affair my mom was like, *Screw this, Renaldo.*"

"You were ten?"

"Almost."

"How'd she find out?"

"He told her."

"Wow. How much do you remember about it?"

"I remember one time them talking loud in the kitchen area, then my mom turning the telenovela up loud (my aunt used to mail her Brazilian soaps on tape), and then them going in the bedroom to yell. Seemed like the next thing I knew, we were splitting for SP. Just like that. But now that I think about it, it must've been a while. I remember it was snowing when they had the fight, and when we went to the plane I was wearing shorts. So it was probably a lot of things, but I'm sure it was mostly the affair. But also my granny died, which opened up some space in the house my tia and tio lived in."

"Sorry, I'm not— The words."

"Oh. My aunt and uncle. My mom's sister and her husband. Vinicius's parents."

"Oh, oh."

"And then there was the fact that America just wasn't catching on for them, I think. They sure as hell tried. But like, they were illegal at that point, so there was all the shit that came with that."

Which is why when an America—for there was nothing more American than Marjorie Miller, who'd never lived more than twenty miles from Boston Common, whose ancestors had fought in the Revolutionary War—sought him out, welcomed him, gave him access to privileged places.... Well.

"Plus the constant worry," Mateo went on. "It was like three big arrows that pointed back to SP."

"How sad for your mom. It's like she was betrayed by her husband and America at the same time."

"Worked out in the end."

He turned over and put his lips on my shoulder, almost as punctuation, and I felt my pulse quicken with the idea that when he said *worked out* he might've been thinking of me. I didn't know if I wanted to be liked that way, or that much. But then against my hip I could feel him getting hard.

"Again?" I said, relieved, because this I knew exactly what to do with.

We quickly found, though, that we'd spent all of what we had overnight, and, boners dwindling, we lay on our backs again and looked up at the ceiling.

"What was the, uh, government like when you moved back?" I hoped it came across as a worldly question.

"Democratic by then. Corrupt as hell. But moving the right direction. Maybe that was the fourth point."

"But it was home."

"It was home."

After naming a few more animals in the ceiling I said, "I think we need a shower." I stretched my arms and discreetly smelled my armpit. My guts felt cramped, too, from going all these hours without passing gas. I'd forgotten how difficult it was to wake up looking OK. And yet Mateo seemed to manage it.

We hauled ourselves out of bed and he wrapped a sheet around us both. Underneath it, like a moving tent, we hobbled down the hall to the floral bathroom at the end, bumping into walls and each other the whole way.

The water felt good

and I liked seeing his body in the full light, especially when his eyes were closed against streams of shampoo suds and I could look with abandon. The tattoo on his arm of Boston was a familiar view of the city. I knew the buildings well — there were only three or four major ones: the Hancock, the Pru, 111 Huntington. He blew at me the suds that covered his lips. The tattoo on his other arm, the São Paulo skyline, was a single shaded block with a serrated top. It looked something like a comb. Not three or four major buildings in this skyline but dozens, even hundreds. I felt lonely and small just looking at its immensity. I focused on the suds working their way down his chest.

"I guess what I'm still missing," I said as he rinsed, "is how you went from São Paulo into the house of your father's mistress."

"Hmm. I don't know. Guess it was two reasons." He pushed back his hair, held up two fingers. "First, I was doing a lot of graffiti. Like a *lot*. Barely went to school. Me and my friend Tiago, we'd miss whole weeks of school at a time. Go out on days-long binges of nonstop graf, like some kind of addicts or something. Stints so long I got sick doing it. Really scared my mom."

"You won't ever get to the Moon if you drop out of school, Mateo."

"That's basically what she said!"

"So she sent you away?"

"No, she sent me away after my dad got shot."

"Jesus, he got shot?"

"Not killed or anything. He and my uncle were out, got held up at a traffic light. SP can be a pretty tricky place sometimes."

"Everywhere can," I said, though my mind ran with images of heavily-armed drug cartels.

He nodded. "But SP more than most. Anyway, he caught a bullet right here." He squeezed my hip bone. "Went right through the door of the car. Shattered part of his pelvis. Went through. By some miracle, didn't hit anything he couldn't live without. They took the bullet out from back here." He ran his hand around my back and circled his thumb against the bottom of my butt. "Walks with a limp and a cane. Always will forever."

"He was lucky though."

"Definitely. Scared the shit out of my mom, though."

"I can imagine."

"They wanted to get me out. Do my last year of high school in an American school. Re-establish myself. And go to college. And go to the Moon. I think my mom still hoped for that."

What happened to facilitate

Mateo's return to America was something that made him think of his mother Sabina as a monument, a wonder of the world, a towering figure like Christ the Redeemer who overlooked Rio. And though he raged against her plan at first and wrote his rage all across São Paulo, his awe at her sheer ballsiness was, in the end, what made him pack his bags.

His mom, man, she called her for help. Back then Mateo could barely wrap his mind around it and these years later he was no closer. The woman who, six years earlier, had nearly sabotaged their family. The woman who Sabina had packed up her family and switched continents to get away from. The same woman.

His mom *called* her.

Marjorie's skin turned to ice

when she heard the voice on her answering machine. She had never spoken to Sabina before but her accent instantly called to mind that time. Six years collapsed to minutes like a wormhole in space-time and all the progress she'd made during that time in overcoming that thing seemed to disappear too. Suddenly it was all right there, rushing back — the sound of his voice, the warble in his throat as he told her about Sabina, and that they were leaving, and that he could never see her again. The anger she'd felt. At him. At herself.

She had pressed delete without listening to the full message, hoping the woman would not call back. What could she possibly want that would cross all those years and all those miles? Her thoughts jumped first to motives of retaliation, then leapfrogged to fear: Had something happened to Renaldo?

Two days later Sabina's second call caught Marjorie on her way out the door, and Marjorie, after the greeting, was going to use that as an excuse.

"I'm about to go out," she was going to say. "Could we talk later?" Later, of course, as in never.

But before she had a chance, Sabina, swallowing every ounce of her considerable pride, told Marjorie, "I need your help. For my son."

At the end of a terrible, wonderful hour, there was a deal, much more than the simple advice Sabina had intended to ask for, or ever imagined, much more than she thought she could accept from this woman of all people — much more than Marjorie had ever intended to offer.

Marjorie questioned her motives in offering it. What business did she have opening her home to Renaldo's teenage son? What did she hope to gain? Did she hope to see shades of Renaldo in the boy? Did she hope to pretend the boy was their own son, a surprise relic of their brief time together?

It felt dangerous, too. She knew nothing about this Mateo Vinicius Armstrong Amaral, who was apparently truant, prone to—what had Sabina called them?—fugues. She couldn't expose her young daughter Phoebe to something like that.

It was when, at last, Sabina revealed *why* Mateo was truant that it all seemed to open up and become justified and right and obvious. It wasn't drugs or theft or gangs or violence. Mateo was an artist. An art student. Just like the ones Marjorie spent all day teaching, encouraging, pushing and helping. An art student. And probably a good one. At the very least a dedicated one. It clicked. And at the end of a terrible, wonderful hour, there was a deal.

That same long night Sabina had lain in bed. Sending her son to live with her husband's old mistress? Insane. Totally, utterly insane. The woman was her arch enemy. She hated her and hated her for years with a passion conjurable only by a woman from the land of the harsh São Paulo sun. She'd changed continents to get away from her. And now she was going to, basically, invite her to shelter her only son?

Sabina felt sick. In bed she rolled against Renaldo. He didn't sleep well anymore, was plagued by constant pain, and as she stroked his belly and side (tickling distracted him from the pain), her fingertips found the thick cord of scar that seemed to tunnel through him like a worm.

In the morning she informed Renaldo of her decision— somehow it had always been her decision. And Renaldo, with much sadness, agreed. Sadness because he understood that, in some way, he was losing his son. Mateo was going to a place Renaldo would never be allowed to follow.

Mateo stood at the top

of the stairs in Marjorie's old Jamaica Plain house, listening, listening. He tilted his head and bent his brow. He heard a car go by outside; the mutt a few houses down barked twice. But from this house there was only silence. Silence and the last few drips from the faucet behind me.

He turned when I opened the bathroom door the rest of the way. We'd run the water cold against the morning heat and there wasn't much steam. I wore a towel around my waist.

"Clean?" he said.

I nodded. "What are you doing?"

"Listening. They're out."

"How'd you get dressed so fast?" I walked down the hall leaving footprints on the wood.

"We should go get your car," he said, following me into his room. Stepping into my underwear, I modestly turned to cover myself, stopped, we both laughed.

"Nudity is so situational," I said.

"It looks good on you."

I pulled up my boxers. "I hope I didn't get a ticket."

"I'll pay it if you did. It's my fault we left it."

"*Fault* is hardly the right word."

We had breakfast and took the T to Charlestown and walked and found the car mercifully free of orange parking tickets.

"Can I get a ride home?" he said as I unlocked the door.

"No," I smirked, and he got in.

For shits and giggles we drove to the street with the construction, where last night, when things were so much different—was that really only twelve hours ago?—we'd painted on the plywood wall. I drove by slowly.

"Would you look at that," I said.

"I know, right?" He clicked his tongue. "What is this neighborhood coming to? Such riff-raff running free."

"Running free and defacing private property."

"A shame, really."

"Such a shame."

"Reminds me," he said, snapping a Polaroid of our graffiti, "I need more yellow."

He bought his supplies

after work, he told me, because a guy in *slacks* and an ironed button-down got less hassle buying spraypaint than a guy wearing jeans and a hoodie.

What did he need today? He thought about which holes in his trunk compartment needed filling. He needed some blue and some lime. He also, as usual, needed more yellow. All Mateo's people were yellow, a yellow the color of honey that sufficed to imply the skin-tone of anyone from a Fletcher to a Jamar to a copper-skinned brasileiro. Meant he had to carry fewer shades, which made his backpack lighter.

He was pretty sure the MBTA ripped off his style for Charlie, the cartoon commuter of ambiguous honey-colored ethnicity, who starred in advertisements for the T and on his namesake, the Charlie Card subway pass. But Mateo didn't mind. He himself had lifted the yellow from Os Gêmeos — The Twins — a pair of brothers, two of the biggest names in Brazilian graffiti. Not all of their people were yellow but a lot were, and those were the ones Mateo liked best.

He put the cans and a few fat-tipped markers on the counter, paid with cash, stuffed the change and the receipt in his pocket.

In the parking lot of the hardware store (one of the many he frequented on a rotating schedule; there were art-supply stores for the exotic colors, but art stores tended to get to know their clientele, and he didn't like people asking questions) he stashed the cans in the trunk, dropping them into the plywood shelves. And when he parked outside his house he left them there, bringing in only the markers.

Marjorie and her daughter Phoebe were eating dinner — hot dogs and mac and cheese by the looks of it — on the stools at the kitchen counter, watching *Wheel of Fortune* on the little TV by the fridge. The kitchen table was overwhelmed by one of Marjorie's huge puzzles, a half-finished Taj Mahal, which she spent Saturday and Sunday mornings piecing together while consuming cigarettes and English muffins.

"Hello," Mateo said, shutting the door behind him. By the edge of the puzzle sat a couple of pieces of mail addressed to him — a credit card bill and a renewal notice for *Rolling Stone*. Also a thin square package, obviously a CD, wrapped in brown paper, bearing colorful stamps from Brazil. He picked them up.

"There's a couple of hotdogs left, if you're hungry," Marjorie told him. She wore her graying brown hair always in a loose bun, and the paintbrushes she stabbed through it on school days were there. Usually too she had on an old flannel shirt, her getting-messy shirt, but that was gone for this weather and she wore only a pinkish t-shirt. Her skirt was paint-splotched tan cotton and on her feet she wore clogs.

"Hello Mateo," Phoebe said, clippy, as though to catch him and keep him from leaving. She was working her way down off the stool.

"Hello Miss," he said, lifting his arms and then putting them on her back when she collided with him and squeezed him around his middle. He stepped back to steady himself. She looked up, her chin just above his belly, and grinned; there was a blob of cheese on the corner of her mouth and a twinkle in her eye. She was only a couple of years younger than Mateo.

"You missed dinner!" she said, imperatively, the way she said most everything.

"I had to run some errands! I'm going to steal a wiener, though. Then I need to get to sleep!"

"Will you watch the dancing show?"

"Hmm. The dancing show isn't on tonight. But I'll watch it with you when it's on, OK?"

"OK."

He helped himself to two hotdogs and a scoop of mac and cheese, banging the spoon against the plate to get it off.

"How you doing, Marjorie? You look dressed for school."

"Today was the first day of Art Camp," she said, waving a fork with a chunk of hot-dog stabbed on the end.

"You go, Phoebe?"

She was climbing back onto the stool beside her mother. She nodded.

"Fun?"

"I asked mom if next time we can bring you!"

"And what did your mom say to that?"

"Yes."

"Haha. Oh she did, huh? But I don't know if my boss, Mr. Larry Bassett, would let me go. I'll have to ask."

"Tell him Phoebe says he has to!" she shouted, angry for an instant, then smiling again.

He opened the fridge and from the shelf marked MATEO he grabbed a bottle of water.

"Thanks for the food. Now I'm out like the fat kid in dodgeball. That's a simile."

Phoebe laughed hysterically.

He took the plate upstairs to the room he rented from Marjorie, set it on his door-desk, and scattered the contents of his pockets across the door: the markers, his keys and wallet and phone, the mail.

He set aside the bill and opened the CD. He chuckled at the name of the album, by a band called Numismata. There was a note, written in English in his mother's hand:

Mateo — Saw V. with this the other day and I had to buy one for you. "Brazilians On The Moon"! Someday. Maybe it will be you! I hope you are doing well. Please think about a visit soon... it has been too long! Pai sends his hello. — Mamãe

He smiled, folded the note, tucked it under his copy of *Porcupine City*. He popped the CD into his laptop. He liked the sound but it struck him as surprisingly low-key for his cousin, who last Mateo knew was in the throes of a hip-hop phase.

He logged on to chat but Vinicius wasn't online.

He ate the hotdogs slowly while checking the weather forecast and perusing graffiti message boards to see what people were saying about him today. When he was done he got out of his clothes, did a hundred push-ups and a hundred sit-ups, and went to shower and shave in the floral bathroom. Marjorie had told him a million times he could tear down the wallpaper and paint it however he liked, perhaps as a way to coax him into doing renovations, but the flowers didn't bother him, and anyway he had more important things to paint than bathrooms. After drying off he put on some shorts and walked barefoot back to his room. It was almost 7:30.

He lay down on the floor and pulled himself head-first under the bed. It was no small procedure to remove his black book, and his night with me had shifted it around, but when he'd fished it out of the panel cut into the box-spring, he sat up and slapped dust off his back. He opened the book on his lap. It was now almost four inches thick and running out of blank pages—he'd have to start a third volume soon. (Or he could finally begin the transition to digital, but old habits die hard.)

This evening, as on most evenings, he succumbed to the desire to look through his old work, and when he reached the first blank page he got up and pulled from his office pants a few Polaroids taken last night, and the one from the night before in Charlestown, with me. None of his Dedinhos stuff appeared in this book—this book was for the special stuff he did on his own—but this one, with my drippy ARROWMAN beside it, made him smile. He glued them in, and with a fine-tipped Sharpie began noting the location of the piece, and the date.

A knock on the door made him streak ink across one of the photos. He flung the black book under the bed, jammed his toes between the mattress and box-spring, flopped backward, put his hands behind his head and said, "Come in."

Marjorie opened the door. "Didn't mean to disturb."

"It's OK, I was just working out." He sat up. He felt funny to be shirtless in front of her and folded his arms across his chest.

"Muscle man," she said, and he blushed. "I just wanted to let you know, Mateo, that—well, I noticed you had a boy over the other night, and—"

Suddenly shirtlessness was the least of his embarrassment. "I'm sorry, I was sure we were quiet."

"Oh— I heard you come in, is all I meant." She looked down at her clogs. "Going up the stairs. That's all I—" She took a breath. "Anyway. What I wanted to say is that you don't have to sneak him around. You're welcome to have him over any time. You know that. Or anyone special."

"Thank you. That's nice."

"Have him over for dinner. I could make something. Or to watch TV. Phoebe loves meeting new people."

"I know." He stood up and sat on the bed.

"I would make one request, though," she said. She seemed to be choosing her words carefully, and that made him nervous. "I don't think Phoebe needs to know exactly *who* he is. Does that make sense? I think it's enough for her to know he's your friend. I think it would be confusing for her."

"Confusing?"

"I don't think she'd understand very well, that's all."

He wanted to say, What's to understand? He knew I would've said that, knew I would've made a sarcastic promise not to blow any guys in front of her daughter. But instead he said, "Sure. And he really is only my friend. He's just a guy from work. We've only—" Spent one night together, he almost said. "He's just an amigo."

"Well." She nodded. "Now that I've made myself look like a total homophobe— How do you say homophobe in Portuguese?"

"Oh, I don't know. *Inimigos dos gays*, I guess?"

She repeated it carefully, and sighed, and seemed to regret the whole thing. "Anyway, I'll let you get back to your exercise."

He lay in bed, the windows turning dark, and looked up at the ceiling at the horse with the elephant trunk. In the whole weird exchange with Marjorie the thing that bothered him most had been something he himself had said: that I was just a guy from work. It seemed right and yet not. Factual but not true.

He tried to put it out of his mind. He rolled over and smelled the other pillow but the smell of me was gone by then. He needed to get to sleep. His day started at 2:00 a.m.

"When do Jamar and I

get to meet this special boy of yours?" Cara pleaded. "It's been like a month, mister!" She had her back against the arm of the couch. Her feet were wedged under my thigh. Every once in a while I'd feel her toes wiggle through my shorts. She held out a half-full joint and I took it. "Assuming he exists. Jamar thinks this Mateo person might actually be a composite character you've created out of a ginormous number of tricks. Mike, Arthur, Tom, Eddie, and Omar."

"I've never dated an Arthur. And it hasn't been a month! It's been like ten days. And jeez, Cara, we're just knocking boots."

"No, you and the Warcraft kid just knock boots."

"..."

"So when, huh?"

"Assuming he's real?"

"Assuming he's real."

"I don't know," I said. "Soon. I promise." She reached for the joint and I waved her away and put it between my lips again, inhaling as deep as I could. "He's a busy guy. He keeps weird hours."

"I can't believe you're dating someone you work with," she said. "It's so scandalous. Do your other coworkers know?"

They did not know, and although I called Cara a prude for saying it was a scandal to sleep with a coworker, I was delighted to be someone who was doing it. At work I couldn't help but snicker every time I realized I knew what the I.T. guy looked like naked. The people who passed my cube did not know about the line of freckles across his left shoulder blade, were not familiar with the spray of hairs at the small of his back. Probably had never seen his tattoos. And certainly had no inkling of a thing far more intimate than any of those others: the knowledge of how the I.T. guy spent his nights.

"It's really not that scandalous," I told Cara. "He's not exactly president of the company. He just installs RAM all day."

"I bet he prefers to install his RAM in you."

"Touché."

"You haven't said much about this one."

"I never kiss and tell."

"Mmhm. You kiss and write whole books."

"Hah."

"How is he? Big? Long?" She laughed. "You've turned me into such a gay man."

"He's just right. He's perfect."

"How many times total?"

"A couple. I told you, he's busy. You're nosy when you're stoned, aren't you?"

"Too busy for sex, and you're hanging out with him anyway?" She leaned forward, withdrawing her feet and circling her arms around her knees. "I think I was right in the beginning: you're in looove." Her face was high and earnest. "And why, because I'm so happy for you, Fletcher. It's so great that you have someone. Even if part of me has always wished it could be me." She made a fist and socked me in the shoulder.

"Ow!" I took another drag on the joint and passed it back. I made a sneaky look. "I would've moved in on that when Jamar was in Denver. I would've made my move. Swoop!"

"Like how again?"

"Like swoop!"

We finished the joint and then lay on the couch through the rest of an episode of *Law & Order*, and when it was over I dragged myself up.

"I'm going to go write for a while," I told her. "I always seem to get interesting things stoned."

"Don't leave me."

"Gotta, princess."

Right away I noticed Mateo's

sneakers on the floor by my bed, and that gave him away. But he was too asleep to notice. He was facing away from the door, moppy hair splayed over my pillow. I closed the door and tip-toed to the bed and lifted the sheet.

"Heavens to Pete. There's a bare Brazilian boy in my bed — *boing!*"

The bare Brazilian rolled over, grinned, put a hand over his eyes. "I wanted to surprise you. Been waiting in here *forever*."

"That's adorable. A-dor-a-ble. Adora-bubble. Did you know your chest hair looks like cotton candy? I want to eat it. *Num num num.*" I leaned down and licked his belly button, pressed my tongue into the fuzzy hole. His whole body went rigid and he grabbed me. "Oh, the bare Brazilian's ticklish!"

Laughing, he said: "What were you doing out there anyway?"

"Couldn't you smell?" He laughed. "How'd you get in without me seeing you?"

"Secret."

"Same way you've avoided the Boston PD for years, I guess."

"Take off your clothes!" He tugged at my shirt.

I sat down on the bed. "You should've told me you were coming, I wouldn't have smoked. I'm totally flaccid stoned."

"No. Totally?" He sat up. He moved to put his hand on my crotch but hesitated. "Anything I can... do?"

"Many men have tried."

"Damn."

"Sorry."

"Well it's not your fault."

"Do you need to...?"

"I was *hoping* to," he said bashfully.

"I could give you a hand. So to speak."

"No," he said with a little smile, but he didn't try to stop me when I pulled aside the sheet. I rubbed my hands together to warm them.

A couple minutes later his hands clenched into fists and with a yelp he filled the four-layer tarpaulin of Kleenex I had ready. It was sexy enough to make me suspect I could've gotten something up after all. But too late now.

"Woooh!" He fell back on the pillow and threw a forearm across his eyes, a big smile showing under his Boston skyline.

"You're welcome." I sat for a second, holding and beholding the tissue. "What am I supposed to do with this now? It looks like one of those bags for frosting cakes with."

He rolled his eyes. "Flush it for me? I'm in my nude." He grinned and yanked the sheet up.

I palmed the tissue and snuck out to the bathroom. Cara was still on the couch. "Gotta brush my teeth," I told her, closing the bathroom door behind me. I lifted the toilet seat but imagined the tissues clogging the finicky pipes, so I dropped it in the wastebasket instead. It landed with a squishy thump. Then I brushed my teeth.

When I came out Cara was straightening up the living room. She had two cups in her hands and an empty bag of Pirate's Booty crumpled under one arm.

"Did you brush 'em up?" she said.

I nodded.

"Let me check." She walked up close to me with her lips puckered and pressed them against mine. It surprised me but was over too quickly for me to react. "Nice and clean," she said.

I whispered goodnight and went back into my room.

I'd been asleep maybe

an hour when Mateo's phone started chirping. I rolled over with a gasp, thought it was the end of the world, glared at the clock radio with eyes that felt as big as planets. 2:01 a.m. I started to lay back down but checked the time again in disbelief. It was an hour I was well acquainted with seeing at the end of a day, but never at the beginning of one. This must be a mistake, then, maybe one of his train alarms he forgot to turn off.

He shifted around under the sheets and reached out and killed the alarm. Beautiful silence resumed. Past midnight I'd laid there beside him, listening to the sounds of his breathing, feeling his movements—but now I just wanted to get back to sleep.

A moment later, though, he was sitting up, the sheets sliding down to his bare waist. He was looking at his phone—it lit his face in an otherworldly glow. He rubbed his hair and yawned. Then he put the phone down and slid against me, circling his arm around my chest.

"Time for me to get up, Arrowman."

"Up?" I whispered, genuinely a little night-delirious but mostly feigning it to keep from having to deal with him leaving. I reached and clutched the back of his thigh. "No up. Sleep."

"If I sleep," he whispered against the back of my head, "how will the walls get painted on?"

"Mm."

"Somebody's gotta do it."

"I know," I said, thinking: *Why?* But by now I was more alert. Sleep was slipping away like an unaffordable luxury. I wanted to be asked to come along but I didn't want to bring it up myself. It was hard to know what nights were off-limits for me. Some nights he went off by himself. I suspected that when we were together he only dabbled; something entirely different went on the nights he went out alone. Maybe tonight was for serious.

"Are you really pretty tired?" he said, his hands cool against my chest. "Come out with me, if you want."

I looked at the clock again. "I'm used to being asleep for another five hours."

"I know."

"And we have work in the morning."

"I know. Bring your office clothes with you. I'll show you how I change in my car. My car's on the street."

I thought for a minute but when he peeled away from me I knew I was going to follow him wherever he went.

The bathroom light nearly blew up my eyeballs. I squinted around for my toothbrush while he peed beside me—an act which seemed to me about the most intimate thing I'd ever experienced, and it sent an unexpected warmth through me. He flushed and stepped out of his underwear and got in the shower, the sound of the water suddenly different when he moved beneath the streams.

I dropped my underwear and peed and noticed the wastebasket. Now that I was sober I couldn't believe I just left his jizzy tissues sitting in there in plain view. (I was one to wrap used Q-tips in toilet paper to hide earwax.) The wastebasket was empty. Tomorrow—today—was trash day. Cara must've emptied it. I hoped she hadn't realized what it was. She would think it was mine. God, that would be embarrassing. I'd never hear the end of it.

I flushed and got in the shower, catching the spray of water that ricocheted off his shoulders.

"Babette told me a while ago that I had to get you into a shower," I said with a mischievous grin as I sealed the curtain against the wall. "Guess I succeeded."

"Babette from work?" His hair lay flat across his face as though he'd had a bucket of black paint dumped on his head.

"Yup."

"What made her say that?"

"Well—" My grin may as well have made a sucking noise as it drained off my face.

He stopped soaping. "I don't like smell or something, do I? Fletcher?"

"Of course not!" I didn't know what to say. "Well it's been really hot out for the past few weeks, and obviously that's the only time she's known you. And she doesn't know what you do on your way to work."

He covered his face with his hands. "Oh god, I smell. How could you not *tell* me?"

"You don't smell. I like it. You just smell like you have a life, that's all. You're not sterile."

"I shower every day like everyone else."

"You don't smell."

"I reek."

"You don't reek."

"I'm like Pig-Pen."

"You're not like Pig-Pen. Come on."

"I'm lucky I don't have flies around me all the time!"

"Stop. You don't smell. You're beautiful. I think you're *beautiful.*"

"Oh." The water streamed between us while we stood averting our eyes, wearing little smiles. "You do?"

"Maybe I do."

"Maybe you do?"

"Maybe I do."

Tired isn't really tired

when it comes from making out with a hot graffiti artist under highway overpasses. Or when it comes from swapping paint-misted clothes for office clothes in the backseat of a gray Civic parked at the rear of the office lot. That kind of tired is more like the kind of tired that comes when you've just had good sex. Not tired but satisfied. Not tired but—dare I say it?—content.

Which is why Mike's text barely phased me. I received it at

my desk not long after having lunch with Mateo. Mike was heading home for a few weeks and wanted to know if I was up for a send-off. I thought the news was best delivered by voice, so I called him.

"Please tell me you're free," he said before even saying hi. "It occurred to me all of a sudden that I'm going to be in the woods for three weeks. Three weeks is that perilous timeframe that has me clawing the walls, and there's not a lot of guys banging down my door in Maine."

"I wish I could," I told him, "but I've kind of started seeing someone. Crazy, huh?"

"Is this the right number?"

"Haha."

"Who is he?"

"Guy from work."

"Nice. Cute?"

"Very."

"Nice," he said again, a little melancholy.

"I'm sorry."

"No no no, don't be. This is part of the deal."

There was a long pause, then—a silence as deep as a dropped call. I didn't know what to say either. This was uncharted territory.

"I could raid my phonebook," I said finally. "Try to connect you with someone?"

"I'm sure you could. But no. Maybe this is a sign. Maybe there's a lobsterman waiting to fall in love with me."

After hanging up I looked at my phone, trying to remember whether I'd ever turned down a hook-up with Mike, other than that first time. I didn't think I had. I wasn't sure I'd ever turned one down, period. Doing it should've felt worse.

"You look busy," Mateo said suddenly, sarcastically. He was standing in the hall outside my cube, holding a monitor. A cord hung swaying against his legs.

"Mike," I said, referring to the phone.

"Your special friend."

"I told him I made a new friend."

"Cool," he said simply, and continued down the hall.

He was only puttering,

I was sure of it now. Sometimes he would ask me what he should paint. Other times he would just doodle, literally: squiggles and stars and the type of things I put on notepads when I was on the phone. It seemed amateur, un-urgent. It was pretty and creative but it wasn't the type of work that would compel someone to get up when the day was a mere two hours old and go out into the night, spelunking through alleys in dangerous parts of the city.

For all the knowledge I was accumulating about my new friend Mateo Amaral—from the details of his mother's yearning for space travel to his thoughts on Da Vinci—this was the remaining mystery. When I was there, he wasn't doing what he did. It was starting to seem obvious. On the nights I was there, he was just playing. Dedinhos was a ruse, a pen name, a—what had he called it?—an apelido. Something to disguise a whole lot more.

The last day of June,

when we'd been hanging out for a month, on a day following one of the nights he slipped out without waking me up, I nearly drove into a parked car. My boss Janice's. In the Cook parking lot I sat idling, staring up at the billboard at the back of the lot, until a car behind me—Randy—tooted.

"Yeah, yeah, Porn Randy, I'm going."

I parked and got out and walked over and looked again, standing below the billboard looking up, probably gaping like some kind of idiot. In green and white bubble letters the billboard bore the words ARROWMAN IS.

My hand met my forehead and ran back over my hair. "You're fucking kidding me," I said aloud. I looked for his car, which wasn't in the rear corner of the lot like usual. I spotted it a few spaces over. So he was here.

I dropped my stuff in my cube and made my way to the I.T. department, offering obligatory good-mornings along the way. He was in his cube unpacking hardware from a cardboard box, bits of foam peanuts static-clinging like snowflakes to his tattoo buildings.

"Hey you."

"Morning, Fletcher."

"So."

"What's up?"

"When you get a chance, can we talk?"

"Sure. What about?"

"Oh I think you know."

"About the—?" He drew a big rectangle in the air, peanut pieces dropping off his arms. He looked sheepish.

"Could be."

He dropped his head and smirked. "I'll be over in a minute."

A half-hour later he entered my cube and tapped me on the shoulder with one green finger. We went outside and sat on the hood of his car.

"How was your night?" he asked.

And I replied, "You write the Facts, don't you?"

He smiled, looking both vulnerable and uncomfortable.

"You know," I went on, "I just thought you were some graffiti guy. I had no idea. I really had no idea."

"I *am* just some graffiti guy."

"When I knew nothing about graffiti I knew about you. Well not you. About the Facts. I'm kind of in awe."

"Don't be in awe."

"You told me it was some oldster."

"I told you that was the rumor. There are a lot of rumors."

"Fair enough. So what do they mean?"

"Aren't they self-explanatory?"

"Well yeah. Individually. But why? Why so many?"

"Why not? Gotta write something. And maybe I'm not creative enough to describe other than what *is*."

I looked at him. He seemed different, suddenly. Bigger. He leaned over and bumped his chin against my shoulder.

"I'll never tell anyone," I said.

"I know."

"The billboard." I pointed. "Did you not finish?"

He crossed his arms on top of his knees and shook his head, embarrassed. "That was my last one of the night—it's probably still wet. I came here to crash in my car for a while before work. I was thinking about you, thinking about what Arrowman is to me. I saw the board. I was painting, you know, and then it hit me that just by writing that, putting your name in the context of the Fact, as you call it—"

"What do you call them?"

"I don't call them anything, I just make them. And by putting your name, which I think only I know—"

"Which only you know."

He flashed a smile. "Which only I know. By putting it there, poof, Mateo is the Fact-writer. I realized it and damn, I froze. I think it's the only slip-up I've ever made doing this. I just didn't have time to go over it."

"Didn't have time or didn't want to?"

"Hmm. That's a question for another day, Arrowman. Maybe another night."

"I can see why you're so secretive. I've read about you in the newspaper. You're like a one-man graffiti army. Some cop is going to make his career off bringing you in."

"Please."

"Don't be modest. You know. You must know. You wouldn't be so secretive otherwise. But I won't tell anyone. I'll never tell anyone. Not just because I'm your— you know, friend. But because I respect you. I think it's art. Like I said that first day."

"Thank you."

"I'm glad we got together before I knew this. I wouldn't want you to wonder whether I thought of you as just—I don't know—an arrow in my quiver."

"I don't think that."

He held out his hand, palm up, and I touched mine to it— a very slow-motion high-five.

"You have no idea how much I want to take you into the back of this car right now," I told him.

"I have some idea. Tonight."

"That's so far away." I slid off the hot hood. "Are you free for lunch?"

He cleared his throat, as though to mark a more professional tone for the conversation. "I wish I was. I've got a meeting. Something about the new website?"

"The perpetually-in-development website? The thing's going to be outdated before it ever goes online."

"But I'll see you, huh?"

"Yeah. Soon."

We started back toward the building.

"Arrowman is!" he yelled, spreading his arms.

"Wait a minute, wait a minute. How were you going to finish it? WELL ENDOWED? HOT IN BED?"

"HOT IN BED is on the side of Symphony Hall," he said. "And possibly one or two bathroom stalls."

"Har har."

"Arrowman is. That's all!" He grabbed me by the shoulders. "You are, aren't you?"

A Fact in the process

of creation was something I never expected to see—as far as I knew, no one, with the exception of a handful of people from São Paulo, had ever witnessed it—and watching it took my breath away. It was entirely different from anything I'd seen him do before. It looked almost like a dance, or some kind of martial art, or a mix of the two like capoeira, with graceful swings and turns of his bare arms and soft, deliberate movements of his legs. It was fast, much faster than how he normally painted when we were together, but it was more controlled, too. He even seemed to close his eyes at times, feeling the paint with some other sense.

This piece, on the base of a support column of the Longfellow Bridge, had been started days or weeks ago, one of the many unfinished he apparently had in rotation. I held a can in my hand but it was like a beverage at a party, just something to hold—I wasn't painting tonight, just watching. How could I paint when this was going on? How could I do anything? Cars thundered over the bridge above us but I barely heard them, and I noticed Cambridge reflecting in the river only as a backdrop to Mateo.

I watched him and grew uncomfortable with the intensity and looked at the paint instead of him. This was serious, more serious than anything we'd done, an intimacy that made sex feel like a handshake.

When he was done he stepped back and looked at his work, wiped his hand across his brow, flicked paint off his fingers. He looked at me and smiled bashfully, as though he were being seen naked for the first time.

I didn't know what to say and said nothing. After snapping a photo he picked up his backpack and we walked away in silence. The greenery of the park along the river enclosed us. Sailboats lined the docks. I asked what he'd really started to write on the billboard outside Cook.

After a slight hesitation he told me, "ARROWMAN IS CREW."

"What's crew?"

"As in my crew. My team. My—"

"Gang?"

"Sometimes. Not for us. My crew."

"You'd let a toy be in your crew?"

He smiled. "Well, you'd have the benefit of my experience so you wouldn't be a toy any more. Per se."

"Per se. So you want to be partners." I felt giddiness mix with fear, and the resulting emotion was bigness, heaviness.

"That's why I stopped writing it," he said.

"Oh. So you're not sure."

"It's a big step."

"It is."

He held out his hand and touched the can in mine. "Want me to take this? Or were you going to paint something?"

"Oh— No, tonight I'm just watching. Thank you for showing it to me."

He smirked. "C'mon, let's walk faster. There's more to do."

"How much more?"

"Infinity much." We picked up the pace and left the newly decorated Longfellow Bridge behind us. And behind that bridge, glowing white in the distance and much closer to infinity, was the Zakim.

There wasn't time to go

home before we had to be at work, so we went straight there and parked at the back of the lot. We'd hung our work shirts, ironed and crisp, from the ceiling handles in the backseat of Mateo's car—his on one side, mine on the other, so there was a shirt blocking each window. We lay together on the seat, the windshield blue with pre-dawn light. He had his São Paulo arm around me, was pretty much holding me onto the seat, my back against his chest. He probably didn't know I had one hand on the floor, holding myself up. He scratched his nose against my hair.

"I'm exhausted," I said.

"I know."

"I can't believe we have to go to work now."

"Not now. Later."

"I don't know how you do it every night."

"I sleep in the evening."

"I guess."

"Go to sleep a while. We have a little while. Get some sleep."

"I can't. I'll fall off."

"I'll hold you."

We couldn't really sleep like that, though, so he moved to the front seat and let me, as much as was possible, stretch out in the back. He pulled a sketchbook from underneath the passenger seat, and with marker he doodled again and again, in different letterforms, sometimes with illustrations, sometimes without—to find out if they really were true—the words ARROWMAN IS CREW.

I watched him for a while and then closed my eyes, listening to the squeak of marker against paper. By the time the first ray of sun came in between his shirtsleeves, I had fallen asleep.

THE PAINTING OF PORCUPINE CITY

PART
TWO

Hanging On Every Word

Thunk.

My backpack, packed for Mateo's, slipped off the back of my chair and hit the floor with a metallic clatter I was afraid would give away its contents. By now Jamar knew about Mateo's — shall we say — *hobby*, but I don't think he knew I was joining him at it. I leaned over and picked it up, hooked the strap once more around the top of the chair.

"Wow," I murmured, sliding back in the chair. Jamar's face was blank, was offering no clues as to how I should be reacting to what he'd just told me. It was big news and I wasn't sure what the proper response was. Meanwhile his life was flashing before my eyes. "How do you feel about it?"

"How do I feel?" He looked at me as though he'd never considered he was supposed to feel anything. He turned and looked at the fan in the window, its blades rotating in the August breeze. "How do I *feel?*" He flung himself back on my bed; the whole thing lurched on its castors, two of which bumped from rug onto wood. He stared at the ceiling. Despite his size he looked like a frustrated boy lying there, bumping his forehead with one fist. Finally he leaned up on his elbow. "I was hoping you'd tell me how I should feel about it."

I laughed, went and sat beside him on the bed, put my arm around his shoulders. "You are going to be," I paused for effect, "an amazing father."

"You think so?"

"I don't have a single doubt."

"I don't know how this happened, though," he said. "I'm well known as the double-rubber guy."

"Do you really wear two?"

"Well, no—but always one, especially since Cara decided to drop the Pill. We've never had one break or anything, that I know of."

"Always?"

"Well I mean I've—*you know*—on her stomach and her legs and stuff. Could it have dribbled in? Is that possible?"

"Like osmosis?"

"Not osmosis, like—" He squiggled a finger down his belly to his crotch. "You know. Dribbled."

"Maybe. It must've? Anyway, it happened, right? It's going to be fine. You love her. You love her, right?"

He looked at me. "Of course I love her."

"She loves you."

"She loves me."

"What's the problem?"

"There has to be a problem."

"Why? You have a good job. Advertising is stable."

He got up and walked around my room. He picked up a paperback of *Sweet Thursday* from my bureau, fanned the pages, put it back. "We can afford a kid if we're careful. I love her. OK."

"And you're twenty-seven now. You're older than your parents were, right? You're older than mine were."

"I'm old enough to have a kid. OK. OK."

"OK?"

"Thank you."

"OK."

"Remember not to tell her I told you, though. She'll kill me."

"I won't. But tell me publicly soon. I don't want to be keeping a secret like this. You know I'm not good with secrets."

"Yeah. I will. Man. A kid. Can you believe it?"

"Honestly? No. Better you than me, sucker."

He grinned. On his way to the door he said, "Going to Mateo's tonight?"

"Yeah. Yup."

"Going pretty well with him, eh?"

"Don't jinx it, Jamar. Seriously."

He flung up his hands. "Sorry!"

He left my room and I got up and looked out the window. The air had that yellow, hazy glow that precedes a summer storm. If it rained there was a decent chance Mateo would stay in bed all night, and that would be great.

Jamar poked his head back in my room. "Remind him that Car and I want to go with you guys to see that street art exhibit he mentioned at dinner. The one at the ICA."

"The Shepard Fairey one. I'll tell him." It hit me all over again. "Jamar, are you aware you're having a freaking baby?"

"If it's a boy we're going to name him Fletcher."

"Really?"

His face blanched. "Um. Oh. Well, I don't know. I was just playing. We haven't discussed it at all. I'm not sure why I just said that."

"Too bad. I'm holding you to it! Fletcher Andrews. Even if it's a girl."

"You got it. OK, I need to get out of here before she gets home. If she sees we're here together, she'll know. She'll know I wouldn't have been able to resist."

"I'll walk out with you, Dad." I put on the backpack, grabbed phone, wallet, keys off my bureau. I still always thought of the key-touching guy when I did that. It'd become a weird habit.

On the sidewalk Jamar, squinting against the setting sun, put his hand on my shoulder. "This is a secret now, remember."

I drove past Forest Hills

and in the humid twi-dark with the windows down cruised down Hyde Park Ave and turned onto his street, winding the car in the heat up the hill. And parked.

In the air was the faint smell of the brick-oven pizza place down the street, a smell that reminded me of the night a couple weeks ago when I brought Mateo there to meet Cara and Jamar for dinner, to prove to them once and for all that he wasn't Mike, Arthur, Tom, Eddie, and/or Omar, but only Mateo. I don't know why I chose such a neutral place to do this, I just felt the need. Maybe it was to keep them in check — at home they might've mauled him like he was some kind of rockstar, the first of my romantic life. They'd both run into plenty of my guys over the years — coming in, going out — but Mateo was the first one I was *introducing* them to. They were aware of the significance and behaved like thrilled parents. In the vestibule of the restaurant Jamar, normally pretty reserved, enveloped Mateo in a giant hug and lifted him a foot off the ground. Cara made googly-eyes at him as though he were surrounded by glowing fairies or some kind of halo, from appetizers all the way to dessert.

"I never thought anyone would be able to tame our Fletcher," she told Mateo. "What's your *secret?*"

Had I been tamed? Things were remarkably low-key so far with Mateo and me. No heavy discussions about our feelings, no labels placed on our relationship — we hadn't even said the word *relationship*. Or *boyfriend*. It had none of the drama I'd learned to expect from romances in Porcupine City. So it was easy to think of Mateo as just a lasting trick, a special friend; the difference was only in the amount of time we spent together. Cara and Jamar saw things differently, though. They seemed more inclined to already think of Mateo and me as a merged unit. I figured it was because they were straight and uber-domestic, though now I think it was because they were in love, and wanted so much for me to have what they had.

I climbed the steps to Mateo's house. Sweaty, I opened the screen door and knocked on the cranberry-colored door. Through the glass and translucent curtains I could see the tell-tale blue glow of a television in the living room beyond the kitchen. I knocked and waited, still thinking of it too much as Marjorie's house to enter uninvited. Beside the door some purple flowers sat wilted in a pot. I noticed then that

Marjorie's car was gone from the tiny driveway. I put my hand on the knob just as it began turning.

He was wearing a white sleeveless t-shirt that showed off his tattoos, shorts, no shoes, and the plastic band that kept his hair back. "You don't have to knock, I told you."

"I know," was all I managed before he stopped my lips with a kiss. "Ooh. Hey, your plant needs watering." I pointed.

He shrugged. "I don't handle the landscaping."

"You mean you don't take after your dad?"

"Haha. No." So his thumbs were many colors, but green wasn't one of them. "Come in."

The house had the natural cool of a brick building and my sweat turned chilly. To warm up I put my lips on his neck and slipped my hands down the back of his shorts.

"Haha. Arrowman, Marjorie's not home—"

"I know."

"—and I'm watching Phoebe."

"Oh." Quickly I withdrew my hands as though his ass were a different type of hot. "Yikes." And wiped my lips.

"Rain check?"

"Yeah. Sure. Of course."

"Mateo you're missing it!"

"On the double!" he called. "Dancing show," he said to me, taking my hand and leading me to the living room; I had to walk funny to keep from stepping on his bare heels. "Miss, you remember my friend Fletcher."

"Er, hi Phoebe," I said, waving awkwardly with my fingers while my thumb stayed hooked in my pocket.

We'd met once before, on the evening I picked Mateo up to have dinner with Cara and Jamar—a mess of introductions gotten over with in one day. She'd kept her hugs to herself that first time and seemed no more inclined to dish one out now. She told me hello, but it was dutiful.

She was sitting Indian-style on the couch with a box of Nilla Wafers in her lap, her straight brown hair splayed across her plump shoulders. A cup of tea sat on a coffee table pulled close to her knees. After looking me over through purple-rimmed glasses that made her eyes look big, she turned to

Mateo. "Kupono is on," she said.

I wondered why she didn't like me—according to Mateo she liked everyone. I wondered if she could sense I was uncomfortable around her. I crossed my arms and stood watching the TV. She made me nervous for all the same reasons little kids did. The unpredictability, mostly. But with her there was an extra awkward facet: it was a little bit cute to not like kids, if you struck the right tone with it. But not liking the handicapped just made you a douchebag.

"Ooh baby. Kupono!" Mateo cooed. He sat down at the end of the couch and when he told me to sit I wedged myself between him and the arm. He said to me, "Kupono is our favorite dancer. He's from Hawaii." On-screen a shirtless guy did multiple back-flips all the way across a stage. "Kupono also happens to be Phoebe's boyfriend."

She laughed—"Yup"—and leaned forward for the tea.

When the show was over

and she'd cast ten telephone votes for Kupono and one vote for someone named Gev (the runner-up for her affections), Phoebe hugged Mateo goodnight, sort of patted me on the forearm as she walked past me, and went upstairs to her room.

"Does she know about us?" I said. "You were holding my hand."

"I think she knows we go together. Does she know it's romantically? I doubt it."

"She must know you're gay, though. You were practically drooling over the Hawaiian guy."

"Funny what computes for her. I can get away with slobbering about how cute he is, I think because to her, objectively, he's cute, and it's not weird to her that I'd be able to see that too. But this one time I said I wanted to kiss him and she laughed like crazy and slapped me on the knee, like, *Hahaha, you silly son of a bitch.*" He took my hand and played with my fingers for a second. "Oh, Miss!" he called up, "I'm supposed to remind you to brush your teeth!" There was no response. He shrugged. "We'll assume she's doing it."

"She's pretty self sufficient?"

"Pretty much. With that kind of stuff. Not so much with cooking or anything like that. I mean, she couldn't live alone."

"Oh."

"She's actually in line to get into a home for people like her."

"An — asylum?"

"Arrowman! Jeez. It's more like a sorority house or something. In Newton. Gorgeous. It's a mansion."

"That kind of reminds me, actually," I said. "I'm not really supposed to tell, but...." Mateo was a neutral party and thus probably fell outside my promise to Jamar. "Cara's *with child*."

His face lit up. "No shit, really?"

"Jamar told me just now. It's still a secret. I'm not supposed to tell anyone."

"Wow."

"Crazy, huh?"

"Crazy!" He pursed his lips and blew out air without whistling.

I squeezed them and his cheeks filled up. "Can we go upstairs?"

We made our way to the third floor and the air grew hotter as we went. I snapped his bedroom door shut behind us.

"It'll be a good-looking kid," Mateo said. "Did you know that when mixed-race babies are born, they get a birth certificate, a Social Security card, and a modeling contract?"

"Haha!"

"That's why us Brazilians are such lookers," he said, stroking his eyebrow suavely, "because so many are mixed."

"But you're the most good-looking and you're just plain old — what are you?"

"Italian and German mostly."

"Spaghetti and weiner schnitzel."

"Heh. What's the baby's name? Have they decided?"

"They haven't gotten that far yet," I said. "He or she is currently the size of a comma." I sat down on the bed and unlaced my shoes. He came over and stood between my knees, looking down at me with his hands on my shoulders. I slipped my hands around his legs and up into his shorts. The coarse hair on his thighs tickled the webs of my fingers. "Actually, Jamar said they're going to name it after *me*. Even if it's a girl."

"That's a girl who'd be very popular. They could call her Fletchinha."

"I'll call *you* Fletchinha. Come here."

We fell backward onto the bed and he was on top of me. I held his painty fingers, looking at the cuticles and hangnails.

"Do you want to have kids, Arrowman?"

I folded his fingers into a fist and brought it in slow motion to my jaw. "*Boooof.* I'm out."

"You're out?"

"Stone cold." I looked up at him. "You mean right now?"

"Ever."

"No."

"Really?"

"Kids suck."

"You were a kid once."

"And I sucked. My dad split and my mom moved to Honduras."

He scrunched his mouth.

"I just can't see myself devoting that much time and energy to another human being."

"Huh." He rolled off me. "But Jamar's glad?"

"Jamar's nervous. But he'll be glad the moment he realizes his head's not going to explode. Cara will be—must already be—ecstatic. Motherhood is so up Cara's alley." I heard a pattering begin against the windows and felt relieved. Rain didn't necessarily mean we wouldn't go out tonight—we'd gone out painting in the rain plenty of times—but when it was raining it was easier to convince him to stay in bed. "How about you? Do you want kids?"

"Would be nice someday," he said. "Yeah, I think so. Maybe just one so it's more of a novelty. If you have too many they probably just blend together after a while. Although it would be really hard with my schedule."

"Yeah."

"Speaking of." He leaned up on his elbow. "Damn, is that

rain?"

"Yeah. Supposed to be stormy tonight."

"They were saying it would pass."

"Yeah. But it's a good excuse to stay in tonight, though, right?"

His hand had been encircling my bicep and as he stood up he slid it down my arm, our fingers catching briefly and pulling apart as he stepped away. He walked across the creaky floor to the window. A flash of lightning silhouetted him against the glass. I went over and stood beside him. We looked out, caught a glimpse of a shard of lightning bolt in what we could see of the sky above the neighbor's roof.

"You really want to stay in?" he said.

"I'm not a big fan of the rain."

"I know."

I put my arm around his waist and we watched the sky flash and listened to it rumble.

"Do you ever get homesick," I said, "for Brazil?"

"What brings that up?"

"I don't know. Family."

The light coming through the rain-spattered window made globs of light dance across his face.

"Sometimes the saudade does creep up," he said.

"*Sow-DAH-jee*," I repeated. "I don't know that one."

"Doesn't really translate. It's kind of like — nostalgia? But with more need or something."

"Different from missing?"

"A little."

"Like longing?"

"Longing is closer. My first paintings are in SP so I'll always feel connected to it."

"And your family is there."

"And my family's there."

"That's a good word, though. I'll have to remember it. Saudade."

"What's your favorite word?" he asked.

"Mine? Boy, I don't know. I like them all."

"A man of words like you must have a favorite."

"I like *razbliuto*. The word itself is kind of clumsy but its meaning gives me a heartache."

"Awh. What's it mean?"

"It's the sentimental feeling you have for someone you once loved but don't love anymore."

"Heavy," he said. "So who makes you feel razbliuto?"

"No one, that's the thing. Not yet."

"So Arrowman's never been in love?" He raised his eyebrows incredulously and drip-lights moved across his forehead and the plastic band in his hair.

"I've been in love dozens of times. But never for more than a few minutes."

"Well when you do fall in love, and then you fall out of love, you'll be all set with the right word handy and you won't even need a dictionary."

"That's what I'm counting on."

I woke up a few times during the night and every time I did I thanked the rainstorm for keeping him beside me. Still, I hoped it wasn't only the rain keeping him there.

Surprised. Noun. The state of

being astonished or amazed. I'd been working on my best surprised face since morning.

"Does this look astonished and amazed?" I asked Mateo, standing in my underwear in front of his armoire mirror. He was sitting on the floor organizing graffiti markers. He organized them not by shade but by width of tip.

"Way too much is going on with your mouth," he said. "Surprise is in the eyes."

"How about this?"

"Closer." He came over and pressed his thumbs upward into my eyebrows. "When they tell you about Fletchinha, don't put on the look right away. Give them a second of blank stare first. And if you really want to look surprised, pretend like you think they're joking. Laugh."

As I sipped at a hard lemonade I recalled his advice, which seemed logical despite his aggressive puppeting of my features. I leaned forward on the couch. Cara was sitting on the coffee table and Jamar towered beside her.

"What's this all about, guys?" I said. "Should I be worried?" I put the bottle to my lips. I was weighing the idea of performing a full-on spit-take when the moment came. If I did I'd definitely get lemonade on the TV, and possibly on Jamar's Playstation. A paperback of Cara's was sitting on the coffee table in front of me and was sure to get sprayed. Was the slapstick worth the clean-up? Possibly —

"We're getting married," Cara blurted. She looked up at Jamar. He gave her a little noogie.

I looked at them — up and down, up and down — and then became aware of lemonade dribbling down my chin. "You're — Really? Married?"

Jamar sat down beside me. "Bet you weren't expecting *that*, Bradford."

Cara's face was a freeze-frame of expectation. She held her clasped hands against her chin. Then she leaned forward and wiped the lemonade off mine with a motherly stroke of her thumb.

"I think — Wow, that's so exciting! A wedding! What, uh, brings that on?"

Jamar smirked.

Cara said, "Fletcher, we've been together since sophomore year of *college*."

"Oh, of course."

"But we've had a push, yeah."

"A push?"

"More like a kick," Jamar said.

"A kick?"

"Not yet!" Cara said. "More like the promise of a kick." She took my hand, the one not clutching the bottle, and put it on her flat, firm belly. "There'll be kicks by Christmas."

"You're kidding," I said, certain Mateo would judge my surprised face convincing.

"You're going to be Uncle Fletcher," Cara said, springing forward to hug me.

She was excited—they both

were—and deeply nervous too. The two competing and complimentary emotions rose and fell like a stock-market ticker over the remaining weeks of August.

Jamar wanted the wedding before the end of summer so Cara wouldn't be showing in the photos.

"There's something tacky about a bride with a belly, isn't there?" he said to me. I told him I'd never, ever thought about it. "I just don't want it to seem like we're doing this just because of the baby," he added.

Meanwhile the quickie wedding was the only point Cara conceded. She vetoed the idea of a minister and a church in favor of a justice of the peace and something outdoors. She nixed all formal attire.

"I want to get married barefoot. In jeans." She and Jamar were discussing the details in her bedroom as I snuck through the kitchen. I heard him groan as I looked around for my keys.

"And we'll get a golf-cart for the JP to ride in," he was saying, "so she can do the ceremony while you're like skipping through the meadow while doves sprinkle flower petals on you."

I made it out of the apartment, quietly closing the door behind me. Their deliberations were going to culminate in either a ball-bust or a fuck sesh, and I didn't want to be there to overhear either one.

"Young love," Mateo said as he slipped off his backpack and opened the zipper. I dug around inside and retrieved a can of pink.

"So Jamar's moving in," I said. "Did I tell you about that?"

"Oh. No. All this news!"

"His lease is up on fifteenth and the wedding is the week after. September's going to be a whirlwind month."

"Sounds like it." He made a big arc with green and closed it off on the other side with blue. I'd given up trying to figure out what he was painting as he was painting it. The images were never clear until he applied the finishing touches. "At least we'll have your place to ourselves when they're on their honeymoon."

"Heh. That's true. We will."

A week to ourselves was something I could get excited about. Jamar's decision to move in laid to rest a less comfortable idea, one that had been sizzling on the edge of my consciousness: that if, after the wedding, *Cara* were the one to move out, I'd be faced with the question of whether Mateo should be invited to move in.

He dropped the green and blue cans in his backpack and made some marks in yellow. "How do you feel about Jamar moving in? Will your place be cramped and stuff?"

"You mean because he's a giant?"

"Haha. I mean with three people."

"It'll be fine. I lived with Jamar in closer quarters than this."

"Tell me."

"We were roomies in college. In the dorm. Our freshman and sophomore years."

"Just two years?"

"He and Cara got a place off-campus after that."

"Ah." He stepped back from his piece and looked and then shook up the yellow and started spraying again. "So they left you."

"They didn't *leave* me. They got together."

"So then how did you end up living with Cara and he didn't?"

"That's a long story," I said. When it was mentioned, which was rare, it was known among us simply as *that year*. It began a few months after we graduated.

I could still remember the

sound of Cara's voice when she called me on what turned out to be the first day of *that year*. There was fear and worry in it, but it was most of all the voice of someone who believes she's been left out of the loop.

"Fletcher," she said, and that was all. Like she was waiting for me to fill in the rest.

"Yeah Cara? What's up? I'm kind of on my way to meet somebody." Tonight's somebody was a Boston College tennis player.

"Do you know anything about what's going on?"

"What do you mean? What's—? Are you all right?"

"I mean about what's up with Jamar's stuff being gone."

That was the moment I knew, with a sigh, that there wouldn't be any love-serving-anything in my immediate future. I stopped walking, leaned against a parking meter, flicked a cigarette into the gutter.

"Cara. What do you mean, *gone?*"

"*Gone.* I got home from work and there was barely any sign Jamar ever lived here. At first I thought we got robbed. Stuff was missing. I went back out to the stairs and started digging in my bag for my phone to call the police. I mean, his Playstation— You look around and stuff's just missing. But then I realized there was no mess. Nothing spilled over. No drawers hanging open. A burglar would leave a mess, wouldn't he? But there's no mess."

"Nothing?"

"Fletcher— He left. Left me."

"Cara, that's—" I was going to say ridiculous, but it wasn't. It may even have been likely, now that I thought about it. Jamar got hit especially hard by all the *rest of your life* bullshit that accompanies graduation. He'd been freaking out at regular intervals. About finding a job. About whether Cara was really the woman for him. About—just freaking out. But we all were. I had paper cuts on my thumbs from wrestling with pages of *Porcupine City*. "Have you tried calling him?"

"It sends me to voicemail. Like it's either busy or he's ending the call."

Some lady needed to get at the meter so I started walking, feeling nervous. There was no anger in Cara's voice, just confusion, and that's what made me nervous, and the more nervous I was, the angrier I got at Jamar. If Cara had been angry too, well, anger is its own damage control. Anger would've contained within it motivation and strength. But she was hurt. Hurt needed help. I resented the hell out of Jamar for saddling me with the responsibility of cleaning up his mess.

"Do you want me to come over?"

"You don't have to," she said, meaning yes. "But could you try calling him?"

"Yeah." I turned and started walking back to the T. I'd worn good underwear and everything.

I wasn't able to get Jamar on the phone, and after a day I gave up trying. Because a letter, probably mailed on his way out from the box a block down the street, arrived from him, telling everyone everything they needed to know.

"A letter, so dramatic," Mateo said, popping the cap off a can of black, shaking it up. "What did it say?"

"*I love you, yada yada, I got a job in Denver.* I love the guy, but it was a wussy letter. Whatever."

"So you moved in with her."

"Yeah. I did."

"That was nice of you."

"She wouldn't have been able to pay the rent by herself. What was I supposed to do, let her go homeless?"

"Um. She could've gotten another roommate."

"Yeah, well, we did what we thought was best."

"Where'd you live before that?"

"I had a bachelor pad. A little studio in the Fenway."

"It's convenient your lease ran out at that same time."

"It didn't. I had to break it."

"Oooh." He was smiling. "That was a pretty big sacrifice."

"What's the smile? You think I was secretly in love with Cara and jumped at the first chance I got to shack up with her?"

"That's not what I think," he said, still grinning. "I think you jumped because you were lonely."

"Whatever."

"But Jamar came back, obviously." *Clack clack. Ffssshhttt.* He highlighted in white a black pupil on a yellow face.

"Like a year later. I barely remember that time because I was still so embroiled in my book. But uh—yeah, apparently he was only in Denver for six months, bailed on that too, moved back to Boston. It was another six months before he got back in touch with her. I remember, he came to the apartment — which had been his and Cara's and was now mine and Cara's. I saw him out on the front steps looking like he was working up the courage to ring the buzzer. And he had flowers. A big thing of wildflowers. Sunflowers and stuff. Cara likes those. And I took the flowers away from him and threw them in the yard. 'This is not a *flowers* situation,' I told him. 'Flowers are for when you forget her fucking birthday.'"

"Dramatic."

"Well, it was. Plus I was well into my celibacy experiment at that point, and not exactly a happy camper. And by then, after living with her for a year and barely hearing from him, I was totally Team Cara, you know?"

"Makes sense."

"She even had a new boyfriend by then. Kind of a douche. Great ass, though."

"Heh."

"Anyway, yeah, so she took Jamar back but they've always had separate apartments since then. Jamar's not a bad guy. He's my best friend. He was just scared. We all were, facing that post-college void, you know? I had *Porcupine City,* Cara immediately swan-dove into grad school, and Jamar ran away to Colorado. It was a crazy time."

"Sounds it."

"What was your first year post-college like?"

"Hmm. When was that?" He fished around in his head for the year and when he came up with it, one year later than mine, he said, "I did the front doors of the library and all the lampposts along the lagoon in the Public Garden."

"That wasn't exactly —"

He laughed. "I know what you meant. I went to SP after graduation, thought seriously about staying. I know what you meant."

"You thought about staying?"

"Yeah."

"What made you want to stay?"

"I don't know. The weather," he said, so I didn't press it.

Clack clack. Ffssshhttt. Some wavy, purple hair formed across the top of the yellow head.

"It feels a little funny to have Jamar moving back in," I went on. "I guess because for him it's a step forward—he'll be moving in with his wife, you know? And their baby. Man, their *baby*. And for me it's like moving back in with my college roommate again after I've been graduated five—six years."

"Houses are just trappings. Do you feel like you're moving backward if you put on a t-shirt you happened to wear in college? Every time you put down a word, that's the important progress, Arrowman. That's how you measure."

"I love when you get all mystical on me."

He smirked. "Nothing mystical about it." He shook his can, shook it near my ear, the *clack clack* loud and familiar. "It's the most tangible thing there is." He held his right hand near the bottom of his piece, splayed his fingers, and dragged a blast of paint across them, leaving in negative their print on the wall. *Fffssshht.*

In typical Jamar fashion

his apartment was stacked neatly with square boxes arranged in towers of varying height like some kind of life-size board game. He was over at my place so often, it was months since I'd been here. The place looked smaller with the walls bare and the carpets rolled up. I wiped sweat off my face with my shirt and bent down for another box. His apartment was on the second floor so the walk down wasn't bad, but it was hot out.

Normally I would've put up a stink, even just for show, about having to help him move in this kind of weather, but a couple of days earlier he asked me two questions: (1) would I be his Best Man, and (2) would I help him move. Once I was buttered up by the first, no way could I say no to the second. Clever guy.

Outside on the street his dad's big diesel pick-up, borrowed for the day to do the move in, was parked in a space reserved earlier with a laundry hamper and a desk chair.

"So you're really not giving me much time to plan your bachelor party," I told him, wiping my forehead and waiting for him to stow his boxes with the others in the back of the truck.

"You're *such* a comedian, Bradford. You agreed."

"You're really not going to let me do *any*thing? No strippers at all? No donkeys?"

"No strippers, no barnyard animals." We went back inside and the stairwell, beneficiary of the drafts from a.c.'ed apartments, was like heaven. "We'll go out for a beer somewhere."

I followed him into the apartment, sighed, grabbed another box extra hot from sitting in the sun. "Are you sure? I was looking forward to seeing some boobs."

"Try the mirror," he said.

"Hahaha. Wait—what? What do you mean by that?"

We did another few trips down to the truck and then, sticky with sweat, I hit up his kitchen to splash cold water on my face.

"I hope it's not this hot for the wedding," he said, plucking at his shirt.

"Me too, I don't want my boutonniere wilting."

"Heh."

"I also hope it's not this hot that day I agreed to help you move tons of heavy shit out of your apartment. Oh wait. That's today." I squeegeed slick water off my cheeks. "Speaking of which, I'm not sure how much more we can fit in the truck. Or at our place, for that matter."

He stood looking around, hands on hips. "Don't worry, anything that's not in a box isn't going."

"Oh. Really? Not even the futon? I was thinking we'd have to do a second trip."

"No. No, just one. You're off the hook. But if you know anyone who'd want the futon, tell me. I have a couple of guys from work coming tonight for the dresser."

"Homos?"

"No."

"Wait, so no Leaning Tower of CDisa?!" I went over and touched the tall CD organizer, wobbling to and fro on its bent metal leg. It was legendary.

He laughed. "I've been debating."

"You should keep it. It's amazing how much stuff you still have from when we lived together."

"It wasn't that long ago."

"Feels like a long time."

"Yeah, sometimes. I need something to drink. Want something?" He pulled open the fridge. "I have—relish and, uh, bagels."

"Much as I enjoy a good relish-bagel smoothie, I'll just have some water."

I started to reach for the cupboard for a glass and he said, "I packed all but one. We'll have to share."

So we did, passing the glass back and forth, each keeping our own side. It struck me as cute, and once again I was happy he asked me to be Best Man, even if my duties were moving boxes rather than hiring strippers.

"How do you feel about, you know, doing it again?" he said. "I realize we didn't give you much say."

"Living together?"

"Yeah."

"It's fine. You practically live there already. So I'm pretty stoked about splitting the rent three ways."

"I don't just mean me, though. You-know-who will be there too eventually."

"Fletchinha?"

"Who?"

"That's what Mateo said you should name it."

"Fletchy-what?"

"It's Portuguese or something."

He smirked. "But yeah. Come winter you'll have a third roommate."

"Yeah. We'll see how it goes. —You ready to finish this up?"

We started down with another load, footfalls heavy on the stairs. A lady coming up squeezed against the wall to let us pass and my elbow grazed her tit.

"Anyway," I said, "to be honest, I figure I'll probably scram in the spring, depending."

"Move out? No. Bradford!"

"You know I love you guys, and I'm gonna love this kid like crazy. But that doesn't mean I want to live with him, know what I'm saying?"

He frowned. "Now I feel like we're kicking you out."

"No, don't. Don't. I'm thinking it might be nice to have my own place again."

After depositing our boxes he lifted the rear door of the pick-up and we had to slam it closed against them—they slid like heavy dominoes across the back of the truck.

"You know," he said, "I don't think I ever really thanked you for moving in with her that year. For taking care of her when I was—" He put his fist to the side of his head and blew out his fingers. "—*Psssh*."

"Cara didn't need anyone to take care of her."

"I know. You know what I mean. Keeping her company."

"Yeah, well. I was glad to do it. It's been good. I've been happy there."

"Good. —I'll go lock up. Don't leave without me."

I leaned against the truck, arms spread to let my pits dry in the breeze. Across the street a stud with a mohawk was walking a chocolate lab. He made me think of the key-touching guy. I wondered where that guy was, and whether he still had the grown-out mohawk.

Jamar came out of his building carrying the Leaning Tower of CDisa, which he wedged into the back of the truck. "I don't know why," he said. "All my music's digital now."

"It's an antique," I said, nodding at the bent metal structure.

"Mateo. Have you ever thought about getting a place with Mateo?"

"I would've been sad to see it go."

"Have you ever thought about it?"

"All the nights that thing woke me up randomly dumping CDs onto the floor."

"It could be good for you."

"Yeah, right."

"How come?"

"*How come?* How about I've only known him three

months. Plus there's no way he'd leave his place. Do you know how much he pays for rent?" We got in the truck and Jamar started it up.

"How much?"

I told him the number and he said, "Does that even cover his electric?"

"Who knows."

"He must be shagging the landlady."

"Not him. His dad was."

"Say what now?"

"It's a long, intercontinental drama. I'll tell you sometime; it's pretty great. But yeah. He's not about to give up that kind of luxury."

"I wouldn't either. Dude must have money coming out his ears. What's he do with it?"

"He sends some home to his family. I don't know. Probably buys stock in Krylon."

"Spraypaint?"

"Yeah."

"Ah, for his— What's the preferred term, anyway?"

"He refers to himself as a writer."

"What's he write?"

"His name. His code name."

"His *code* name. Wow." He smirked. "You in love?"

"Don't."

"Heh."

"To tell you the truth Jamar, I'll never have room in my heart to love another until I find a way to get over *you*."

"Oh shut up, you silly homo."

The first week of September

had always been for me a magical time in the city. That song people sing about Christmas—about it being the most wonderful time of the year—is something I hummed during that week at the end of summer. For during that week the population of Boston swelled, eventually doubled, and the entirety of its doubling was due to an influx of college students—half of which, of course, were male. The most wonderful time of the year was the sudden arrival of 300,000 horny college boys, kissed by summer sun. And 15,000 of them, give or take a few thousand, were horny for other guys.

The most wonderful time of the year felt like standing on a diving board, bouncing, plunging into a pool of them, swimming through them like Scrooge McDuck through his money. The backstroke past countless butts in skinny jeans, the breaststroke through shaggy haircuts and scruffy cheeks, the doggy paddle amidst football pads and beat-up guitars, the butterfly into cramped dorm rooms smelling of cheap cologne and lit with lava lamps and reading lights. The most wonderful time of the year.

But this year things were different. When the college boys flooded the sidewalks I had Mateo at my side, his paint-sprayed hand in mine.

"Hold me back, hold me back!" I whispered to him, feeling his hand grip mine tighter.

"Back!" he said. "Down boy!"

This year as I strolled down the shop-lined Newbury Street, it wasn't to find something to wear to a club, but something to give at a wedding.

"Wait a second," Mateo said,

his hand frozen on the doorknob. He looked at us quizzically. "Thought I was late," he added, shutting the door and stuffing his hands in his pockets. "And you guys aren't even dressed yet?"

Cara clicked off the TV. Jamar stood up, stepped easily over the coffee table and a few boxes of his not-yet-unpacked stuff, crossed the living room in two strides, shook Mateo's hand.

"It's casual. Cara decided we're shunning tradition. You look cool. Thank you for coming."

"But I'm overdressed," Mateo complained, looking down at his tie, his hand still hanging absently in Jamar's. I was wearing jeans and a gray vest over a mint-green v-neck t-shirt. Cara wore jeans too, and just a t-shirt she planned to exchange later for the white, lacy shirt we'd picked out together.

"Don't worry about it," Jamar said. He had on shorts now but they weren't much less formal than his wedding attire: gray plaid pants and a solid black t-shirt that looked a little snug when he paraded through the kitchen last night. He gave a tug on Mateo's skinny blue tie. "Lose this if you want and you'll be fine."

"Jamar," Cara huffed, "this is why the invitations shouldn't have said *casual*."

"I was thinking business casual," Mateo said.

"See? They're going to think *business casual*." She turned to me. "Why didn't you tell him?"

"I told him casual!"

"There's going to be so much confusion about this, I can tell already." She looked at Mateo. "Our policy is wear what you want." She took a breath, hugged him. "Sorry I'm acting like bridezilla. You look gorgeous in yellow." Jamar had disappeared and he called to Cara from the bedroom to help with the suitcases.

"Do you, er, need a hand with those?" Mateo said, glancing at Cara's belly. She was just barely showing.

"Oh he's got it, he just needs me to supervise." She grinned and went off down the hall.

Mateo smirked. "And what's got *your* tongue, pretty boy?" he said, sitting down and squeezing my thigh.

"Nothing. I'm just rendered speechless by your killer looks."

"Shush."

"She's right about yellow."

"Why didn't you tell me I could dress cool? Should I lose the tie?"

"I don't think you should change a thing."

"Don't want to look like a dumbass." He took his hand back and started undoing the tie, reverse rabbit over the log.

"You don't. It reminds me of the first day I saw you at work. You had a tie on."

"I looked like a dumbass then too."

"Hey—" I leaned in to kiss him and he stopped fumbling with the tie to kiss me back. It was too nice for an inopportune moment. At the sound of rolling luggage he took back his tongue and finished removing his tie.

Jamar came dragging a suitcase. Cara had a pair of small backpacks. Mateo stood up to help with the luggage and got shooed away again.

"We've got it, Mateo. Bradford — do you have the rings?"

"I have the rings."

"You're sure? Because they're kind of key."

"Right here in my pocket." I patted my thigh.

"Fletcher that's your wiener," Cara said.

"Oh. Well they're around here somewhere." I grinned. "Are we ready? Can we go? You know there's always that weird traffic past Worcester. You don't want to miss your own wedding."

"You know, I think I should change," Mateo said. He asked me if I had a shirt he could borrow.

"Let's go look." I grabbed his hand and yanked him into my room.

I closed the door with my foot and slid my hands inside his yellow button-down. His chest was fuzzy against my palms. He laughed, his teeth on my neck.

"Let's," he said. "Real quick."

"Teo." I laughed. "We don't have time. You're supposed to be the responsible one."

"It'll be a long day otherwise. A three-hour drive...."

I laughed, pushed my lips against his grinning mouth. "Don't tempt me any more. I can't take it. Tonight."

"All right. Tonight. It'll be worth the wait."

I dug through my dresser while he got out of his shirt. He laid it carefully over the back of my chair.

"How about this?" I held up a white v-neck t-shirt with a subtle argyle print. "The wrinkles will come out."

"That's fine." He grabbed it and pulled it over his head. The short sleeves showed off his tattoos. He looked in my mirror and swooped his hands through his hair. "Ready."

One last time before leaving

the apartment I touched my pocket to check for the black velour bag containing the wedding rings. It was there. As I did this I thought of how the key-touching guy had checked for his keys.

"Wait, what about their gift?" Mateo said.

"We'll leave it here. I don't want to bring it there just to bring it back."

"Oh. OK."

"They can open it when they get back."

We descended the narrow, brown-carpeted stairs, Mateo a few steps in front of me. I looked down on the loopy dark curls of his hair that my fingers knew so well now.

"I like this shirt," he said.

We emerged from the house and found Cara and Jamar leaning against my car with their luggage lined up on the sidewalk.

"You want me to drive?" I said.

"We remembered you kind of *have* to," Cara said, "since we're not coming back with you afterward."

"Oh, man. Yeah. That's right."

Jamar, Cara and I traded blank stares. I could tell we all were wondering, in light of the fact that we'd totally overlooked this pretty significant detail, what else we'd forgotten.

"You have the rings, right?" Jamar said.

"Relax, future husband. Yes. I have the rings." I reached up and grabbed his shoulders and pretended I was going to jump on his back. "It's fine. I'll drive. It's not a problem."

"Won't you guys need a car to get back?" Mateo said.

"Nope. We're flying out of Albany and flying back into Boston," Cara told him. "Very convenient!"

"This is a day you two should be chauffeured anyway," Mateo said, and added, "You have that shirt from the coat rack, right?"

"Right here," Cara said.

The luggage was loaded into my trunk, so bland and empty compared to the trunk of Mateo's car.

Cara patted the backseat after hanging her shirt from the hook above the window. "Are you going to fit in here, Jammies?"

"Jammies," Mateo snickered from the front.

"I'll fit just fine, thank you very much," Jamar said, sounding a little embarrassed as he put one leg in, then tugged the rest of his height through the door. "Now drive, Bradford, before I sneeze and break open your car."

I looked back and Jamar's knees were not quite but almost up by his ears. I moved my seat forward as much as I could. "Better?"

"You can sit up front, Jamar," said Mateo, twisting back. "Want to switch?"

"Nah. S'OK."

Cara asked me, "Do you know where you're going?"

"Pittsfield, Massachusetts, lady. I'm good until we get off the Pike. After that you have to navigate."

With that, I put the pedal to the metal. The little car protested a bit, and we were off.

The a.c. was too weak

for four bodies so we kept our windows open. Cara leaned against hers, smiling into the highway air that was whooshing through her hair. Her eyes were closed and her teeth showing through her grin were as white as the white cotton shirt billowing behind her head.

I looked at her in the rearview. Another girl on her wedding day would've been freaking out about her hair getting messed. Here Cara was, not only enjoying it but looking more beautiful for every minute the breeze kissed her.

She opened her eyes and saw me looking and I smiled and she smiled.

We'd been on the road

for maybe two hours when Cara leaned into the front seat.

"So Mr. Amaral," she said, draping her arms across the headrests. She had that tone middle-school girls use when they're undertaking the business of finding out who you like.

"Yes?" he replied, very cautiously. He may have gone to middle school in São Paulo but some tones are universal.

"Do you *like* my friend Fletcher?"

He smirked and caught my eye. "Guilty."

Jamar swatted her knee. "Leave the homos alone, Car."

"Shush." She swatted back without turning. "Are you guys in *love?*"

Mateo thought for a moment. "The only love that's important today is yours and Jamar's."

I laughed. "Well played."

"Harrumph," Cara said, and slumped back into her seat.

Cara's step-father—short, slim,

and bald with heavy sideburns a leprechaun red that grayed at the bottoms—was affixing a pair of balloons to the mailbox when we pulled into the driveway. One black balloon, one white one.

I turned the car off (not a minute too soon for the radiator) and Cara got out first.

"Hey Wayne."

"You made it!" he said.

"We made it."

"Happy wedding day, Cara."

"The yard looks lovely."

"Let's hope the weather holds." He looked up at the sky before giving her a quick hug. "Where's the groom?"

The groom was unfolding himself from my backseat.

"Can you get out?" I said to Jamar.

"My legs are asleep. Thrombosis!"

He hobbled over to Wayne with the crumpled posture of an orc. It put them at eye level.

Wayne shook Jamar's hand in both of his. "Happy wedding day, Mr. Andrews!"

"Very happy," Jamar said. "Thank you for putting so much work into everything. The yard looks really nice."

I pointed at the two balloons and said to Wayne, "Is the black one Jamar?"

Cara rolled her eyes but Wayne's face turned to glass. "The groom—" he stammered. "Black is always for the—"

"He's kidding with you, Wayne," Jamar said. "It looks fantastic. Thank you."

"Oh. Well. Thank *you*," Wayne said, re-gathering himself, but looking more comfortable than before. He'd definitely been thinking about the colors himself and now it was out in the open, a joke.

"Looks like my parents are here already?" Jamar said, noting their car further up the driveway.

"Your parents and your brother. Yes. They got here, oh, a little while ago."

"How's my mom?" Cara said. "She freaking out?"

"Freaking out? *Your* mom?" Wayne chuckled. "That's one way to say it. But so far everything's going according to plan. I think she's pulled herself together since the Andrews— Andrewses?—got here." He turned to me, gestured at the driveway. "You're going to want to pull in all the way, Fletcher. It's going to fill up."

The house, an old colonial,

was big with blue siding and a porch that wrapped around the front. The backyard was big too and was bordered with pine trees. This city boy wondered what anyone could possibly do with all this land. It'd been a long time since I'd had any grass at all, so it was ironic that I was assigned to the last-minute yard work. The ceremony was to be done on the front lawn, in front of a tall bush bursting with little pink flowers. I was handed a pair of pruning scissors and told to edit out the expired flowers.

Mateo came out with a dishtowel over his shoulder and sat down in the grass near where I was working. He stretched out his legs, pulled the towel off his shoulder and whirled it around.

"Jamar's mom is hilarious," he said.

"What's she doing?" I dropped a cut flower to the ground.

"Blessing the cake." He paused and I like to think he was admiring my ass when I bent over to rake the clippings into a pile. "It's a giant cake. Thought there weren't too many people coming?"

"I think you're supposed to have leftovers. And then eat a little piece every year or something."

"Every year?"

"Or maybe just the first anniversary? I'm not too up on the minutiae of wedding tradition."

"Ever want to be? Up on it, I mean?"

"Do you mean do I want to get married?"

"Yeah."

I was silent a moment, the kind of silence that's never more pregnant than the one that follows that question. I made a few snips and stepped back to survey the flowers.

"Well, if the person I am now were to continue unchanging into the future, then no. I'd never get married. But I do plan on evolving. No one wants to be static. And some small part of me does hope I evolve in that direction, yes."

"In the direction of marriage?"

"Theoretically."

He laughed. "You're such a politician, Arrowman. You should run for office. Don't worry, I'm not proposing or anything."

I smiled and made a few more snips. "Do you see any more dead ones?"

He pointed, the towel hanging from his colored fingers (he'd used a lot of lime green last night, which had gone well with the yellow shirt he'd chosen earlier but it was too busy with the argyle he wore now). "A couple there. Near the bottom. That you missed."

"I see." I bent down and clipped a flower and sprang back up and heard myself whisper: "*Ow.*" I looked, almost absentmindedly, in the direction of the sudden pain down by my heel, before grabbing my elbow and jumping, dropping the scissors, running. "Fuck! Bees!"

There was still one in my pant-leg. And now more were swarming and Mateo was running alongside me thrashing me with the dish towel.

The guy was *laughing.*

As I ran I flailed down and pounded my shin with my fist. I felt a pinch and a poppy crunch that took care of the one in my pants.

On the porch fifty feet away we stopped and looked, bent over with our hands on our knees.

"Only twice?" Mateo said.

"I think so."

"Could've been worse."

"Could've."

"You're not allergic?"

"No."

He stood up, tossed the towel back over his shoulder. "I hope Cara and Jamar weren't too set on that spot by the bush."

"Yeah." I twisted my arm and pulled the skin around to look at the angry red bump on my tricep.

Jamar's sixteen-year-old brother,

Robbie (a.k.a. Robot), wanted to pour gasoline down the bee-hole and torch it.

"Let's nuke them," he said. He looked like a shorter, nerdier version of Jamar at that age. He had big glasses that made his eyes grow to saucers over the idea of blowing something up.

"Um, no," Jamar said.

Robbie frowned.

"We'll just move the ceremony," Cara said. "It's not a big deal."

"But that was such a pretty spot," her mother said. She looked a lot like Cara, had the same bright hair and slight build. The only difference was that Diane's face had an anxiety that rarely touched Cara's.

"Well Mom, maybe if you go ask the bees nicely, they'll leave us alone."

"Fine, do what you want. We'll move it." Diane turned to the sink and started filling a vase. "We'll do whatever you want."

" —I'm telling you, a little gasoline...."

"Robot, give it up."

"Diane," I said, touching Cara's mom's arm to get her attention, "is there something I can get to put on these?"

"Fletcher, of course." She dumped some water out of the vase, shifted the flowers around. "Upstairs," she said, setting the vase on the window sill, "in the bathroom, under the sink, there's a Tupperware box. Inside that box—a clear Tupperware box—I think there's some insect-bite cream stuff."

"Thanks." I turned to Mateo. "Come?"

We went up the stairs. The wall was decorated with family photos that spanned a hundred years. Cara was a baby halfway up. Jamar started appearing near the landing and had a healthy presence at the top.

"He was cute, huh?" Mateo said.

"He was. He's a good-looking guy."

"Were you totally in love with him in college?"

"I've never spent much time pining for straightboys. Always had plenty of other dicks in the fire."

"You thought I was straight."

"I was unsure."

"And yet you pined for me."

"I sensed the truth. Where's this bathroom?"

All the doors of the rooms upstairs were closed, but we found the bathroom after one wrong try that revealed Cara's old room, full now with dusty exercise equipment and piles of winter clothes. Under the bathroom sink, just as Diane said, was the insect-bite stuff, only it was a spray, not a cream. I sat on the edge of the tub and rolled up my pant-leg.

"Gimme the stuff," Mateo said. He sat down on the toilet and took my foot in his lap.

"Oh woe is me!" I threw my forearm across my brow.

"Are you ready?" he said. "I am about to apply the medicine. It will hurt. I should find something for you to bite down upon."

"Just hurry and spray me with your magic serum, doctor."

"Oh god. OK." *Skwwsht.* "There. Let it dry. Now give me that arm of yours." *Skwwsht.* "OK. You're done."

"Thank you, doctor."

"Mmhm." He placed the cap back on the spray, rubbed it

with his thumb— "Feels like paint but not," he mused —and stood up. "But you won't be good as new until I apply my final secret remedy," he told me, leaning forward, but before our lips met I fell backward into the tub.

We waited in the house,

in the room adjacent to the front door, for the guests to arrange themselves in the getting-married area beneath the branches of an apple tree a safe distance from the killer bees. Yellow and white wildflowers swayed lazily at the edge of the lawn and rays of sun came down through the apple leaves in visible beams.

At the head of the group, standing under the tree, was the justice of the peace, looking like a younger Ruth Bader Ginsburg in a lacey white collar and black robe that fluttered against the tree trunk at her back.

Mateo and Robbie were standing awkwardly at the side of the group. Jamar had tasked them with ushing people around the yard. It meant a lot to me that he gave Mateo that duty when there were other guys he knew better. From time to time guests cast glances at the house for signs of the bride.

Meanwhile the Pachelbel was running out.

"They're getting antsy," I said, letting the curtain fall back.

Jamar had his arm around Cara. "Think we've made them sweat long enough?"

"I think so," she said. "Let's go get married."

"So Bradford and I will go first."

"Just like we discussed."

It was my idea for Cara to be escorted out by the Best Woman. Sandra, Cara's best female friend, seemed thrilled: both women had been squealing nonstop for the past ten minutes.

Jamar changed the song to the Bob Dylan they'd chosen. He kissed Cara, and put a peck on Sandra's cheek.

"You have the rings, right Bradford?"

I tapped my pocket. "I have the rings."

"All right ladies," Jamar said, "catch you on the flip."

He did a little soft-shoe as we left the living room, but by the time we made it to the door he was more earnest.

"Thank you for doing this," he told me, clearing his voice.

"OK," I said, wishing instantly and ever after that I'd said something more meaningful.

But he laughed and opened the door. The air was warm and the sun bright and we were walking. Everyone was watching. I found Mateo's eyes and locked on. He did look beautiful in that shirt.

I followed Jamar beneath the tree and stood at his side with my hands clasped in front of me. I felt as though all eyes were on me, even though probably only two actually were.

And then I realized when the front door opened a second time that there were no eyes on me at all, and none on Jamar. A wedding really is all about the bride, and although the music was Dylan and she wore jeans and her feet were bare in the green, green grass, she looked every bit a bride, the most beautiful one I'd ever seen. My breath caught in my chest and it occurred to me for the first time that *I* would've liked to have walked her down the aisle. Jamar, grinning, stood up straight, to his full height. His head went up into the leaves of the apple tree.

Once the knot was tied

and hugs were exchanged and pictures-pictures-pictures were taken and we'd all gathered in the crowded kitchen, at the behest of Cara and Jamar, I raised the glass I'd already emptied a few times during the lengthy photo shoot.

"Cara and Jammies tell me that as Best Man it's my duty to say a few words. Although why they had to choose this particular moment to cling to tradition," I pointed to Cara's bare feet, "is uncertain. I offered to write them a letter but they said that's no good. So I'll do my best.

"I first met Jamar Andrews when we were teenagers, when we were freshmen at Shuster College in the great city of Boston. We were roommates, two-thirds of a triple. And before I'd even known him a month, it's safe to say that Jamar saved my life. That third roommate was so obnoxious I would've thrown myself out the tenth-story window if not for

Jamar's radiant sanity."

There were some chuckles, and Jamar nodded to confirm.

"We weren't especially close at that time, Jamar and me, even though we roomed together again our sophomore year. To be honest he was a little too *conservative* for my taste. A little too old-*fashioned*. But he welcomed me, silly homo that I was, even if he did cover his ears and say *la la la* when I tried to tell him how this or that date had gone. He lightened up, though." I looked up at him. "Maybe it was because I kept trying to put the moves on him. Ha ha. But fear not, Cara," and here I turned to her, "he never bit that fruit. So to speak. Which is not to say that over the years I haven't kept trying. And now that we're going to be living together again...."

Some nervous glances. I felt Mateo's fingers slip into my belt, as though to hold me from going over the edge.

"I'm kidding, I promise. But anyway. Jamar's lightening up, his relaxing, wasn't about me, and it wasn't about Shuster or age or the anything-goes attitude of the big city. It coincided with the year this woman came into his life." I put my hand on her shoulder. "She taught him to chill out, to smell the flowers and to walk barefoot. And he kept her grounded. They made each other into people I'm proud to know, people I really love, people who are my best friends. What else can I say about these two? They balance each other. They belong together. They always have, even when things were hard. They're yin and yang. And they're going to make lovely, lovely parents. I just hope by then they've found their own apartment."

We all drank and Mateo, at last, exhaled.

We walked around to the

back of the house, Mateo and I, in the shade away from the people and I wiped white frosting off my mouth.

"You didn't really think I was going to say anything *lewd*, did you?"

"Of course not," he said, a twinge of sarcasm riding shotgun on his accent.

Beside the breezeway staircase was a wide patch of shade. I sat down in the grass with my back against the house's cool concrete foundation. He joined me, stretching out his legs. He slipped off his flip-flops and rubbed his feet in the grass.

"Remind me how long they'll be away?"

"Two whole weeks," I said.

"That sounds nice."

"It sounds great."

I picked a long blade of grass and put it between my lips and let it bob there like a lollypop stick. Music was coming from the house, and voices and laughter floated through the open windows, but it seemed far away. I lay down and put my head on his thigh, slipped a hand down to his ankle and fingered the black band there, and closed my eyes. It was nice here. The blade of grass drooped back and tickled my nose.

It wasn't something I noticed but from the moment we sat down he must've been admiring how clean and smooth and blank was the wall of concrete behind us. Without disturbing me he slipped his fingers into his pocket, withdrew a marker, popped the cap. On the concrete he began drawing two interlocking wedding rings, each about three inches tall.

I opened my eyes and scratched my nose and saw what he was doing. By then he was writing words too. "Hey!"

"What?" he said, like a little kid caught.

"Are you drawing on their *house?*"

"Yeah."

The matter-of-factness was dumbfounding to me and the little-kid routine wasn't cute. "It's not permanent, is it?"

"Of course."

"Of course it is or of course it's not?"

A pause. "Of course it is."

I sat up. "Wait a minute. What? You're *drawing* on someone's *house?*"

"It's a wedding gift."

"But how do you know they even want it there?"

He frowned. "How do you know they'll want what you give them?"

"They can *return* what I give them."

"So you want me to stop."

"Yes! Jesus Christ, Mateo. My mind is boggled right now.

You're drawing on someone's house!"

"So you want me to stop *now*." Under the rings, which looked, I had to admit, remarkably three-dimensional, was the word CONGRATU.

I groaned. "You can't turn the U into an S, can you?"

He scrunched his lips. "Not without making it look like a fuck-up."

"What's worse? Having your house graffitied or having the guy fuck up while he's doing it?"

"What's worst is not having him do it at all."

"Jeez, Mateo, just finish the goddamn thing and let's get out of here before someone sees." I stood up and looked around — we were the only people in the backyard, for now.

While I looked fruitlessly around the yard for something we could drag up against the foundation, he added LATIONS and then started in on the date. When he was done he pressed the cap back on the marker.

"I think it looks nice," he said. "You act like I was drawing a swastika or something."

"The point isn't *what* you drew. The point is that you *drew*. You can't just draw on other people's property."

He looked at me, dumbfounded. "Newsflash, Arrowman: that's what I *do*."

"Would you draw on their car? Would you draw on their *face*?"

"If I could get them to hold still."

"Man."

"This is news to you why? Far as I remember, we've sunk a bunch of hours into doing this very thing."

I sighed. He was right, but *that* had never felt like *this*. "You think this will be well received?"

"Sure. What do you think they'll do, be all like *screw this person for celebrating the wedding of our daughter?*"

"I don't know. It doesn't seem right."

"You know how when parents mark their kids' heights on the kitchen wall or on bedroom doors or whatever? Know what that is? That's family graffiti. They could record the numbers in a notebook just fine but they don't, do they. They write it on the wall and it has more meaning that way. They look back on that stuff twenty, fifty years later and coo about it, and when they finally move out it's the hardest thing to leave behind. Family graffiti. That's all this is."

"It's not the same."

"You're sexy when you're being so anti-art, Arrowman."

For the first time, the nickname bristled. "I'm not anti-art. I just respect other people's property."

"Property. *Pfft.* It's all up for grabs."

He was still sitting in the grass and he reached up and pulled at my pocket. I sat down. We sat for a minute together. I stretched out my legs and smoothed my pants and nudged his foot with my shoe.

"You're a communist," I said.

He shrugged. "I need more cake. Coming with me?"

"Harrumph."

"Awwh." He brushed his lips against my cheek as he stood up. He wiped grass off his butt and squeaked back into his flip-flops.

"Hey, do you always have a marker in your pocket?" I asked.

"Lot of the time."

"Oh. And here I thought you were always just happy to see me."

Everyone had cake or the

remnants of cake on plates in their hands, but the cake itself was still about three-quarters full. I forked a pre-cut slice onto Mateo's plate.

"Would you...?" said a guest, one of Cara's aunts, holding out her plate at me when she saw me serving Mateo. "Not too big now, just another taste."

"Sure."

"I'll be spending an extra hour on the treadmill tonight as it is." She looked over at Cara, who was dancing with Jamar to a slower, sweeter song than the one that was actually playing. "I used to have her figure, a thousand years ago."

"Easy come, easy go," I said, sliding a fat piece of cake

onto her plate.

"Thank you. You're the Best Man," she said, and to me it felt like getting *recognized*, a life experience *Porcupine City* had only once provided. "That was some speech."

"Oh," I said. "Thank you." Mateo snickered behind his fork.

"You've known our Cara a long time, have you?"

"Since college. Yeah. A thousand years of our own."

She nodded, sunk the fork in her cake.

"And now she's going to be—" I was thinking of the baby but caught myself, realizing I didn't know how public that information was yet. Auntie raised her eyebrows, waiting for the rest. "Married and stuff," I continued. She seemed suspicious. "Uh. Have you met Mateo, my—" And again I stopped, which felt like I was only making things worse.

Mateo supplied the word. "His boyfriend."

"No, my pleasure." Auntie shook Mateo's hand quickly while they balanced their cake one-handed. Then someone— another aunt; Cara had like sixty of them—called to her and she smiled and slipped away.

"Why'd you hesitate?" Mateo said. He forked cake into his mouth.

"I don't know. We've never talked about it before. I didn't want to get all presumptuous."

"Presumptuous? We've been sleeping together for like four months. What else would we be?"

I agreed about the timeframe, although to me it meant virtually nothing as a criteria for relationships; before him I'd been sleeping with Mike for fifteen. "But you never did ask me to be in your crew. So I wasn't sure how—serious you considered us."

"Oh." He looked down at his cake and his cheeks flushed pink.

Robbie sidled up to the cake table and tipped another slice onto his plate. "Hey guys," he said. His thumb caught a blob of frosting and he stuck it in his mouth. "Fletcher," he said after pulling it out clean, "you still keeping up with *Blue Beetle*?" He shuffled his plate around to reorient the cake away from the edge.

I had to laugh at him. Robot made me wish I had a sibling of my own.

"Dude," I said, "I had to drop out of comics."

"No. Why?"

"Too frustrating. I'd go to Comicopia and they'd be sold out by the time I got there. And when you miss one issue it's hard to catch up, you know?" That was true, but it was only after I'd treated the emo shop clerk to dinner and a roll in the hay that I really lost interest.

"Do you not sub*scribe?*" Robbie said.

"Ah. No. I should've, huh?"

"Of course. Then you never miss anything. They hold it for you. — Comicopia?"

"It's a shop in Boston. Pretty cool. You should check it out."

"Comicopia," he said again, forking cake into his mouth.

"Come visit your brother some time. We'll go."

"That would rock."

I looked down at the floor. "You know," I said to Mateo, "you said you thought the dress was business casual, and yet you're wearing flip-flops."

Robbie looked and chuckled. "Lucky," he said.

Mateo shrugged. "Acceptable? Yes? No?"

"I don't know," I said. "I'm pretty against flip-flops anywhere other than the beach."

"Don't look at me," Robbie said, "I tried. My mom made me put on these shit-kickers." In lifting his foot to show us his new brown boat-shoes, he knocked into the cake table and sent three slices splatting onto the floor.

"Oh." "Oh." "Oh my." Some of the aunts gasped.

"Don't worry," I said, clapping Robbie's shoulder. "Five-second rule, remember?" And in two we were on our hands and knees, scooping.

People didn't stay long.

The newlyweds and Robbie and me and Mateo and Sandra and her boyfriend and a pair of Jamar's coworkers sat around the tables arranged in the front yard for an hour or two until it began to rain. Mateo and I and Jamar and Robbie hustled rented tables and chairs from the grass onto the front porch, while Cara and the others took them from us and stacked them against the house.

When that was done we stood on the porch making puddles. Mateo's white t-shirt had gone deliciously transparent and he stood with his arms crossed to cover his nipples.

"Car, why don't you go stand in the rain so your shirt goes clear like Mateo's?" Jamar said, nudging her arm. "Pretty please?"

"I would if I had a tat as cool as those."

Mateo smiled and turned pink through the hair that clung to his cheeks.

"So—" I announced, feeling ready to get on the road and ready to get this wet boy undressed, "anything you want me to bring back home?"

"I don't think so?" Cara said. "Oh—yeah, hold on." She disappeared into the house and returned a moment later carrying a foil-wrapped slab of cake the size of a cinderblock. She held it out. "Can you put this in the freezer when you get home?"

I took it, and my goodness, it must've weighed twelve pounds.

We said our soggy goodbyes in the garage, traded damp hugs.

"I'm going to lend you some *Blue Beetle* next time I see you."

"Make sure you put that in the freezer—not the fridge, the freezer. Remember."

"Bring me something good from Cancun. A Mexican twink or two."

"Don't burn the apartment down. Mateo, make sure he doesn't burn the apartment down."

"Nice to see you again."

"Safe flight."

"Miss you guys."

"Miss you too."
"Congratulations."
"Bye!"
"Bye!"
Waving. Blowing kisses. Running to the car.

We traversed Massachusetts

in the pounding rain, me hunched over the wheel trying to make sense of the four feet of Mass Pike I could see in front of us at any given moment through the dark water knocking back and forth over the windshield. Before we were even halfway home my back was sore and my neck ached. Mateo had put some Brazilian rock into the CD player, a CD he left in my car a few weeks ago, and while normally I thought his music was sexy, not understanding the words was just another layer of confusion right now.

"Can we switch to something in English?"

He'd been looking out the window, drumming his fingers on the edge of my seat. He looked over. The air vents were aimed at him and his shirt looked almost dry. "Don't like it?"

"I like it but I'm really trying to concentrate on the road. I can't see a fucking thing." A blurry pair of red taillights glowed a few car-lengths ahead of us. "Can you?"

"Oh." He turned down the stereo. "You should've said something. I'll drive for a while if you want."

"Nah, it's all right."

"OK."

"You don't mind?"

"Nope."

"Hmm. OK." A few minutes later a yellow blotch in the distance revealed itself to be a rest-stop McDonald's and I pulled off. Ludlow plaza.

"Maybe we should get something to eat," he said.

"Eat? We ate like four pounds of wedding cake and have a dozen more in the backseat."

"All that sweet makes me want salty. Like fries."

"Yeah, fries sound good actually."

I pulled around to the drive-up ordering speaker thing

and found a soggy piece of cardboard duct-taped to the front of it. The sign said, BROKE.

"That's succinct," I said.

"*Broke*. Ouch. That must send your copyeditor sensibilities crazy."

"I'm used to it, luckily. Maybe we can order at the window?"

I continued up. There was no sign there, and no human either.

"Should we go in?" I said, turning and noticing Mateo looking lasciviously out the window. I looked too and, seeing the white brick wall of the building, rolled us farther along. "Do you want these fries enough to get wet again?"

"We should go in. Yeah."

"No, buddy, *you're* going in. I don't want them bad enough to ride home wetter than I already am."

"OK."

Around to the front again, I parked as close as I could to the doors. It was a short distance to run but the downpour was at Niagara levels.

"Oh," he said, pulling his t-shirt, "I just remembered. If I get wet you can see my nipples."

"They'd be the best thing this place has ever witnessed."

He looked coy. "Will you go?"

"But I don't want— All right, fine. Large?"

"Sure, what the hell. Want money?"

"My treat." As I said it I thought, *Fletcher, you're whipped*.

He watched through the water rushing down the windshield until I was inside. Then he unbuckled his seatbelt and dove into the backseat, careful not to smoosh the cake. He felt around under the seat and came out with a can. He held it at the window to check the color. Red. Not what he would've preferred—alone red looked too aggressive, too graffiti cliché—but it would do in a pinch. His stash in my car was bare-bones. He had others all over the place; this was just one of the many he'd spread throughout my life.

He pulled his legs into the backseat and sat up and peered through the windshield. He saw me in line behind a good four or five people. He had time. He reached forward, grabbed the keys from the ignition, stuffed them in his pocket, bailed.

The rain hit him hard and made his white t-shirt go clear instantly. He didn't care about that but it'd been a good ploy — I fell for it. The rain was warm. He pushed his hair aside and plastered it against his forehead.

His flip-flops squeaked and muddy water flooded his toes. He ran and slipped and swung his arms to catch himself. He hadn't intended to run today and that's the real reason he'd worn flip-flops: because today was one of the few days he could, because at all other times he had to be ready to run. But this was a good new place and he wasn't going to pass it up just because he was wearing inappropriate footwear.

Now he was beneath an overhang and walking close like a spy against the brick wall, dripping. He touched the wall but it was damp, was catching too much spray from the overhang. He continued around to the back, dragging one hand against the brick until he felt it was dry, shaking the can in his other.

Clacka clacka clacka. And let the red flow.

I pushed my wallet back

in my pants and popped the bag of fries under my shirt, the paper hot against my belly. I took a breath at the door and dove back out into the torrent. I assumed by now that Mateo had moved to the driver's seat, so I ran to the passenger side and jumped in — there were worse things than to fall into his lap. But the seat was empty, and so was the driver's seat. And so was the backseat (apart from the cake).

I put the fries on the dash and squeegeed water off my face with my thumbs. Had he gone in to use the bathroom or something? Unlikely. With my sixth sense for hot guys, especially green-eyed ones in transparent t-shirts, I would've noticed.

I tried looking through the windshield but it wobbled like a hallucination. I reached to turn on the wipers and found the keys were missing — so wherever he'd gone, he cared enough to keep the car from getting stolen. Which probably meant he was coming back.

I looked out the window but the rain was so thick it was hard to see anything. So I opened the bag and took out a fry. I munched it and looked at the CD he'd had playing: *Brazilians On The Moon*. The album cover showed five figures in space suits chilling on the Sea of Tranquility, the green-yellow-blue of a Brazilian flag dazzling against the surface of the white moon. I opened the case and plucked out the liner notes—all in Portuguese. I decided that if Mateo and I were going to be boyfriends I'd have to invest in a Rosetta Stone or something.

On the windshield above the bag of hot fries an oval of condensation was growing. I drew an A, pointed it into arrows. ARROWMAN IS. And I'd let him fill in BOYFRIEND.

Suddenly my door yanked open, my finger streaking through the condensation, and he was climbing onto my lap, or starting to, through a curtain of water.

"Oh good you're back here take this!" He dropped a can at me. "Start the car!" He slammed the door. Three seconds later the driver's side opened and he jumped in.

I stared, a wad of potato paste in my mouth. "Wha—?"

He held out his hand. "Keys! Keys!"

"You have them! Don't you?"

"Shit!" He twisted around in his seat, banging against the armrest and steering wheel, squirming to get his fingers into the stiff, soaking-wet pocket of his pants.

Then the flat of a hand was thumping furiously on my window inches from my face. *Thumpthumpthumpthump.* On the other side of the rain-streaked glass someone was yelling, mouth and eyes big and distorted like in a fun-house mirror.

Mateo stopped fumbling for the keys and pressed the locks. He was giggling now.

"What did you *do?*" I said, but of course I knew. I remembered the wall. The white, blank wall. I looked down at the can in my hand, the evidence. I was angry but it manifested as a weary calm.

He stabbed the keys into the ignition and we were moving.

"Jesus, don't hit him."

"I won't."

And we were off, tearing past the gas station down the ramp to get back on the Pike. The motion sluiced clear the windows enough for me to see a big woman in a dripping McDonald's cap raise a fist at us.

"You got caught," I said.

He turned and grinned. Water was running out of his hair and down his face. Plump drips clung to his nose and his chin. "Almost. But that bosomy lady back there came a lot closer than the Boston PD *ever* has." He turned his head to me, keeping his eyeballs on the highway, and opened his mouth. "Shoot me a fry?"

In Framingham we pulled ahead

of the rain and the night opened clear around us. He picked up speed, shut off the wipers and the air, lowered my window a crack. The glass squeaked against my cheek and I sat up, giving up the illusion of being asleep. We hadn't said much since the rest stop.

"Home?" I said now, my voice croaking salty from fries.

"Almost."

A few minutes later my eyes were closed again and I heard him say, "Did you feel that?"

I looked out the window. "Feel what?"

"We just crossed into Boston."

"Oh." We were indeed back in the city. I could see the lights. The traffic was thicker. "Was there a sign?"

"Probably," he said. "But I can just tell. It's like—I don't know. An *ahhh* feeling. Like a Coke on a summer day." A moment later as he rolled up to the toll booth, he reached down into the cup holder for his wallet and gave it to me. "Can you fish out some dollars?"

The apartment was hot and

stuffy and I went around opening windows, letting curtains billow and blinds rattle.

"We can sleep on the pull-out if you want," I told him. "Living room gets a better breeze. Since we have the place to ourselves."

We pushed the coffee table and some of Jamar's boxes back against the wall and tugged out the mattress. Got some sheets from my bedroom. White ones.

"You were quiet on the way back," he said gently as we unfolded the sheets.

"I guess."

Rather than mentioning the rest stop, which is what I expected him to be thinking of, or even the wedding graffiti he'd put on the side of the house, he mentioned the cake table. "I should've explained," he said, shaking the sheet over one end of the mattress while I grabbed from the other side, "why I never actually asked you to be my crew."

I started to say that that's not the reason I was annoyed, but this topic was worth talking about too. "So do you not want me to be?"

"Arrowman!" He clutched the sheet to his chest balled up in his fists. It was a simple thing but the way he did it—like a Victorian damsel—lightened the mood and made me feel sure that neither this nor the kafuffle at the rest stop were going to impede our night. "It's just a really big deal for me," he said, "having a crew. I've been working solo for so long. I started the Facts solo. I'm totally ready to be your boyfriend. I want to be that, you know? But crew. That's big for me. That's more like—"

"Marriage?"

He laughed. "Because it wouldn't be *you* joining *me*, or whatever. We'd be joining *together* to make something that would have to be different. And that means I'd be doing something new. And there'd be what I *used* to do, and what I do *now*, a whole different thing. And I'm not sure I'm ready to give up working solo." The sheet floated into place and we smoothed out the wrinkles; he was so intent on getting each one that my watching him do it smoothed out the invisible ones too, the ones between us. "Do you think the plane could take off in the rain?" he said, tucking the corner under the mattress. He sat down and kicked off his flip-flops. I was surprised that he dropped the topic so quickly, but it at least was tagged, and that was enough for now. The bed was ready. I stood in front of him between his knees and he put his feet on the tops of my shoes.

"Do you think your pants can come off in the rain?" I said.

"Heh."

I undid his belt and button and zipper, feeling the soft fuzz of his belly against my knuckles. We threw our soggy clothes around the living room and warmed our skin against each other. The wobbly fold-down legs of the bed thumped the hardwood floor.

"Wait," I said, twisting out of his cityscape arms. "I almost forgot. I bought us something."

"Huh?"

"One sec." I rolled off the sofa-bed, skidded when I stepped on some damp pants, and in my room fought open the sticky bottom drawer. I returned to the living room with a small shrink-wrapped box.

"O que é *isso?*" he said, sitting up, smirk all curious. I jumped onto the bed and placed the box in his hands. "Oh boy. Edible body paints?"

"Isn't that funny? I was out with Cara helping her buy wedding-night sexy-time stuff and she made me get it."

"This is *good*. This is perfect." His grin was huge. He already had the box open. "Lay down." Like an alchemist he took the squeezey tubes and unscrewed their caps and lined them up side by side on the mattress, the way he did when he was organizing his markers. He ran one of his red fingers back and forth over them, choosing a color.

I smirked and lay down on my back. "What are you going to do?"

"You'll see."

He scooted over and kneeled between my spread legs — the little tubes bounced around as he got into position. He was pretty hard already and that made me happy I listened to Cara.

He squirted some blue, ostensibly blueberry, onto his finger. "Ready?"

I nodded and squeezed my eyes shut, feeling ticklish all

over in anticipation and then ticklish in a specific place on my belly where his finger dabbed blue onto my skin.

"Don't move," he warned, wagging his finger at me, "or you'll ruin it!"

He waited for me to stop laughing, then applied more paint to my belly, but tentatively, ready to stop to avoid a smear in case I got ticklish again. Whenever I started laughing he told me to stay still, stay still, come on Arrowman, seriously! As punishment for my wiggling he leaned down and put a row of teasing kisses along my penis.

It took a while and while he was painting I began to feel more peaceful than sexy. Content, as though I'd be happy to have this moment stretch to the end of my life. Sometimes watching him, sometimes just feeling him. He worked with concentration; his tongue crept out from the corner of his mouth when he was trying to get something just right; his hair fell back and forth over his eyes. When he was done he sat up and surveyed me, idly licking paint off his fingers.

"How is it? The taste."

"Tastes like a Fruit Roll-Up," he said. "Here." He leaned forward—his penis, soft now from the focus on his painting, slid wonderfully against mine—and pressed his fingers against my waiting tongue. I touched his wrist to hold it there.

"Mmm. It does." I let go of his hand, licked my lips. I was desperate to pull him down on top of me. "Finished yet?"

"Came out a lot better than I expected," he said, grin huge. He leaned back onto his heels and stood up, wobbling on the mattress, and gave me his hands to lift me up. "I like it a lot. One of my favorites."

"I want to see."

We went in the bathroom and, standing behind me with his chin on my shoulder, he positioned me in front of the full-length mirror.

"Wow. It's your bridge." Across my torso from my sternum to my thighs was an abstract rendering of the Zakim Bridge, its two main structures like giant divining rods pointing to my face, cables hanging between them and supporting a highway that ran along my waist like a belt.

He said, smiling, "You make a good wall." Then he turned me and kissed me, leaving smears of paint on my lips. "I want to sign you now!"

We returned to the sofa-bed and I lay back down, careful not to smudge myself. He looked me over, tapping his chin. He ran his hand up my inner thigh. It tickled.

"How about here?" he said. "I like this place."

I raised my leg a little. He took the tube of blue paint and squirted what was left into his mouth. He swished it around like mouthwash, mixing it with spit. He spread his fingers evenly on my inner thigh and leaned down, bringing his mouth close to my skin. He blew a hot, fine blend of paint and spit against his fingers, his dedinhos, using them as a stencil against me, so that when he removed them their negative image was left in the blue place on my thigh.

I sat up to have

a look and he was harder than hard and I was too and I was worried he might not want to splatter his masterpiece so soon. But then he pushed me down and did just that.

We laughed during it,

something he'd always done and which I was only beginning to get used to. Sex, for me, while never formal, had almost always been serious — but he brought a glee to it that you had to just roll with. When we were done he started cracking up, squirming beneath me, making a squiggly snow-angel in the rumpled white sheets. They were so streaked with paint it looked as though rainbows were pouring out of him.

"What's so funny?" I put my hands on the mattress just below his armpits and lowered myself onto him, making a jizzy splat when our bellies met.

"*Oof*," he said.

"I'm tired now."

"Me too." He crossed his legs over the backs of mine, ran his foot back and forth against the inside of my thigh, over the place where he'd made his mark. "And hungry. That paint wasn't very filling."

"So hungry," I said into his hair. "I could eat a foot-long sub."

"I could eat forty-two pancakes."

"I could eat a turkey." I felt his hands on my back, fingers tracing my shoulder blades.

"I could eat an entire Thanksgiving dinner."

"I could eat a cow," I said.

"I could eat a flock of cows."

"You mean a herd of cows. A flock of geese."

"A gaggle of geese."

"Smarty pants."

"I'm not wearing any pants."

"Heh."

"I could finish that wedding cake."

"Me too. They'd be pissed though. Want me to make you a sandwich?" I blew raspberries against his stubble.

"Yes please."

"I must look such a mess now," I said. "And I don't know if I can move." I feigned trying to push myself up. "I think we're dried together forever."

"We'll have to go to work like this," he said.

"They'd love that. What do you want on your sandwich?"

"What do you have?" His arms crossed again over my back and his legs tightened around my thighs.

"Honey ham. I think some turkey." I knew we weren't any closer to getting up.

"I'll have ham. And cheese?"

"All the cheese you could want."

"Mayo if you have it."

"Miracle Whip."

"That's fine."

"Mustard too?"

"Mustard too."

It was another fifteen minutes before I finally got up to make it. We ate sandwiches paint-splattered on paint-splattered sheets like some kind of performance art piece.

At 4:30 his phone started

squawking. To me it was squawking, but I guess to him it was like a starting whistle. *On your mark. Get set.* I snapped awake and clenched the sheets. *"Wha — !"*

He reached for the glowing device and stopped its squawking. "Only my phone," he whispered. *"Sshh."* Squinting, he held it up to his face and worked the buttons with his thumbs. I grumbled and buried my face in the back of his head.

"You forgot to turn it off," I mumbled, his curls sticking to my lips.

He rolled onto his back and my nose settled in his ear. "I didn't forget." His tone was normal but the words sounded ominous.

"You're not going out tonight—are you?" I pulled away— in light of those words it was no longer cutesy that my nose was in his ear.

"Why wouldn't I?"

I was silent a moment. Why indeed? "It's our—wedding night."

He laughed. "Come out with me then."

"I don't— I don't *want* to come out with you. I want to stay in *bed* with you." I leaned up on an elbow and stared at him, a stare I felt was glarey enough to argue my case. "I want to sleep with my boyfriend through one continuous goddamn night, for once."

"Hm."

I sighed. "I'm sorry." I touched his hand. Never once had I seen it fully clean, and that was starting to bother me. "Can't we just sleep? You already painted tonight anyway. And almost got caught, if you recall. And you painted on *me*. We were up late."

"That's why I gave us extra time to sleep."

"Teo—" But I could see it was pointless. I rolled over and stared at the wall.

"Are you coming?"

I closed my eyes.

"Fletcher. Are you coming I said?"

"No."

He sighed. "Fine."

I opened my eyes. There was something resigned in his voice that made me believe I'd won, and with a quiver of excitement I waited for him to lay back down. Any moment now the bed would squeak under his shifting weight and his stubbly chin would fit itself back into the curve of my neck and shoulder. Any moment. *Any moment.*

Instead there was a rustling of clothes, the sound of the bathroom door, the sound of mouthwash swished and spit. After a minute I felt lips on my cheek, and then the sound of clinking cans muffled in a backpack, the sound of a door opening and closing and quiet footsteps growing quieter as they receded down the stairs.

I sat up, wide awake.

He didn't feel guilty, exactly —

he felt that I should be used to this by now, and he wasn't going to make any apologies to anyone about doing what he did. Least of all to me, his boyfriend, his almost-crew, who should be totally supportive of this part of his life, who should give him the benefit of every doubt on this topic. But he did wonder whether tonight was a night he should've stayed in bed. He could've pretended it was raining....

No. There was work to be done, paint to unleash, words to write.

With his hood up and his thumbs hooked through the straps of his backpack he walked a half-mile from my apartment to an area where the city was almost rural, to a bridge that went over a gulley and a stream. He'd started a Fact months ago on the concrete wall abutting the stream and he was surprised to find it still there. It must've rained shortly after he stopped working last time because the paint was bent into drips and cut with clear lines as though someone had squirted thinner at it. He tried to remember if the rain was what stopped his work last time. Really this should just be whitewashed and put out of its misery, but he had no rollers on him and anyway was in the mood to try to salvage *some*thing tonight.

He shook his can. I was not, he was beginning to admit to himself, exactly into graffiti. At least not as into it as I'd been in the beginning. In the beginning he and graffiti had been entwined, an indivisible, exciting new package, but that was no longer the case. Now he was *the boyfriend*, linked, partnered, to graffiti on one side and to me on the other. It was a love triangle.

Love?

A *fssshht* of spraying paint not his own interrupted his thoughts and he looked up, startled, thinking at first, and hoping, that I'd followed him, that the sprayer was me. Someone was reaching over the overhang of the bridge and painting upside down with light-colored paint on the green-painted steel. In the dark he could see only the can and a shadowy arm but he could tell by the letterforms that it wasn't me.

The guy then spotted him too and Mateo lifted his chin and the guy gave a little nod and finished his tag.

Mateo tried to work out from the angle whether the guy could've been able to see what he was painting. He decided he probably couldn't, but nevertheless considered his options. He ended up walking casually six feet closer to the bridge, leaving this ever-in-progress Fact alone, and whipped out a decoy DEDINHOS in fast, tight letterforms.

While he was doing this the guy on the bridge disappeared, and Mateo felt relieved. But a minute later he heard him behind him, coming down the slope, pea-stones skittering ahead of him and plunking into the stream.

"Yo," said the guy. Rather, the kid—he was young. Celtics sweatshirt and flashy sneakers.

Mateo lowered his can and took a breath. He nodded and looked up at the kid's work and back at the kid. "You write MAKO?"

The kid nodded. "Yeah." He examined Mateo's decoy. "You write DEDINHOS?" Mateo said yeah and the kid said, "I seen your tags around. What's a dedinho anyway?"

"Just my name," Mateo said. "Cousin stuck it to me."

"For real."

The wind moved the trees and the light and shadows changed and the kid noticed the other piece. "Holy shit, that yours?"

"Huh?"

"Do *you* do the Izzies?"

"The what? Oh—I fucking wish. No." He swiped his hand over an old part of the Fact to demonstrate that the paint was long dry. "I just write DEDINHOS. Just DEDINHOS." He prayed the kid wouldn't step closer and find that some parts were still wet.

"Oh." Mako looked a little disappointed.

"Yeah. Sorry."

"Ever seen the guy?"

"No. Actually, from the rumors I hear, it's a girl."

The kid laughed and Mateo wondered why. "Right. I hear talk he ain't even human, though."

"What is he then?"

"Fuck if I know. Fuck if I know how he gets all those places all those times. Not human is a good guess. People say he's a shapeshifter or some shit. So when he's handling his business and a cop comes by, dude just morphs into a trashcan or some shit till the coast is clear."

Mateo hadn't heard that one. "That's what they say, huh?"

"For real."

"What do you say?"

"I *don't* say. Mako is silent on the matter. Mako observes. For all I know dude's shapeshifted into that fucking tree right there. I do not speak ill of the Izzies." The reverence in the kid's voice was both chilling and thrilling.

"Good idea. You never know, right? Maybe *you* write them."

Mako looked at him intently, narrowing his dark eyes, trying to decide whether Mateo was being serious or poking fun. He shrugged. "All right, I'm out."

"Later."

The kid started walking back up the slope, slipped down hard on his knees, got up, wiped his legs, said "Dedinhooos!"

when he saw Mateo had seen him fall, and continued up past the flickering trees.

Mateo put some finishing touches on the decoy and pressed the cap back on his can. The Fact would have to wait again—he'd come back to it another night. He was done for today. Two close calls in one day was a record he wasn't thrilled with setting.

He walked slowly back to my place, climbed the stairs, and had already undone his belt when he found me not in the bed but sitting on the edge of it, tying my shoes.

"Oh," he said.

I stood up.

PART
THREE

The Writing On the Wall

His fingers went: blue, orange,

red, purple, blue, green, yellow (a bright lemon, not the honey of his humans), red, pink, blue, blue, blue, blue, blue, yellow, orange, green, green, lime, purple, red, blue.

As his fingers changed colors so did the trees, and soon at night we were spotting lumbering trucks and teams of men sucking up piles of dead leaves off the sidewalks with vacuum hoses as big around as barrels.

"Do you think people ever get sucked up into those?" I said.

"Definitely."

The night workers were like wild animals, like something you'd spot while fishing, something coming down to the edge of a lake for a drink. And like woodsmen we walked among them in an unstated truce. Surely they knew what we were doing but it wasn't their concern what walls got graffitied that night—they had a job to do—so the leaf-blowers, the street-sweepers, the electricians coming up out of holes in the street, they left us alone.

Sometimes being out in the wee hours doing what we did was exhilarating. Often it was. When he was suddenly grabbing me to run, when he most had that intoxicating, contagious thrill in his eyes. When we slipped into Cook in the morning and no one knew we'd spent the last hours of the night in his car, making space-constrained love in the backseat or just holding on to each other to keep warm.

But the weeks were creeping by and it was getting colder. One night in mid-November I noticed his typewriter-ribbon–dark hair collecting grains of white crystal. The first snow.

"*Brrr*," I murmured, suddenly feeling colder. I looked up and saw snowflakes shivering in the glowing air around a streetlight. I could feel them on my face too, pricks of cold on my eyelids and nose. I stopped in the middle of an ARROWMAN, leaving ARRO, and capped my can.

"Not going to finish?" he said.

"I'll come back to it."

"OK." He dragged a spray of paint across his fingers to mark a finished Fact. "Let's go. You're freezing."

Winter that year had a premature climax, day after day in November burying the frosty city in wave after wave of snow. Like one of Pavlov's dogs I started shivering at the first chimes of Mateo's pitch-dark alarm-clock reveille. But by early December the winter was spent. Christmas decorations went up in lukewarm weather and lots of breath was expended on the subject of climate change.

The weather was killer for painting, though, that's what Mateo said. But my nose was always runny, my lips were always chapped, my eyes always felt tired, and the days always began too soon. Too many afternoons I was falling asleep at my desk, slumped backward like a drunk or falling forward onto my keyboard like a dead drunk. One afternoon I woke up to find seventy pages of Y's on my screen. An unrelenting question.

Why was I doing this every night? Why was I going out spraying paint on things that weren't mine? It was true that since college, since my *Porcupine City* awakening, I'd fancied myself a bit of a bad boy — but why? Because I banged a lot of guys? Because I slept with people who wanted to be slept with? When I was out at night with a can in my hand defacing people's property all my previous bad-boy escapades seemed as morally questionable as returning an old lady's lost purse. Meanwhile Mateo painted away. Bad boy. Sometimes it was exhilarating, yes. When he was really in the zone there was no more beautiful sight on Earth. But other times it left me full of guilt, made me want to turn myself in. The rest of the long winter still loomed, and maybe I didn't really *want* to be a bad boy. Maybe all I'd ever wanted was to be warm.

"Relationships are all about compromise," Cara would often tell me, her advice seeming more legit and persuasive the more pregnant and Buddha-like she became. "You shouldn't feel like you have to go out with him *every single night.*"

So I started to think of a tactful reason to limit my nights out with Mateo, to stay in bed when he got up. It wasn't long before I got one. Unfortunately it happened by accident. And it was anything but tactful.

Outside a post office hub,

in a fenced-in lot where they keep the postal trucks parked at night, we were doing the back doors of two trucks side by side. He'd gone over the tall chain-link fence with an ease that was always a pleasure to watch—the sight of his nimble acrobatics was worth a few hours of runny nose—and from the other side opened a gate for me to slip in with his backpack. But when he headed for the trucks I felt queasy. I already had more of a problem with vehicles, for reasons he couldn't or wouldn't understand. Vehicles felt to me more tangibly property than a wall or a bridge did, more owned by some particular person who wouldn't be happy to discover our handiwork, even if it was a public vehicle like a bus or a T car or these postal trucks.

"I don't like how it makes me feel to paint on stuff like this," I told him, lowering my can after just a couple of strokes, the metal rim clinking like a reholstered gun against a rivet in my jeans. "It makes me feel like a vandal."

"Don't be silly. It's all the same. You don't like to paint on private property, so we try to stick to public. Now you want to cut out half the public stuff too?"

"But what gives us the right to—"

"We've talked about this. No one *gives* us the right. We

take it."

"OK. But this is a public thing. Consensus demands this truck be white, not covered with"— I looked at his work— "yellow people in postal caps."

"Consensus is bullshit," he said without looking at me. White clouds of his breath billowed out from his hood. The angle, which revealed only his lips and the tip of his nose against the black fabric of his hood, made him look sinister in a way that would never actually suit him—but perhaps it was my glimpse of him that way, however unfortunately wraith-like, that made me realize the level of his dedication. In the face of it I felt lonely, second-rate. "If everything was decided by consensus," he went on, "everything would be white because no one could agree on any other color. Every building would be a cube and have X number of windows with X type of awnings. The world would be fucking boring, Arrowman. There's no reason or need for anything to be uninter—"

In a split second we knew we were spotted and had to run. And we were moving. The sudden jingle of keys, the bouncing flashlight beam playing over us—these were familiar and at first we reacted on instinct, on that old refrain: *Don't get caught.* I'd gotten pretty good at not getting caught.

But this time things happened differently, because things went wrong. I'd entered the parking lot carrying Mateo's backpack, had put it down somewhere, and the black of it on black pavement in the dark made it practically invisible. We wasted valuable seconds looking for it.

"It was right around—" I was saying, right before my hand snagged one of the straps. I flung it on and Mateo stuffed his cans in. Just then a second flashlight beam lit up a truck near my face before searing my eyes—there were two guards. And then three. Had they seen us on a camera? Had they rounded up a fucking army?

"It *is* them!" I heard one of them say, one who must've seen Mateo's work on the truck and recognized the yellow people. "Shit, it *is* them!"

And I thought, *It's them?* And not, *It's him and some other guy?* As in, the guards thought we were a crew? As in, they thought I was equally responsible for the Facts? I didn't know how that made me feel, and now wasn't the time to think it over.

They gave chase with a lot more doggedness than guards and cops and citizen vigilantes usually did, because they knew we were *them!* (*Them!*) And we ran, weaving between boxy postal trucks — I didn't know to where, not in the direction we came — and I followed Mateo hoping he had a plan. Because it was closer and because they were on us, he brought us to plain fence. No door. Just plain fence.

"I can't make that!" I blurted.

"Yes," he said, and he was grabbing my jacket and was beginning to scramble up the fence, as though his plan was to haul me up along with him. Hands were laid on his hip and his leg by the first guard, and a moment later by the second.

"Stop, we want to talk to — Stop!"

"Hey — You guys are — Wait — "

I didn't even know where the third guard was.

Mateo's sneakers, despite the pull of the guards, were going up the fence as though it were stairs, while mine slid off as though it were greased. I heard my jacket rip and then Mateo was pulling my backpack strap instead.

If he'd been doing a Dedinhos rather than a Fact, I think he might've stopped and faced the music; Dedinhos was a small-beans writer. But he'd been doing a Fact and the Facts were big-time. These guards knew it too. They'd gathered an army.

"Go," I told Mateo.

"You can do it." Pulling me harder.

"You guys are — *Stop! —* "

Adrenaline surging, I saw Mateo's panicked eyes the moment he knew they'd gotten a hold on his belt and started pulling him down off the fence. I saw one of the guards readying a zip-tie. I saw the many opportunities Mateo didn't take to land his heels in the guards' teeth. And I saw the hands on him that were not my hands and that didn't belong there, trying to get Mateo's second wrist into the zip-tie.

"Don't you fucking touch him!" I screamed at the guards,

probably the only time in my life I full-on screamed. And then like a thug I shoved the son-of-a-bitch zip-tie guard hard, his belly and shoulder soft beneath my hands. "*Fuck off!*" He was older than I thought at first, less steady — my decision to fight him dropped a curtain in my mind that revealed him to be an old man, a desk-jockey night watchman with a loop of ribbed plastic. I pushed him again as he was going down, and he collided with the other guard hard enough to make the other guard stumble backward and lose his grip on Mateo. Before I knew it Mateo had me by the sleeve and we were running again. With a rattle of chain-link he got the gate open and we escaped through it, chased only by a single flashlight beam (the third guard?) that bobbed around at our feet, then faded, then disappeared.

Mateo walked with wide eyes afterward, running his hands through his hair again and again.

"I have my wallet," he said, feeling himself over. "Nothing fell out. I have my wallet." He clutched at his pants and it made me think of the key-touching guy, who was probably in bed right now asleep, warm and dry. "I have my keys. I have my phone."

"I have your backpack," I murmured, slipping it off and holding it out to him by its worn nylon straps. But I knew and he knew that my ultimate success in locating it barely made up for misplacing it in the first place.

The near-miss could've happened anywhere — *had* happened a lot of places — but usually it was just unlucky timing. And although we had to run all the time, we'd never had to fight until tonight. And that was my fault because, first, I'd been yammering on, forcing him to mount defenses of street art that distracted his special danger sense until it was almost too late — and then all the seconds we spent looking for his backpack, full of items covered in his fingerprints. So I said nothing, even when we were many blocks away and my heartbeat was back to normal and we were sure the sirens in the distance were not for us.

I couldn't stop thinking of that guard, though, and of the way he yelped when first his knee and then his shoulder hit the pavement. I still had a can in my pocket and I took it out and set it down on the curb.

Mateo leaned against a parking meter, tapping a clump of frozen snow with his sneaker. "That sucked," he said matter-of-factly.

"I'm sorry."

"Not your fault." But he didn't look at me when he said it.

A close call, the stuff of nightmares—but it was a good excuse to limit my nights out with him. A few days later I told him it was too much, too often, that I was too cold and too tired to keep going out every night. Fridays and Saturdays were the best I could do. He didn't try very hard to talk me out of it.

And he didn't tell me so, but he'd been thinking that one of the reasons for the close call, and for the near-miss with Mako in September, was that graffiti had grown too comfortable. With me along it had come to feel more like hanging out than robbing a bank, and the second it stopped feeling like robbing a bank—the second that sense of danger and hyperawareness mellowed to chillin'—he was in trouble. He could never be at ease doing this, could never get sloppy. That was Rule #1. He'd figured that out with Vinicius years ago. So it was OK that I didn't come out every night anymore. He needed no crew.

Thanks to his electric blanket

his bed was always warm when I climbed in. Although I was feeling increasingly alienated from him out-there, being in bed with him always felt like a reboot, a recalibration of my feelings to their most tender and affectionate and confident. I always knew what to do in-here. We still fit into each other perfectly and when we were done I could tell he was satisfied.

I breathed in deep and let it out, pulled the blanket back up and rolled onto my side, facing the middle of the bed. He got up to clean up and then got back in. His skin was chilly but warmed quickly.

"Did you get that office email?" he said, his voice in that place between normal and whisper. He smoothed back his hair and I could smell the remains of deodorant under his arm. "The one about the holiday party?"

"Sure."

"We're supposed to bring a grab gift? Have you done this before?"

"The past couple years I bought books I wanted and then grabbed them myself."

He smirked and was quiet a minute. "Think I'll try to skip it."

"Don't skip it, it's fine. I'll be there."

"We'll see."

Quiet settled in around us. He put his hand on my hip and nudged me, which I knew meant he wanted me to roll over so he could spoon me. I did. His São Paulo arm came around and then his thumb went back and forth in my chest hair.

"We haven't talked about Christmas," I whispered. "Do you have plans?"

"Not really," he said against my head.

"You're not going to SP?"

"Don't think so."

"Oh, I was thinking you'd go."

He turned his face so he could speak. "When I go home in the here-winter I don't go for Christmas, I go for Carnival."

"Ah."

"Usually I just kick it with Marjorie and Phoebe in the morning and do whatever when they take off for grandma's."

"I was thinking about going to Honduras to see my mom."

"Getting pretty late to just be thinking."

"I was only thinking. I always tell her I'll think about it. Then I chill with Cara and Jamar. Either we go to her parents' or his. I kind of just tag along. I always feel welcome enough. But this year I'd rather just be here with you."

"Good."

I liked the feel of his breath on the back of my neck and the way he squeezed my feet between his. I closed my eyes. I was content being with him in-here, and there were so many out-there things this closeness could undo.

The door squeaked open,

breaking the spell of the dozey morning, and Phoebe entered like a drill sergeant. She said, "Mateo!"

If I'd had time to decide what to do, I likely would've drawn the covers slowly up over my head and pretended not to be there—but the surprise made me sit up quick and then, upon seeing who was at the open door, gather the blankets up against my chest.

Mateo sat up too but his nakedness under the covers prevented him from leaving the bed. So we were forced to continue to be in it together. "What is it, Miss?"

Phoebe's scrunched mouth, a sign that she was processing, suggested she hadn't expected to find me here. She looked at us for a minute with concentration, then her face relaxed and she walked quietly across the room and sat down on the foot of the bed.

"Guess what Mateo?" she said. She didn't acknowledge me.

"What's up?"

She put her hand to the side of her mouth to impart a great secret, but did not whisper. "I'm going to Sunfield." She laughed.

"You got a place?"

She nodded. "A lady is moving. They said Phoebe we want you here right now!"

"That's very exciting!" He put out his hand to shake, and she clutched it and pressed it to her shoulder in a sort of hand-hug.

"I told them my friend Mateo is going to visit me all the time!"

"Totally. Of course I will. We'll have to celebrate. I was just talking to Fletcher about some things, so why don't I see you downstairs in a little bit?"

"OK." She started sidling off the bed. "And you can bring your friend," she said with a glance at me.

"That'll be fun. Can you close the door when you go?"

She nodded and did, and we were alone again. Her footsteps were heavy on the stairs.

I flopped back on my pillow. "Jesus Christ. Has she ever done that before?"

"Nah. It was good news. She just wanted to share."

"It's lucky we weren't screwing, Mateo. Can you even imagine?"

"Relax, Arrowman. It was fine. All we were doing was sleeping and that's all she saw."

"Naked." I lifted the covers.

"She couldn't see that."

"I'm so not used to kids."

"She's not a kid. She's almost the same age as us."

"You know what I mean. What's—what did she say? Sunfield?"

"It's that place I was telling you about before. This is good news. They've been waiting literally years for a room to open up."

"She'll live there?"

"Yup."

"For how long?"

"Long as she likes, I guess."

"So she's moving out?"

"She's getting her own place."

"So it's just going to be you and Marjorie?"

"Unless you want her room." He nudged my hip.

Back and forth, tick

and tock, cold and hot. A can, a blanket. A hoodie, bare skin. Angst, contentment. One minute I had him in my arms and the next, on the other side of his alarm clock's ear-splitting blare, all I had was a backpack.

From under the dank, dark

overpass where we were painting on a Saturday night—or, rather, where Mateo was painting—I could see Christmas lights glittering in a few of the windows in the buildings that lined Commonwealth Ave. They looked pretty and warm and I imagined I smelled sugar cookies baking inside.

Twenty feet away, against one of the overpass's concrete support columns, a bum slept on a bed of cardboard, mummified in a cocoon of gray shipping blankets he probably ganked from the back of a U-Haul. He'd already peered out once to check us out before withdrawing back under the blankets. I kept an eye on him. Like so many things that are harmless in daylight—coatracks dangling hoodies, the shadows of tree branches—hobos seemed more threatening at night.

Mateo, in just a thick hooded sweatshirt, added some finishing touches to the Izzie, or Fact, or whatever you call them, while I sat on a concrete block shivering, shoes scuffing back and forth on the stiff dirt. His backpack sat between my feet and I rubbed the zipper teeth to make sure my fingers still had feeling.

"What do you think?" he said finally, stepping away from the wall, flicking wet paint off the back of his hand.

I gave it a glance. GIVE IS GET. The letters had bells and ornaments hanging from them, a Christmas theme—but when I thought of Christmas I didn't think of overpasses.

"Looks good," I told him. "I like it. Want your camera?"

"Hey. You barely looked."

"I looked. I've been watching. It's nice."

He frowned and took the camera, and when my hand was empty I pulled it back into my sleeve. Next time I'd wear gloves, even if he said gloves were too restricting. When he turned around with the photo I was already wearing the backpack and starting down the little slope back to the sidewalk. I gave the sleeping bum a parting glance to make sure he wasn't going to chase after us with the jagged edge of a soup can or something.

"Hold up," Mateo told me, and when I stopped he unzipped the backpack and put the camera inside—a new camera he didn't like as well; his old one got broken during the incident at the post office.

"Are we good for tonight?" I said.

"We can be. Feeling tired?"

"A little." My hat was pulled down to my eyebrows and

my nose wouldn't stop running.

"OK. We'll go home now."

"My place or yours?"

"Let's go to mine." He put his arm around me and pulled me against him. Even though smiling cracked my chapped lips, I couldn't help it.

Tick and tock. Cold and hot, so hot.

We did Christmas.

I strategically forgot about an invitation from Alex to his and Jimmy's Christmas Eve bash, reason being that a meet-and-greet with Jimmy Perino wouldn't be the best thing in the world for me. Instead Mateo brought me to Mass at a church I never knew he dipped into from time to time. In the cavernous, candle-lit place we sat on the benches and I whispered, "You're really Catholic, aren't you?"

He shrugged. "I just like the windows," he said, pointing to the stained glass. "They're like graffiti."

I got him a digital camera, which I thought would be easier for him to carry around than that bulky Polaroid but which I don't think he ever used. Also a pair of fingerless gloves, which he did use. I braced myself to receive from him some kind of graffiti paraphernalia—a black book, an array of markers—but in what turned out to be a disappointing realization that he understood I wasn't exactly into that, he gave me a box of fancy stationery and a giftcard to Urban Outfitters. I looked at the giftcard and suddenly felt as though our relationship was running on fumes.

We did New Year's.

We didn't go out, the city too crowded to be painted on unseen. Instead we watched Times Square on TV with Jamar and Cara and threw handfuls of foil confetti at each other when the ball fell.

And then January began chugging

along. The most striking measure of the passing winter was Cara, literally—the growth of her middle. It started slow and then, suddenly, every time I saw her she was like ten sizes bigger.

"I'm a whale," she announced in early February, on the evening after her baby shower. Her eighty aunts had swarmed her that afternoon and now the living room was strewn with boxes of stuff bearing pictures of cartoon animals and giggling infants. She slid farther down on the couch. "I feel like a whale. I look like a whale. My bulk extends through all these products."

"You don't look like a whale," I told her.

"I'm a whale in a Shuster College t-shirt." It was Jamar's—it fit her like a dress.

"Shush, you're not a whale. You're barely a bottlenose dolphin."

"I'm a whale with a bottlenose dolphin inside me."

"Heh."

Jamar came out of the kitchen with an industrial-size bag of M&Ms—a gift from perhaps the most practical aunt—and offered it to Cara, who plucked at the sides, growling, and then handed it back for him to open. He did and she sank her hand in.

"She says she's a whale," I told him, jamming my hand in the bag after Cara had withdrawn a fistful of candy.

"I heard." Jamar lifted her legs and sat down on the end of the sofa, replacing her feet on his lap. He lay his hand on her belly and gave it a squeeze. "Nope, not quite ripe yet."

"It's probably not a good idea to refer to your kid as a sea mammal, though," I said. "He might get the wrong idea and start growing flippers."

"Flipper baby," Jamar said.

"Heh."

"The Penguin."

"Haha. If your unborn child was a member of Batman's rogues gallery, which supervillain would he be?"

"I keep telling her we need to start picking out names,"

Jamar said to me but really to Cara.

"Well I'll tell you one thing, ya jerks," she said, "he's not going to be named *The Penguin*." She frowned, cupped her belly in her hands and whispered, "Listen to those creeps calling you a rogue. You're not a rogue, are you? Here, have some more chocolate." She tossed back a handful of M&Ms and chewed. To us she said, "I told you we can't know the name until we see his face. Or her face."

"You should at least have a pool of options ready," I said. "You know what? Hold on." Naming characters was one of my favorite parts of writing stories, and I wasn't about to let slip the chance to influence the name of a real live human being. I went to my room and perused my bookshelves. Grabbed some Tolstoy, some Salinger, a few others, and—what the hell—the Bible. I dumped the books on the coffee table.

"What are these?" Cara said.

"Let's pick a name." I stood up in front of the TV. "Zooey," I suggested, holding up a book. "Used here for a boy, but in modern times has been adapted for use by girls. Unique, playful, looks wonderful on a lunchbox *and* a business card."

"Ew. Zooey. No." Cara scrunched her face, crunched some candy. "Although maybe we could add Zoë to the girl-pool?"

Jamar said, "Doesn't Zoë have one of those things over the E?"

"An umlaut," I said.

"Right. No kid of mine is having an umlaut." He grabbed a handful of M&Ms. "What else you got?"

"Vladimir?"

"No."

"Petunia?"

"Next."

"Charley. With a *Y*. For boy or girl."

"A *Y*? No."

"Piscine Molitor?"

"Piscine?"

"I hereby decree, Bradford, that you're never allowed to

have kids."

"Jamar Jr.," I said to win back his good graces.

"Hey, I kind of like that."

"You would," Cara said.

"You could call him JJ."

"Hear that, Car? We could call him JJ."

"No."

"Hey, aren't you going to Mateo's tonight?"

"He's got some thing at work and I'm chilling with my peeps tonight. How about Seymour?"

Later that evening I looked

long and hard at my phone after it chimed: a text from Mike. I hadn't heard from him much since last summer when I told him about Mateo and had to decline his request for a pre-vacation hook-up, but he still, from time to time, made himself known.

I made Level 80 today!

It wasn't what you'd call a come-on, but it was hard not to take even the blandest message as a form of invitation—even if it conveyed nothing more than that he still existed, and, by implication, still had a bed and a body. And it was getting harder to ignore the invitation and offer a neutral response. All the sexy/cheesy possibilities flashed through my mind. *That sounds like cause for celebration.* Or, *You deserve a reward.* All the things that in the past—before I had a boyfriend—would've set a visit in motion.

Lately I'd been craving him. Mike. In particular I couldn't stop thinking about a yellow thread from a pull in his bottom sheet: I remembered the thread curling up and licking his ribs before rolling back and getting rolled onto. I looked long and hard at his text and thought I'd just about die if I never saw that yellow thread again.

Congrats, I texted back. The bare minimum, stripped even of an exclamation point.

I lowered the phone and looked out the window, checking for Mateo's car. A second after spotting it I heard his voice. He was in the living room talking to Jamar. I deleted the texts, though they were nothing I should feel guilty about, and pushed back over to my desk. Soon there was a knock on my door and Mateo came in.

He dragged his fingers against the back of my neck as he walked by, then hit my bed on his stomach. He was still wearing his work clothes.

"How was your meeting?"

"Fine," he said. "Got roped into conversation with Porn Randy afterward, though. For like twenty minutes. He was asking me about the new website."

"He was at the meeting?"

"No, I think that's why he was asking about it."

"Why was he even there so late?"

"I don't know." He lifted himself up on his elbows. "How's the writing coming?" He looked at the sheet hanging out of the typewriter. "Using your Christmas paper yet?"

"Not yet. I'm saving it for something good."

"Ah. Then that's no good?"

"Nothing special."

"You seem a little distracted the last few days. I was hoping you had something good going."

"Do I?"

"A little."

"Oh."

"Everything OK?"

"Just a little worried about Cara, I think," I said, lowering my voice.

"She's huge, huh? Is it possible she's even bigger than when I saw her the other day?"

He seemed perfectly serious. I laughed. "I don't know. The doctor said she's supposed to take it easy."

"Like bed rest?"

"I don't think it's officially *bed rest*, but she's supposed to take it easy. And eat lots of M&Ms, apparently."

"She's still got another month to go, right?"

"Mm, three weeks. The twenty-seventh."

"Bet she'll be glad to have that kiddo out of her."

"I sure would be."

"I sure would be too." He rolled onto his back and sat up, unbuttoned his shirt. "Want to come out with me tonight?"

"... It's Tuesday."

"You don't have to." He got up and opened my closet and put his shirt on a hanger. "Just thought it might be nice since we didn't get much of an evening." My grease-stained shirt with his knuckle print still hung on the inside door; he must've seen it a bunch of times but he never said anything about it. He took off his pants and hung them up too, carefully maintaining the creases, then put on a pair of my shorts that he had, over time, commandeered as his own. He tucked his t-shirt into the shorts.

"You're funny," I said.

"*You're* funny. I need to pee."

He left my room, kissing me on the head as he walked by, and as he passed through the kitchen I heard him say, "Three weeks!" and Cara responded, "I'm a whale!" and that cued Jamar to start singing *Baby Beluga*.

I smiled. He fit in so easily here, almost suddenly. I turned back to my typewriter, unrolled the page, crumpled it and dropped it in the trash.

I did end up going out painting with him that night. I hadn't planned on it, and his alarm clock felt like a cattle-prod to my brain, but when he was out of my bed I didn't want to stay in it without him.

I went back and forth

like that a lot. Tick and tock. There were things I liked about being in a relationship. All the weird, physical things that anchored me to it. I liked the way his clothes looked hanging in my closet. I liked the way the colored lights played over his face when he stared into my fish tank. And the way he would randomly show up in my cube at work, put a cup of coffee on my desk and leave without saying anything, only smiling. I liked the tastes of his body and the feel of his scratchy throat against my mouth. I liked hearing his stories about São Paulo and Vinicius and the mysterious Tiago, who I suspected he once cared for.

But other things, as trivial as any of those, would up-end me. A text from Mike. A guy checking me out on the sidewalk. Another invitation from Alex to hang out with him and Jimmy, which I decided not to turn down. Every single thought of the key-touching guy. Sometimes I'd be perfectly content with Mateo in bed, and an hour later I'd be following him around the cold city, wondering why it felt like I was in two separate relationships: a Mateo-Fletcher relationship and a Mateo-graffiti-Fletcher triangle. What made them so different? Was it the warmth of the sheets versus the cold of the street? Was it his bare fuzzy belly versus his chapped bleeding hands? Was it the horizontal versus the vertical? After all, both of our identities had been defined on flat objects: mine on mattresses, his on walls. Was bed just my turf? Or was it more basic than any of that? Was it simply that in our warm naked moments I had him all to myself — and out there, the rest of the time, I was sharing him with a *city?*

There were good things and there were bad things. But I tried to focus on the positive. I tried to stay in the groove. Because it was February, and February is a month for romance.

"So what's Jammies getting you

for Valentine's, huh?"

"Hopefully a vasectomy," Cara said. She was lying on the couch with her feet up on the arm and a *People* magazine sledding slowly down the slope of her belly.

"Haha. Be nice."

"Heh. Diamonds. Jewels."

"Diamonds! Here you go." I handed her a bowl of steaming cream of wheat.

"Awh, you put an M&M smiley face on it!"

"There's more underneath. They kept sinking."

"Even better."

"Aren't I amazing?"

"Truly you are."

I sat down on the coffee table. The baby gear filling the living room hadn't moved much since she unwrapped it at her shower, although some of the bigger boxes—a playpen, a crib—had migrated into a partition that resembled a baby-festooned cubicle wall. Wouldn't be long now before they'd have to start unpacking it and setting it up. I made a mental note to be away that day.

"In exchange for my food preparation services," I told her, "you can advise me on tie selection."

"So then this is a dress-up dinner?"

"Alex wants to do it fancy. I don't really care either way. Are you sure you and Jamar don't want to come?"

"You know I hate Alex," she said nonchalantly, the way she'd turn down lima beans. "I can't be seen in public, anyway, especially on Valentine's Day. I'm a poor advertisement for sex these days." She sucked an M&M off the spoon. The magazine slid off her belly onto the floor.

"You're more like a cautionary tale."

"Heh."

"You guys should come, though. You can hold me back so I don't climb over the table and rape Jimmy Perino during dinner."

She rolled her eyes.

"What, you've seen him."

"Like ten years ago."

"From the pics I've seen he's even improved with age."

"He's a four."

"A four? C'mon, he's a ten. Dude's gorgeous. He should be in that calendar with all those naked French rugby players."

"He's a seven, max. And I just mean physically."

"Whatever."

"Mateo's an all-around ten, babe."

"I never said he wasn't."

"So what do you care about a seven when you're hot and heavy with a ten?"

"I wouldn't say we're *hot and heavy*."

"You would be if you weren't pining for five minutes with a five, dumbass."

"..."

"Why are you going out with them anyway? Valentine's

Day is for couples."

"They asked us. It's a double date. I haven't seen Alex in forever and he's been pestering me. I turned down Christmas. I couldn't turn down Valentine's too. It'll be fun."

"Fun. Sure." She sucked in another M&M. "*Alex* and *fun* don't go together for me. He's like a fingernails-on-chalkboard concert."

"You're terrible."

"Am I wrong?"

"You're just terrible." I smiled. "Maybe I'll be able to ditch him and get some Jimmy time solo. See if the sparks fly."

"And where will Mateo be during this?"

"He can join in if he likes." I offered her a dramatic wink.

"Mateo aside," she said, "I don't see Alex sharing anybody. Or, if he did, he'd share just so he could yank Jimmy back afterward and leave you out in the cold. A free sample so you'll know what you're missing."

"Jeez, you make him sound sinister."

She smiled, swirled the spoon in the cream of wheat, turning up a melted M&M that left an orange streak along the bowl.

"This one time," I said, "in college, at the silverware thing in the dining hall, Jimmy and I both reached for the same fork at the same time. And the way he looked at me, I could *tell* he wanted me."

"Oh you could, could you?"

"But he wasn't out yet, which is obviously why he didn't act on it. Alex said he came out late—and now he's trying to make up for lost time."

She could tell what I was thinking. "Don't *even*. Leave him alone. I know you're kidding— I *hope* you're kidding, Fletcher. Seriously, leave Jimmy alone."

"Of course I'm kidding. I have a boyfriend."

"That's right, you do. An amazing one, by all accounts."

"I know."

"I mean, Fletcher, have you seen those swoon-worthy tattoos on those magnificent arms? Have you heard that to-die-for little accent of his? Have you seen the way he *looks* at you?"

"The way he looks at me?"

"Keep an eye out for it," she told me. Then she went digging in the cream of wheat for more M&Ms, was close to being disappointed, and then turned up a red one. Licking the chocolate off the spoon, she said, "I know the relationship thing is new for you, but it suits you. So don't screw things up with the Brazilian." She booted my leg with her slippered foot. "Seriously. I'll pound the shit out of you if you do. Someday, you know, you're going to look back and realize he's been the best thing that ever happened to you."

"Cara, *you're* the best thing that's ever happened to me."

"Well, me and Mateo both."

He was giving me a look.

"Remind me again why we're doing this," said the best thing to ever happen to me.

"Because Alex is my friend, Teo, and he asked us to go. That's why." I turned away from the mirror, satisfied that my tie was straight, and found him pulling off his shoes. "What are you doing?"

"They hurt my feet. I'm wearing my Chucks, fuck it."

"You can't wear Chucks with a suit. Come on."

"Guys wear sneakers and suits all the time. Turn on MTV."

"We're going to a nice restaurant, not the VMAs."

"Then my feet will be under the table and it won't matter what I'm wearing. Could go barefoot. Maybe I will!"

I looked up and took a deep breath. When I lowered my eyes he was lacing up his paint-misted sneakers.

"I'm wearing a suit, Fletcher. That's good enough. I'm going out with these strangers."

"They're not strangers, they're my friends."

"I don't know how good a friend this Alex can be if you haven't seen him since last summer."

"Well it's not like people who go to sleep at eight o'clock have a lot of opportunities to socialize."

He glared at me.

"I didn't want to say no to the first invitation he gave us. —They're going to be here any minute."

"Cara says Alex is weird."

"She barely knows him. Come on, Teo, it's just dinner."

"Just dinner. OK, I'm ready. I'm ready."

He looked good—I was too annoyed to admit that he looked fucking great. His suit was tailored, a hip cut. It even looked good with the sneakers. I resented having an off-the-rack suit myself.

Alex texted me to say they were out front. The cold air slapped our shower-warm skin and we ran coatless (because who owns a coat that goes with a suit?) from the door to the waiting coupe. As we arrived at the car I heard the click of locks and Jimmy grinned from the other side of the driver's window. From this angle, shoulders-up, he was like Alex's post-coital photo sprung to life. He had a shirt on now of course but my imagination effortlessly removed it.

"You better let us in!" I said, tapping on the glass, playing along. In the reflection I caught Mateo roll his eyes.

"What?" Jimmy cupped his hand around his ear. Nice fingers, clean nails. In the passenger seat Alex was laughing. "I can't hear you!"

Right before it would've become awkward the locks clicked again and the door swung open. Jimmy got out, blue tie swinging against his chest. He was tall, eyes the color of the tie, with short brown hair you know would lighten in summer.

"I'm Jim."

"I remember," I said, excited to have his hand in mine. "This is my boyfriend Mateo."

He gave Jimmy a quick, wimpy shake.

"You guys look killer," Jimmy said. "I don't own a suit." He had on Dockers.

"You look great anyway," I told him.

"So can we get in?" Mateo said, breathing on his hands as though he weren't used to spending every night in the cold.

"Sure, sure." Jimmy pulled forward the seat.

Mateo held out his hand to say *after you* so I got in first and slid across the backseat, annoyed that I wasn't getting to sit behind Jimmy. When Jimmy uprighted the seat and got in I had a good view of his profile, though, so all was forgiven. He'd just had his hair cut and the edges met his skin in razor-sharp lines.

"Hi," I said, reaching forward to squeeze Alex's shoulder. "Sorry it's been like forever."

"Yeah, yeah. I forgive you."

"This guy's been keeping me busy. Mateo, Alex, Alex, Mateo." They shook hands against the armrest.

"Happy V Day!" Alex said.

"Vagina day!" said Jimmy. "Not!"

Mateo slumped forward and closed his eyes.

The restaurant we went to

was one Mateo had tagged the side of three years earlier. He claimed the piece ran for less than six hours before it was whitewashed by a frantic maitre d'.

The table was round, the lighting dim, the food French and expensive. The waiter sported a yellowed comb-over and wore a white towel on his forearm. He sold us on a bottle of wine. Alex and Mateo got carded; I didn't, and didn't know how to take that.

"None for me, Jeeves," Jimmy said. "I don't do alcohol. This body is a temple."

I thought: *Understatement.*

A loaf of bread on a wooden board was placed on the table and Mateo took the thick knife and began to cut, gently at first, and then grabbing the bread to keep it from sliding.

"Excuse my fingers," he said.

Jimmy laughed. "What's with those fingers anyway, Mr. Brazil?"

Mateo tipped over the first slice, the heel, and resumed sawing. "Huh?"

"He means the colors," Alex said.

"I mean the colors," Jimmy said, grinning as he lifted his chin slightly. "You a painter or something? Do a lot of painting?"

"Oh. No. Not really. I was, uh, coloring Easter eggs."

With a curious smirk Alex leaned forward. His plate clinked his water glass, which in turn clinked his wine glass. "In *February?*"

"We do Easter in February in Brazil."

"Do you really?"

"Um. Sure. Yup. Bread? Anyone?"

Jimmy took a slice and offered the board, littered with crumbs, to Alex. "And next I bet you'll tell us you have Christmas in the summer," Jimmy said.

"Oh. We do, actually. Yeah. Southern Hemisphere and all."

Jimmy laughed. "Southern Hemisphere. That's hilarious." He looked at me. "Your boy's hilarious, Fletcher. Not only a stud but a comedian too."

Alex laughed, reaching across the table to pass me the bread. I took a slice and noticed Mateo aggressively buttering his.

"This table reminds me of when we met," Jimmy said to Alex.

"Darlene's wedding."

"I think these are the same candles. Aren't they the same candles, babe?"

"They look the same," Alex said. "But then again I wasn't exactly focusing on the *can*dles." He let that sit for a second before adding, "I had some other *long thing* on my mind."

"You guys should've seen it," Jimmy said, tearing a piece of bread with his teeth, lips shining with butter. "It was love at first sight basically. Totally storybook. I knew nothing was going to keep me from getting this guy in the sack that very night."

"Not even your boyfriend," Mateo mumbled under his breath. Under the table I kicked him in the goddamn Chucks.

Jimmy said, "After I got him good and sweaty on the dance floor, I invited him back to my hotel room for a shower."

"And the rest is history," Alex said, bumping his head against Jimmy's.

A trio of servers arrived with our meals and set them in

front of us, removing metal dish covers and releasing lots of steam. Coq au vin for me. Mateo got some kind of salad that he quickly began stirring around.

"I actually saw some photos of you guys' first night together," I said, not wanting the conversation, amidst the arrival of the food, to lose the thread of Jimmy's nudity. "Alex showed me."

Jimmy turned to Alex. "You *showed* him those?" But he didn't look upset. More surprised. "What'd you think, Fletcher? Good stuff?"

"There wasn't a whole lot to see." I ruminated for a second and then added boldly, "Unfortunately."

Jimmy laughed. "Well that's a darn shame." He sliced into his chicken and a burst of steam wafted over his face, either making it or revealing it to be a little pink, the kind of pink that looks good against a white pillowcase. "You wouldn't believe what X is like in the sack," he said.

"Yeah—" I started to laugh but when I realized the implication of his comment my laugh became more of a choke. Alex flicked his eyes away after briefly meeting mine. Why would he not have told Jimmy about our weekend together? How could Alex do that to me? What I thought I had with Jimmy—the link, however tenuous, in the sex-chain—hardly mattered if he didn't even know about it!

"How's your chicken?" Mateo said to me.

I lowered a forkful of mashed potatoes back to my plate. "Sure I would, Jimmy. Did Alex never tell you about how I quote-unquote *kept him company* last summer?"

"You guys were to*gether?*"

"More than once," I said. "When he was house-sitting. Right after you guys met, I think. So you and me, Jimmy, we're just one link apart."

"I need the bathroom," Mateo said, pushing back his chair.

"X, you never told me that." Jimmy looked at me. "What other secrets do you guys have?"

"I barely remember it," Alex said. "It totally got lost in the shuffle."

Ouch.

"So was there chemistry?" Jimmy said, nudging his plate forward with his elbow so he could get in closer. He didn't seem the least bit uncomfortable or jealous. "Were there sparks?"

I looked to Alex to find the right answer. I wasn't sure what to do with Jimmy's encouragement, and I balked. "It was just a friend thing," I said finally. "Alex and I go so far back. It was only ever a matter of time."

"It was a friend thing," Alex affirmed. "And it was just what I needed." He said to Jimmy, "After we met I was so bent out of shape about *you*. Fletcher gave me some solace."

"Well that's what friends are for, right?" Jimmy said, and he winked.

We dropped two credit cards

on the plastic tray with the bill and the waiter returned them with two slips, two pens, and four little green mints. Mateo unwrapped one and chewed it.

Jimmy was watching me fill out the receipt. "Are you going to leave a good tip for your coq?" he said. Alex laughed and swatted him. "How *was* your coq, Fletcher?" To Mateo he said, "Did you taste your boyfriend's coq?"

Mateo stood up, balled up his napkin, dropped it on the table, and pushed in his chair. "This was fun, guys," he said. His accent was unusually thick; I wondered if that was because he was angry. In a vague way that I knew meant never, he added, "We should do this again." He buttoned the first button of his jacket, clapped me on the shoulder. "We'll just grab the T out here at the Pru."

"Hey, it's early though," Jimmy said. "You guys should come chill at our hotel a while. We're at the Marriot down on Tremont."

Mateo laughed.

I said, "Really?"

Mateo said, "Why'd you get a hotel?"

"A special Valentine's Day hotel. Our apartment's kind of a dump."

"We could watch a movie or something," Alex said.

Mateo frowned. "Don't you guys want to— I mean it's Valentine's Day."

"We'll order room service," Jimmy said. "It'll be fun."

"What do you think?" I asked Mateo.

"I dunno. Room service? We just ate."

"Sure, we'll come for a little," I told Jimmy.

The waiter came by and Jimmy placed the signed receipts into his hand. "Delicious," he said.

The hotel room was small,

devoted mostly to the king-size bed and a love-seat, which I was sitting on now. The TV was tuned to the Pay-Per-View menu but we hadn't selected anything yet. The room was just starting to warm up again after Mateo opened the big sliding door to step out on the balcony "for some air."

Jimmy and Alex sat side by side on the bed, bending big gullies in the outrageously fluffy comforter. Jimmy threw himself backward and said, "You guys are beating me!"

"Fletcher beats me too, though," Alex said. "He slept with a guy named *Scotch Tape*."

"Scotch Tape?" Jimmy said, sitting up again, lips full of hysterical smile.

"Legally Scotch Tape," I said, "a full-on legal name change. I saw his license."

"That's crazy. *Why?*"

"Beats me."

"Was he sticky?"

"Haha."

"OK," Jimmy said, "my guy who wouldn't take off his socks during sex is definitely not the weirdest."

"I could probably even top Scotch Tape if I really thought about," I said.

"But you've traded the weirdness for the Brazilian, huh?" Alex said. "He seems pretty normal."

"He has his moments."

"We like his accent," Jimmy said.

"*Love*," Alex said.

"Me too," I told them. "I think it's more pronounced when

he's angry."

"Then let's get him furious," Jimmy said, and Alex busted up laughing. "So how about when you're fucking? What's it like then?"

I looked at Jimmy for a long time while I decided how to answer. My brain searched for witty retorts; my eyes felt like they were crossing; my pulse cranked up; a shiver went up my back. Finally, when Jimmy raised his eyebrows in expectation, I said, "Why tell you when I can show you?"

Mateo stood on the hotel

balcony with his arms bent across the brass railing, suit jacket flapping in the wind. His fingers glowed dully in the light from the window nextdoor. They were cold but he was used to it. Out and below was the city, his city. From here he had a great view of the South End, full of brick walls and stone monuments waiting to be tagged. The city was a never-ending canvas — when they blasted away his work or painted over it with those silly gray squares, that only made the canvas bigger. More blank space. He smiled.

I shut the sliding glass door behind me and reached around him, gripping the railing against his hips. His tailored pants needed no belt and had no loops.

"It's freezing out here."

"It's not too bad."

"Whatcha looking at?"

"Just looking. Thinking about where we could paint later. Any ideas?"

"Oh. No, not really."

He turned and faced me, put his lips against mine — we exchanged clouds of breath. Last September on the night he painted my body he showed me how to press our mouths together and share the same air back and forth, from my lungs into his and back — this reminded me of that.

"Happy Valentine's Day," he said.

"You too."

"We about ready to go off by ourselves?"

"Are you ready?"

"Been ready for a while." He shrugged. "Since before the appetizers."

"Ah."

"I hate them," he confided, making a funny grimace to keep it light.

"Why do you hate them?"

"I don't know. I just do. They make me nervous."

"They really like you."

"They don't even know me. Maybe that's why I don't like them. They're too familiar. They act like we're old pals. I don't like people like that."

"They're just friendly. They're nice."

He shrugged. "So you're ready to go? Lead the way. I'll follow you."

"Actually," I said, my teeth chattering, both from cold and excitement, "I was thinking we could stay a little while longer." I grinned sheepishly. "They, uh." I couldn't stop the grin. "Wow. Yeah. They want to, like, hook up with us. Jimmy especially, I think."

"Hook up?"

"I'm supposed to come out here and see what you think."

"You mean like—group sex?"

I smirked. "Well yeah. I was kind of thinking it might go this way. Valentine's Day and stuff. You know. A hotel room. Four homos." I felt him go rigid in my arms.

"You were *kind of thinking?* So this was all planned out?"

"No, it wasn't planned, but— C'mon, it's hard not think of it as being in the air."

"I didn't think of it as being in the air. I thought this was a double date, not one big single date. And what do you mean, *four homos?* What does that mean?"

"It just felt in the air. Have you ever done anything like that before?"

"No."

"You don't think it would be fun? Or something new, at least? A fun experience?"

"Have you done it?"

"Three. Never four. Never Jimmy."

He looked away and scrunched his face. His eyes had that blur of moisture that can sometimes be caused by cold wind. "I don't even like them."

"But he's so hot."

He turned back. "Let's go paint. OK? I know a place that's practically a heaven spot. You'll like it. You'll like it."

"Teo, I go painting with you so much. And when I'm not painting with you, I'm by myself. It's freezing out. Why can't we do something I want to do?"

"We can. Whatever you want. But come on, Arrowman. Not this. At least not with *them*."

"You don't have to be jealous."

"It means something to me, Fletcher. It doesn't have to be sacred. But it has to mean more than them." He nodded at the glass door. The curtains moved; we were being watched. The discomfort in his eyes flared to anger and his lip quivered.

"Well I want to do it."

He looked at me for a long time. "OK. Then I'll let you get right to it then." Again he waited for me to acquiesce but it didn't happen and it wasn't going to happen. A gust of wind lashed his hair across his eyes; he brushed it back behind his ear. And again he said, with more urgency this time, "We won't paint tonight. We'll go back to your place, watch a movie. We'll get Cara and Jamar to hang out. We'll do anything you want."

"I don't think you understand, Mateo. I want to do *this*. I want to know what he looks like. I want to know what he feels like. And tastes like. And sounds like."

"*Who?* Jimmy?"

"Jimmy."

"Fletcher, newsflash! He looks like all the rest! Tastes like *all* the others. Like all the other fuckwads from Porcupine City."

"I want you to be there, Mateo, but if you won't be there, that's fine too."

He exhaled through his nose. "Well then that's it."

"What's it? What do you mean, *that's it?*"

He stabbed his finger into my chest. "You know what?"

He pursed his lips and I could tell he was about to really lay into me. But then he just sighed. His finger rolled into a fist that pressed against my sternum. "Fuck it. Never mind." He let it drop along my buttons and fall to his side.

Then he raised it again and pushed me away. "Be safe at least," he said. He pulled open the sliding door and pushed through the curtain, and in the room Alex and Jimmy were falling back onto the couch, having scurried away from the door when they heard him coming. Mateo charged toward the main door, keeping his eyes on the glossy sign indicating what to do in an emergency. He forgot to undo the chain and yanked the door and one of the chain's screws popped out of the wall with a loud *thwunk*. He closed it, undid the plastery hanging mess and, with the door open and his hand on the knob, he turned. "We don't fucking color Easter eggs in Brazil," he said.

And then he left.

I watched the plaster dust

settle. Clouds of it turned the bright carpet gray.

"Did you guys just break up?" Alex said.

"I don't know. No. Maybe."

Jimmy: "So I take it he said no?"

"Are you sure he's even *gay*?" said Alex.

I walked to the door and pressed my cheek against it to look through the peephole, expecting to see him standing against the opposite wall, but there was just a distorted expanse of floral wallpaper. I put my fingers against the hole where the popped screw had been.

Jimmy again: "So that must mean *you* said *yes*?"

And then Alex: "What do they do if they don't color eggs?"

I knelt, felt around on the carpet for the screw, found it and stood up to press it back in the hole.

"I don't know what they do," I said. Then I took my suit jacket off, stood twisting it slowly. I was stalling. Not thinking about going after Mateo, but wondering how to get this started. They were sitting on the bed, side by side, looking at me. I felt out of my element, and although I really wanted to do this, I was afraid. Promiscuity is, ironically, a refuge for the sexually vanilla. A new person is all the novelty and spice one needs. Rarely on the first date did I ever need to go beyond the basics.

I looked around. Why were there no drugs here? Pot wouldn't help me but why not some ecstasy or at least a little alcohol? Something to loosen me up. Jimmy was some kind of health nut, but Alex— On the other hand, maybe I wanted to be sober for this, to capture all the details.

"So are you staying?" Jimmy said, and because it was Jimmy I said yes.

"I don't know if he'll come back," I added, and to buy myself a few more seconds I went back to the door and had another look through the peephole. I felt lightheaded. I was even shivering. Tingly.

When I turned around again Jimmy and Alex were gone and the white bedspread was now a large, ill-defined, wobbling hump.

"Fletcher," said the hump in a muffled voice, "come see our cave of solace."

That's how it started. Imagine. Such a kiddy thing to initiate something so adult. I stepped out of my shoes and went around to the side of the bed, wondering if I should be getting undressed yet. I lifted the edge of the bedspread and stole underneath, a runaway slipping into a circus tent.

"There you are," Jimmy said. "Welcome. Nice suit."

"Thanks."

They were sitting Indian style with their heads bent under the weight of the bedspread. It was totally uncomfortable but it was serving its purpose. Alex had his hand on Jimmy's crotch, rubbing lightly. I sat facing them, my knees touching one of each of theirs. I tugged closed the flap of the tent. Light came in pink through the blanket.

The closeness and the humidity from our breath beneath the polyester paralleled the touch Alex had delivered the night we slept together. What started warm got hot quickly, and buttons were fumbled with, t-shirts abandoned, and when they were, lips fell onto shoulders and clavicles, and fingers wormed through chest hair and unzipped flies.

The tent got pushed off — like a metamorphosis we'd gone in separately and come out entwined. At first the air was cold on my skin. And then warm when they were against me. And then hot. Sweat and spit made it moist.

It was clumsy, awkward, but if they noticed they didn't seem to care. Neither did I. I was so glad to have my hands and my everything on Jimmy Perino, the one who until now had gotten away. He became the center, with Alex and me orbiting — kissing, licking, sucking — like desperate satellites. The bed creaked, sheets came unfitted and snapped away from corners. We switched places and wore serious expressions and after a minute I found myself on my back. Jimmy was straddling my chest — his bent knees seemed to grow out of my armpits like we were one pale, hairy creature. Alex was blowing me, reaching around with one hand to tug Jimmy's dick; he thumped it against my nostrils.

"X said you've been a fan of this," Jimmy said, taking his dick from Alex and touching it to my lips.

I had been — what I'd imagined of it. A fan, I mean. It was big, as big as Alex had said. Bigger. And now that it was here I felt only intimidated where I should've been aroused. Instead of giving the blowjob he was angling for, I skirted my lips across the cock and dipped against the balls, fanning my tongue across them. I don't know why I thought this would be better, but it was — perhaps because it was a thing much more difficult to critique. Also because I knew Alex was pretty anti this. The hair was thick and the smell was of sweat and soap. I nudged Jimmy forward and shimmied myself down, my head sliding off the pillow. I zigzagged my tongue along the taint (t'ain't the balls, t'ain't the ass), back and back until it was the latter indeed. The cheeks closed off my nostrils and I gasped through my mouth and gagged, and then tipped my head back some more, made a couple quick and tentative touches of my tongue to the wrinkled place, and with an increasing and increasing urgency and devotion went, as they say, to town. It was a feeling that alternated, quick as a tick-tock, between being the greatest and worst thing I'd ever done. I felt a cold flash on my own dick and then a crushing pressure as Alex mounted me. The bed shuddered. My stomach turned. Jimmy thumped his hand flat against the wall again and again, vibrating the framed landscape above the headboard. He moved his leg to let me go deeper, and through the open slider window I caught a glimpse of the dark, bright city and I wondered where in all that Mateo had gone.

And so the night passed.

I awoke with the light

alone on the couch, shivering, a pillow against me as though I'd been trying to use it as a blanket. I was naked and my ribs on the left side hurt. My face was hot and scratched from their stubble. My lips felt big, and the taste. When I imagined the taste my stomach curdled.

In the bed Alex and Jimmy were under the covers sleeping, spooning, in a way that looked innocent, in a way that might even be called domestic. I hated them because they had come out of the night together and Mateo and I hadn't.

I turned over and rested my head on my bicep and looked out the big glass sliding doors. The curtains were pushed open all the way — we'd fucked against the Boston cityscape — and I stared for a long time at the orange sky. On a tall building a light pulsed blue. Mateo was probably still out there somewhere, writing his Facts, his simple Izzies, across the city. Things seemed so clear for him, so black-and-white, even as they burst with color.

I started to sit up and the couch squeaked and I stopped. I knew if they woke up, regardless of whatever I felt and thought at this moment, one inviting look from Jimmy and I'd be in their bed again. Yet again. I rolled over, careful not to squeak the couch any more, and dropped to the floor on hands and knees. I crawled over to the bed, finding my outfit on the carpet piecemeal, a sock here, t-shirt there, mixed in with theirs. I found a complete set but couldn't be sure it all was mine, and when I crept into the bathroom to get dressed I found that one of the socks wasn't mine. I put it on anyway.

The pants were mine, and that was the important thing. I looked at myself in the mirror, smoothed my hair, was slightly surprised to find my lips clean. Jimmy had been clean—had been, probably, prepared. That helped my stomach a little. I tip-toed out and grabbed my suit jacket off the back of the armchair, checked to make sure it contained phone, wallet and keys (and thought of the key-touching guy, still, with a stab). On the way out I grabbed my shoes.

The hallway was long

and bright and quiet, the narrow runner carpet piled here and there with half-eaten room-service meals. My walk of shame. I noticed something on my hand, white powder—plaster dust from the doorknob, remnants of Mateo's exit.

I was waiting for the elevator when my clothes started singing.

I slipped my plastery fingers into a pocket and withdrew my phone. I hoped it was Mateo and was glad about that, was relieved by the clarity of my gladness: *Teo is who I want.* But in fact it was Jamar, and that was even better. If Jamar was calling me at this hour—it wasn't yet 6:00 a.m.—he was about to provide a bonanza of distraction. I pressed the green button and said hello.

"Bradford— I'm sorry to wake you up."

"S'OK. I was up. What's up?"

"Fatherhood is imminent."

"Baby's coming?"

"Very imminent."

"She's not due for two weeks."

"Tell that to the baby! I called my family. I wanted you to know. Diane and Wayne are on their way. I'm about to go in. They're trying to find a johnnie-gown thing that's tall enough for me."

I was smiling and absently dropped the phone away from my ear. The morning had bloomed and the night and the taste and the hurt in my ribs seemed part of some other life. I returned the phone to my ear. "Brigham's?"

"Yeah, you know how to get here?"

"I'll cab it."

"Hey, where are you, anyway?"

I considered. "With Teo."

"The tao of Mateo! Bring him. I'm having a baby!"

The revolving hotel door released

me into the freezing dawn. I took a breath, stuffed my hands in my pockets. Beside me was a Stonehenge of yellow caution signs arranged on the sidewalk. Sudsy water tinted blue streaked through the circle in numerous streams, icy at their edges, across the concrete, pooling near the base of a parking meter and flowing over the curb into the gutter. I turned around, faced the front of the hotel. Two men in maintenance coveralls, big brushes in their hands and a hose on the ground between them, were frantically scrubbing an expanse of brick. The brushes flicked blue foam against their shirts, against the surrounding brick, out into the air. Foam ran down the brick in glistening streams like that fake spray-on snow people put on windows. I couldn't tell what was under the foam, what was getting scrubbed, but I recognized the shape, the height, the size—and I knew it was for me. I took a deep breath, crossed my arms over my chest to try to warm myself, stepped to the edge of the sidewalk to pretend to watch for a cab.

I heard one of the guys say, "I don't think this is gonna come off."

"I bet it was that faggy guy came through in the suit," the second guy said.

"The one was crying?"

The second guy nodded. "OK, let's give it another rinse."

I turned casually and saw them step back, foam like pompoms on their boots. One grabbed the hose, aimed, released a blast of water at the wall while the other raised his arm to shield his face. I could feel the mist on my own face. The air grayed-up, ice crystals freezing, and then, when the guy shut off the hose, it cleared.

"Awh Christ," the first guy said. The soap was all on the sidewalk and the letters were mostly still on the wall. The guy looked at his brush in defeat, shook soap and water off the bristles. "When will they catch this motherfucker already?"

I turned to face the street again. Sudsy blue water flowed around my shoes until a cab saw my shivering finger and stopped.

"Brigham and Women's," I said as I got in.

"You sick?" The cabbie was peering at me in the rearview and then turned around for a better look. "You look like you just saw a ghost."

When I caught the first

glimpse of Jamar I skidded to a halt on the baby-blue line on the tile I was following. He was there in the waiting room, which was odd. That was the first thing.

The second thing was that he didn't look the way I imagined a new father should look. He was sitting on the edge of one of the beige vinyl chairs, legs stretched out in front of him. Over one leg hung a folded blue johnnie. He was leaning forward, hands clasped between knees. He looked like he was praying. A maternity ward was a place for hopping hallelujahs, not silent, tense praying like this, especially from someone I'd never seen pray.

In the seats beside Jamar were his parents. They were angled toward each other, knees touching, but weren't talking. Robbie stood by the big windows wearing flip-flops and baggy Spider-Man sweats. Their expressions stood in sharp contrast to a scene of Norman Rockwell contentment going on on the other side of the waiting room: a father rocking a drowsy preschooler on his knee, every so often leaning forward to whisper in the girl's ear.

A woman I didn't immediately recognize spoke to me, and I realized it was Cara's friend Jenna, and with her another friend whose name I couldn't recall. Good friends of Cara's— they'd been to the apartment, they were at the wedding. Coworkers, I thought. And I found it strange that I knew so little about them—how I so often remembered so little about women. If they were men I'd have remembered their birthdays and what they were wearing last I saw them. If they were gay or bi or curious men I would likely remember them wearing nothing at all.

"Jenna. Hi. Is something wrong? I expected a — less somber mood."

"Us too."

The other girl, perhaps sensing she wasn't remembered, extended her hand. "I'm Shelly." When we shook I realized she hadn't merely been introducing herself, she'd been looking for camaraderie — someone to get through this with. It sent a chill up my spine.

"Fletcher."

"I know. Cara talks about you all the time."

I smiled and excused myself and went over and slid into the chair beside Jamar.

"Hey Papa," I said, choosing to ignore the scene.

"Bradford. You're here." He sat up and leaned back in the chair, dragged his legs in under it.

"I came right over. It's a bad time for cabs — took me a while to get one. Why's everyone look so mopey? Is the baby as ugly as you or something?" He showed the smallest of smiles. "I thought you were going in with her?"

"They were bringing me in and then someone came out of the room and they turned me around and I've been here."

"Oh. Have you heard anything?"

"A nurse came out once. It's going difficult. They're going to do a C-section. But we're not supposed to worry or anything. So, you know, since they told me not to worry, I'm not worrying at all. Easy as pie."

I smiled and put my arm around his shoulders. "I'm sure it's going fine. I bet the kiddo's as tall as his dad and he won't fit out through little Cara. I'm sure everything's fine."

"Thanks." He looked around. "Where's Mateo?"

I started to explain and then just shrugged.

We waited. Robbie bought Jamar a Snapple and it sat on the floor unopened, sweating. After a few minutes I got up to stretch my legs, walked over to the window, looked out. There wasn't much to see, just the building across the way, a FedEx truck parked on the street beside a mailbox someone — not Mateo — had tagged in silver marker. I reached into my pocket to pull out my phone to text him, and it made my boxers pull taught and sharp against my pubic hair—someone's dried come still there. I realized I was still wearing last night all over me, hadn't even brushed my teeth. God only knew how I looked, with my burned cheeks and tired eyes.

HEART IS BROKE. That's what it said on the wall outside the hotel; that was the message the maintenance guys were scrubbing away. HEART IS BROKE. That's what he'd written after leaving. I wondered, did he have to run before finishing it? Or was he purposely trying to offend my copyeditor sensibilities? Or did he mean exactly what he wrote? Not *broken* at all but literally *broke*: poor, destitute, bankrupt. And whose heart did he mean?

I looked at myself in the glass, at my burned cheeks and tired eyes. I knew he meant mine.

I was lowering my phone back to my pocket when I heard a shriek, something that can only be called a shriek, and it made a swallow of saliva catch in my throat and my balls pull up tight inside me.

It was Jamar and my first thought was just never to turn around. To stand here forever. I looked at the reflection in the window of the room behind me, trying to prepare myself at least a little before I turned. And when I did turn I saw a flash of white coat and the blur of Robbie leaping forward with his arms out, but mostly what I saw was Jamar, Jamar's knees knocking together and Jamar melting down to the floor, the folded blue johnnie billowing out around him.

I took my arm back

from the girl called Shelly and put both hands over my face. Squeezed my eyes shut, tried to keep my breathing going, tried to keep from vibrating right through the chair, or melting, or exploding, or wailing, or dying. Stood up and my phone fell off my lap and went skittering across the tile, and through blurred vision chased after it after kicking it once by mistake and then stuffed it in my pocket and found once more the blue guideline on the tile and followed it around corners around gurneys to the lobby and spun through the wide revolving doors and the cold air steamed on my burning wet cheeks.

But I know her, I kept thinking over and over. *But I know her.*

I kept it together in

the cab but started crying again the moment it pulled up outside of our apartment. I realized that I absolutely didn't want to go into our apartment. That was when I finally called Mateo, but there was no answer. I tried three more times. Then I called Mike, and I got him right away.

A hand touched my shoulder

tenderly. I didn't turn my head but opened my eyes and saw purple fingers splayed against my collar bone. The purple fingers slid gently down my chest, met a clean hand on the other side. They entwined against my sternum in the same place they had once pressed a smear of motor grease. And then a scratch of stubble against my cheek as a chin settled on my shoulder. Hair tickled my ear.

"I heard. I'm sorry, Arrowman. I'm so very, very sorry."

I briefly imagined my response and some kind of conversation following, but the words to say it were nowhere to be found—my language was gone. Instead I reached up with both hands and threaded my fingers through the ones against my chest, and in response to this welcome he moved in, hugged me harder. And my floodgates opened and I started to cry.

But this was a dream, except for the crying. I awoke with wet eyes in Mike's loft, the ceiling a few feet from my face. I had all my clothes on, even my shoes, and Mike's arm encircled me.

Marjorie pulled open the fridge

to get Phoebe a strawberry milk night-cap. When she turned she noticed Phoebe standing near the kitchen table, a creased sheet of paper in her hands, her mouth scrunched in concentration as she tried to decipher the writing.

"What do you have there?" Marjorie said.

"It was under the puzzle."

"A note?"

"It's from Mateo, I think," Phoebe said.

Marjorie went over and held out her hand, trading Phoebe a glass of strawberry milk for the paper. It said:

Gone to SP. Tell Miss I'm sorry for missing the dancing show. M.

Across the street and across

the T lines, across power lines, across phone lines, past train stations, gas stations, fire stations—on the other side of the city in an apartment on the third floor of a three-decker, I sat by myself.

In the apartment there were no sounds of babies laughing or crying. There were no sounds of Cara giggling. There were no beeps of camera or heavy footsteps of Jamar twisting to record every moment of this first day.

He had taken the infant—a horrible healthy boy—to his parents' house in Waltham. The apartment was quiet. The only sound was the bubbling whir of the fish tank in my room. I sat on the floor with my back against the bed and watched the colorful, translucent bodies flickering across the fish-tank light. I put my phone to my ear again to call Mateo, and again there was no answer. And suddenly in a flash of comfort it came to me: the idea that I could go out and fuck. That it would be just that easy—would fill my head, would occupy my mind, would kill the night. A few keystrokes on my laptop. A text message, maybe two. An email. And the night would be full.

I watched the fish swim around. And in the glow of the light, by the base of the tank stand, behind a shoebox of CDs, I saw two cans.

Thinking: I can fuck. Or—

I reached and picked up one of the cans. Popped the cap and, for no particular reason, smelled the valve. Put a finger on it and wobbled it back and forth, not enough to spray, but almost.

PART
FOUR

The Night Would Be Enough

São Paulo wind rushed over

him, washing him of the smell of the plane. São Paulo wind and the sour-sweet smell of the driver's mahogany skin. Over his t-shirt the driver wore a flapping meshy smock, bearing like a soccer jersey a big yellow 24. Mateo, through his helmet, couldn't hear the flapping over the *rrmmm* of the motorcycle.

The city streamed by in a blur as the motorcycle devoured the street. The familiar city: buildings, restaurants, little shops were the same. Push-cart vendors were the same too — some were even in the same places. The crippling morning traffic was letting up now and the traffic was only bad — the driver navigated it boldly, once driving a whole block on the sidewalk, shooting back a warning to Mateo to hold tight when they jumped the curb.

When they made it out of the city center the traffic mellowed and Mateo was able to ease his grip on the bike and relish again the taste of the air in his mouth.

At last he patted the driver's shoulder and made a motion with his hand and the driver slowed and pulled to the edge of the street, put his bare foot down to steady the bike.

"Obrigado," Mateo said, and when the driver told him the fare he put into the boy's hand some crumpled reais from the stash he had kept in his dresser drawer 5,000 miles away. He took off his helmet and handed it back to the driver, who stashed it and sped off. *Rrrmm* away into the summer morning the way they had come.

Mateo stretched, shook out his helmet-hair, jostled his backpack and let out some slack on the shoulder straps. His butt was numb, his fingers stiff from clutching. The moto-taxi ride somehow felt longer than the plane ride. Whenever he came back he had to realize all over again just how big SP was. You could drop Boston into São Paulo six times and SP would still have room for overnight guests. That's land area. In people, you'd have to multiply the population of Boston eighteen times before you got close to the number of Paulistanos in SP.

But this area, his neighborhood, on a winding cobblestone street called Rua Giacomo in the neighborhood of Vila Madalena, reminded Mateo a little of Boston's North End—not because it looked much like the North End but because that was the closest point of reference Boston had to offer. The way Marlborough Street in Boston reminded him of Paris, and how something about the edge of the Charles River, down by the Science Museum, made him think of Toronto.

But Boston and São Paulo were his two cities—the two he'd branded himself with—and his comfort in each fed off his comfort in the other. They both felt like home. He liked the North End's curvy, narrow streets, its stone pavement and its old men who sit in lawn chairs on the sidewalks, passing time in loud voices—because it reminded him of Vila Madalena. And here, the colors and the cooking smells and the voices reminded him of all the dark mornings he'd gone into Bova's, the twenty-four-hour bakery near Prince Street, 5,000 miles away, for warm bread and cookies on the nights when his work took him near there.

He liked these cities because he liked the way they felt when he painted on them.

The tall walls that divided Rua Giacomo from the houses that abutted it looked different now—they'd been painted over again and again in the two years since he'd last been home. Layer upon layer in stories of paint. He wondered if perhaps the street had not always been so narrow. If you sunk a knife into the wall, just how deep would it go? How many layers of paint would it pierce?

He hiked his backpack up on his shoulders and walked up the street. His neighborhood was shaped like an S, a snaking canal of street weaving between residences that stood on the other side of the high walls. It was the perfect place for painting because it was out of the way and the walls made a ready canvas—and because no one in the neighborhood ever seemed to mind. Well, they minded if they caught you in the act—old people especially would throw little rocks until you ran away—but the paintings that appeared overnight were greeted like any other part of a new day, as ever-present and changing as trees.

A spot where one of his own tags had been now sported a huge tropical bird rendered in neon blue. It was signed TUCANO. He wanted to add something next to it, to take the spot back. His palm began to itch. His hand craved a can. No spraypaint allowed in his carry-on; he was twenty hours away from his supplies. All he had was a marker.

He put his backpack down and was digging to find the marker when he noticed a guy, blond and wearing shiny aviator sunglasses, coming down the street, his white button-down shirt open and flapping against his chest—and Mateo's attraction recalibrated to love of a different kind when he realized it was his cousin. Vinicius was on the other side of the street, and when he was about to pass Mateo, Mateo said, just loud enough to be heard, "*Pssst. Primo.*" And stood up smiling.

Vinicius stopped short, stepping out of one of his flip-flops. He pushed his big sunglasses up over his wavy hair and squinted at Mateo. "É você?" He had a spray of dark freckles across his tanned nose. "Primo Mateo?"

"Yup," Mateo said with a grin. "It's me."

«Just wanted to make sure,» Vinicius said in Portuguese, «before I maul a stranger!»

He bounded across the street, nearly getting clipped by a scooter buzzing by. "Haha!" A clap on Mateo's shoulder tugged him roughly into a hug and a hard, quick, scratchy kiss landed on his cheek. "Oh!" Mateo smiled against his cousin's hair and then returned the fast, hard kiss.

Vinicius held him at arm's length and gawked. "O que você está fazendo em SP?"

"What do you mean, what am I doing here? I told you I was coming, didn't I!"

Vinicius frowned and shook his head and smiled. "Em Português, primo. The English of me is fuck. You know."

With his shaggy blond hair and mischievous grin Vinicius looked like he should be carrying a surfboard under one arm and a stolen purse under the other. His features were sharper than Mateo's, and his hair was unique in their family—Mateo had always given him crap about it, saying blond hair like that was proof he was adopted—but there was clear relation in their eyes. Vinicius had corneas of the same striking green as Mateo.

«You messaged me last night...,» Vinicius said.

«And told you I was coming.»

«Well I didn't fucking believe you, primo! I thought you were fucking with me. Or drunk!»

«Heh.»

«When did you decide to come? You could've given us some warning! Shit!»

«About a half hour before I messaged you.»

Vinicius looked at the sky and shook his head. «Homeboy's in fucking SP. Your mom's gonna flip!»

Mateo blushed. Vinicius grabbed him again and tried to pick him up.

«OK, OK.»

«Ha!»

«Somebody painted over me over there,» Mateo said, catching his balance and swiveling away from Vinicius, but with Vini's arm still clamped over his shoulder. He lifted his chin at the wall. «Who's the toucan?»

«That would be Edilson. You remember him? From up the street.»

«Edilson Soares? Little Edilson?»

«He's good, huh?»

«Not bad. I guess. For a toy.»

«Haha, don't pout like that! You go away, this is what happens. You gotta stay here if you want to protect your turf.»

«Maybe I'll take the spot back.»

«You can try. Not sure *I* would. Little Edilson's not so little these days.» He floated his hand flat a few inches above Mateo's head.

«I've been gone a long time, V.»

«Not so long.» He squeezed Mateo's shoulder. «Not so long between cousins.»

«My mom leave for

work yet?»

«Yeah. Uncle Renaldo might still be there, though. He was just leaving.»

«Auntie and Uncle?»

«My dad's in Belo Horizonte doing set-up shit for Carnival. Mom went. This is what happens when you give no notice! Olivia's here though. Somewhere.»

«Why Belo? Ours not good enough?»

Vini shrugged. «Hey, are you home for Carnival?»

«I wish. Well... jeez, when is it this year?»

Vini's jaw fell slack. «You mean you don't *know?*»

«I lose track of this shit up there, V.»

Vinicius told him the date and Mateo frowned. «Don't think I can stay that long, no.»

«Well how long you home for?»

«Week or so.»

«OK. So at least we have some time. I can't wait to show you my stuff. I've been getting into stencils. I tell you that? Hey, can you get in the house?» He fished in his pocket, pulled out his keys, and wiggled one off the ring. «Here you go,» he said ceremoniously, pressing it into Mateo's palm and closing Mateo's fingers around it. «Some things never change,» he added about Mateo's blue fingers. He turned Mateo's hand over so he could read his watch face. «Who wears a watch anymore?»

«Had to turn my phone off so it won't roam.»

«This SP time yet?»

«Yup.»

«Then shit, I'm late. I gotta get to work. Tiago's gonna have my ass. Not the way he wants it, of course.»

«You guys still carpooling?»

«Yup. He's still got the armored car so that's how we roll. I pay him in blowjobs. Just kidding. That's your job.»

«Sure.»

«He asks every once in a while what you're up to, you know — wants to ask more often. You must be a hell of a lay, primo, because that boy's still hung up on you.»

Mateo shook his head.

«Wish I could take the fucking day off and kick it with you!»

«Me too!»

«Can I tell Ti you're home, or is it a secret?»

«Secret for now. Unless you can't control yourself, I guess.»

«He's gonna be happy.» Vini wiggled his eyebrows.

«We'll see.»

Vinicius grabbed him again and hugged hard. «So fucking good to see you!»

«I know. Go to work.»

«Booo!»

Mateo walked slowly up the

street. It took some figuring to find his family's door — the outer door was part of the wall that ran along the street, and like everything else around it, it was covered in graffiti. And that graffiti too had changed since the last time he'd been here. Like ever-changing landmarks. He had to look up beyond the wall to the houses and rooftops — those colors stayed the same. That was how he found his door. Filling it and a few feet on either side of it was a pink and blue sunset, across which flew a dragon-bodied creature with the head of a toucan. It was gorgeous. Must be little Edilson again. Mateo sighed.

He pushed through into a tiny yard. The stiff grass was brown in places and there were plastic lawn chairs set up around a grill, and some flower pots. He walked across the patio to the bright blue front door and used the key Vini had given him.

"Olá!" he called into the warmth. "Bom dia!"

No reply. The house was quiet.

He left the door open so the air could circulate. He dropped his backpack on the couch and took off his shoes and socks, feeling the cool tile floor beneath his feet. This was one of the feelings of home. The whole house was floored with this same beige tile, even the bedrooms; there were little brightly-colored rugs here and there, but no carpeting. It made the house seem more airy than the houses up north, especially Marjorie's big old house with its thick carpets and hardwood floors.

He squiggled his toes on the slippery tile and left shaded evaporating footprints.

"Mateo está em casa! Onde está minha família?"

In the corner by the television a birdcage hung from the ceiling. Two little birds, yellow and gray, hopped around inside tweeting.

You're new, he thought, wondering what else was new around here. "Oi, passarinhos," he said to them. *Hi, little birds.* He poked his finger through the pale blue bars of the cage. "Onde está minha família?"

The birds went on cheeping, but it was clear from the silence in the rest of the house that he was here alone. That was a relief. He was exhausted, had not slept for countless hours, not since briefly during his layover in Panama and fitfully on the plane, and the short interaction with his cousin had drained all his remaining energy.

He yawned. His bare feet carried him across the tile into the kitchen and his fingers reached for a bowl of fruit and a piece of chocolate cake. His hands brought the food to his lips and his mouth made him chew. He looked out the windows at the neighbor house, at a basket of wet laundry waiting to go on the line.

Then his feet carried him into the bathroom and his hands undid his fly and he peed. Then he was carried down the hall into his bedroom, and upon seeing it filled with Vini's things his tired brain reminded his feet that this room was no longer his. He turned in the doorway and his feet carried him back to the living room. His toes tipped him forward and his heels let go of the smooth floor and he flopped onto the couch, where he sprawled out, rubbing his cheek against the cushion until it found a comfortable place.

And he slept like the dead.

There was a gasp and

a crash and a *glugluglug* of liquid and then Sabina was upon him with kisses.

"What are you doing here? Meu Deus! What a surprise! The door was open! I thought you were a thief! What are you doing just laying there—help me clean up this milk!"

"Mamãe," he said, sitting up, rubbing his eyes.

She stopped amid the spilt groceries and all was quiet except for the birds cheeping, and she clasped her hands against her belly and smiled all the way from her hair to her chin. "My baby," she said.

I'm told the people in

Brazil are more about lunch than dinner, but that night, in celebration of the return of their American boy, they did it American style and had a feast. The prodigal son was given the head of the table. Sabina plunked in the middle of the table a big bowl of spaghetti with a dozen tiny meatballs rolling around on top.

«Vinicius, go get your sister,» said Renaldo, who was standing behind Mateo's chair squeezing his son's shoulders. Vini leaned out the back door and yelled up to his sister's window.

Renaldo released his son's shoulders, rolling his eyes at Vinicius. He hooked his cane on the back of the chair beside Mateo and sat down. His shiny bald head reflected the overhead light, and a graying mustache hugged his upper lip.

"You look good, son," he told Mateo. He knew his English

wasn't what it had been sixteen years ago but he made an effort to speak it all the same. "Big. Strong!"

"Dad."

"So. Your flight was good?"

"Felt longer than usual, but yeah. They had good movies."

"Good." Renaldo crossed his arms on the table and leaned forward. There were limits to what they could talk about, areas he could not venture into. Mateo's home life, particularly. "How is your work going? Your job."

"It's fine."

"The computers."

"Yeah. It's good."

"Do you like it?"

Mateo laughed. "No. But I'm not really concerned about liking it. It's a necessary but minor part of my life."

"Like pooping?" Renaldo said with a smirk.

Mateo blushed.

"And you are still doing a lot of—?" Renaldo made the motion of a spraycan.

Vinicius saw the gesture and said, «Ah, his favorite topic.»

Mateo replied, "Yeah. A lot. And I'm getting pretty big. People recognize my work. They write about me on the Internet. Sometimes even in the newspaper. They don't know it's me."

Renaldo frowned and looked at his son's hands clasped on the table. "You have to be very careful."

Mateo could sense his father's old alien fears—the need to be unseen, perfectly law-abiding in all ways but the one. "I'm a citizen, Dad. If they catch me they can't deport me."

"Hmm. Maybe. But there are other things." Sabina handed Renaldo a big wooden spoon and he stuck it into the spaghetti. "You still have to be careful. It is not like here there. I know here sometimes you can get away by saying, *OK, sir, I did it, but at least I am not one of those horrible, scribble-writer pichadores! My work has beauty!*"

"Heh."

"Right?"

"They'll never catch me."

Renaldo laughed and began stirring the pasta. "The moment you really believe they won't, filhinho, they *will*."

After the spaghetti they

finished what was left of the chocolate cake. And after that, when everyone else retired full-bellied to the living room, Mateo joined the younger of his two cousins at the sink.

«I'll wash if you dry,» he told Olivia, and she took the striped towel he was holding.

«Deal.»

«We should've used paper plates,» he said. The tap offered only cold water and he swirled his hands in the sink to help grow the suds.

«What, afraid you'll get dish-pan hands?»

«No.»

«Heh. Well it won't hurt you to get a little soapy, maybe some of that paint will finally come off.»

«Then how would you recognize me?»

He gave her a wet plate and she rubbed the towel across the front and back and placed it in the drying rack.

«I told my friend Gabi you're home and she wants me to ask you if you know any American movie stars.»

«Movie stars?»

«Or if there's anybody in a band or something.»

«Like a rock star?»

«Mmhm.» She pressed her lips together and nodded nonchalantly, her dark hair — more the color of Mateo's than Vini's — coming untucked from behind her ears.

«Is this Gabi your t-shirt business partner?»

«She thinks we need an American contact. She says if we can get Americans wearing them first they'll take off here.»

«Ah.»

«So do you?»

«Sorry. I'm the most famous person I know up there, but no one knows it! Is that one of yours?» He pointed at her shirt.

«Yup.» She threw the towel across her shoulder and used both hands to stretch out the t-shirt, showing the detail. The design was a stenciled sea turtle swimming in water highlighted with sewn-on silver and blue beads.

«Cool. Do you have other ones besides the turtle?»

«We can.»

«I'll buy a couple off you. My friend Phoebe would like one.»

«Cool.» Olivia took a plate and resumed drying. «Wait. Phoebe the retarded one?»

«She's a Downsie.»

«Ah,» she said, placing the dry plate in the rack. «I see how it is.» She smirked. «You see my shirt and your first thought is, *Oh, that would be a smash-hit with the retards.*»

«Heh. I thought no such thing!»

She laughed. «Did too! Take that!» And because no one in the Amaral-Bittencourt clan had ever passed up a soap fight, the kitchen was soon dripping with suds.

When Sabina and Renaldo went

to bed and Olivia hit the phone to discuss t-shirt plans, Mateo and Vinicius loaded into a backpack a few cans, a pair of small rollers, and two Coke bottles full of watered-down latex paint. Then they slipped out into the muggy night.

Mateo was glad to be outside again. The streets, the walls — these felt more indisputably his domain, a domain that seemed no longer to include his house, especially since Vinicius had commandeered his bedroom. At the house he had no *place* — his belongings were scattered across the living room couch, and even that had already been cleared off once when people needed space to sit. The streets welcomed him more fully, as they always had, as they did everywhere. He breathed in the air.

«Where do you want to go?» Vinicius said.

«I don't know. I'll follow you. Anything interesting up at the Buraco da Paulista?» He meant the big overpass downtown, prime graffiti real estate where the big boys played.

«I think there's a giant Nuncamais piece up now. Least there was last time I was there. I wish some of these guys would leave some prime space for us smaller outfits.»

«Wah wah. You got the whole city!" Mateo said. "The legal guys have it harder. Only so many places you can do it legal.»

«Well— Let's head down that way, check it out. There's some stuff I can point out on the way.»

«Yours?»

«Yup.»

«Cool.» Mateo rubbed his arms. The moist night air was making him damp.

«How are the tats holding up?» Vini said. «Need any touch-ups or anything?»

«They're good.» He held out his arm. «No touch-ups exactly but there's a couple new Boston buildings you could add at some point.»

«Lots new here too. I could see if Zé will let us into the shop?»

«Eh. Don't bother. Too sweaty out to be wrapped up in plastic.»

At the bottom of a concrete staircase leading from a plaza to the street Vinicius said, «Down here,» indicating the direction with a tilt of his head. He went down around to the side of the stairs. «Good, it's still here. This is mine.» He wiped his hand across the piece, clearing away pollen and street-dust.

«Wow.»

«Like it?»

«Definitely.»

«This is one of the first things I did with stencils. One of my favorites too. Beginner's luck. This part is all regular latex—»

«Uh-huh.»

«—then the details, this, this, this is all sprayed stencil on top.»

«Very cool. —Can I riff on this?»

Vini grinned. «Of course.»

«Wouldn't want to fuck up your piece.»

«You won't.»

Mateo shook his can and began waving it around Vini's

work, teasing out the lines he wanted to make before he let out any paint. He sketched out a dragonfly that would be holding Vini's original work between its wings like a crest.

Vinicius watched closely, feeling like he was learning something. He'd always been enamored with his cousin, even instantly upon their first meeting when Vini was six and Mateo ten. Back then Mateo was the faraway cousin whom Vini had only ever seen photos of and talked to from time to time on the phone. Short exchanges of whispered sentences, which cannot even be called conversations, shared when the boys' mothers pressed the phones to their ears and said, «Say hi to your cousin!»

When Mateo first moved to SP Vini thought of him as the boy, big and ten, from the country where people walked on the Moon—his Aunt Sabina was still going on about it even though by that time it had been nearly twenty years since anyone set foot on the Moon. But it was family lore, one of those legends that develop in families. Mateo was tied to the Moon, and Vini suspected Mateo had even been there on secret missions. Mateo never seemed inclined to talk much about his space travels—but on Vini's birthdays or when Vini was crying over a stubbed toe or a spill out of a hammock and needed cheering-up, Mateo would sometimes drop hints about his visits to the Sea of Tranquility.

That faded as they got older, though, as Mateo shed his alien Americanness and became almost indistinguishably brasileiro. But the respect of the ten-year-old for the fourteen-year-old stepped up to replace the awe of the new and the alien. Mateo grew hair under his arms so Vini stood in front of the mirror with his hands in the air, watching for sprouts of his own that would not come. Mateo grew tall so Vini hung upside-down off the end of the couch, to try to stretch himself and match his cousin's height. To no avail. But when Mateo started copying the paintings that covered Rua Giacomo, Vini found his hand liked a can too, and they took off together in a direction that welcomed them both regardless of their ages.

Only once did Vinicius's idolatry of Mateo waver: it was the summer between Vini's first and second years of high school, when Mateo, again an American, now a college student, was in SP on break. On the Metro on their way home from the art museum, Mateo had told Vinicius he was gay. Vini thought at first his cousin was joking, but when he gathered from Mateo's watery eyes that it was true, the pedestal on which he'd always kept his cousin rocked and pitched Mateo off and Mateo seemed to lay prostrate on the ground with dirt in his face.

A homosexual. Um baitola. Vinicius's heart quickened and they were silent for the rest of the ride.

For weeks afterward there had been a quietness between them. And then Tiago came out too, not a coincidence of timing but something shared and planned between he and Mateo away from Vinicius. Suddenly Vini was in the minority, and in his isolation he wondered if perhaps Mateo had caught on to something that he wasn't able to see. If perhaps Mateo was still, as always, intriguing in his alienness, the boy from the Moon.

They walked for a little

while and Vini pointed out other pieces of his. He was happy when Mateo looked close and sometimes seemed to study the work, even past the point of awkwardness, as though Mateo thought they were the most interesting things in the world.

«How's your *bridge* doing?» Vinicius said coyly when they were walking again. He was speaking, of course, of the Zakim. «Your beautiful bridge.»

«Heh. I'll pummel you.»

«Your sweet, precious, lovely, darling *bridge*.»

«You'll be sorry.»

«Heh. So you haven't tagged it yet?»

«Don't rub it in.»

«Just do one of the thingies, the cables.»

Mateo shook his head. «I don't want to do a cable, I want to do the obelisk. As high up as possible.»

«What if you just start with a cable, though, just doing a cable? Or the bottom part. Might take some of the edge off.»

«V, it's not like fingering a girl or something or feeling up her titties till you can round the bases."

"The bases of what?"

"I mean I'm not going to dabble with it. I'm going to wait until I can do it right.»

«You're saving yourself for your true love.»

«Call it what you will.»

«As high up as possible, huh?»

«Preferably the tippy-top.»

«You're sure there's even a way to *get* to the top?»

«Has to be. It's got lights on the top. Which means there has to be a way to change the light when it burns out.»

«True. Unless they change it by helicopter.»

«They're not going to change it with a helicopter.»

«I guess.»

«So there's gotta be stairs. Or an elevator, although I think it's too narrow for an elevator, because if there's an elevator there has to be stairs too, for emergencies.»

«You've thought about this.»

«Sometimes it's all I think about.»

«You can't just go online or something?»

«You know they don't put this stuff online. This is top-secret shit. Someone would try to blow it up.»

«You can't just wing it?»

«I'm not going to wing it. I need to have a plan.»

«You know,» Vini said, «from all the pictures you've sent, it looks a lot like the Oliveira Bridge here in SP. Over the Pinheiros. Practically identical, right?»

«Actually the Oliveira is bigger.»

«It's bigger and you don't want to paint on it?»

«It's not that I don't want to paint on it, but it's not the one I want to paint on.»

Vini sighed. «But it's pretty much the same, right?»

«Guess so, in terms of construction they're pretty similar. Both cable-stayed, both have obelisks with lights —»

«If we could figure out *that* bridge,» Vini said, "then you'd have a pretty good idea about how to get up inside *your* bridge. Right?»

«Theoretically. But the Oliveira is a highway too. And the

traffic's even thicker than in Boston. I don't want to see you get flattened if we make a run for it.»

«Sweet of you.»

They were passing a familiar street that turned onto another familiar street. Mateo looked up that way. On the corner there were a lot of young people standing around. He could hear the faint sound of rock-and-roll.

«You still go to Colonel Fawcett's?» Mateo asked.

Vinicius looked up the street and back at his cousin. «All the time. Want to stop in? I bet you can't get any decent cachaça in Boston.»

«Tiago will probably be there, right?»

«He might be.»

«Need a good night's sleep before I tackle that.»

They continued on to Buraco da Paulista and stood on the opposite embankment looking down at the highly-decorated wall at the mouth of the tunnel, into and out of which cars were still streaming at this hour of the night. They didn't paint anything, and kept their hands in their pockets. Finally Mateo started walking back up the embankment and Vini followed.

The morning would soon gather

its strength for another bright, loud day, but right now it was wee and quiet and their sneakers clapped on the cobbles of Rua Giacomo. As they got closer to home their footsteps were joined by the tell-tale *ffssshhtt* of paint meeting wall.

"*Tucano. Oi,*" Vinicius whispered loudly, cupping his hands around his mouth.

The writer stopped and looked and grinned and capped his can. «I know you,» he said, pointing at Mateo. «I heard a rumor you were back.»

«Who are *you*, though?» Mateo said. «The Edilson I knew was only up to here.» He held his hand against the teenager's sternum. Edilson grinned, blue eyes gleaming. «This looks good,» Mateo said, nodding at the unfinished piece. «Saw you grabbed some space from me down the street.»

Edilson flinched. «You know how it is. It just kind of happened. You went away. There's only so much wall.»

«Only so much wall, sure. This is one of the biggest cities in the whole world. You got all the favelas!» He meant the shanty towns, the slums, where some boys dribbled soccer balls along the winding roads and others not much older walked with black pistols tucked in the waistbands of their colorful swimsuits.

By now Edilson realized Mateo was playing. He thumped his can against Mateo's arm. «*You* go paint the favelas, Dedinhos.»

«We're going to go in there. You and me, Edilson. And V. And we'll trade their guns for cans. They can spray paint at each other instead of bullets.»

«Yeah. Right. So how long you back for?» Edilson said.

«Few days.»

«You guys stop at the Colonel's?»

«No,» Vini said. «Around there though.»

«Where'd you guys go?»

«Around. Avenida Paulista.»

«Oh. Still Nuncamais there?»

«Yeah.» For a minute they looked at Edilson's piece, which looked to be the start of a smiling motorcycle, and then Vini said, «We're going in.»

«OK. I'll see you guys later. Welcome home, Dedinhos.»

Edilson watched them go and then resumed painting, wondering if Mateo was serious about the favelas.

Mateo came into Vinicius's

bedroom wiping toothpaste off his mouth. «Give me one of your pillows.»

«Where are you going?» Vini said. He was lying on the bed poking at his phone, checking for texts.

«To sleep on the couch.»

«Awh, don't stay way out there. How will we shoot the shit?»

«I need to sleep somewhere.»

Vinicius scooted over and patted half of the bed.

«I'm not sleeping in the bed with you, V.»

«Why? Oh, I forgot—you Americanos get all sketchy

about bodies. So uptight.»

«I'm not uptight. It's because you fart all night.»

«I do not fart. Hey, will you stay if I get you the bitch pad?»

Mateo sighed. «Where is it?»

«I'll get it.» Vinicius hopped off the bed, maneuvered around the stool in front of his PC, and rummaged in the big particle-board armoire. With some effort he pulled out two big foam pads rolled into tubes.

«Bitch pad,» he said, tossing them one by one at his cousin.

Mateo caught them and unrolled them alongside Vini's bed. Vini pushed down a pillow and a threadbare sheet with Buzz Lightyear on it.

Mateo wrapped the sheet around himself like a toga and lay down on the pads. Under the bed were a few pairs of sneakers, a cardboard box and, lined against the wall, a row of clear soda bottles of latex paint reflecting the weak orange light from a power strip. At the other end was a bundle of rope and a climbing harness. Mateo stretched out his foot and touched one of the buckles. He felt dust on his toes.

«Don't use the harness much anymore?»

«Nah,» Vini said in the dark. «Not for a long time. It's too hard to stencil when you're swinging around on the end of a rope. Plus I don't know how much I trust Tiago. It's not like when it was you on the other end.»

«Yeah. It was fun though.»

«Heaven spots have to be hard or else they're just spots.»

«Yeah.»

«Edilson offered to buy it. But I didn't know if maybe you'd want to come back for it some day.»

«Nah, go for it.»

«You don't want it?»

«You need a crew for that stuff.»

«What about your boy?»

«I work solo.»

Vinicius was quiet so long Mateo wondered what kind of shit it was he'd wanted to shoot. Finally his voice from a few feet above and over, disembodied in the dark, said, «So how is Fletcher?»

Mateo rubbed his hair and pulled the sheet up around his shoulders. He didn't feel like talking about me but he wasn't home often enough to be evasive. «We're in a rough patch.»

«Break-up rough?»

«Yeah. Pretty rough.»

«Oh. ...That why you came home?»

«Guess so.»

«You go kissing on someone else?»

«No. But Fletcher and I both have other loves.»

«I can guess yours. What's his?»

«He's a bit of a — playboy.»

«Oh.» And then, gently: «He go kissing on someone else?»

«Someone elses.»

«Hmm. Oh — you mean not at the same time, right?»

«You ask too many questions.»

Vini laughed, softly, then was quiet a long time. Mateo thought he had fallen asleep, but then Vini cleared his voice. «Tiago asks about you.»

«Yes. You mentioned.»

«You could probably pick right up,» Vini said gently, «if you ever wanted to.»

«That was a long time ago.»

«He keeps asking me if you've joined Orkut yet. He wants to friend you.»

«You mentioned that too. He's just hoping I'll post hundreds of shirtless pictures of myself like all you guys can't resist doing.»

«Well we gotta advertise, primo!»

«What are you advertising? Aline's got you roped like she's a gaucho and you're a cow.»

Vini slid to the side of the bed and peered down, shook his head. «Aline dumped homeboy's ass all over town.»

«Again? You didn't tell me. When?»

«Two days ago?»

«Why this time?»

«She thinks I was getting with this chick Camilla.»

«Were you?»

Vini grinned. «Primo, you should've seen this girl, though. Hot enough to make you like girls.»

«So was it worth it?»

«No. But all we did was kiss a little. If she had let me»—he slammed his pelvis against the bed, knocking the legs against the tile—«*bam bam*, then it would've been worth it, right?»

«You're terrible.»

«I can't help it. I try.»

«You're just like Fletcher.»

«Whoa, let's not go all Greek tragedy, primo!»

«Hm?»

«The one where homeboy goes to town on this chick who turns out to be his *mom*.»

«Oh. Yeah. What?»

«Family lusting, primo.»

«I missed something.»

«You were saying I was like your boy.»

«You're crazy.» Mateo reached up and smacked his shoulder. «You're not even my *family*, V.» He grabbed a twist of Vini's blond-blond hair. «Where'd this come from? Ain't Amaral. Ain't Bittencourt. That's for sure. You find out who your papai is yet?»

«Is too Bittencourt.»

«Is not. You're adopted.»

«You're lucky you're sleeping on the floor, or you'd be sleeping on the floor.»

«Haha.»

They were quiet a long time.

«I'm glad you're home,» Vinicius whispered.

«Go to sleep, V.»

You're adopted, Mateo had told

him. He'd always kidded Vini about that, even right from the start. A classic case of a transplanted ten-year-old's insecurity.

He listened to his cousin breathe and looked around the room—his old room—at the posters and clothes and books and computer that weren't his and that were even more unfamiliar at this angle from the floor that wasn't his beside the bed his cousin slept in now.

Adopted. Maybe that was actually true. Not by Vini's own parents but by Mateo's. Vinicius was living in Mateo's room, in Mateo's parents' part of the house, while his own family lived upstairs. While Mateo lived in another country, on another continent, in another hemisphere. Figure that out.

A few hours later when Vinicius's alarm went off and bleary-eyed he stumbled off to the cellphone stand, Mateo crawled up into his old bed and went back to sleep.

During the day he slept

or went off tagging the walls of São Paulo with Portuguese translations of his Facts. If it ever occurred to him to call me or get in touch with me, he didn't follow through. His phone stayed off.

But I wanted him. I could've had Mike but avoided him for the same reason I was avoiding Alex and Jimmy: I didn't want to see anyone I knew.

I would like to say that grief over Cara's death gave me permission to go crazy, and that I seized it, and that rolling on E for three days straight I fucked so many guys I had to go in for a penis transplant halfway through. I would like to say that I drove crying through the night at treacherous speeds with the windows down, that I sat wailing at Cara's grave in the slushy mud. I would like to say that I burned down our apartment to turn all memories of her to ash. I would even like to say that Jamar and I pummeled each other to bloody bits in a terrible, blame-hurling rage.

Nothing like that happened. What happened was: I hid in my room. For three days I hid in my room. I called into work bereaved and sat in my desk chair and looked out the window. Watching the light change. Watching the birds. One afternoon it snowed.

They all missed her, I knew, but I missed her the most because the hole her absence left in my life was the hugest. She hadn't lived with her parents in years; Jamar was at home with his, and he had the baby to occupy him. *I* was the one who had to step around her things. *I* was the one who had to see her toothbrush sitting dried-out on the bathroom sink. *I* was the one who had to shut off her alarm clock when it throbbed beside her empty bed. *I* was the one who had to separate her mail from mine, who had to decide what to do with that fucking unfinished *Metro* crossword she left on the kitchen table.

I was the one who had to live here, in an apartment that seemed snapped back away from the goal it'd been building toward, the one who had to feel the whiplash of a stretched elastic cut. Everything here looked off-kilter, a little wrong, as though it all belonged in some other universe. Baby things that had been given and received with such happiness and such joy became, in an instant, purely utilitarian. I let in Jamar's father and Robbie and they pawed through these items, taking the essentials with them, the bottles and the diapers and the tiny clothes, leaving the rest lying dormant on the living room floor. A home that had been so ready to burst with new life now hung quiet and dusky with death.

Caleb. Jamar named him Caleb. Cara had liked it.

I sat in my bedroom and looked out the window. The two cans continued to stare back at me from underneath the fish tank. And I didn't write a fucking thing.

Despite the size of São Paulo,

or maybe in reaction to it — a pushback against anonymity, a wall against loneliness — their circle was small, close, tough and incestuous in a way that called to mind a telenovela. Before he had bedded Aline, Vini was with her best friend Olive (a name so perilously close to his sister's the affair couldn't possibly last), whose brother was none other than Tiago do Nascimento. The same Tiago do Nascimento, of course, who, in the back of an armored Volkswagen, first got Mateo to admit, under penalty of releasing his earth-shaking grip on Mateo's boner, that Mateo liked boys.

Depending on whose story you believed, Olive was now dating Edilson, a.k.a. Tucano, but that would make her something of a cradle robber, as he was nearly six years her junior. Edilson who, again, depending on whose story you believed, had once kissed Tiago's left butt-cheek on a dare.

Colonel Fawcett's happened

on the third night. Vini had told Tiago days earlier about Mateo's return and there was coordination between the two to make sure Tiago would be there on the night Vini showed up with Mateo.

The Colonel's was a little bar known for its manioc fries, its live music and its cheesy Amazonian decor.

Upon entering through the doorway, across which hung green streamers of plastic vines and a rubber snake, Mateo stuffed his hands in his pockets and Vini scanned the crowd. The light was dim and people flickered in shadows. Still, it took Vini only a moment to spot Aline and then he made a bee-line for where she was standing near the bar with two other girls. He'd worn his nice shirt and put something shiny in his hair — tonight he was going to make up for that thing with Camilla and win Aline back.

Ditched, Mateo looked around and sighed. He reached onto the bar and grabbed a few of some guy's fries when he wasn't looking and, biting off the ends, wandered farther into the small, crowded room. At the far end a band was playing on a stage which stood only about two feet off the ground so it was hard to see them through the patrons' heads. One of the lights above the stage had a broken fixture — a bulb was hanging by a wire, rotating gently. The light lashed Mateo's face before continuing its rotation and returning him to the shadows. He leaned against a vine-covered post and looked around, eyes following the spotlight.

It drew his attention to the side of the room, where a row of two-person tables lined a wall festooned pith helmets, machetes and taxidermy birds. Tiago was sitting at one of the tables. The chair across from him was empty but his sister Olive was standing behind it rocking it forward as she leaned across the table to tell her brother something. Tiago shrugged and laughed. His front teeth were crooked and he'd always been embarrassed about this and rarely showed them, preferring instead to make his introductions with his body, which was lean and strong and over which he had much more control. Because the smile was rare it had always stopped Mateo in his tracks, and still did tonight.

Some people between Mateo and Tiago shifted around, blocking Mateo's view, and when they shifted again, like a magic trick, Olive was gone.

Mateo took a deep breath and released himself from the viney post. The spotlight hit him once more before he arrived at the table.

«Hi Tiaginho,» he said.

Tiago looked up, not surprised, not un-surprised, fleetingly hating Vini for setting this up, fleetingly feeling the stirrings of a boner, fleetingly feeling his hand clench into a fist, fleetingly wanting to cry. He had on a black t-shirt that matched the black, half-inch plugs in his earlobes. His dark hair was as short as it could go without being shaved.

«Just Tiago is fine,» he said finally. His voice was deep and he was making it deeper. «We're not exactly familiar. In fact I'm having trouble *placing* you, estrangeiro.» He put his finger to his caramel-colored chin and scrunched his heavy eyebrows.

«Awh, don't be like that. I missed you too.» Before sitting down he lay a kiss on Tiago's cheek. Tiago frowned but didn't pull away. «What are you drinking?»

«Cachaça and Coke.»

«Give me a sip?»

With one finger Tiago pushed the glass across the scratched table. «Finish it. I don't care.»

«I just want a sip.» Mateo lifted the glass to his lips and felt the ice knock against his upper lip and realized his whole face was hot. He held the liquid in his mouth for a second before swallowing. It tasted harsh and sweet and like home. Maybe he'd finish the drink after all. «You look good.»

Tiago shrugged. «You grew your hair out?»

Mateo rubbed his own head. «Yeah. You like it? I had a fugue a year or so ago and came out of it with my hair long. Kind of liked it that way. What do you think?»

«I like it better how it used to be.»

«Ah.»

There was silence.

«You still have those? Your fugues?»

«I don't know. From time to time.» Mateo looked across the room and saw Vinicius talking with Aline. Hard to say how it was going — Vini was making big gestures, but she had her arms crossed and wore a look that made it clear that whatever Vini was saying, she'd heard it all before. Mateo knew she had.

He rubbed his thumb across the glass, turned to check out the band. «Is he singing into a megaphone?»

Tiago didn't respond and after a moment he said, «Your cousin tells me you've got yourself a shanty queen.»

Mateo put down the glass. «His name is Fletcher.»

Tiago made a sharp motion up and over with his eyes. «Gotta be a shanty queen saving cash on airfare. Why travel here when he can get a brasileiro all his own without leaving America, right? Does he suck your toes and tell you how *exotic* you are?»

«It's not like that.»

Now Tiago narrowed his eyes. «It's always like that with the gringos.»

«It is?»

«Yes.» He looked away, then up at a bird on the wall over his head. «I don't know.» For a while they looked at their hands and devoted an inordinate amount of attention to the band. Finally Tiago touched the tabletop to get Mateo's attention and said, «So why'd you come back?»

«Just realized it'd been a while.»

«A while? Two years. More than a while, Dedinhos.»

«Fair enough. A long while.» He touched the glass, took another sip, the ice cold on his tongue. Vini was holding Aline's hand now. «How's V doing?»

Tiago leaned over to see through the crowd. «Well he's wearing his get-back-together shirt. He says it looks nice and comes off easy. It'll work again. They'll get back together. It never lasts long.»

«I don't mean tonight, I mean like in general.»

«OK I guess. What do you mean? You talk to him like every day, according to him.»

«I mean things he might not tell me about. He steering clear of the favelas and that kind of shit? The drugs?»

«Far as I know. But *I'm* not his cousin.»

«You'd tell me, right?»

«Probably.» He looked down at the table, at Mateo's hand on the glass, the familiar colored fingers, and then at that foreign city tattooed on the sweetest, most vulnerable part of his arm. «You know you can't just come in here and sit down with me and have a heart-to-heart with me about things like we're still together or like I'm your friend or like, fuck, like we've even had a word in the past two years, Dedinhos.» He looked Mateo in the eye briefly and then looked down again. «I mean when you take off, you take off.»

«I know.» Mateo smiled, a defensive smile he could only sustain for a moment before it dropped away. He rocked the glass from side to side.

Tiago felt his cheeks grow hot and prickly and his mouth dry out. «Do you want the rest of that?» he asked. Mateo looked up; when he didn't say anything Tiago pulled the glass back and swallowed the last of the cachaça-and-Coke. Finally he sighed and said, «Come on.»

He led Mateo outside because it was too hard to talk in Colonel Fawcett's. And they started walking because it was too awkward to stand face to face or even shoulder to shoulder on the sidewalk. Better to be moving.

The night was sticky and there was a light, hot breeze. They saw a guy standing on another guy's shoulders, scrawling with a two-inch roller above the door of a Metro station in the scribbled, messy style of the pichadores. Tiago rolled his eyes.

«Go show them how it's done,» Mateo said.

Tiago shrugged.

«Do you still go out?»

«Sure,» Tiago said. «Not as much. It's not like when we were little kids and could go out painting as long as we liked and still have a home and breakfast to come home to. Paint doesn't pay bills.»

«Word. So you're hawking cell phones now, huh?»

«Vini and me.»

«That's cool you guys work together. Must be fun."

«He's a fun kid. Crazy sometimes. A flirt. He can't let a pretty girl go past without trying to kiss on her. Usually gets away with it too. He sells twice the phones I do.»

«I bet you sell plenty.»

«Sometimes.» Tiago smiled and there it was, the smallest revelation of crooked teeth. «And no, to answer your question, I don't think he's getting into any trouble. At least not in the favelas. And most girls don't carry guns.»

«Good.»

«He's doing some crazy shit with stencils lately, though.»

«I've seen.»

«He's better than you,» Tiago said. He'd intended to say it with bluster, like a jab, but it came out almost as a question.

And Mateo just laughed.

At the top of the plaza stairs, the bottom side of which was one of the places Vini had stenciled, they sat down side by side. Across the street a pair of old-men fado singers were standing on a corner spitting rhymes back and forth, cheered on by a few passersby as though it were a spontaneous, late-night boxing match.

«Last I knew you were in construction,» Mateo said after watching the singers for a minute.

«Concrete.»

«Right.»

«Bitch-ass boss fired me. Right when I was doing the patio at the library.»

«Sorry. Why?»

«I don't know. I guess he heard something about me he didn't like.»

«Oh.»

«Before I left I made sure to tell him he has a tiny dick.»

«How do you know?»

«I saw it in the bathroom once. Like a little bean.» He

measured on his finger.

«Heh.»

«How about you? Vini says you publish books.»

«I'm just the computer guy there.»

«Is that where you met your boy?»

«Yup.» They watched a street vendor push a closed-up cart down the street, taking the long way to the top of the plaza to avoid the stairs. «I wonder how Vini is doing.»

«By this time he's usually fingering her in the alley outside the Colonel's.»

Mateo laughed.

«I'm telling you, he's a ladies man.»

«I don't get it.»

«What?»

«Ladies.»

Tiago laughed. «Me neither. How could I find one who could throw me over her shoulder the way you used to?» They could hear the street vendor's push-cart rattling somewhere behind them.

«Do you remember how we used to sit and count helicopters?» Mateo said.

«I think of it every time I pass by there.»

«Do you?»

«Of course.»

«Huh. Want to go?»

Tiago smiled, showing his teeth again. «I guess.»

They lay on their backs

on the edge of the roof, end to end so the tops of their heads were almost touching, Mateo's dark waves meeting Tiago's buzz. From above they looked like the propeller of a pinwheel, or a helicopter. They each dropped one leg over the edge, as they always had done, keeping the side of the building against their calves to remind them of the place where relaxing would become falling.

They were up to four helicopters when Tiago raised his hand to point out another one.

«Yup,» Mateo said. He threaded his fingers over his chest

and rubbed the side of the building with his heel.

«Do you do this in Boston,» Tiago said, «with your boy?»

«Count helicopters?»

«Yeah.»

«No.»

«Oh.» There was a smile in Tiago's voice.

Quickly Mateo added, «There aren't any helicopters in Boston.»

«There aren't? How do the rich people get around?»

«They just drive. There's helicopters but they're just news helicopters looking at traffic. And sometimes hospital helicopters. But that's all.»

«That's boring.»

«It's quieter.»

«Oh.» Tiago shifted himself on the ledge and Mateo felt the tops of their heads rub together. «I'm sorry what I said before, I guess,» Tiago said to the sky. «About shanty queens.»

«It's OK. Fletcher and I aren't together anymore, anyway. He dumped me.»

«Oh.» Tiago was quiet a minute. A new helicopter was buzzing somewhere but they couldn't see it yet. «Why you defending him then?»

«I don't know.»

«You love him?»

«I plead the Fifth.»

«Huh?»

«Never mind.» Mateo pointed at some tiny lights in the sky. «There it is.»

«I see,» Tiago said, and he moved just a little so this time their heads rubbed together on purpose.

Three days seemed quick

to bury someone, though it didn't seem hastily done. It was fast as a result of surprise, like a sleeping cat jarred into motion by a shattering plate.

The calling hours and the funeral that immediately followed were a series of disjointed blurs separated by startling interludes of crystal-clear reality.

I don't remember putting on my pants or my suit jacket but, for some reason, I remember putting on my belt, fitting the stiff leather through the loops and then feeling to make sure I hadn't skipped any. And I remember taking off the suit when I realized it's what I was wearing when Cara died. I don't remember driving to the funeral home and I don't remember entering it, but I remember the cold gleam of the casket wood at the front of the narrow, flowery room — the first sight of which made my bowels feel full of bricks. Jamar had wanted cremation but her parents pushed hard for a burial and he relented. And here she was, my Cara. I hadn't wanted to see her, had intended to slip as far back in the room as I could. But once I saw her I couldn't look away.

If you've ever seen on any of those *National Geographic* shows a mother animal, of any species, baffled over a dead baby, you have some idea of what I probably looked like standing at Cara's casket, my fingers bridging the plush inside and the cold wood — wanting, not wanting, to touch her. I'd never been more reminded that people are animals too. Just as confused, just as powerless to reverse this. Everyone wondering at the most basic level, what is *dead*? How is she dead? She looked so much the same. She was wearing lipstick. I'd never get to talk to her again. Her son would never know her.

I skipped the receiving line — Jamar was doing his best to stand up straight but his eyes fixed were with a glaze in the direction of Cara — and retreated up the aisle and slid into a chair near the back of the room.

I watched the door for distractions, for comfort. Everyone I knew who failed to come through it to provide one or the other, I hated. It surprised me. I wouldn't have expected to care so much but I knew, sitting there, scraping my shoes against the dark green carpet and watching the door, that I would later categorize everyone in my life by who showed up to that funeral and who did not.

But some people came. Babette, from work, was the first. She held her purse at her belly and waited in line, stopping beside Cara and spending a moment there — older people who'd done this before seemed to have a routine—then making her way down the receiving line. She spotted me and came to give me a hug.

"Such a pretty girl," she said, shaking her head. "Such a shame. Such a shame. But the baby is OK?"

"The baby's fine."

She nodded.

"It was really nice of you to come," I said.

She put her hands on my cheeks and squeezed my face between her palms. She smelled of spearmint. "How are you doing, sweetie?"

"Fine," I said, and then: "Horrible."

She smiled and cleared her voice. "I don't have any say-so, of course, but you just take as much time as you need, and I'll do what I can at work."

"They've been fine. They gave me the week."

"Good."

She left a minute later and I resumed watching the door.

I missed him come in, but when I looked up Alex was in the receiving line talking to Jamar. Then I felt a hand on my shoulder—Jimmy Perino was standing beside me. He was wearing the same shirt and khakis I had taken him out of four days earlier. Four days? I stood up and he gave me a hug, and I hated myself for wanting to press closer and feel him all against me one more time.

"I came right to the back," he said. "I don't really do— death."

"That's OK."

"I don't like to think about it."

"Yeah."

"So," he said, finally, "I'm real sorry."

"Thank you. Thank you for coming."

"No problem." He looked around. "The flowers are nice. Hey, I haven't seen Mr. Brazil around here anywhere. Are you guys still—?"

"He went to visit his family."

"And left you?" Within a chuckle he disguised the word *asshole*.

"He didn't know. About her."

"Double asshole," he said, with no disguise this time. "So how'd she die?"

"Childbirth."

"Does that still happen?"

I wanted to say, *Well she's in a fucking box so apparently it does*, but instead I just said, "I guess."

"She passed away on Valentine's?"

"Early the day after."

"Oh," Jimmy said. "After our...?"

"Yeah."

"At least something good happened that day, though, right?" He nudged my arm. "Was that why you snuck off? I woke up hoping for another round but you were gone."

"I guess. It was early. So." I saw Mike come through the door, look around uncomfortably and slink into line. He was wearing a tie.

"That reminds me," Jimmy said, "I think you have one of my socks."

"Oh. Yeah. Sorry."

He went on, grinning, "I know this really isn't the right place to say this—"

"Then don't fucking say it. Excuse me."

I pushed forward the chair in front of me and slipped out of my row. Walking down the aisle and against the flow of the receiving line, I squeezed Alex's arm when I passed him on my way to the door. Mike had let some of Cara's cousins cut in front of him and he was farther away from the casket now than when he'd started. His face was white and I walked into him and hugged him, bumping him backward into a piano.

"Fletcher," he said, "I don't know if I can look—"

"You don't have to. Please, will you get me out of here?"

They counted fourteen helicopters

and then they went back to Tiago's apartment. It had pale green walls, small windows, and a mattress on the floor. They did sleep together that night, Mateo and Tiago—and it wasn't the fling I'd like to imagine it was. It was the sex of old boyfriends falling back into a comfortable habit made of all the best things. It was, I think, sex fueled by two of my favorite words: *razbliuto*, the sentimental feeling you have for someone you once loved but don't anymore, and *saudade*, a deep longing for the return of something lost. One word for each boy.

As the sun came up Mateo idly traced with a painted finger the perimeter of the plug in Tiago's left earlobe. He stared up at a twist of bare wires sticking out of the ceiling plaster, where a light fixture once existed. The previous tenant of Tiago's little apartment must have taken it with him when he left.

«I have to go to work,» Tiago said finally, looking at his phone—it was one of the fancy ones—before dropping it into the folds of the sheet. «Your cousin's waiting for me.»

«I know.»

Tiago got up and kicked his long caramel legs back into his underwear. He wore thin black leather bands on both wrists and one around one ankle—the missing one was the one that had long been on Mateo's. He pulled on a t-shirt with a rip under one armpit.

After flinging a purple towel over his shoulder he left the apartment. The towel was wet when he came back a few minutes later. Mateo asked where he'd gone.

«My showerhead sparks like a motherfucker so this guy down the hall lets me use his.» He spread the towel over the back of a folding chair to dry, then took his yellow work t-shirt off the arm of the same chair, pulled it on. «You'll have to get moving. Or I could just give you my key?»

«That's OK.»

«We should do this again, though.»

«I'm not in SP for long,» Mateo said, sitting up.

Tiago handed Mateo his shorts and sat down on the mattress. His bare knees came up high in front of him. «But we'll do this again.» He started to get up and then looked back at Mateo. «You know, we both know Vinicius. And we know how he is. I don't know exactly what he's told you, but I'm guessing he's painted you a picture of me where I've just *spent my life* crying over Mateo Vinicius Armstrong Amaral. That I'd slash my wrists and bleed all over SP if that's what it took to get you back in my life. We both know Vinicius. So I hope you know all that's not true. But I never really stopped loving you. OK? I know you're not home long enough for me to waste any time acting like I don't. It's exhausting being nasty and so much easier to admit to feeling sad. So I love you. And I think last night was pretty great, the two of us. I've hoped for it for a long time. Since the last time. You know who I am. I'm your Tiaginho. I'm not going to slit my wrists. I get by; it's what I do. So listen: It's not about me when I say I don't know what the fuck you're doing up there. Why you keep going back there. What you have there that's so great. In my guts I know someday you're going to be up there and suddenly realize that everything that makes you you is here in SP. It'd be a lot easier if you would just realize it now. If there's any way I can get you to stay a little longer— If there's anything I can give you that would make you want to stay here where you belong, I hope you'll let me know.»

Mateo looked at Tiago's crooked white teeth and the beads of water that dotted his throat. Then his green eyes met Tiago's dark brown ones. He crawled across the mattress and sat on the edge. «You always did give a good speech,» he said.

«Is that all you have to say?»

He pressed his chin against Tiago's shoulder. «Remember the night we painted at your heaven spot? All that rope and all that patience. Never saw anyone happier than you were when I pulled you back up with your empty can. What I want is a place that makes me that happy. The craziest, awesomest place to write, ever. I'm looking for my heaven spot. Know any?»

Tiago frowned and said, «I'll see what I can do.» He didn't say what he was really thinking: that the reason he'd been so happy that night wasn't because he'd just sprayed paint on a building. It'd been because the person holding him up, holding his life in his hands, was Mateo. «Now I need to go,» Tiago said. «Vini's waiting.»

Outside Tiago's building Vinicius

was standing near the busy street watching a vendor selling kitchen knives from a push-cart. There were only two or three others observing the demonstration but the salesman was wearing a tiny microphone attached to a crackling speaker. First he cut paper into thin strips, and by the time he'd gone through various vegetables and graduated to slicing a pane of glass as though it were cheese, Vinicius was gawking at Mateo as he and Tiago emerged from the building.

"Oi, primo," Mateo said.

«Didn't expect to see you here together,» Vinicius said. «You guys look like you didn't sleep much. Doing some smooching?»

«We were hanging out,» Mateo said. «You didn't notice the bitch pad was empty last night?»

«I was at Aline's.» He grinned.

Tiago said, «Dedinhos, don't you recognize his famous shirt? Always good for a second day, he says. Let's go, blondie, people need new phones.»

Tiago tossed his keys in the air and caught them before Vini could. He put his arm around Vini's shoulders and shot a smile back at Mateo as they walked down the street toward Tiago's armored car. Mateo made his way back to Rua Giacomo and crawled into the hammock on his back patio.

They slept together three times,

according to Tiago. The next night after this, and the night before Mateo left. And perhaps one other time that Tiago wanted to keep for himself.

Jamar called me the day

after Cara's funeral and thanked me for going. He sounded stressed but told me he was doing OK. I wondered if he really was. I wondered how much time would have to pass before I could really be sure. When I could decide that he was not only getting through the day but getting through his life. Weeks? Months? Years?

"How's the baby?" I said, gritting my teeth to say it. I wanted to be the first to mention him, though. I'd been working hard on thinking of him as a baby and not as the monster who killed Cara.

"Caleb's OK," Jamar said. "He sleeps a lot. I've been feeding him with the bottle. My mother taught me how to change his diapers. He doesn't cry as much as I expected. I should've learned all this stuff earlier. I guess I figured Cara would just know, or something, and she'd teach me what to do." He paused. "He misses his mom."

"I miss his mom too." I took a deep breath and blinked fast.

"Have you been staying at the apartment? I hope Robbie and my dad didn't leave too much of a mess. Thanks for letting them in, by the way."

"It's fine. Don't worry about it. Yeah, I've been staying here."

"I wondered if you would've been staying at Mateo's."

"He and I aren't really — involved anymore."

"Oh. I'm sorry, Bradford. I wondered, when I didn't see him at the funeral."

"He's in Brazil. I talked to his landlady."

"Oh. Brazil?" There was a mechanical, uninterested quality to it I would've resented under other circumstances, but I knew Jamar had bigger things to worry about than my failed relationships.

"So do you think you'll be coming back here?" I said. "I mean like ever? Will you live here at the apartment again?"

"I hope so. I want to. I want to come back soon, actually."

"Really?"

"I don't want you to have to move out. Or replace me."

"I could swing the rent for a few months by myself. If you need time."

"No. My parents have been awesome, but — If I stay too long I'll never leave. I want to leave before I get into a routine here. Or get too dependent. Does that make sense? And I want to be at Cara's house. I want Caleb to be around her things. Is that morbid?"

"No. It'll be good to have you back."

"Do you mean that?"

"Jamar, it's so quiet here."

Mateo got up and went

to the living room to poke his finger into the birdcage and found the little food tray that clipped to the inside bars empty. There must be seed around here, he thought, and he found it in the second drawer of the bureau on which the television stood. He unlatched the cage door, careful to block it with this other hand to keep the birds from flying out, and shook some tiny yellow seeds into the tray. The birds peeped in offense, hovering near the top of the cage, and then, when he'd withdrawn the box and closed the door, they flew to the tray, peeping and nodding into the seed.

"Be careful not to let them out," his mother said as she came through the door. She was wearing her white nurse's shoes and purple scrubs. She put her bag on the couch and went in the kitchen. Mateo heard the refrigerator door open.

"I didn't," he said. "Are you home already?"

"My short day," she said, returning to the living room sipping a glass of juice. "They're pretty, no?"

"When did you get them?"

«My last birthday. Your father bought me one.»

«Just one?»

"One, and he just sat there. He didn't sing. And we said, *What good's a bird who doesn't sing?*"

"Heh. He was lonely."

"He *was* lonely. A week later your father came home with a little paper box and said, *Here's the other half.*"

"Did they sing then?"

"You have ears," she said, waving at the cage. «They don't shut up!»

"It's nice."

"It *is* nice. And the weather is nice today too." She finished her juice and was quiet a minute while they watched the birds knock seed out of the tray. Then Sabina said, «Put on your shoes.»

They walked slowly down Rua Giacomo, past the dragons and the flame-maned horses, past Edilson's new smiling motorcycle, past the purple waves and the googly-eyed jaguar, past the dancing woman with the skirt made of jungle, and all the way past the planet Saturn.

"Edilson got big," Mateo said.

"Well, he grew up," Sabina said. "They say he's going with Olive. Do you remember Olive?"

"Sure. Tiago's sister."

"She's *much* too old for him."

"He paints like he's thirty."

"Hm. He may paint like he's thirty but if he's not careful his little ding-dong will make him a papai at sixteen."

"Mom."

She smiled. "Remember when your cousin was with Olive? Aye!"

"He seems pretty happy with Aline."

"For today. We'll see about tomorrow. So many different people to meet in this city and these kids just keep dating each other."

"Heh."

They walked further along the arc of the S that was their neighborhood. A moto-taxi went by, then a scooter. A scrawny yellow dog barked at the scooter. They passed an underwater sunset.

Sabina said, "Vinicius says you have a little bird of your own up in Boston?"

It took him a moment to realize what she meant and when he did he blushed. "Kind of."

"Well that's good," she said, nodding. «Does he make you sing?»

"He did. I showed him everything, all of it. And in the beginning it felt like I was showing him a whole new world or something and he seemed so open to it. But then I don't know what happened. He hurt me pretty bad, right before I came here. Think maybe I've been hurting him longer than that, though."

"Ah." It made her sad to know that he had come home to

get away, and not simply to be home. But then it was a relief, too, to know that when he was hurt he wanted to be near her, still, even though he was a man now.

«It's complicated,» he said.

«Very. Yes.»

"I told him once about how I ended up in the States again. About how you sent me to live at Marjorie's."

"Oh?"

"He was amazed that you could do that, send me to live with someone who caused you such sadness. He was pretty impressed."

"She caused me no sadness. *She* wasn't unfaithful."

"I guess."

She shrugged, moved some hair out of her eyes. "Has it been good for you? To be there?"

"Yes."

"You answer so fast. Then I did the right thing."

"It was a big thing."

"Well you always have to make the best of a bad thing. Could I have left your father? Yes. For a while I wanted to. But I married a man, not an angel. You have to always remember the difference."

Thinking of the difference, and of the strange place in between, he said, "I've seen Tiago."

"Oh?"

"A couple times. He looks good."

"He's always had that in his favor."

"Heh."

"But Tiago has — troubles," she said.

"...What kind of troubles?"

"Well." She shrugged, apparently unwilling to go through the door she'd opened. "They say he goes with — older men. And the men give him things in return."

"They say that, huh? *Who* says that?"

"The kids."

"Vinicius?"

"Olivia, sometimes, when she and Vinicius fight. She says that Vinicius goes off with Tiago and that's what they do. I think — well."

"Tiago does what he has to do. His parents were not like you and Dad when they found out. His parents never even cared enough to put an H in his name and it was downhill from there. Everything he has he's gotten by himself. He's never kept anything from me. I always knew. Always."

"I know." She could see that he was angry and she wanted to touch him, hold him. Instead she said, to change the subject, "Did you see, a while ago, in a magazine they had new pictures of the Moon, of the landing place? Somehow they had a camera in space and you could see, very very tiny," she held up her pinched fingers at the sky and squinted, "the footprints, the flag of America, the piece of the gold spaceship they left behind."

"I didn't see that, no."

She grinned. "I looked for an hour."

And he said, "Do you know some people don't believe humans have ever really been to the Moon? They say it's just a sham, that the landing was filmed on a stage in Arizona or something." He was still feeling angry and he added, "Their evidence is compelling. Sometimes I really wonder."

"I have heard that." She touched her chest, as though newly appalled by the old idea. "I believe because I've seen pictures and read newspapers and because I watched it on the TV when it was happening. But if none of this proof existed I would still believe." They passed a shooting star in blue and purple and a satellite rendered in silver; an old explorer's galleon sailed on the tail of a fiery comet. "I would believe even if there was no evidence. I would believe because it's the most beautiful thing I've ever heard, and so I choose to believe. A man on the Moon. A man on the *Moon*, Mateo. Who can possibly benefit from denying such a beautiful thing?"

He was dreaming, and in

his dream he was a can. A person-size can with legs and arms, and his arms ended in hands that were cans. And he was almost finished painting the world. All the continents were done and the oceans were complete, but one obstacle stood in his way. He stood at the bottom of it, at its base, its shadow falling across his glinting metal body. He felt hopeless.

A jab on his shoulder

woke him. He rubbed the spot and rolled over, tugged up the sheet.

«*Psst*. Primo.»

When he looked up Vinicius was standing over the bitch pad, looking down at him. «What are you doing?»

«Get up.» He nudged Mateo again with his flip-flop.

«Shit, V, I have to travel in the morning. Leave me alone.»

«Get *up*.»

"Fuck off."

Vinicius knew enough English to understand that, and responded accordingly: he seized Mateo's wrist and dragged him off the pad, Mateo's bare back squeaking across the tile.

Tiago's car was waiting outside. They ushered Mateo into the backseat and closed the door. Vinicius went around and got in the passenger side.

«Here,» Tiago said to Mateo, handing back a grease-stained paper bag, «eat these. You'll need some energy soon.»

Mateo took the bag with two fingers, could tell by the smell it was last night's manioc fries.

«Not exactly breakfast, I know,» Tiago said. «It's all I had.»

Mateo said, «Am I being kidnapped?»

Vinicius laughed.

«You guys know I have to be at the airport in the morning, right?»

«We'll see,» Vini said.

The bullet-proof windshield of Tiago's armored car made the clicking streetlights look as though they were under water, as though the Volkswagen were a submarine. The reds were more pink, the greens more lime, and everything, through that glass, had the gauzy glow of an old movie.

Mateo ate the cold fries one by one and didn't ask any more questions until twenty minutes later, when they arrived at the power plant.

«No, primo,» Vini answered with a laugh, «we're not

taking you to the power plant.»

They drove through the parking lot and came out at the back, navigating a pair of bumpy, curving side-roads. From there they continued for a long time down a single-lane dirt access road with the Pinheiros River on one side and two sets of train tracks on the other.

When Tiago stopped the car — when their destination was clear — Mateo stopped chewing, letting the manioc gather in his cheek in a thick paste. Then he carefully swallowed it down as he looked through the bulletproof window up at the Oliveira Bridge.

«We're here!» Vini exclaimed, turning around, clapping the headrest. Tiago looked up in the rearview and grinned.

The main structure of the Oliveira Bridge was a gigantic X, through the bottom triangle part of which ran two highways, one curving above the other as they split in two directions on the far side of the river.

They got out and stood by the hood of the car, looking up at it. Colored lights at the top, and the glowing suspension cables, and the headlights and taillights of cars moving in both directions across it had the effect of making the whole thing look like a quirky alien spaceship. Mateo half expected it to lift into the air and streak across the navy-blue sky.

«Dedinhos,» Tiago whispered, threading his fingers through Mateo's and feeling them squeezed gently back, «I can get you inside.»

Mateo let go and took a lurching step forward. Behind him Vini grinned at Tiago, who put a finger to his lips.

"You can get in?" Mateo said.

Tiago slung his arm around him. With his other hand he dug in his pocket and withdrew a key-card, half the width of a credit card and twice as thick. He held it out and Mateo took it.

«How'd you get this?»

«You asked me to find your heaven spot,» Tiago said casually, though anyone could see he was practically bursting. He took Mateo's hand again. «Let's go in. C'mon, V.»

They walked to the nearest of the structure's two bases,

the first of the surprisingly delicate concrete feet of the X. The highways rumbled like constant thunder high above their heads.

«Didn't know there was an entrance at the bottom,» Mateo said.

They noticed how he seemed to inspect the gray door, bumping the heel of his hand against it and examining the control pad before sliding the key through.

When the door beeped and let them in Vini clapped Tiago's shoulder and mouthed: *We've got him.*

They noticed how he memorized the large room beyond the door—part vestibule, part storage shed for highway equipment. He walked around the perimeter and stood in the middle and looked up at the harsh fluorescent light and then down at the concrete floor, as if orienting the place in his mind.

They noticed how carefully he proceeded to the back of the vestibule, as if counting the paces to the first steps of the metal staircase. They noticed how he thumped his sneaker against it before taking the first step.

Delighted, they thought he was savoring it.

He was learning it.

Mateo and Vini slid open

the heavy door on its dusty steel tracks, while Tiago kept one hand firmly through each of their belts in case a rush of wind tried to suck them out. But it didn't, and when they had the door slid to an opening of about a meter, they stopped, and stood, and stared.

They could see the sparkling Pinheiros in the first light of dawn, and the buildings and hotels beyond it, and on the outskirts the favelas huddling against the city. The slums had a discordant beauty in this light.

«Wow,» whispered Tiago.

«Wow,» said Vinicius.

«It is pretty,» Mateo admitted.

«I wanted to give this to you, Dedinhos,» Tiago said, lacing his fingers through Mateo's hair. «You asked me to find you a heaven spot and I don't know how I'd ever do better than this.»

«Thank you.»

The moist river air made their faces glisten, and through their own silence they could hear the sounds of highway traffic many meters below.

«Fuck!» Vinicius slapped the door. «We forgot the paint!»

«How could we have *forgotten?*» Tiago exclaimed. But of course they had carefully planned to forget. If they'd remembered they wouldn't have been able to tell Mateo, as Tiago told him now, «We can come back another night. Now that we have the key. We'll do this again. You should stay in São Paulo.»

"Stay," Vinicius told him in English. «You could be a king here, primo. This could be your castle. You have the key now!»

Mateo smiled. He looked at their faces, so excited, and out at the city, and down at his fingers holding the key. He shook his head. «I couldn't be king in SP,» he said. «It's too big, guys. There's too many others.»

«A knight, then,» Vini said. «Stay. Knight can be enough, right? We're all here. It's so much more *fun* when you're here.»

«Up there, I'm king. I will be. You guys, I love you but I have to go back. I love you so much but I have to go back.»

He looked at Tiago and Vini and shrugged, and because he could find nothing else to say he looked out at the vast megacity again. When he turned around he saw that Vini—sincere, gentle Vini, master strategist Vini—was wiping tears out of his eyes.

«Awh shit, V, come here,» Mateo said, and he pulled his cousin into his arms and felt Vini's close around him. With his cheek against Vini's blond head he wondered what the fuck he was doing, turning down this gift. His family was here, yes, Vinicius was right about that. And despite what he'd said he knew he could probably be a king here, too—he was good enough; in time he could be good enough. But he wanted to go back, felt compelled to go back. Standing at the top of this bridge that was so like the Zakim, he was now itching to be back.

He stood still, looking out at the city. He took a deep breath. He gripped the door in his painty fingers and started sliding it closed. Vini helped him. When they turned around they found that Tiago had already started back down the stairs.

For the past few days Jamar

had been acting as though my very existence offended him. For the past week, actually — almost the entire time he'd been back. He seemed so happy at first, a fragile happy but happy nonetheless, carrying the squishy new baby into the apartment. I'd made and taped to the living room window an IT'S A BOY sign that Jamar went gaga for, even though it was practically impossible to see from the street. "That's awesome," he kept whispering as we stared at the backward letters through the translucent paper. "It's a boy."

Maybe it was because the boy cried his entire first night at the apartment. Maybe it was because all our life-filled things made Cara's seem more dead — our wet toothbrushes beside her dry one; a finished *Metro* crossword beside the one she left forever incomplete. Maybe he was still angry, as I was, that he'd allowed Cara's mother to talk him into putting her in the ground. Whatever it was, on his second day back he turned on me, subtly at first — that night he didn't say goodnight — and then more alarmingly. Several times I noticed him move Caleb out of a room I was in, into a room I wasn't in — as though he didn't want me near his son.

So I was surprised to find him sitting at my desk when I returned to my room after showering off a date with Mike. He was holding a few sheets of manuscript that he put back in the box on my desk. He looked like he had an agenda.

I secured the towel around my waist. "I'd prefer you didn't read that."

"Oh. Sorry. Been out boning college kids again?" In his voice was both sarcasm and accusation.

"Yeah, actually. And I really made him *squeal*." I pulled on a sweatshirt even though my back was still wet. I started to move toward the socks on the floor but they were too close to him and I abandoned them. Wasn't like I needed them, anyway—he insisted on keeping the thermostat at 73, for the baby. Instead I walked around to the other side of the bed. "Don't turn around," I told him. I exchanged the towel for underwear and pants. Then I told him I was going to make some oatmeal. A moment later he followed me out of my room and joined me in the kitchen, his hands in the pockets of his khakis.

"You need to grow up," he said.

"Jamar, I'm not sure what it is, but you've been on my case for days and frankly I'm getting a little fucking sick of it. What were you doing in my room, anyway?"

"I want to ask you something."

"Oh, ask away. Just ask me to move out and be done with it."

"Do you think I'm a good man?" he said. I looked at him, startled. He was unshaven and his eyes were dark. I should've felt a pang of guilt—he was going through a *Porcupine City* of his own and I had failed to stage an intervention—but instead I just felt pissed that the kid was taking such a toll on Jamar's looks.

"A man? Well I assume you have a penis. I mean, you made Caleb."

"Fucking-hell, Bradford, I'm being serious."

I put aside the oatmeal, dragged out a chair across from him and sat down, knocked the heel of my palm against the underside of my chin, looking terribly attentive.

"A good man as opposed to what, Jamar? A good laaady?"

He didn't tell me to go fuck myself and that made me worry I'd crossed a line.

"A dude. A guy. A bro," he said. "I don't want to just be a guy, but that's all I've been since I was a kid. I'm not even comfortable saying the word *man*."

I sighed. "I guess I've never thought about a difference."

"There's a difference," he said. "There's a difference."

"Both have dicks."

Jamar shook his head. "You're a guy."

"Fuck you."

"*Fuck you*, you say. So you know it's better to be a man than a guy. Because being a man is the harder thing to be. ...And I'm asking you." He shook his head.

"Maybe I'm not the one to ask. Maybe it takes one to know one."

"Maybe it does. You don't care about being one?"

"I'm still not clear on what we're even talking about. Do I want to wear a suit and tie to work and kiss my vacuuming, pearls-wearing wife every day when I get home? No, I don't. Sorry. Sorry!"

"That's not what it's about."

"Then what *is* it about, Professor Andrews? Educate me."

"It's about— What have you done since college?"

"What do you mean, what have I done?"

"You sit at a job you don't like. You've been with more guys than I can begin to imagine. You dumped the only good one just so you could fellate some loser."

"I didn't fellate him, actually, I tongued his asshole."

"Oh, awesome."

I looked down at the floor while I gathered myself. "I published a book, which you seem to have left out of your glowing biography."

"And who pushed you to get it published?"

"Cara. So? That makes it less valuable? That someone cared enough to encourage me?"

Her name seemed to have startled him and he looked off-balance now. "I don't know," he said. "No, it doesn't. I'm sorry."

"And what the fuck business is it of yours how many guys I've been with anyway, Jamar?"

He pressed his face in his hands. "Fuck fuck fuck." He sighed, and I knew the lead-up was done and now it was going to come out, whatever it was. And it did. He looked directly at me and said: "I think I hate you."

I hadn't known what to expect from this but it wasn't that. It certainly wasn't that. "Uh. Come again?"

He didn't say anything. He looked down at his hands.

"So Jamar, you hate me now? Care to elaborate on that or

anything? I think I've been pretty fucking accommodating of your little *project* in there since you've been back." I looked at him for what felt like a long time and when he didn't respond I pushed back the chair and got up. "Happy Saturday night to you too, shithead." I'd never called him anything like that before and it made my stomach turn. I tried to pour some sugar into the bowl of dry oatmeal but the little door was sealed shut because no matter how many times I told him Jamar would not stop holding the sugar container above his steaming coffee thereby moistening the sugar and turning it into cement on the hinge of the little sugar-door. I unscrewed the cover and dumped on way too much. Sugar dust caught in my lungs and I coughed. "Mother*fucker*."

Jamar said, "Caleb is yours."

I turned and the sugar top clattered into the sink, stainless steel on stainless steel. My teeth rang. "Fine, Jamar, fine. I'll babysit your kid all night if it'll get you out of my fucking hair."

"Caleb is your boy."

I put down the sugar before it had a chance to slip out of my hands. "If you're trying to get a smile out of me you'll have to try harder."

He looked at me and his eyes were red and full of tears. "Please don't make me say it again, man. It just about killed me to say it once." He crossed his arms on the table and rested his chin on his wrists.

"Jamar— *What*? What are you talking about? I don't know what you're talking about. You think I'm his father? You think I had an affair with Cara? I'm a fag, Jamar, for fuck's sake! I don't sleep with women."

"Bradford," he said, "that's the only reason you're still standing."

It chilled me and I laughed, a laugh that sounded to my own ears desperate and maniacal. "Well, I would've thought you knew about this by now—but you kind of have to sleep with a girl to get one pregnant."

"No. You don't." And then he said it again: "You don't. Not if they love you enough." He got up and went in the bedroom he and his wife had shared. I stood in the kitchen, oatmeal forgotten — I was shivering. Goosebumps covered my arms but my face felt hot. He came out with a notebook, one of Cara's journals. He threw it down on the table — it slid and stopped against her unfinished puzzle. "June fifteenth. I don't want to be here when you read it."

"Are you — ?"

"I'll take him out."

Through the living room window

I watched Jamar's car drive away with Caleb hastily stuffed into a snowsuit and packed in a car-seat in the back. I paced around the apartment wracking my brain, trying to figure out what that journal might say that would give Jamar the ridiculous idea that Caleb was mine. I didn't want any more surprises tonight. Cara and I had kissed exactly twice — once theatrically on a Halloween and that other time when we were stoned. And I'd once accidentally walked in on her in the bathroom and seen her nude from the waist up. But we certainly had never had sex. Caleb certainly could not be mine. When I'd assured myself that this was all a laughable misunderstanding I picked up the journal and flipped to the fifteenth of June.

I did something real

gross last night — I can barely even write it down — but at the same time I'm excited to write it down because that makes it real. Fletcher and I smoked-up last night. Then he went to write. Then he went into the bathroom. Then I cleaned up around the apartment and then I went into the bathroom after he'd gone to bed. I was still a little stoned, feeling good. I was peeing and I glanced down at the trash which I'd already emptied for trash day and saw, sitting there all alonely in the can, what was obviously a Kleenex of his Fletcher's cum. I don't even know what made me do it. OK, I know what made me do it. Because it was there, because I was there, because there was no one to know. Because he is what he is to me. It was still warm, I could feel the heat through the tissue. I held it and felt silly and then felt not silly. I was there to pee and now peeing was the farthest thing from my mind. It was like a little bit of Fletcher, a souvenir of a togetherness that will never be. And you'd have done it too, if you were there and if it was there. If you adored Fletcher like I do. Because in the moment it was close enough to the real thing, and it was exactly how the right-afterward of the real thing would've been. Not like being with him but exactly like having been *with him (he would love the nuance of those tenses). But I feel bad, too. Not for Fletcher — his cum has been pretty much everywhere. So I don't think he'd mind. But bad for Jamar, who I love. He'll never have to know. This is mine. This is make-believe.*

I was shivering so much

the flapping notebook fell from my hands. It hit the linoleum and although it closed it couldn't take back what I had read in her swirly handwriting.

It felt as though she had reached through my belly button and was squeezing my stomach, digging her fingernails in. My eyes were running. My entire life felt suddenly veiled in uncertainty and I had no idea what was going to happen. I leaned forward, rested my forehead against the edge of the kitchen table. I was barely out of the chair making for the bathroom when I threw up all over the linoleum.

Putting the floor cleaner back under the sink, my eyes still wet, I saw a can of Lysol and my mind leapt to paint. I remembered the cans Mateo left under my fish tank last summer.

I went in my room and picked up the cans, two cans. Green and blue. Popped the cap off the green and shot a blast into my palm. It looked good still. I squeezed my hand into a fist and the paint pushed out over my lifelines.

I grabbed a backpack out of my closet and dropped the cans inside. Yanked on a hat. Rummaged in my closet for fingerless gloves.

Where was Jamar? When was he coming back? Was Caleb OK? For the first time ever I wondered if Caleb was OK. All I knew was that I didn't want to be here when Jamar came back.

I pulled the strings of my hoodie tight and stumbled down

the stairs. The night was cold. I was on the sidewalk. Jamar's car was gone. I wondered where to go. Where to start. What to write.

I squeezed the can.

The frigid metal numbed my fingers. I held it to my face, soothed my burning cheeks with it. And then, rubbing my finger back and forth over the white valve, remembering its feel, I pointed it at the wall.

Behind me two cabs zoomed by, as if in a chase.

I hadn't yet decided what to write. Or if I could write. Anger boiled from my twisted stomach. What was I even doing here? I was here because of her. Here because of what she had done. And she wasn't even here to have to deal with any of it. Once upon a time Jamar left me a mess with Cara and now Cara had left me a way bigger mess with Jamar. Had she even known? Had she ever even suspected? Would she ever have *told* me? Anger warmed my hands and there was only one thing in the whole world I wanted to write now.

FUCK YOU, CARA. I wrote it huge, each letter three feet tall, using both colors, all of both colors, going over it and over it until they ran out. When I was done, it was there and it was true, as true as any Fact Mateo Amaral had ever written.

I dropped the empty cans on the ground and ran.

I walked the entire Freedom

Trail, which took a couple of hours, and then I grabbed a cab back to the apartment.

Caleb was crying in Jamar's bedroom and I could hear Jamar making cooing noises to try to quiet him down.

I thought about just slipping into my room.

I put my backpack on one of the kitchen chairs. Very slowly washed the paint off my hands in the sink. Took a deep breath while it swirled down the drain. Made myself go into Jamar's room.

"How is he?" I said.

Caleb was wriggling on his back on Jamar's bed, naked

from the waist down. A gnarly scab sat where his belly-button would be. Jamar taped a dirty diaper across itself and put it in the trash. The room smelled like poop.

He looked at my face for a minute. I wondered if he'd thought I would just flee into the city and never come back. "He's OK. He just had some poopy problems— Didn't you, coolguy?" He looked up at me with an ambiguous expression. "You read the journal."

I nodded.

"And then—did you clean? It smelled like Lysol."

"I threw up."

He nodded. "Me too."

He put a fresh diaper on the baby and packed him back into his blue feetie pajamas, set him in the crib at the foot of the bed. I didn't know how Jamar learned how to do all this stuff so fast. I couldn't imagine doing any of this stuff at all.

He stood up and rubbed the small of his back and looked at me hesitantly. "So. Now you know."

"Yeah. Um, Jamar—" I started to tell him I was so sorry for what happened—that was what I was going for, anyway, but I ended up just crying all over the place. And then Caleb was crying. And then Jamar was crying too. And then we were laughing and Caleb was sucking on a pacifier. And finally we were talking, which did not come as easy as crying.

"Were you just reading her journal," I said, "or did you go looking?"

"I went looking. I suspected."

"What made you?"

Jamar laughed, this welcome laugh. "Bradford, have you *seen* Caleb? Kiddo's white!"

"Oh—I guess I just thought he was fair-skinned or something."

"I guess you haven't seen lot of black babies."

I shrugged. "I haven't seen a lot of babies, period."

"I thought at first he might've been, you know, *switched*. In the hospital. But no, they noticed it right away too. They said it was *interesting* but that I shouldn't necessarily worry. Everyone's different, right? But I dug out her journal from early summer, and read through to see if there'd be any, you know, clues. I was pretty scared, man. I had no idea what to expect."

"Yeah."

"I mean, was I going to find she was cheating on me? I know she'd never do that."

"Of course."

"When I saw it was you. That was a whole different can of worms. I mean, I *know* you. What would happen to *me?*"

"What do you mean? Nothing'll happen to you! You think I'd try to take him from you?"

"You think a lot of things, reading something like that. A lot of things go through your mind."

"I wouldn't ever do that."

"He's all I have of her now, Bradford, and I'll never let him go. And I love you, man, but I'll pick him over you every time."

"I know."

"That also means I'll never pawn him off on you."

"Jamar, but I think—"

"So just remember that."

"Jamar—"

"I'm telling you all this because I want to be a good man."

I could see in his face that he was determined never to look back and think of this year as *that year.* And when I realized that I was standing here now for the same reason I moved in with Cara *that year*, I said goodnight without telling him what I was thinking.

I went back the next

night to paint over my piece, to get rid of it, and found it defaced. Most of it was blocked over in white, and new words had been added. FUCK YOU, CARA now read CARA IS MISSED. In the corner of the D was a familiar wiggle of paint, yellow and white. I boiled.

At least he was back.

Before I'd even taken off my jacket Monday morning, I went stomping down the hall, the I.T. department a flashing target on my shit-list. I turned the corner into his cube and my eyes lit like laser beams on the back of his head. The way he was sitting, I knew he was doing the sleeping trick.

I put my hand on his shoulder and spun him away from the desk. His eyes snapped open and his wing-tip shoe knocked against my shin.

"Let me see your hand."

"Hi Fletcher — How are you doing?"

"Show me your hand." I exclaimed it in an office yell through clenched teeth.

"My hand?" He held up his left hand.

"Your other — "

"Fletcher, I don't know what you're — "

I grabbed it and saw that his fingers were yellow.

"I knew it was you. You had no right to touch my stuff, Teo. That was mine. You had no right to change it."

He sighed. "It wasn't true, Fletcher."

"Like hell it wasn't true, it was totally true. You of all people have no idea how true. It was true when I wrote it. I was angry. And what gives you the right to decide what is and is not true? To deface my work? Huh?"

"You used my paint."

"...So? That gives you ownership over everything I do with it?"

"Fletcher, it wasn't true."

"That's for me to decide, not you."

I turned and walked out of the cube. I heard his chair squeak but then Bassett was there and he said:

"Amaral, where have you *been?*"

In the movies and on

TV they always carry a box, a cardboard box that seems to have been designed specifically for clearing out desks and cubes of the laid-off and the fired. Boxes about twenty by sixteen, always coverless so we're allowed to glimpse sad belongings protruding: picture frames, coffee mugs, employee-of-the-month ribbons that scream weakly against the injustice of this. Are these boxes marketed just for this purpose? Do companies keep stacks of them in their supply closets?

When Mateo passed by my cube and said, "Meet me in the parking lot," he was holding no such box, but he was wearing his coat and he had some papers in his hand and the H.R. woman, Allison, was walking beside him, all business.

His car was running so

I opened the passenger door and got in. It was warm in there.

"Teo."

"Fletcher."

"At first I thought it was only *me* you didn't tell you were going away. But then they started asking around."

He shrugged. "You told them?"

"Of course. It'd been days. I didn't want Bassett filing a missing persons. — Why didn't *you* tell them?"

"I forgot?"

"You can't miss ten days of work without telling anyone and expect to just walk in on the eleventh day as though nothing happened."

He smirked and looked at me, slapped his hand against the wheel. "That's *exactly* what Bassett said!"

"It's common sense."

"Well."

"Well what?"

He shrugged. "Doesn't matter now."

We sat quiet for a moment. I looked at my hands, and at Mateo's hooked over the wheel. "I stopped by your house and Marjorie told me you went to SP."

"Yeah."

"Why?"

"Wanted to."

He was acting like a child but he still looked beautiful, I'll give him that. Even fired and miserable he looked beautiful. He had a tan he could not have gotten at this latitude, and new short black scruff on his chin made his eyes all the brighter.

"Was it good to be home?"

"Boston's my home. But it was good to be there. I left right after I left—the hotel. Valentine's night."

"I stayed."

He nodded. "So. Everything you hoped for and more?"

"It was fine. You were right—he was like all the others. Most of the others."

I expected him to ask if Jimmy was better than him, and maybe that's actually what he said when he said, "Was it worth it?"

I looked out the window. "To be honest I haven't thought about it much. Kind of got overshadowed, you know?"

"Yeah. I'm really sorry," he said, "about Cara. Marjorie told me."

I shrugged. He knew and still hadn't tried to contact me?

"I feel very bad about it," he went on, "and I don't really even know what to say."

"It was hard. It's going to be hard for a long time."

"How's Jamar?"

"Dealing."

"And the baby?"

"Caleb. He's OK. Someday he'll be sad but right now he's a baby. So."

"Caleb. Like Superman? Kal-El. Kal-elb. Not really, I guess. Close."

Despite everything I found myself smiling. My anger at him had softened with his firing. The firing had been his punishment for leaving and I was satisfied with that for now.

"How did you know the Cara piece was mine?"

"I knew," he said. "But I could tell by the comma. It was the graffiti of an editor. Not a lot of us bother with commas."

I smiled. "Yeah. Probably not."

He was looking away out the window and I used that chance to really look at him, and began to remember us, shades of our times in this car. "So where are we now, Mateo?"

Tonelessly he said, "At the place of my former employment, Fletcher."

"I mean where are *we*?"

He sighed. He looked out the window, which had fogged,

and he wiped his hand across it. "I think we made our choices on Valentine's. The unstoppable force met the unmovable object."

"But I think we—"

"I just got fired. OK? Another time."

"Yeah." I reached for the door handle. "That's fine."

Through the fogged window he watched me cross the lot and go back in the building. He cranked up the defroster and put the car in drive.

He felt a certain relief, a knee-jerk relief that never had to consider consequences. *You don't have to go to work anymore!* this relief told him. *You can paint 24/7. You haven't a care in the world.*

The sky was overcast and while he was driving a few snowflakes whisked across the windshield, but after five minutes they stopped. Then they started again and went for ten. It was hot chocolate weather, and he went through the drive-thru of a Dunkin Donuts to get one.

I thought maybe he'd call

me that night, but he didn't. Instead he laced up his painty shoes, pulled a wool hat down to his eyebrows (he always felt colder in Boston after being in SP) and started down the dark staircase of Marjorie's sleeping house.

He'd already entered the kitchen when he saw her sitting at the table, pressing a puzzle piece into its place, pressing hard and then abandoning it in search of one with a better fit. An ashtray sat amidst the scattered cardboard shapes; a wispy column of smoke rose from it and orbited the carnival-glass lamp hanging over the table.

"Marjorie—" His sneakers squeaked on the linoleum. "You surprised me."

"Sorry." She waved some of the smoke away from the ashtray and clasped her hands on the table. Then she looked him over. "Haven't seen you around much lately, stranger."

"Yeah. Sorry." He put his hands in his pockets. She asked him how his trip had been and he told her, "It was nice. Just needed to get away for a bit."

She took the cigarette from the tray and put it to her lips. "Happens to the best of us. Lots of comings and goings around here lately."

"When does Phoebe — ?"

"Tomorrow," she said. "My god, *tomorrow*."

"Guess I lost track...."

"It snuck up on all of us. Funny, we waited in line for years to get her into that place and now that it's here — *Psshh*."

"That why you're still awake?"

She smiled. "I'm so afraid, Mateo!"

He could tell she was serious but the funny way she bugged her eyes gave him permission to smirk. He walked closer to the table.

"Of what?"

"All kinds of things. Am I doing the right thing? Is she going to be happy? Am I going to be happy? It's been just the two of us — three of us for so long."

"You said she's loved all her visits there."

"Oh she *loves* it. And that's another fear. If she's happy there, will she forget me?"

"She's not going to forget you."

"I know she's not. But I'm a mother and I worry! What can I do?"

She took a big drag on the cigarette and put it down and rifled through the puzzle pieces. She picked one up and pressed it but it didn't fit and she flicked it aside.

"Well — "

"I'm going to sell the house," she said. She crossed her arms and leaned forward. The corner of her mouth pulled up in what would've been a smile if there'd been something in her eyes to match. Instead it was more of an invitation for him to chew that over.

"You're — Really?"

"Mm. I won't need this whole place with Phoebe gone. Too big. Too much to take care of. It needs a new roof, you know that better than anyone. I don't want to bother. You understand, I hope."

"Oh. When?"

"Not until after she's settled. Spring."

"OK." He hadn't told her he lost his job at Cook and now he knew he would keep it to himself.

"I'm just telling you now. So you have some time."

"OK."

"Don't worry," she said, touching his hand gently, then lifting it by the thumb to search beneath his palm for puzzle pieces. "You'll find another place. Get a roommate. Or shack up with that boyfriend of yours." She reached out and rubbed his arm through his sweatshirt — her mention of me had raised goosebumps on his skin. "Are you warm enough in this? When you go out?"

"When I go — out?"

"To paint."

"To paint?"

"Oh don't look so surprised." She tapped the cigarette on the rim of the ashtray, knocking free a tiny avalanche of ash. "And don't look so worried, for Pete's sake, Mateo."

He looked at her quizzically. "How?"

She looked back at him. She understood that he really wanted it to be a secret, so she left out the point about so much of his laundry being spattered in spraypaint. She left out all the nights she'd heard him or seen him creeping out of the house. She ignored his hands.

"A long time ago your mother told me about your graffiti," she said, "and once something like that gets into a person I guess it doesn't ever get out of him. Plus, I'm an art teacher. I sensed it. Magic."

He smiled.

"But I understand that it can be a kind of secret thing. Since you've never mentioned it, I haven't either. But I've kept my eye out. And I *think* I know which ones you do, but I've never been sure. The ones that are everywhere. The beautiful ones. The words. Am I right?"

"The Facts?"

She leaned forward. "Is that what you call them?" Her breath moved the smoke.

"That's what Fletcher calls them. What makes you think

those are mine?"

"Oh, because there's so much Brazilian influence in them. It's more, I don't know, *grand* than the dumb tags you see around here. It's more than just tags. Tags are about the person doing the tagging. They say, *I was here. This is me. I exist. Pay attention to me.* Yours are about the reader and writer coming together. Yours are about *community.* Typical of what you see on a lot of streets in cities in Brazil. Hey, come on, don't look so surprised!"

He was blushing beneath the yellow kitchen light. This felt more like coming out than coming out ever had.

"At first I set your rent so low as a favor to your mother. God knows I owed her. But I've long since thought of it as my way of quietly patronizing the arts. My civic duty! They're really beautiful, Mateo. I can't say I've ever seen one that didn't make me think or make me smile. And make me glad we've had this little arrangement over the years. You've made me feel like a benefactress."

He looked at the smoke and the puzzle pieces and after a moment he said, "They wanted me to stay. In SP."

She looked at him. "Your family?"

"My cousin. And my friend."

"Well, that's something to think about, definitely. You can decide what you want to do now. Maybe it's good timing, with the house. But whatever you decide, I'm thankful, Mateo, that what you do, you've done in a place where I've been lucky enough to see it."

"That's nice of you."

"Pish posh." She picked up her cigarette but it was almost burned down to the filter. "Go, go. And be careful." She took a quick puff before it went out.

PART
FIVE

Small Steps, Giant Leaps

March came in like a

lamb that year, and then had second thoughts. The sky had a big pile of snow in reserve and dumped it down all at once mid-month, its last chance to make up for the warm winter. We knew a big one was coming — the *Globe* called it THE IDES OF MARCH — and Jamar took Caleb to his parents' house out of fear that we'd lose electricity during the storm. We didn't, but the drifts on the sidewalk made it practically impossible to leave, so I sat in the apartment wrapped in blankets by myself — reading, writing, but mostly thinking about Cara. Everything gets a little more supernatural in a blizzard — the way the lights flicker and the TV goes in and out, the way the snow climbs high against the windows and muffles the street sounds. During the blizzard it was even easier than usual to imagine her shuffling groceries in the kitchen or camped out at the end of the couch with her journal.

Her journal. I only ever read one page in that multi-notebook, multi-year journal of hers: the entry of June fifteenth. What she wrote had been the truth as she'd known it, but her facts were wrong. I was sure of that by now. There was never a eureka moment inside my head, no lightbulb ever hovered over it — it was more like the slow and careful excavation of memories to back up a theory I'd felt from the start. It was a terribly lonely realization, one that held no obvious place for me. The windows rattled and I wished I'd gone with Jamar and Caleb, as he'd invited me to do.

I called Mike, just to talk, but he was so deep in a raid he hadn't even realized it was snowing.

I called Mateo, even though we hadn't spoken since the day he got fired. I do things in blizzards I wouldn't do otherwise. There were things he would have to be told, sooner or later.

"If you happen to be in my neighborhood," I told either him or his voicemail (the connection was so poor I couldn't be sure), "you should stop by." It cut out before there was any reply. I didn't call back to make sure he heard.

A couple of hours later, though, when I was halfway through watching *Wonder Boys*, he walked through my door. I would say that he waltzed, were he not so loaded down in winter gear; it had that nonchalance. The nonchalance annoyed me. It had taken me a lot of effort to make the call and apparently none for him to show up. I paused the movie and stood up.

He was wearing one of those ski masks bankrobbers wear (if not for the unmistakable eyes I probably would've reached for a weapon); it glistened with snow and a tuft of hair stuck out through one of the eyeholes like an overgrown eyebrow. He pulled off the fingerless gloves I'd given him for Christmas and dropped them on the floor. Snow skittered like diamonds across the wood and commenced turning into dozens of little puddles. He pulled off the mask. His hair stood up big and staticky for a second before gravity weighed it back down. His cheeks had a week's worth of beard that mixed into the scruff on his chin, and darkness cradled his eyes.

I asked if he was all right.

"Sure," he said, looking at me curiously. "What do you mean? I got your call, thought I'd come by and say hello."

"Oh. Yeah. I wasn't sure it went through."

He started unzipping his jacket and I noticed his fingers. They were covered in layers of paint and the knuckles and backs of his hands were dry and cracked. I couldn't tell whether the cranberry-colored grooves in the chapped places were paint or blood.

When he had everything off—the jacket, the snow pants, a sweatshirt—he was standing in my living room in a gray waffle shirt and white long-johns—underwear—and I wasn't sure what to do with that. I could see the shape of his penis through the thin fabric. It seemed too familiar for what I thought we'd become. I felt turned-off in an uncomfortable way.

"Have you been painting during the day?" I asked.

"Yeah. Blizzard makes a good disguise."

"But how can you run, with these drifts?"

"How can they chase?"

I looked at his face and hands again. "But the blizzard started yesterday. You look like you've been out longer than that."

"I have. There's lots to do."

"I guess so. I thought you only painted at night so you wouldn't get caught?"

"Huh? Oh. No. Only painted at night because I had to work during the day. But now that I'm unemployed, no holds barred."

I didn't find that comforting. There was something in his eyes that was making me nervous.

"Do you want something to eat?"

"Nah, I'm OK." He was still standing at the door, a wind-blown vampire waiting to be invited in.

"Some hot chocolate or something, at least?" I wondered why I was offering because in fact I wanted him to put all his gear back on and leave.

He accepted the hot chocolate and came and sat in the kitchen while I boiled water and worked the flimsy plastic scoop into a container of powder. Then we moved to the couch, just touching our tongues to the liquid until it was cool enough to drink. I could smell him—not like at work; it was more intense—mixing oddly with the chocolaty steam.

For a time I thought we were enjoying the quiet, relishing the pressurizing cabin that silence can be for two people who've been apart, but soon I realized he'd dozed off. I took the nearly empty mug off his lap and he woke up. He got up. I thought he was going to the kitchen but then I heard him flop onto my bed.

With the mugs in my hand I went to my room. He was lying face-down on my bed and I could tell from the way the long-johns stretched across his bum that he wasn't wearing underwear. I looked away.

"Mateo, what are you doing?"

"I'm a little tired," he said, rubbing his face into my pillow.

"But you're in my bed." I put the mugs on my desk. "I guess I don't understand what's going on here. You told me the unstoppable force—"

"I just want to sleep. No forces. Come sleep."

I was getting angry enough to show it. "I don't want to sleep with you. You stink. You're dirty. When was the last time you showered?"

"Yesterday," he said, frowning into the pillow. "Uh. Two days ago? I don't know, Fletcher, I've been busy."

I sighed, angry that I wanted him. But it was the old him I wanted. Seeing him in my bed made me remember how it'd felt with him in it when things were good, how it'd been my favorite thirty-square-feet in the universe. Now it was just growing sour beneath him.

"Fine," I said. "Sleep here. But you have to shower first. And there's razors under the sink."

Without a word he got up and walked past me and I didn't know what to do. I wanted to help take off his clothes. I wanted to shampoo his hair and rinse it with water from a cup. The bathroom door closed between us and I just listened to the water run. One thing was clear: I wouldn't be telling him anything about Caleb tonight.

I lay on my side on the side of the bed, thinking, watching the fish swim around their simple, well-lit world.

The shower ran for a long time and then the sink went on and off, on and off. Then he came back to my room and walked around the bed and sat down on the floor, Indian style, so he was face-to-face with me. He was wearing only a towel wrapped around his waist and his tattoos popped against the skin of his arms and his damp hair was pushed back behind his ears. He'd shaved and his smooth cheeks glowed tropical blue in the fish-tank light.

"I don't want you to be worried about me," he said.

I rolled onto my back to get away from his eyes. "How can I not be? You seem like you're—" I wanted to say *crazy*. I meant *crazy*. "You seem like you're getting way too deep into this."

"It's just what I do," he said gently. "It's just what happens. Don't be worried." He reached up and took my hand. "Do you know that between Cook and the job I had before that, I didn't work for four months? I take these opportunities to do what I really love and then when another opportunity comes along, I pull out of it and get back to normal. Don't be worried."

"I don't like seeing you looking like a—homeless man."

"Awh Fletcher. Come on. Come on now. No one's homeless." He took my hand that he was holding and touched it against his cheek. "See? All smooth." He stood up and climbed over me and lay down on the other side of the bed. I scooted over to give him room, but not too much—I wanted to be close. He smelled like soap now, and shaving cream and Listerine. "You told me once, that when you were writing *Porcupine City* you got so obsessed with it that you forgot about everything else in your life. You told me Jamar actually tried to stage some kind of intervention because you were ignoring your friends!"

"Yeah."

"Well see? We're just the same, you and me—that's all."

I fell asleep in my clothes with my face against his hair and my hand locked tight in his against his belly, but when I woke up at 5:00 a.m. the towel he had slept in was folded neatly on my desk chair and there was no other sign that he'd been there, other than the puddles of snowmelt left by his boots.

The rest of March passed

and I didn't see him even once, although I started noticing a lot more new Facts around the city, which I took to mean he was still at it full time. I also counted two separate articles in the *Globe* — with headlines like VANDALISM ON THE RISE or some shit — noting the increase in graffiti and calling on the mayor's office for some sort of crackdown.

None of the new Facts seemed targeted at me, though, and that hurt. One evening I drove past Marjorie's house, for no other reason than to catch a glimpse of Mateo's car, to feel that feeling I got from being in on his secrets. But the car wasn't there, and near the driveway was a snow-covered sign featuring the face of a grinning realtor. To this sign a second sign had been appended: SALE PENDING.

That sign brought a funny mix of feeling. Funny strange. Mateo's absence — and the further absence the sign portended — made me feel less like I was carrying a secret of my own. But still I worried about him. And I kept my eyes on the walls.

April came and Jamar's family

leave time away from work was drawing to a close. It was something we both were aware of and tip-toed around. On the calendar in our kitchen the date throbbed like a cold-sore. Jamar hadn't quite figured out what he wanted to do with Caleb when he had to go back to work.

"I guess Jamar's mom told him she'd take the kiddo a day or two each week," I told Mike. I lay on his mattress looking at the ceiling a few feet above my face, while he crawled around gathering up our clothes. Mike had given up Warcraft for Lent, and so had been calling me almost every day for the past week, to help fill the void.

"That's nice of her," he said.

"But I'm thinking I want to help Jamar out with him, you know?"

"Do you, though? Have you seen my shirt?"

"I think it went over the railing. But I'm afraid to make

any significant motions toward that because, like, I don't want
Jamar to freak out. I don't want him to think I'm trying to
move in on him. On his kid. Because I fully support the idea
that Caleb is his. That's what the birth certificate says and
that's good enough for me."

"Cara's journal says otherwise."

"Which is why I want to help him out. I want to be there. I
feel some responsibility."

"You didn't ask for the responsibility," Mike said. "You
didn't ask her to do what she did. It was a huge violation, if
you think about it." He gave up sorting our clothes and
dropped back onto the mattress. All he had on was his glasses;
he pushed them up on his nose. "Actually, if you're inclined to
see it a certain way, it was pretty much the biggest violation
one human can commit against another human. Creating a
person's offspring without their consent, even if it was
accidental."

I looked at him. And at the ceiling. "Well I'm not inclined
to see it as a violation."

"No. Of course not. I'm sorry."

"It's OK, I just— I mean, it's not like I'm going to get a lot
of other opportunities, you know?" I slid my hand under him
and squeezed his butt. "As much as I like these."

He grinned.

"I've never really had a family," I went on, "and I don't
think I want one. But if I get all writerly on myself— If I look
at the narrative of my character or whatever, sometimes I
think every single thing I've ever done, since the time I was a
kid, was basically an attempt to get one."

"A family?"

"Whether it was boyfriends, whatever. I moved in with
Cara so fast her head spun."

"Well, maybe here's your chance. But it's quite a
commitment. You can't do it half-assed."

"No."

"As for telling Jamar, you just have to tell him. Something
tells me he'll be glad. He trusts you, or else he wouldn't have
told you about the journal in the first place."

"You're right."

"Of course I'm right. I didn't get to level 85 by being a dumbass."

"Touché."

"Oh Warcraft," he moaned. "Fucking Lent! Why did I *do* that?" He kicked his heels against the mattress. Then he reached out and traced his finger around my groin. "Hey," he said, "what do you think about going again?"

Jamar and I were sitting

on the couch later that night watching Conan and he had his feet up on the coffee table. Caleb was wedged into the nook between his thighs, chilling there in the Jamar-hammock.

"So I was with Mike after work," I told him during a commercial.

"He graduate yet?"

"Soon. Next month. And anyway—and don't laugh—he was giving me some parenting advice."

"Your sex buddy, who can only recently order a beer, was giving you parenting advice?" But he said it with a smirk.

"He's a pretty smart guy. And a pretty cute guy. Really I wonder what he's been doing with me for the past two years."

"You should've gotten together."

"He has another love."

"Don't you all."

I waited a full commercial length before I went on. "He, uh, promised me that when I tell you—*ahem*—that I want to help you take care of Caleb, fifty-fifty, you won't worry that I'm trying to usurp you."

Jamar wiped some drool off Caleb's chin with his thumb and then cleaned his thumb on Caleb's sock. "He told you that, did he?"

"Yeah, he did. Did you just wipe your hands on your kid's clothes?"

"Socks aren't clothes, socks are napkins on your feet."

"Ha!"

"Mike sounds like a pretty smart guy."

"Told you."

"You feel that way, huh? About us going fifty-fifty on this guy?"

"I mean, I don't know anything about raising a kid. You seem to know so much already. But I figure, when he's hungry I can feed him. You know? When he's got shit on him I can clean it off. When he needs to go to the doctor I can drive him there. When he's bored I can wiggle toy animals at him or whatever. I can teach him proper grammar. I can do what needs to be done. And beyond that, maybe the big picture will just take care of itself. Or is that just totally wrong?"

"No, Bradford, I think that sounds about right."

"But, big picture, I'm against using socks as napkins."

He laughed and bumped his head back against the cushion. "Actually, Bradford, I've been thinking a lot about how I want the big picture to be. But I didn't want to say anything until you said something first. And I'm glad you did."

"OK."

He was quiet a minute and then he grabbed the remote and turned the TV volume not down, but up. "OK, I'm just going to come right out and say this." And then he said, "I think we should get married."

"*What?!*"

"Fucking-hell, Bradford, you'll wake him up."

"OK. I get it. You're joking."

"Partly. Only because I'm afraid to be serious."

"I'm confused."

"We share a son. We should be married." His tone was very matter of fact. "It's no more complicated than that."

I stared at him blankly. I had always assumed that when Cara found out she was pregnant, she pushed the idea of marriage. Now I realized it must've been him.

"Jamar, I know you have a conservative streak in you a secret mile wide, but I'm not marrying you."

"It's the biggest commitment I can make to you and I want to make it. As proof."

"Proof of *what?*"

"I don't *know.*" He crossed his arms and looked at Caleb.

"Here's how I want this to go. You're my best friend. You're also the biological father of my son, as admittedly insane in the membrane as that sounds. OK?"

"...OK."

"Here's how I want this to go."

This had taken a turn for the ridiculous and I no longer felt quite so threatened by the M word. It would be like getting hung up on your fear of heights if someone told you he could help you grow wings.

"I have a good job," he said. "I make pretty good money. And there's the life insurance money too. You have kind of a shitty job—no offense—which you don't even like. What you're best at, you can't devote the proper time to. You should be writing. Full time. Do you disagree?"

"Well no, not in theory. But I reserve the right to." I imagined this was what he was like at work, pitching an ad campaign to a skeptical client. All he was missing was some kind of visual aid. Or maybe the visual aid was right here, sleeping in his lap.

"You quit your job," he went on, "I pay the rent, et cetera."

"*Et cetera?*"

"You stay home during the day."

"Jamar!" I laughed. "You want me to be a kept boy?"

"Fuck, Bradford! Christ! What you'll be—what you *can* be—is a stay-at-home dad."

On the face of it that sounded to me much worse than being a kept boy. I started laughing. This definitely had taken a turn for the ridiculous. Flap flap with those new wings.

"Jamar, does a stay-at-home dad go out sleeping with a college boy in the off-hours? Does a stay-at-home dad, from time to time, sneak out with a can of spraypaint and commit random acts of vandalism?"

"You still do that?"

"Sometimes."

"Hmm." But then he did something that made my breath stop and my future, until now so uncertain, smooth out as though he had fixed the rabbit-ears on an old, staticky TV: he slowly raised his shoulders, and with them went his eyebrows and the corner of his mouth; a dark wrinkle appeared in the corner of his eye. It was a gesture that said—reluctantly, but it said: *Why not?*

He patted the couch cushion like a judge calling for order, though I hadn't made any noise and was in fact speechless. "If you'll think about it you'll see it's completely logical."

Still I stared.

"See, during the day, you look after Caleb. You know how much he sleeps. You'll have so much time to work on your books."

"He sleeps a lot *now*. What happens when he's like two and crawling all over the place 24/7?"

"Bradford—" He sighed. It was the first hole.

"Go on," I said, though. "I'm listening."

He regrouped and came slamming back with more enthusiasm than before. "I'm home by 5:30. The evenings will be yours. You can go out and slip it to Mike or whoever as often as you please. You won't have to stay home and write because you'll have done it during the day. And I'll be with Caleb."

"Everything you've suggested," I said, "seems part of its own complete puzzle. I don't see where marriage enters into it."

"The reason we should get—hitched—is so you'll trust me. So you can do this with confidence. It's my promise to you. It's to prove I'm not going anywhere."

"Jamar, I don't think you're going—"

"*And* for purely legal stuff like getting you on my health insurance." He looked at me for a minute, waiting. "Bradford, it could be good. You know it could."

"You sound like you're trying to line up a nanny."

"Bradford—" He looked at me deadly serious, and hurt. "I'm trying to line up a family."

I felt my throat tighten. Something within me fluttered.

"But what happens," I said, "when you find a girl you want to be with? I know that's not something you want to think about now, and it probably won't be for a while, but you're a young guy and it's going to happen eventually. And you're already going to be married to your college roommate slash baby-daddy?"

He sighed. "So we put an expiration date on it."

"How long?"

"I don't know. How long do you think? What would you be looking for?"

"I don't know. Until he starts school?"

He smiled. "Pre-school or kindergarten?"

"When do they start kindergarten? Six?"

"Five, I think."

"Kindergarten, I guess."

"Five years."

"And then what?" I said. "We get divorced?"

"I guess so."

"How do you think that would make him feel?" I said, nodding down at the kid sleeping in Jamar's leg-hammock. "Wouldn't it be as unsettling for him as if we'd really been together? It would require the same explanations and the same reassurances about the family not breaking up. No. We can't make a family with an expiration date on it, Jamar."

"So we eliminate the expiration. We make it permanent."

I flopped against the other arm of the couch and picked up the remote, lowered the volume. I still didn't know why he'd turned it up—perhaps to keep his weird proposal from echoing. I looked at him. He was fixing Caleb's sock.

"You're scared, aren't you, Jamar?"

"I'm not *not* scared."

"You don't want to screw him up."

"No. That's something I definitely don't want to do."

"Neither do I. So. You really think this is the best thing for him?"

He nodded.

"And you think Cara would want this?"

"Don't you?"

We were quiet for a while and then I said, "Let me think on it, huh?"

"Yeah, Bradford. Yeah. Take your time."

I got up and went in my room, closed the door, feeling, for

the first time, guilty about leaving Caleb with Jamar every night.

I took off my clothes and got into bed, but I couldn't fall asleep. The question on my mind was not whether I would marry Jamar—it seemed to me very clear already that I would do that. The question was what to do about Mateo. A story, Mateo and I had both agreed, did not have to be factual to be true. Cara's journal entry told a story, and that story, though unfactual, was true. And the truth of it was this: Cara's love for me resulted in Caleb.

I took a deep breath and closed my eyes.

Boston City Hall is widely

recognized as the ugliest building on planet Earth. It's a massive, labyrinthine structure made entirely of concrete, even the offices and hallways inside. It resembles a cross between an M.C. Escher painting and a parking garage someone slapped local government into. Down into the bowels of this building we descended via narrow escalator—Jamar, Caleb and I—and we got at the end of the line at the Registry Division.

It was a place I never expected to be and Jamar never expected to be again. Three other couples, three opposite-sex pairs, were ahead of us, waiting for marriage licenses.

Jamar was fidgeting. Whenever I looked at him he was looking at Caleb, who squirmed in the kid-pack that hung on Jamar's chest.

"You OK?" I said.

"Yeah."

"If only Cara could see this, huh?"

He smiled.

Before long we were second. The first couple in line, having filled out their paperwork and raised their right hands, smiled big, over-welcoming smiles at us and at the little boy on their way out.

"They want to show they're cool with the—same-sexers," I whispered to Jamar when they'd passed—careful, for his sake, not to call us gay.

"Huh?"

I realized he hadn't even noticed them. "The big smiles? You must get the white people who're overly friendly to show they're not racist, right? Gays get the same thing from people who want to make sure we don't think they're homophobes."

Jamar looked back at the people going up the escalator and then glanced at the window ahead of us. "Oh. Yeah."

"We don't have to do this," I told him.

"I know, Bradford. I want to. I promised."

Still, he was looking ashy. I looked down at his hand, which was cupping Caleb's butt under the kid-pack, and saw it shaking—and I noticed for the first time that he was still wearing his wedding ring, the one Cara had given him beneath the apple tree last September. That was when I knew for sure this shouldn't be done. Since the partnership of Bradford & Andrews would never involve sex or romance or many of the other things that knit a marriage, it would have to depend even more on the things all good partnerships share: loyalty, compassion, the occasional willingness to take a bullet for the other person. I'd been willing to walk up to that window for Jamar—more than willing, I *wanted* to—but I was willing to walk away from it for him too. To be the one to bail.

When the couple in front of us cleared out and there was nothing between us and the clerk with the long, cherry-red nails, I slipped out of line and slunk over to a concrete bench near the bottom of the escalator. Jamar stared at the empty space between him and the window and then turned and followed me. He sat down hard on the bench and sighed.

"I just can't do this, you know?" I told him, just as he was beginning to speak. "I'm sorry, Jamar, but I can't do it. Too many gay people have worked too hard and wanted this too badly for too long for me to come along and marry my roommate for *insurance* benefits."

But he seemed barely to hear me. He was looking at Caleb. "I can't do this either, Bradford," he said. "I thought I could but I can't. I don't ever want to be married again."

"I miss her too." I sat down.

"Damn it," he said, squeezing his hands in his lap. Caleb

was reaching up at his chin but he didn't seem to notice. "I feel like I've already broken my promise to you."

I looked around the big concrete space, trying to get my bearings or at least spot a sign, but this place was not only ugly but poorly labeled too.

"Look, Jamar, there's something else we can do. Something that's way more right for us."

"What?"

"It's called a domestic partnership. Have you heard of it? All it means is that we depend on each other. It's exactly what we're going to have."

The little office was in a different part of the dank labyrinth that is City Hall, but we found it eventually and filled out some paperwork with ceremonious signatures, standing tall, because this had a weight for us both. When we left City Hall we left as a weird little family, with a certificate stamped with the Bostonia seal, as proof. We stood on the wide brick plaza looking at it, then Jamar slid it back into its envelope and tucked the envelope in the kid-pack, for Caleb to hold.

I pressed the ribbed switch

and the oil-smelling typewriter stopped humming. Cara had given me this typewriter some time after *Porcupine City*, when I was trying to start a second book but kept getting mired in false starts and derivatives of the first. She'd gotten it at a thrift store in Jamaica Plain for $8 — it was worth at least twice that, haha. I'd cleaned it up, scraped gunk out of the letters with the end of a paperclip, and scoured the Internet for new ribbon. I hadn't expected to actually use the thing, if only because it was so young-writer cliché, but the clacking sounded nice and the pace was closer to my thoughts, and I got a pretty decent short story out of it right away.

I cranked out tonight's product and put it face-down on top of some other pages in the manuscript box.

I turned in my chair, leaned forward, rested elbows on knees, looked at my feet. Yawned. Got up.

Jamar's door moved open when I knocked. He was lying

on his bed with his legs hanging off.

"Whatcha doing?"

He put his hands against the foot of the bed and pulled himself up to a sitting position. His back was slouched. "Laying."

"He sleeping?"

"Sounds like."

"Wanna do something?"

"Eh. I'm feeling sort of tired."

"Oh come on, big boy, you're not going to leave me alone on our honeymoon night, are you?"

He smirked and perhaps blushed, it was hard to tell with Jamar.

"What do you say I break out the Scrabble?"

"Bradford, I've learned never to play a copyeditor in Scrabble."

"Hmm. Good point. How about a video game? Can I interest you in a little Guitar Hero?"

He was going to say no but then he said, "Ha. Sure. Set it up."

"Sweet."

"You want some tea or something?"

"Whatever you're having."

"I think I'll have some tea," he said, and I stepped aside to let him out.

Giving my two-week notice

was difficult because I didn't know exactly what to tell the people at Cook. Just what *was* I doing next? Even I wasn't sure. I ended up telling them all different things, variations on possible futures. To my boss Janice I said there'd been renewed interest in my book and I was leaving to become a full-time writer. I told Porn Randy I had a new job selling bear-skin rugs (he obviously got the reference and quickly changed the subject). Only Babette was given most of the truth. It wasn't a very talkative workplace and I had little fear these stories would ever interact. And if they did I'd be long gone by then, content to be thought of as nuts.

The end made me introspective,

though, as endings tend to do. My cubicle had always been pretty bare, and only now that it was time to clear it did that make me sad. I took down what little there was — a Christmas card from Babette from two years ago, a sympathy card from more recently, a couple of thank-you notes push-pinned to the wall — wishing there was more. Four years here and I suddenly wished there was more to show for it.

No sixteen-by-twenty boxes for me. Not even metaphorically. I'd invested very little in this job, had only ever seen it as a way to pay the bills, had only ever been waiting for 5:00. And that always seemed fine, as far as I'd considered it, which hadn't ever been very far.

At least I wouldn't have to deal with these mojo-killing fluorescent lights anymore.

I emailed myself some files I wanted to keep, mostly snippets of unfinished stories, and then began cleaning off my computer. Scanning through my archived emails, I came across the first one I'd gotten from Mateo, back when he was still New Guy, asking me to lunch. That was barely a year ago but seemed so much more distant, given all that'd happened. Mateo's Cook email address didn't even exist anymore.

At 4:00 I went to H.R. for my exit interview, where I handed over my office key, was given some COBRA literature on continuing my health insurance (weird to think I was covered through Jamar now), and was told I had about $3,000 in a Cook pension account or something that I'd receive with my final paycheck.

I shook H.R. Allison's hand. "Take care," she said, and she told me to let her know if there were any problems with my paycheck. I told her I definitely would — it would be my last one for the foreseeable future. Would I be getting an allowance now? How much had Jamar really meant by *et cetera?* Maybe I'd have to look for some freelancing.

When I got back to my desk I found my phone showing a missed call. I didn't recognize the number. There was a voicemail to go with it.

"Fletcher, it's your, um, old boyfriend," the voice said. A

touch of accent. My heart pounded. "Sorry to call while you're at work, but yours is the only number I know by heart now that Marjorie is moved. And I'm only allowed one call. So you can probably guess where I am. And what happened. I'll tell you where I am. I have it written down." He shuffled something and told me he was at the Newton Police Department, and he gave me the street address. "They don't know who I am. I mean I gave them my name, but they don't know *who I am*. So it's going to be minor. But I'm scared. And I'd like it if you'd come. Sorry I've been out of touch for so long. Will you come?" He told me the address again and then someone said something to him and he hung up.

And that is why I

rushed out forty-five minutes early on my last day at Cook. At least it spared me the handshakes and the nostalgic departure, which probably would've felt forced and false anyway. I was a little ahead of rush hour but I-95 was still a bitch, and in the slow-moving traffic I had time to pick out a total of four Facts just from the view from my car. He really had been everywhere; it was a wonder he hadn't been caught sooner. It had only ever been a matter of time, I think even he knew that, so what worried me was not *how* or *why* but *why now*? I hadn't seen him since he came to my house in that snowstorm, but then I'd been afraid. He'd seemed one step away from this ever since he got fired. Maybe even before that.

I was used to being surrounded by cruisers, but not the police car variety, haha. I laughed too loud at my own joke, realized I was trying to distract myself. What would he look like? What was going to happen? Would he have to go to jail?

If that girl Pell Mel got six months in prison for writing graffiti at Back Bay Station, what the hell would Mateo get? Mateo tagged Back Bay as a warm-up on his way to wherever he was actually headed. I knew he could be looking at serious time. It was scary, the idea of him in prison. But another part of me thought it might be good for him—an addict going to rehab.

I pulled into a space, walked slowly across the lot, held

open the door for a woman and her kid, followed them inside.

I'd never been inside any kind of police building before and I was expecting the Big House. I was expecting a rat-infested dungeon, a Turkish prison like in *Midnight Express*. But in fact it looked a lot like the RMV and I tried to pretend I was just there to renew my license. Not that it put me at ease, but it could've been worse.

The woman in front of me with the kid walked up to a counter and gave a name. She seemed to know what she was doing—even the kid gave off the uninterested air of someone for whom this place was old news. I looked down at my shoes to avoid making eye contact with criminals and by the time it was my turn at the counter I was shivering.

I told the woman I was here to see Mateo Amaral, who'd been arrested. She was not unfriendly but had the air of a government employee with no need to satisfy me because I needed everything from her and she needed nothing, not even money, from me.

"Mateo Amaral," I repeated, wanting to give her his full name just to prove that I knew it. Mateo Vinicius Armstrong Amaral. Then she asked my name and I gave her that too.

"Have a seat," she told me. "We'll call you. Could be a while."

I settled onto a wooden bench. The woman with the kid was reading a magazine. Not flipping through a magazine like other people were doing, but actually reading it. She had the attention to spare. She'd definitely done this before.

Eventually they called my name.

Again I imagined a dungeon and again it was more like the RMV: fluorescent lighting, glossy gray tile floors, walls of that rough brick with shiny pale-blue paint like in elementary school cafeterias. We went up a rubber-treaded ramp and around a corner and another waiting area and here, like some kind of zoo, were the bars.

"Do not touch the bars, do not pass anything through the bars."

"I won't," I said in case I was supposed to respond.

My god, he looked so small in there. Like a caged bunny

among bigger beasts. One flinching glimpse of him was all it took to make me take back my earlier thought—no way could jail ever be good for him. I somehow knew without doubt it would kill him. He was sitting on a bench with his colored fingers clasped between his knees, the toe of one shoe crossed over the toe of the other. His head was hanging and his hair covered his face.

"Teo," I said, and he looked up. The bright eyes popped against the darkness of his hair and his glossy, month-long beard.

He smiled. It broke my heart. It filled me with rage. I lifted my hands to touch the bars, to fucking rip them apart, to grab him and hold him and carry him away from here.

And on the heels of that fantasy came the realization, with surprise, with a gasp, with perfect clarity: *I love him.*

He stood up. "There you are. You got my message."

"Of course. I came right away."

"That's nice of you."

"What happened, Mateo? When are you getting out of here? Do you have a lawyer? I can try to get you a lawyer. Jamar's dad would know—"

"...One will be appointed to me," he recited in monotone.

"A public defender? No. You want someone good, goddammit, Mateo."

"He's nice. Young. Cute. You'll like him."

"This is serious."

"It's going to be OK."

"Mateo." I didn't know how much I could say here. Certainly I couldn't risk revealing to anyone nearby that Mateo wrote the Facts. "When do you get out?"

"Oh, won't be long." He scratched his beard and pushed his hair up away from his face. "Before night, I think."

"What do you want me to— Jesus, Mateo, you've got paint in your hair." Running along his hairline was orange paint, dried and flaking like neon dandruff. I reached through the bars and touched his forehead with my thumb.

"Hands, please!" an officer shouted and I looked at her, confused, and withdrew my hand. What the hell did she think was going to happen?

I was ready to cry. I wanted to scream. "What do you want me to do, Mateo? You called me and I'm here and now I don't know what to do."

He seemed to be thinking about it. "There's only one cure for me." He raised his finger and pressed an invisible valve on an invisible can, and smiled.

"No no no. You need a break."

"No breaks."

I sighed. "Do you want me to wait for you?"

"You don't have to wait. Thank you for coming. It was good just to see you. I'll be OK. I'll call you."

I looked again at the paint on his forehead, wondering how you even *get* paint on your forehead. Had he been kissing a wall? Would I be surprised if he was?

I turned the ignition and

started to back out of the space. I stopped. Stared for a long time at the police station doors. Turned off the car. Pulled out my phone and called Jamar. And sat.

When a parking space opened near the main doors I moved so it would be harder to miss him when he came out. Twice I went back inside to the vending machines for soda and Snickers. I listened to the radio long enough to hear the popular songs three or four times. I would've thought that if I had to kill an indefinite amount of time in a parking lot, a police department lot would be a good one to do it in — the foot traffic would be entertaining, right? Cursing pimps in feathered hats. Stumbling drunks. Murderers bathed in their victims' blood. Prostitutes calling officers *sugar*. But there was none of that. While I watched, two men and one woman were brought into the station, all three with that perturbed air of being under arrest, but one of the three wasn't even handcuffed.

That I was afraid Mateo would sneak out of the station and slip past me is perhaps a sign of how far I thought he had gone. But after all, he'd called me — he didn't have to. And he did wake me up, did reach through my open window and gently touch my hair when he finally came out and I was asleep.

Night had been going on for hours and he looked shiny in the glow of the station floodlights. I opened my door, got out, stretched my legs. I wanted to hug him but didn't.

"Thought you were going home," he said.

"I started to." I stomped the blood back into my legs. "I didn't want to leave you here."

"That's nice."

"Are you OK?"

"Yeah, I'm OK."

"What's in the bag?"

"My stuff." He tore open the heat-sealed plastic and pulled out his phone, wallet, keys — it made me think of the key-touching guy, even here, even all this time later. "They kept my paint, though. Evidence."

"Well, you have more where that came from, I'm sure."

He smiled.

"So what are you doing now? You said in your voicemail that Marjorie moved. Where are you living?"

"Boston," he said, gesturing east, and he smiled again. "Boston!"

"I don't understand."

"I think you do."

"Are you — homeless?"

"No. Homeless is one thing I'm definitely not."

"Are you houseless?"

"What do I need a house for, Fletcher? A house is a place to be when I'm not painting. And I don't want to ever be not painting."

Suddenly I felt scared for him again. "Get in the car?" I asked, not thinking he would.

But he did; it felt like a miracle. I waited for him to put on his seatbelt and then I started for my place.

On the phone he'd sounded sad, and he still looked sad, but his sadness had a veneer of betrayal too. He truly didn't understand.

"I always thought of it as kind of a game, you know?"

Driving down Route 9 toward Boston, his Facts blinked by here and there on billboards and retaining walls and bridges. "The cat would chase the mouse and that's what makes the mouse the mouse. I mean I can't imagine doing what I do with their *consent*. Wouldn't be the same. But it's a game. The cat isn't supposed to catch the mouse. Why would the cat want to catch the mouse? Even Lex Luthor always gives Superman an out." Then he shook his head. "Newton. It's because I was in Newton, that's why. Boston wouldn't have done this to me." He shook his head again. "Boston wouldn't have done this."

He'd gotten caught while

painting on the back of Sunfield Hall a life-size mural of Kupono, Phoebe's favorite dancer, doing a back-flip. A gift for her, a birthday present. A neighbor spotted him doing it and called the police. The piece was very lifelike so Phoebe would recognize the dancer — not in Mateo's usual stylized style, not yellow — and this was his saving grace. Otherwise the police would've known right away that the guy they cornered against a garage and a swimming-pool fence was *the guy* and not just some random vandal. The women of Sunfield watched from the windows in varying states of interest — Phoebe was the only one crying — as Mateo was handcuffed and led, book-ended by officers taller and wider than him, to the cruiser, and put inside, and driven away.

I looked over and he was rubbing his wrist. He had a court date. Would probably have to pay a hefty fine. But it could've been worse.

"Can you imagine what would happen if they knew you write the Facts?"

"Three years in jail, a fine, and millions of dollars in cleanup fees. I would imagine."

I opened my mouth to say something but nothing came out. I just kept looking at him. He looked back at me and shrugged.

"Almost home," I told him.

It was starting to feel like a routine: he would arrive at my apartment smelly, scruffy, looking slightly bewildered, and I would find him soon afterward clean, fully Mateo, in my bed. As though my apartment restored him. As though my bed brought him back. It was nice to believe that. I wanted it to be true.

He was thinner; the

baby fat I knew before was gone. But his mouth was still smooth and sweet and his hands went right to the places I liked to be touched. He pressed against me as though he couldn't get close enough, his toes pushing off against the tops of my feet. And when he was inside me I held the back of his head and pressed his face to my neck, felt his lips on my throat. He'd looked so small in the holding cell, but against me he felt huge, a city-size giant capable of surrounding me and filling me all at once, capable of picking me up and carrying me in any direction he wanted. I whispered into his hair, in a voice he could hear only if he wanted to, *I love you, I love you*, and meant it.

"Arrowman," he said.

It was May and not since before Valentine's Day had we done this. I didn't know when it would happen again, or if it ever would, and because of that I wanted it all, as far as we could go, and because of that, I hated the presence of the condom. I hated it even more than I'd hated the glove I was wearing on the first night we painted, on that wall outside Jamaica Plain, when he put his valve-finger on mine and helped me to paint. I wanted him to come inside me, to fill me. I wanted to feel the heat of him course through me. I had never wanted that from a guy before, had thought of condoms as happy facilitators of the life I wanted to lead, like bicycle helmets and boxing gloves, not a hindrance. But here I felt hindered. I wanted to feel him.

I thought: *Cara, I understand.*

He stretched his legs out behind me and heaved me up so I was sitting on his lap with my legs locked around his waist, our bellies and chests together as we moved. I slipped my arms under his and clasped my hands against the small of his back to hold myself up. His back was sticky there, wet—wet with sweat. No, something more slippery than sweat. I raised my hand, expecting to find my fingers shiny with lube, and gasped when they came up purple. The edible body paints? When had he gotten them out?

I put a purple finger on my tongue. It tasted of salt.

In the morning when Jamar

woke me up I was surprised to find Mateo still in my bed. I sat up and Jamar retreated to the door. I showed him a finger to tell him one minute. He nodded and disappeared into the kitchen. I got up, pulled on shorts and a t-shirt. It was normal to be getting up at this time on a weekday but today my alarm hadn't been set. From now on I was on Jamar's schedule.

I closed my door behind me. Jamar was standing at the sink rinsing one of Caleb's bottles. There were baby food jars scattered on the counter, some with rubber-coated spoons still sticking out of them. The kitchen was kind of a mess.

He turned off the water and put the bottle in the rack. "Mateo, huh?"

"You could tell?"

"By the hair. So you sprung him out of jail?" He said it and smirked and then we both laughed. How silly it sounded.

"For now."

"Well. Sorry to wake you up. I have to go. We need to perform the Caleb switch."

"Of course, yeah. Where is he?"

"My room."

I went in. It was a mess in there too and I had to kick aside shoes and laundry to wheel the crib out to the kitchen. Caleb was contentedly sucking a pacifier (Jamar and I agreed to call them that, not a *binky* or anything even worse).

"He just ate," Jamar said, "so he should be good for, oh jeez, probably five minutes!"

"Haha. OK." I put my foot against one of the wheels, spun it against the slick linoleum. "So today's your big day, huh? First day back."

"I'm a little nervous."

"Don't be nervous. It'll all come back to you."

"I know." He dried his hands on a towel and tossed it on the counter. "I need to go."

After re-confirming that I had all necessary phone numbers (numbers ordered by urgency from idle question to life-threatening peril), he leaned into the crib to kiss Caleb on the head, squeezed my shoulder, jingled his keys, and headed out. It was Jamar's first day. It was mine too.

"It's you and me, kid," I told Caleb. "Crazy as that sounds."

I took a deep breath and blew it out full of disbelief, and wheeled the crib into my room.

Normally what I would've done

while I showered was roll Caleb's crib into the bathroom, but because Mateo was there—amazingly still there, all these hours later—I asked if he'd keep an eye on him for a few minutes. As far as he knew, I was babysitting.

He agreed, and I left Caleb in the crib and Mateo sitting in his boxers on the edge of my bed. When I came back twenty minutes later he was lying on his back on the bed and Caleb was now lying in the center of the bed. There was a large space between them but Mateo's arm was stretched out and one finger, colored blue, was touching the bottom of Caleb's bare foot, as though maybe Mateo had been tickling him.

I secured my towel around my waist and entered the room.

Mateo sat up.

"Thanks," I told him. "Hopefully someday I won't feel like I need to keep an eye on him every single second."

"Yeah. Hey. This boy's white." He said it matter-of-factly and cocked his thumb down at the baby.

"What?"

"He's not mixed. Brazil's like the most mixed-race country on Earth. I know what mixed-race kids look like."

My heart was pounding. "So what?"

"Nothing, no, I'm just saying. Jamar know?"

"Yes."

He shrugged. "Well, he's cute, that's for sure. Hair

reminds me of my cousin."

To that I said nothing.

"Do you know what happened?" he asked. "Was there a screw-up at the hospital? Or was Cara—?"

I scooped Caleb up off the bed—he felt like a wiggling sack of potatoes—and returned him to the crib, popped the pacifier back in his mouth. I pushed the whole crib over to get it out of the sun. For a minute I stood there bent over it. Caleb's brown eyes followed mine, almost expectantly.

I had never come out of the closet—I'd never been in. When I started having crushes on boys I let the world know it. I told my mom. I told my friends. I told the boys. I never had anything to hide. It was no cakewalk, that's for sure, but indecision and pretending had never been part of the difficulty. But now I felt like I was in a closet, one where indecision was everything, where pretending was key. A closet full of what-ifs and fears for how things might be, and how things might change, if I were to come out with the truth. A closet based on what the people around me might think and might say, and about what was best for the people I cared about. I felt like a teenager, a common type of teenager but one I'd never been. A teenager struggling to become a man in one instant, with one breath, with one sentence of words.

I felt my pulse throbbing, as though I might pass out. I sat down beside Mateo.

"You look nervous," he said, putting his hand gently on my leg.

"A little."

"It's OK. You can tell me."

"I don't know how to start."

I saw him look at my lips—they must've been trembling. Then his face opened up with sudden realization and he hugged me. His hands were cool on my bare back, refreshing, like ice on a fever.

"Oh my god, Fletcher, it's you!" He laughed into my neck. "Why didn't you tell me!"

I pulled away from him just a little, keeping the side of my face against his cheek, and he left his hands clasped against my spine. In this huddled embrace I told him the story from Cara's journal, almost word for word what she'd written. I told him what she found. And what she did. And then I said, "But that's not what really happened."

"OK. What really happened?"

"It was last June," I whispered. "When we were going out." My lips felt dry.

"You and me?"

"Yes."

"OK." Against my cheek I could feel his brow crinkle as he wondered how he factored into this.

"It was the night you snuck over."

"Snuck over?"

"The night I was stoned and you snuck into my room."

"Oh. OK."

"You were horny."

And then, with a twinge, transmission—an idea conveyed. I felt his skin go rough with goosebumps and then get smooth again. His hands unclasped and slid down my back. "And you weren't," he said.

"OK?"

"You left it in the bathroom. She thought it was yours?"

I nodded against the side of his head; his ear brushed my lips. "OK?" I said again.

For a long time he said nothing and I didn't breathe, and then, finally, he laughed. There was such relief for me in that sound. He pulled his arms back and his hands lay on the towel stretched across my lap. He had tears coming down his cheeks. He rubbed them away with the heel of his hand.

"I have to figure out what to write about this," he said.

He got up, beautiful in the morning sun, and walked over to the crib and stood over it, looking in. Again he wiped his eyes. Suddenly I felt very afraid. What would I do if he wanted to take Caleb? If he picked him up and wanted to leave? But he didn't pick him up, merely reached down and cupped Caleb's blond head in the palm of his painty hand. "Well Vini," he whispered, "maybe you weren't adopted after all."

When Mateo was leaving a

few hours later I carried Caleb, in one of those basket-chair things with the handle, down to the street. I set it on the sidewalk and he squirmed inside, kicking at the air.

"Nice out today," Mateo said, closing his eyes, lifting his chin, taking a deep breath of the spring air. His hair was still wet from a shower. He pushed up the sleeves of his hooded sweatshirt, still warm from the laundry. "Could be a hot one later though."

"I heard it's supposed to hit eighty."

"Eighty, huh?"

"That's what I heard."

"Should go move my car to a shady place so my cans don't blow up in the trunk."

"Want a ride there?"

"No, it's OK. Thanks for, you know, taking care of me yesterday with that whole thing."

"It was no problem. Keep me posted on it."

"I will. — And for telling me."

"Yeah."

"We'll have to figure something out."

"OK."

"I'd ask you guys to come painting with me, but... kind of young."

"Yeah. Hey. Before you go. I'm sorry I chose Jimmy over you that night."

"I've made choices too, Fletcher. Things'll end up OK."

For a moment I looked at him. "I know you have stuff to do. I know there are a lot of blank walls still. But you should come back soon. Whenever you want a place to sleep or something. Or to see Caleb. You're always welcome here, Mateo. And maybe eventually we could try to work things out between us?"

"I don't think I ever told you," he said, looking off down the street and squinting against the sun. "When I was in SP, I got to go up in this bridge that's basically their answer to the Zakim. So I have an idea of how it works now."

"That's incredible."

"So now I'm just waiting for the right time."

"When's that?"

"I don't know. But I'll let you know, OK?" He looked again down the street, and I realized it was the direction of downtown. From where he was standing he could probably see the tops of the same buildings that were tattooed on his arm. "Hey, maybe I'll stop by, bring him some finger paints. That would be fun."

"You should."

"Maybe I will."

"Mateo?"

Maybe he heard me wrong, maybe it was just habit—but he said it again: "Maybe I will." And then he added, "See you, Fletcher."

"OK."

I watched him walk up the street and when he turned a corner I sat on the bottom step and watched Caleb watching a butterfly fluttering around overhead. I was going to shoo it away if it tried to land on him, but it didn't.

"All right, kiddo, let's go up." When I reached down for the handle on his chair-thing I noticed, on the sidewalk where Mateo had been standing, a few small circles of paint. I kneeled down and pressed my thumb against one of the circles, an orange one, expecting it to be dry and smooth, but my thumb came away wet. "That's weird." But what was even weirder was that I then put my thumb in my mouth. Salt.

Maybe I will, he told me. He looked like he meant it, he really did, but although I saw new Facts in new places nearly every day of the week, and although that meant he was OK, it was months before I heard from him again.

It took almost that long

for Jamar to start talking to me again. I totally deserved the fury he unleashed—for not telling him as soon as I knew, and then for telling Mateo first. "That," he told me, jabbing his finger at the domestic partnership certificate that hung on our fridge, "that means you always tell me everything first!"

It was an anger I'd never seen him show before, especially

to Cara. He screamed at me. "He asks for one fucking DNA test, Bradford, and I'm nothing! *One fucking test!*"

While he was yelling I felt two inches tall. I wondered if this level of anger was something he would only unleash on a guy, never on a girl, or whether Cara had just never hurt him, in all the years they were together, as much as I had on my very first day.

At the end of May

Mike graduated and moved out of his little apartment on Beacon Street. On the day he was leaving he invited me over one last time. I anticipated a little goodbye rumble, but instead we ordered pizza and I helped him move his mattress down out of the loft. Kneeling on the wood platform, ducking the low ceiling, we pushed it over the rail. It hit the hardwood floor with a slap and coughed up a cloud of dust, fluttering the pages of dog-eared textbooks. There was a stain near the top that was probably coffee or something but it reminded me of everything Mike and I had done together on this mattress and I thought, *One last time*. But he looked so young, had that fear in his eyes, that post-college void fear I filled with *Porcupine City* and felt so far beyond.

"Come on," I told him, bending down, "let's stand this up against the wall so you'll have some room to walk around."

And we did. The mattress looked funny there, vertical, no longer a bed but now more like a piece of art, like a canvas, a portrait of a time that was both more and less complicated.

We ate the pizza out of the box, then stood on the sidewalk near the place where, many moons ago, we made our little arrangement. His parents were on their way with a van. A summer respite in Bangor would be followed by a move to Irvine, California, where he planned to wait tables for as long as it took him to convince the creators of Warcraft to give him a job.

"You'll be fine, you know," I told him, "out in the real world."

"You know, you should come up to Maine this summer...," he said, using that tone people use to mean goodbye.

"Yeah."

"If you're not too busy being a dad." He smiled. "Thanks for the lovin', Fletcher Bradford."

"Thanks for the friendship, Mike Stepp."

After that life settled into a routine, albeit not the one Jamar and I anticipated. Crazy how naïve we were when we imagined our lives with Caleb. *You can write all day when he's asleep*, Jamar had advertised when we were new at this. An infant left no time for writing! And even if I'd had the time to go out, as Jamar had suggested, I wouldn't have had the energy. And money, too: Jamar's paycheck wasn't enough and we had to dip into Cara's insurance money more than we liked, to make ends meet. It was hard. But we were doing the things that needed to be done, letting the big picture take care of itself.

And then things went dark.

The blackout happened on July 20,

and when it happened I was on the T, on the Green Line underground. I was standing inside the pivoting connector between two subway cars with Caleb hanging in the kid-pack against my chest, another backpack of his supplies hanging off my back. I didn't like traveling with him on the T but I had to pick up some freelance work downtown and it was the easiest way. We'd gotten on at Park Street and were stopped somewhere between Boylston and Arlington stations, with either the Common or the Public Garden above us. There was no cataclysmic screech of brakes when the lights when out, just a quiet whoosh of powerlessness and the quick resumption of a dim, yellow light as the train rolled to a stop. I sighed and leaned against the wall, glad for the cushion of new diapers against my spine. This kind of delay was hardly unheard of, and I figured we'd be moving again in a minute. Then a passenger with a good cell signal reported that the entire city, not just our train, had gone dark.

Amidst the groans of other passengers I looked at Caleb and tried to send him telepathic signals. *Please don't start crying now*, I told him. *And please don't poop.*

Above us in the sunlight

the streets were a mess. The power vanished right before rush hour, so within minutes buildings were emptying streams of commuters who had nowhere to go. Intersections with dark traffic lights became snarled with vehicles blaring their horns. Cars, buses, trucks. People on foot had the herky-jerk motion of commuters knocked out of routine, unsure where to go or how to get home. Horse cops had suddenly more to do than pose for tourist photos. In seconds the city was reduced to a giant web of parking lot. Rush hour all in one place, not rushing, not moving. Just waiting.

And out of this unmoving

chaos Mateo came running. From wherever he'd been he came running. Running, at last, not to escape but to chase.

It doesn't matter what streets he used. There are a dozen different routes he might have taken but they all would've looked the same in that web of traffic. It's likely that at some point he crossed through the Common to get there. Very likely he ran right over our heads. Backpack clinking like mad. Hair bouncing against his ears and face. Sneakers pounding the pavement as he dodged pedestrians, cars, newspaper boxes and push-cart vendors. And smiling. I like to imagine that when he ran over my head I felt him, that my heart made an extra beat for him. My god, he was beautiful. I wish you could've seen him. I wish I could've watched him, seen the smile on his face as he ran.

He thought, the moment he saw the lights were out: *This is my chance.* And he came running. A blackout was one of the scenarios he'd imagined and when he was presented with one he didn't waste a second. He came running.

It called to him. Its bright blue lights were as dead as all the others in the city — but in his mind they were still flashing like a beacon, marking the place.

His heaven spot.

People were herding across

the Zakim Bridge, turning the highway into a footbridge and moving with the speed and steadiness of lava around cars paralyzed in traffic. He came out of the tunnel and made himself part of the herd for as long as it suited him, and then he separated himself. He stopped at the first structure, the one closer to Boston than to Cambridge — the forked obelisk, the gigantic divining rod, the perfect place.

He hopped a concrete barrier that at any other time on any other day would've marked the edge of the highway on which cars would've been barreling seventy miles per hour. At the base of the structure was a blank white door. He smiled, touching it. This was a soul in the moment it's been waiting for. This was a heart on fire. This was liftoff. And hugely he smiled.

There was a guy standing

a few feet away from me — cute, short brown mohawk — and the realization came to me very slowly that this was the key-touching guy. Only when the guy actually touched his keys did I realize. Until then I'd been focused on Caleb. The guy had gotten up from his seat and was holding the overhead rail, stretching, head hanging between his arms.

Then he lowered his right hand and tapped idly at his pocket. My pulse quickened. Him.

The fuzzy sides of his head indicated that the haircut I'd seen last summer had been grown-out, and he did in fact razor them down.

He turned and kicked at the floor, and sighed.

Minutes went by. Caleb squirmed in the kid-pack and tried to put his fingers in my mouth. I spat them out.

The key-touching guy was looking and I saw him looking and he said, "Kiddo seems pretty content."

"He's a good kid."

He smiled. I smiled back.

"Yours?"

"No. Yeah. Long story."

"Sounds like," he said. Then he put his headphones on.

Mateo closed the door, its

powerless lock clicking back into place with all the security of a pantry cupboard. It was smaller in here than he'd envisioned. Perhaps the dim emergency lighting made it look smaller. Unlike the Oliveira Bridge there was no room for equipment of any kind. He wondered in a panic if this bridge was different enough to render his lessons from the Oliveira moot. Maybe, but the biggest hurdle was already crossed: he was inside.

He pushed a chest-high stack of traffic cones against the door to keep it from blowing open. He looked up. The angled ceiling went up into space-like darkness that choked out the weak yellow lights that ran along the ladder—a ladder, not stairs. The ladder was probably meant as a back-up; beside it was the lift, a platform with a railing and a control panel with three buttons: up, down, emergency stop. He didn't think it would work but he got on anyway, pressed UP with his knuckle. Nothing.

He rummaged in his clinking backpack and found a pair of old rubber gloves, which he pulled on over his fingerprints. Then he secured his backpack, gripped a ladder rung above his head, stifled a gigantic smile. And climbed. It was easier than climbing a normal ladder—following the angled wall, it was more like climbing a very steep slope. A tubular cage running the length of the ladder encircled him. But still it was difficult—twice his foot slipped past a rung and scraped against granite—and it was higher than any ladder he'd ever climbed. When he arrived at the landing where this angled prong met the vertical part of the obelisk, at around 175 feet, his heart was pounding—whether from exertion or excitement it's impossible to say.

When he was ready he started climbing again, up into space. Tiny lights on the ladder above him glittered like stars. This vertical ladder was more difficult, but every fifteen or twenty feet there was a landing, which helped to lessen the abyss below. Finally, at 260 feet, the ladder ended at a steel floor bordered by bright yellow railings. He slipped off his backpack and lay down on his back, breathing heavy, imagining the air was thinner up here. He snapped off his gloves. He touched his face, felt his beard, wished he'd had a chance to clean up for this.

"I'm here to paint," he said, an affirmation of purpose, and his voice sounded big and echoey in the capsule-like room.

The maintenance door was dark steel (on the outside it had a granite façade) that slid open on big tracks, very similar—virtually identical—to the one in São Paulo. He pushed it open, wishing Vini could be here to do this with him, to be his Buzz. Wind whistled through the crack and as he pushed it entered the capsule like a flood and made a breathy *oooohh* as it filled the hollow obelisk. He wished Tiago were here to hold him by the belt, to be his orbiting Collins.

The staging, a fancy hydraulic system, responded to his gentle push and yawned out like a drawbridge, raising a railing as it lowered. It clanked into place and became a balcony offering access to the big blue lights at the top of the obelisk.

It seemed to him like a portal to another dimension. Here he was in a tiny, echoey, dimly-lit capsule—and through the doorway ahead of him lay his entire city.

He picked up his backpack, slipped it on, and stepped outside.

The guy took his headphones

off and wound the cord around his hand, stuffed them in his pocket. "Color me curious," he said.

I'd been sniffing Caleb's butt; he had a look on his face that usually signaled pooping. Thank god it seemed to be a false alarm—there was still a chance I wouldn't have to do a presto-changeo on the floor of the train. "Curious about what?"

He nodded at the baby. "His daddy issues." He squatted down near me with his back against the wall. Sliding down, he stretched out his legs.

"His daddy issues...," I said. "OK."

I was careful about what I said but I kept talking because I couldn't believe I was talking to the key-touching guy. I ended up delivering some approximation of the truth.

"Quite a story," the guy said. He stuck out his finger and Caleb's hand bumped against it. "Hey kid." He took out his keys and jingled them at Caleb, who no longer seemed interested. "I have one of my own," he said.

"How old?"

"Four. She's biologically mine but they live near Seattle. I donated to my friend and her *lesbian lover*." He said it with aplomb.

"Wow." A kid. The fact brought with it the realization that a year ago it would've had me running for the fucking hills. "That was cool of you."

"Well when they put a cup in—uh—well." He smiled. "Never mind."

"I—saw you," I found myself saying. "I think. About a year ago, I guess. On the T. Around Brighton? It was a really hot day and I was grouchy and I saw you check your pocket to make sure you still had your keys. It was a little thing but for some reason I've always remembered it."

"Just me checking for my keys?"

"It sounds weird when I say it."

"I do that a lot," he said. "Compulsively. I'm always nervous about losing them. It would be so difficult to replace them and meanwhile, how would you get into your house?"

"That's what I thought."

"It's a little piece of metal that stands between you and the place you belong."

He touched the valve,

rubbed his finger against it. The can was cool in his hand.

He turned, too fast, felt the spinny disorientation of extreme height. Then turned more slowly, put his hand on the rail, looked out. It was beautiful. This should've reminded him of other places—other places this high, other places this windy, Bunker Hill, the Citgo sign, the Oliveira Bridge—but it wasn't like anyplace else.

It was silent, too. All he could hear was the rush of the wind, the air filling his hood and banging his hair against his ears.

"*Are you ready for this, Boston?*" he yelled happily, the wind swallowing his voice. "*Are you ready?*"

When he felt steady enough he kneeled down, knee clunking the platform. The wind was blowing his hair in his eyes and he pushed it back and pulled up his hood. He reconsidered his color, because what he had planned to write wasn't what he was going to write. He unzipped the backpack, rooted around again. The cans clinked but the sound was muffled here. He chose blue. The words would be blue.

He stood up with the can in his hand. The hood keeping his hair out of his eyes also cut his peripheral vision, disrupting his view of the city, so he pushed it back again. It, too, blew against his face, along with the strings, and the zipper bit against his belly. He shrugged out of the hoodie and set it down on the metal grating, but in seconds the wind sent it flying over the edge, out and away. Barely noticing, he picked up the can, popped the cap.

He put his hand on the granite, feeling the words he would coax out with paint, practicing the strokes in his mind. He pressed the valve. The wind affected the release of the paint but after a few strokes he learned to compensate. The paint took hold, the letters grew.

He could feel his city rumbling beneath him and through him. Tears came to his eyes. He cried *Wooooo!* and made a cautious hop with his fist raised high. He could feel the Acela slipping through Jamaica Plain, past the concrete wall where he and I painted that very first time. He could feel passengers helping each other out of stranded aboveground T cars. He could feel wheezing tourists dragging themselves up the last few steps of the Bunker Hill Monument, oblivious still that the city had gone dark. He could feel pizza shops in the North End being bombarded by commuters with nowhere else to go; the wheels of baby strollers in the South End. His blood ran with the sound of sirens and horns and satellite radios and the thump-thump of heavy bass idling in the stalled streets.

The letters went on.

He looked out. There was the Prudential Building conducting the skyline like a maestro. There was the Charles River lapping the edge of the Esplanade. There was the Citgo sign on the edge of Fenway Park. Sailboats dotted the river and he could feel those too. There was the Longfellow Bridge and Old North Church. Below him, hundreds of feet below him, the tail-end of an Orange Line train peeked out from beneath the bridge. In the distance Mass. Ave, measured in Smoots, reached across the river into Cambridge, quivering with the movement of tiny pedestrians.

And on the other side was the rickety Charlestown Bridge, where he and I once stood and where he'd pointed to the Zakim and told me, "Someday, Arrowman. Someday."

That day was today. It was now.

He reached into his pocket and pulled out his phone but he had no signal, not even here. Then he got one bar—maybe some tower in Cambridge—and tried a second time. He was kicked directly to voicemail, and the recording that answered was full of static.

"Fletcher," he said after the tone, "I'm at the Heaven Spot. I'm here!"

That was all he needed to say. Anything more would've been superfluous; everything he could say about its beauty was implied in the simple, single fact that he was here. He pressed END and looked at the phone and let it fall from his fingers. He put down the can and rooted for yellow, popped the cap, pressed the valve. He outlined his words.

He could feel his city rumbling beneath him and through him. Alive, more alive powerless than usual. He laughed.

"Is this your first time in Boston?" Marjorie had asked him when they were leaving the airport.

"We came once, for July Four. To the Cap Shell. Hat Shell?"

"Hatch Shell. There's lots more to see than that. We'll get you a subway pass. And the city will be your playground. How's that?"

He reached to point the can and felt a tickle roll across his ribs. If he'd stopped to wonder what it was he would've decided it was a drop of sweat making its way down his torso. But he didn't, he swatted it with his free hand and kept working.

When he reached down to take another can into his empty hand he found that hand covered in red, red that exploded against the blue already there. Frantically he searched for a wound under his arm but found none. When he looked closer he saw it wasn't blood, it was paint. If he'd thought more about it he would've suspected a can had exploded somewhere in the pack for all the jostling of his earlier running—but he didn't. He started painting with both hands. His left hand seemed to know the can even though he'd never used it for painting before.

A coolness, licked by the wind, spilled from the corner of his eye, pooled in the slope of his cheek, and then rolled down, leaving behind a trail of blue. It hit the dark scruff along his jaw and spread out, lacquering the stiff hairs and reaching from hair to hair up to his ear and across his sideburn and on to the other side, around past his chin. When the hair could hold no more it released blue down the curves of his throat. Blue gathered again in the nook of his clavicle before continuing down his chest.

Yellow came from the hair on the back of his neck and traced bright lines, zigging and zagging across his back as he moved, soaking his shirt and the stretchy white band of his boxers.

Purple came from the back of his knee, making its way down his calf, dripping around to the shin when he knelt. It traced the curve of his ankle, slipped along his heel and disappeared into his sneaker. He hadn't worn socks today.

The hips of his jeans turned orange, moving into the pockets and toward the fly.

He pulled off his shirt, swiped at the colors on his chest, mixing them on his belly. He marveled, all his excitement turning to wonder. Laughing, he dropped the other can. Colors were running down his face now and he could feel them between his toes. He kicked up a leg and tugged off a shoe and his foot was pink and yellow. He pulled off his other shoe: white and green. He stood holding one shoe, looking out, colors dripping from him, pattering like raindrops on the balcony. Clutching the handrail behind him with both hands he pressed first one foot against the wall and left a footprint there, then lifted his other foot and stepped one small step, then another, up the granite, leaving a trail of dripping footprints. Then he dropped back to the metal grating. He stood and touched the bridge, dragged his hand across it, leaving a fiery smear of red and purple behind.

"É verdade," he whispered, pressing the sole of his foot once more against the granite. *It's true.*

At the bottom of the

bridge a crowd had gathered of commuters more interested in what was going on at the top of the bridge than anxious to get over it. Something was falling toward them and they looked up and it was pants. Jeans. They caught on one of the bridge's white suspension cables. A t-shirt made it to the ground and a man picked it up and looked up, shading his eyes, before dropping the shirt again and not knowing what to do with the colors on his hands. Then two things hit hard, *clump clump* — they were shoes, a pair of sneakers — sending outward a splattery circular rainbow where they hit, one on the asphalt, one on the windshield of a Volkswagen Golf. A pair of multi-colored underwear surfed on the wind. At last a watch exploded against the bumper of a pick-up. All of these things soaked through and through with colors.

The people — the drivers, the walkers — looked up and saw the blue words at the top of the bridge, and something else too. But in that moment the power returned, and with it the lights, and with those the order, and suddenly they were moving, they were moving, and Boston crept back into rush hour.

Everyone clapped wildly and

for a pleasant moment we all seemed like friends.

"Here we go," said the key-touching guy as the train took its first lurch forward. "One big happy family for a change."

At the next station tons of commuters, impatient to be off the platform and on their way home, piled in with us.

The key-touching guy and I stood squished together with Caleb hanging off my chest like a chubby gargoyle. He reached out and pulled at a button on the guy's shirt. I rotated to put him out of reach.

"I'm the next stop," the guy said. "I guess I should start making my way down." He meant to the door; the crowd was tight enough to make it a journey. He stood on his toes to peer above the passengers' heads.

"Good luck," I told him. "It was nice spending the blackout with you."

"Same," he said. "Would you, heh, be interested in grabbing a coffee sometime or something? You could bring your little friend here."

"That would be cool. Yeah, I'd like that."

"I think I have my, uh, card around here somewhere. That sounds so pretentious of me." He sunk his hand into his shirt pocket and then into each of his pants pockets and I thought, *Yeah, this is him.* He withdrew a bent white card, flattened the crease with his thumb, and handed it to me.

"*Ollie Wade,*" I read, thinking it was a good name. "Oliver?"

"Only legally."

"Freelance photography, huh?"

"Hah. Well. No. Formerly freelance. Recently downgraded back to hobbyist."

"I'm Fletcher. This is Caleb."

"Fletcher. Do you make arrows? Ohhh. Zing! Sorry, I bet you get that all the time."

I smiled. "Just once before actually."

"Then I'm not *quite* as embarrassed." He tilted his head to listen to a muffled loudspeaker announcement. "Uh-oh, this is me. So I'll talk to you later?"

"Yeah, definitely."

"Cool. Call me. Normally I'd say don't forget, but if you

remembered me after a year, I don't guess you'll forget me by tomorrow."

"I won't."

"I bet you get a kick out of this fate type shit, huh?" He smiled.

I watched him push his way through the commuters with a series of *Excuse me*'s and *Coming through*'s, and then he was off the train and we were pulling away.

Midnight, and on the other

end of the world, where July is the dead of winter, Vinicius da Cunha Bittencourt felt like he was falling. Since sundown he'd felt restless, nauseous, had gone to bed early. Now he lay on his back with his palms pressed flat against the mattress and the *Toy Story* sheets, trying to slow what felt like a frictionless, airless tumbling, like falling down on the Moon. He snapped open his green eyes and sat up, mouth dry, skin clammy. He looked at his hands in the dim light. No Moon dust. He looked down at the floor beside the bed. Nothing there. No one there.

He got up.

The sidewalk was cold on his bare feet. He zipped his hoodie, pulled his hands into his sleeves, looked around, not even sure what he was looking for.

"Primo?" he whispered, and felt silly. But of course it wouldn't have been the first time his cousin showed up unexpectedly.

Vinicius took a deep breath in and out. And again.

A step down off the curb and his bare foot touched cobblestone wet and slick. He hopped back and kneeled down and found his toes covered with brown sludge. If it was something truly gross he would've smelled it already, so he touched his toes, examined the sludge between his fingers. It was paint, but old paint, stripped as with thinner. He looked up. From the wall on the other side of the street this sludge was dripping, and from the wall behind him, too—dripping from specific places with unique shapes. Clean lines, defined curves. Letters.

He crossed the street, sludge sliding between his toes like

thick gravy. After tapping the wall to make sure it wasn't hot, he smeared clear an area of sludge with the palm of his hand. Under the sludge was an early Fact, one of Mateo's first. Vinicius turned and looked down the street, and understood: Mateo's old paintings were ridding themselves of all the layers they'd acquired over the years.

It wasn't just on Rua Giacomo. It happened that way all over the city, the *cities*—not to everything Mateo had ever done but to all of the special ones, all of the ones his heart had been in and now was in again. Tomorrow Vini and Olivia, Aline, Tiago, Edilson and Olive would spend the entire day looking. But tonight— Tonight Vini sat down on the curb, his feet in the street submerged to his ankles, and he cried.

"Jamar," I said, my heart

pounding. "Come here. Come look at this."

"OK." He sipped the last of his morning coffee and slowly rinsed the mug in the sink. "Have you seen my keys?"

"Now, Jamar! My god!"

I pushed the laptop over so he could see. On the *Boston Globe* website I'd followed a link to a gallery of photos about the biggest story of the day, the story that had pushed the blackout way off the front page: the sudden, overnight appearance, or *reappearance*, all over Boston and beyond, of a vast number of graffiti paintings.

Jamar leaned down and looked over my shoulder at the photo on the screen.

"This was him," I said. "This was his heaven spot. His ultimate goal. He did this one yesterday."

"Well I'll be. How'd he get all the way up there?"

"I don't know. Patience."

"What'd he write?"

"I can't see. It's too small."

"Drag it to your desktop and enlarge it."

I did and the image was still too pixelated to read, so I paid a visit to the Zakim later that day to confirm it. From where I stood on the shore of the river the sun was too bright and the obelisk too tall for me to make out anything clearly. As

I was walking along the shore to put the sun behind the obelisk, I spotted, lying in the gravel, a thin leather band the circumference of an ankle. It was covered in dry colors, and it was still tied. I picked it up, squeezed it in my fist. With the sun out of my eyes now I looked up at the obelisk. In blue letters outlined with yellow, tall and proud because they were true, were the words CALEB IS LOVE. And beside those words on the white granite was a series of colorful footprints that seemed to lead right into the sky.

It took me a week

to find the gray Civic, driving around all the places I thought he might've parked it. I finally found it shackled on its front driver's-side wheel with a bright yellow boot. I was lucky — it was in the kind of neighborhood where the sidewalks glitter with window glass and when someone sees a car being broken into, they keep walking or close the curtains.

I went back that night with Jamar. He paced on the sidewalk while I peered in.

"Come on, Jamar," I whispered. "You're black, don't you know how to break into a car?"

"Bradford, why don't you stuff the car up your homo butt and we'll take it home and deal with it later?"

"Heh."

"Heh." He shoved his hands in his pockets. "You're positive this is his?"

"Yeah."

"Then let's get this going. If we get arrested we're going to owe Marcy a fortune." Marcy was our babysitter, a highschooler who lived below us.

"OK, here goes — *Ow!*" My elbow bounced painfully off the window.

"Oh goddammit, Bradford. You're sure it's not alarmed?"

"He never had one when I was —"

"OK." He pulled loose from the broken retaining wall behind us a crumbling piece of concrete the size of a softball and thumped it against the window once, twice. And coughed to mask the sound of tinkling glass.

"You *do* know how to break into a car!"

"Hurry up. I'll be at the car."

There were two blankets on the backseat. I shook them to knock off the glass, climbed in, sat down and closed the door.

The Zakim had gotten some attention because, of all the paintings that appeared that day, the one on the Zakim was the only one people saw being done. At and around the bridge the authorities found a complete set of men's clothes—t-shirt, hoodie, jeans, boxers—belonging, they said, to someone around five feet ten inches tall—all stiff with dried colors. A pair of size-ten sneakers. A backpack containing six cans of spraypaint, none of which were empty and which did not appear to have contributed to the condition of the clothes. And pieces of a phone so smashed to smithereens in the 270-foot fall and further decimated by traffic, they could barely tell the brand.

Thank god that was all they found.

Me, I pulled his wallet out of the glove compartment. Opened it, gazed at his license photo, pushed it into my pocket. Ran my hands under the driver's seat and then under the passenger seat, crinkling PowerBar wrappers and water bottles. I turned up his sketch book and his black book, a new volume—there were only a few pages filled with what must've been recent stuff. But no laptop yet, and I had come for the laptop. My worry was that it would be in the trunk, and that was looking more likely.

There was nothing under the backseat among the snaking seatbelts except his winter jacket and snow pants and boots. I pulled them out and balled them up.

The laptop must be in the trunk. How would I get it?

Think, Fletcher. Think.

I spread one of the blankets open on the seat and started piling things on it—the black book, the clothes. If I was taking some stuff, where did I draw the line? If I took some I had to take it all. There would never be anything more. I leaned forward to the glove compartment and pulled out its entire contents—registration, insurance info, phone charger, napkins and ketchup packets—and added that to the pile. I gathered up the clothes on the floor and added those too. Then I pulled the corners of the blanket together and tied them like a hobo's luggage. I shook open the other one for the rest.

Still thinking, *How can I get in the trunk?*

With bundles on either side of me I slunk down in the seat and opened my phone.

"Jamar," I said. I asked him.

"Minus a crowbar or something?"

"Yeah, minus a crowbar. Unless you have a crowbar on you."

"Um. No. But you can— Jeez, Bradford. Hold on."

Moments later we were both in the back of the Civic, ripping off the back cushion. It came apart with ease but the fabric behind it was thick. Three kicks and a push was what it took to get through. The tearing and the clink of a staple sounded loud in the car.

Jamar twisted around. "Are we taking these— parcels?"

"Yes."

He grabbed the sacks off the front seat and pulled them onto his lap.

"Be careful with it," I said.

"I know. I hope you find what you're looking for. I'll be in the car. I'm cramping up."

I hadn't wanted to turn on the ceiling light but I couldn't see into the trunk without it. The light was bright; the car battery was pretty new. I thought of that first day and had to stop for a minute with my hand over my mouth. My shadow covered the plywood shelves and the cans sitting neatly in them, still neatly. Here was the maintenance of all the order he cared about.

"Oh Mateo," I whispered.

Here at last were his important things: a backpack, his camera, his laptop, and the first two bulging, heavy volumes of his black book.

I tucked this all into his backpack and then I reached back in and grabbed can after can and a box of markers. I couldn't leave anything. Vinicius would want some. And I had to make sure I had enough to pass down. I took it all.

I took it all and left one thing, on the back window, in bright green: ARROWMAN IS.

Jamar helped me carry it

all to my room and then left me alone while he went to pay Marcy.

"It was an easy one," I heard her say. "He slept right through. What's in all those blankets, anyway?"

I put the sketchbook and the three-volume black book under my bed and sat down at my desk, pushed aside my typewriter, opened the laptop in front of me. Whatever was on here was everything I was ever going to have. I hoped it was enough.

It booted up fast and showed me his desktop. The wallpaper was the Zakim. I found hundreds of pictures of graffiti, arranged in folders according to artist. I found dozens of saved PDF files, all information about the Zakim Bridge, from scrapped plans to preliminary blueprints to photos of its progress that must've offered some glimpses inside, to photos of elephants making the inaugural crossing. I also found what I'd come for: his address book. It held all the connections I would someday use when I figured out what to say.

While I was perusing through his hard drive an IM popped up. It was from *ViniBitt*. It said, "PRIMO!!"

I took a deep breath. Felt myself shaking. I was now speaking for him.

"Vinicius," I typed. "This is Fletcher."

I went to Brazil to

see and to ask, so I'd know the whole story, as much as could be known. I went to fill in the blanks, as much as could be filled. And maybe to fill in some blanks for his family.

I went to the Brazilian consulate and got my visa and crammed a *Portuguese for Dummies* and Jamar drove me to the airport on a frigid afternoon in the middle of January.

"I really wish you would've waited until I could go with you," he told me as he pulled up to Terminal E. "You know this makes me nervous, you going there by yourself."

"It'll be fine. Vinicius will be there."

"He doesn't even speak English."

"It'll be fine."

"No language. It's your worst nightmare."

"It'll be OK. Don't freak me out."

"And if you do decide to tell them about Caleb," he said, "and if it goes badly—"

"Jamar, I told you, if any part of me feels like it might go badly, I just won't tell them at all."

He sighed. "So you have your passport?"

"I do. I need to go. I'll call you when I get to Panama."

"Panama. Fucking-hell. These are places in high school textbooks. Be careful, huh? Pay attention to your surroundings."

"Oh Jamar." I closed the door and slipped on my backpack. Caleb was strapped into the backseat and I put a kiss on his little pom-pom hat. He'd be turning one next month.

As I was leaving Jamar lowered the window and said, "Bradford, come here a second."

"I'm going to miss my flight."

"Back, you know, right after Cara, when I said you were a guy and not a man. That was wrong and I was wrong to say it. It's not about who you sleep with, or—whether you know about sports or tools or have a pearls-wearing wife or whether commercials make you cry. I think it's about whether you step up. When something hard comes along. A man steps up. He doesn't dodge it or run away from it or try to push it onto someone else. He steps up. Even if it isn't his responsibility. And that's why there are so many guys and so few men. Because stepping up is hard. And yet there's never been anything in your life you haven't stepped up to. I mean, from the time you were twelve, to moving in with Cara, to Caleb, to everything. To this."

When he was done I let it sit for a beat, just long enough so he would know I would remember this forever. And then I said, "Did you want to get that off your chest in case my plane goes down?"

"I was saving it so I wouldn't have to see you for the week it'll take your massive ego to calm down now."

"Haha."

"Tell them I say hi. Or *oi*. Or whatever."

I traveled for almost

a day, which felt like forever. I guess since São Paulo time is only one hour ahead of Boston, I imagined it couldn't be that far. But it was winter when I took off, and it was summer when I landed.

I walked into Arrivals drowning

in Portuguese. It was easily the most afraid I'd ever been. It was as Jamar had said, one of my nightmares where I mysteriously forget how to speak. It was scary not only because I couldn't communicate, but because it stripped me of everything I thought I was. I liked to consider myself a master of words — my job had been built around perfecting them, my hobby was about stringing them into stories. Words were my identity. And suddenly I couldn't understand a single one. I was not a master of words, it turned out, but a master only of English. And here that was worth virtually nothing. I felt more isolated than I'd ever felt, and that's maybe saying a lot.

I followed the passengers exiting the plane and found my way through customs, showed my passport and visa. But when the crowd was no longer moving in a single direction I felt even more lost and I stumbled and gawked and felt the first stirrings of panic. I thought that if I could only find the ticket counter I'd book myself a seat on the next flight back to Boston.

And then I saw him. My first thought was: Mateo. That's how much alike they looked. Silly that Mateo ever joked about them not being related. He'd been watching for me and when he saw me he smiled and took off his sunglasses.

We had talked so much, so tentatively and with so much effort, on the webcam and through auto-translated IMs for so long, that when I finally saw him it felt like I was dreaming, and not just because I'd been traveling for twenty hours. When Vinicius put his arms around me I didn't know what to feel. It was so many things. Most of all I was thinking I loved him. Because he knew Mateo. Because he had those green eyes. Because I knew Caleb was going to look so much like him.

"Welcome," he said in slightly rehearsed English, and it made me feel suddenly at home in this place. "Welcome, Maker of Arrows, Fabricante de Flechas."

I rode a moto-taxi,

Vinicius on one in front of me, looking back from time to time to make sure my young driver hadn't lost his and to flash me a thumbs-up and that wide, white grin.

I stayed at the Amaral

house. Mateo's parents and aunt and uncle were friendly and gracious but I think, when they understood I had no new information about Mateo, they didn't know what to make of my presence. They treated me politely as a guest and didn't know that in some weird way I was family — and I hadn't yet fully decided to tell them or Vinicius. But I slept on the couch and woke up each morning to the cheeping of the two little birds in the cage across the room, and I felt content.

I met Tiago, who was

breathtaking and angry and wanted nothing to do with me. He did not shake my hand or even respond when I placed Mateo's ankle band into his, and he withdrew into the crowd at Colonel Fawcett's the moment Vinicius seemed willing to let him go. I think he still believed I was the reason Mateo rejected his gift of the Oliveira Bridge and returned to Boston. While I would like to believe that, I know it wasn't true. Tiago hated me and didn't understand we were so much the same.

For most of the week

it was just me and Vinicius. He took off work at the phone stand and we spent the days walking around the city. He showed me Mateo's São Paulo Facts. He showed me photos from when Mateo was a boy, pictures from Framingham and then, when Mateo was a little older, from São Paulo. He showed me some of Mateo's things and his old school books, and suggested I help myself to these. I took the dog-eared Clarice Lispector book Mateo had once mentioned, though it was a long time before I could read the words.

And finally Vinicius brought me

to the top of the Oliveira Bridge. Mateo had given him the key and he came up here from time to time, sometimes with Tiago, sometimes to make up with Aline, once or twice to get in trouble with Aline, but most often by himself. We slid aside the rumbling door and sat down.

Looking out at the looming, colorful city, I wondered why Boston. Why was Mateo drawn so much to Boston? It was the one thing I wasn't willing to take a guess at—it seemed beyond knowing, something where fiction may have been far from fact. What did Boston have that São Paulo, in all its immensity, did not? It wasn't me, as Tiago thought. It wasn't the chance to be a king, like Vinicius thought. Perhaps it was simply the place that called him home. And maybe these days I could relate to that. Maybe. Maybe yes.

Vinicius was sitting beside me, his knees drawn up and his hands clasped against his shins.

"I want to tell you the real reason I came to meet you," I said to him in English and he looked at me, perhaps catching every second word. "I think I know enough words to tell you, Vini, but I don't know nearly enough to explain it."

He pursed his lips. "Um segredo?" *A secret?*

"Sim," I said. "Um grande segredo."

He put his hand on my shoulder for encouragement and I told him, in halting Portuguese, the simple truth. I had nowhere near enough words for an explanation of it, even though he clearly was waiting for one.

"How?" he said finally.

I thought, trying to find the right words. «A lot of people,» I told him, «loved each other in a lot of different ways. So Caleb.» It was a simple explanation but it was perhaps the best one.

«An accident,» he said.

«A good accident. A happy accident.»

Always when I imagined telling him, which I'd done daily for the better part of a year, I would tell him and without hesitation he would jump up, dance a samba or something, heels slapping the floor. That was the Vini Mateo had told me about and the one I had gotten to know over the computer. I would swipe a tear or two from my eyes and he would grab my hand and pull me up with him and show me how to dance and I would dance. And, feeling for the first time my favorite word, I would think of Mateo. That's how I imagined this ending.

But instead Vini slowly stood up. Wind through the open doorway rushed between us and flapped his hair against his cheeks. He wasn't dancing, merely looking out. Above the favelas that sprawled over the land like rigid flora, the Moon was low and bright in a halo of yellow haze. I wondered if Vini was looking, as I always did when I looked at the Moon, for the sudden, wondrous appearance of one of Mateo's paintings across the face of it, big and eternal as the Sea of Tranquility. But, as always, the Moon was a blank wall, a blank page, blank save for the tiny cluster of footprints that had been there since 1969.

And that's a fact.

EPILOGUE

Facts and Fiction

There are a lot of names

for that day, none of which are very creative. But if you think about it, names for this kind of thing rarely are. When the Japanese attacked Hawaii, it was known simply as "Pearl Harbor." When Neil Armstrong made his famous first step, it was simply "the Moon landing." The day all the Facts appeared in Boston, most people call "Paint Day"—which sounds to me like one of the made-up holidays they're always celebrating at Caleb's school. The more skeptical among us refer to it simply as "the event." None of them know what to make of it, still, though by now it's a simple fact of city life. At first they thought some electrical currents during the blackout—either resulting from the blackout or caused by whatever caused the blackout—had reacted with a chemical in a particular brand of paint to melt off whatever other layers had accumulated on top of it. Perhaps that was how so many paintings overcame so many gray squares that day. That or else it was a gigantic publicity stunt by Krylon. Those theories quickly fell apart when it was discovered that the Facts could not be removed or ever painted over again. People fought against them with chemicals and sand-blasters but it was useless. Specialists were brought in to figure out what they were, research teams flocked to investigate—but it wasn't anything magical, wasn't any kind of new molecule or space-age technology. It wasn't even all the same. Some was latex. Most was various brands of aerosol spraypaint. It was just paint. Very persistent paint. They shrugged and went away and searched for other things to explain.

Two years after Paint Day, Boston's Department of Tourism launched a nationwide campaign celebrating the Massachusetts capital as "the Painted City." While somewhat controversial at first, that small action gave people permission to begin thinking of the paintings not as a pest but as a beloved celebrity. Street vendors began hawking t-shirts emblazoned with some of the most popular Facts. There are tours you can take. They're a part of Boston now — the Red Sox, the Freedom Trail, and the Facts.

Nobody calls it Beantown anymore. Or Porcupine City, for that matter.

Some people think the Facts have religious significance, that the paintings have a collective meaning beyond each piece, that their presence in Boston is evidence of... you name it. A guy with a website painstakingly marked on a satellite map of the city the location of every single known Fact. That map has become like an ink-blot test or tea leaves in the bottom of a cup: everyone has their own theory about what shape this guy's pushpins make. An animal rights group bought a giant pop-up ad on the *Globe* website making its case that the shape advocated veganism. For his part, this website guy sees it as a signal, literally a bulls-eye, which he speculates will mark a landing pad for extraterrestrial visitors. I like that one. There are a thousand other theories. Some are better than others. You can see whatever you want. You might see a horse with an elephant trunk. Me, I see Mateo. On every street, around every corner, on every wall. Everywhere. Always.

My publisher wants more sex.

"Don't we all, Lou," I say with a smirk. Lou is the woman behind the desk, my literary agent. We're in a cramped office in her South End condo. I lean forward. "I've been married three years, you know. *Don't we all.*"

She laughs. "Well. They're willing to pay for it."

"Touché. But I think there's enough."

"In a gay book there's never enough. You know that."

"Maybe they just don't recognize the sex scenes because I haven't likened genitals to any variety of fruit or vegetable."

Lou smirks. "So it's a no?"

"This one's dedicated to my son. I don't want it reading like a porno."

"How is Caleb, anyway?" Lou says. "School going well?"

I lean forward a little more and smile. "School's going lovely. And no changing the subject."

"Right."

"There's already a blowjob. Heck, there's *two* blowjobs." I put my hand against my mouth and whisper, "I even threw in a rimjob—much to Ollie's chagrin."

"All right, I'll tell them we talked about it." She jots something on a yellow legal pad and then taps the pen on the desk. "But you know, Fletcher, you're not exactly Updike. They want to publish but we don't have a super-ton of leverage here."

"If I were Updike I'd have spent more time contemplating anuses."

"The man was weirdly fixated on bums, wasn't he?"

I lean back in the chair. "I won't get weird about it. Plane tickets to São Paulo don't pay for themselves. If they want more sex I'll take another look at it—but I'm too in love with these characters to make them skeezy."

"Good enough." She smiles.

"And anyway, I don't want to be Updike, I want to be Steinbeck."

She laughs at our joke. "I'll let them know."

"So that's it? They're good to go otherwise?" I drum my fingers on her desk.

"Well, also...."

"What?"

"The ending."

"Oh boy."

"The other books in the *Surfboy Forever* series were realistic, and then this. They want to know what happens to

Govinda."

"What happens? He catches the perfect wave. His heaven wave. It says so right in the book."

"Yes, but afterward. The salt, the water. Jones finds Govinda's swimsuit and his surfboard. And then—?"

I shrug. "All I can say is the ending's based on a true story."

"A factual story?"

I don't answer. She stares at me, a small smirk on her lips. I drop my eyes and examine my folded hands. There's a flake of blue stuck under my fingernail.

"Turn around," I say finally. "Look out the window." When she obliges, I add, "What do you see?"

"Hm. A car with a parking ticket. A mailman."

"From this angle there's at least two paintings visible."

"OK, sure, two of the paintings too."

"Not even five years and you already don't see them anymore?"

"Fletcher." She can tell I'm lecturing. I tend to lecture on this topic, obliquely, careful never to reveal what I know—which I'm sure is perceived as obnoxious.

"What are they? The paintings."

"I don't know," she says. "*No one* knows."

"We live in a world where those paintings somehow exist, and they can't accept what happens to my surfer boy?"

She's looking at me again.

I put my hands on the desk and stand up, just enough to see past her out the window. Down on the street are the two paintings I knew were there. One of them had been finished in my presence—it was a stripe of green that went across his fingers that night.

"I'll add more sex," I say to Lou. "The ending stays."

I stop at the supermarket

on my way home—it seems like I'm always buying groceries—and in the produce section a woman with basket in hand is picking out summer squash.

I reach for the broccoli and we see each other and pass

between us what I'm sure is vague but mutual recognition. I know I know her but I don't know from where. I smile. She puts a squash in a clear plastic bag, twists it and drops it in her basket. She's turning and then I guess it hits her—she tilts her head and smiles and says, "Mateo's friend."

And then I remember her too. Of course. His landlady. She's wearing a floral cotton skirt with a purple streak on the thigh, as if from a stray magic marker. "Right."

"Peter?"

"Fletcher."

"Fletcher. That's right. How are you?"

"Good, good. And you?"

"Just buying our dinner." I wonder who she means by *our*, if she means Phoebe or if she's met someone.

She looks about to turn away but stops, and for a moment words catch on our lips but we don't say them.

"Well, nice seeing you," she tells me.

"You too."

She walks past the deli and I keep glancing at her as I pick out vegetables. She's looking at the baked stuff. I pick up a box of blueberries for Caleb—I heard they're some kind of miracle food and he won't get within five feet of that shitty-tasting noni juice we brought home after visiting my mom in Honduras. But I keep my eye on Marjorie. Only after she's disappeared around the corner do I regret not hugging her. I leave my cart to follow and then stop and pull it behind me, wheels squeaking as I catch up.

"Marjorie—?"

She turns, a box of breadcrumbs in each hand as though she's weighing them.

"Do you—" I stop, feeling bad for indulging in doubt. "Have you ever heard from him?"

She knows who I mean, of course. "No," she tells me. She smiles but looks sad. Just by asking her the question I've told her something too. "I was going to ask you."

"Not for years." I shake my head. "No. Not since Paint Day. He left me a voicemail that day, but—nothing since."

"No clues?"

I shake my head.

"At first I was sure he went back to Brazil," she tells me. She places one box in her basket and returns the other to the shelf. "But then his mother called me looking, and I learned he hadn't. Still, I like to imagine he found his way back there eventually."

"He didn't go back to Brazil," I say, though immediately I regret it. She closes her eyes and smiles a little smile that chastises me for cheating her of her illusion. "I've kept up with them," I add. "I've gotten pretty close with them, actually. I've been down there with my son."

"Then where?" she says. "Another city, maybe?"

I smile. "Maybe. Yeah, maybe."

"Well," she says, "if he comes back, we'll know. There'll be signs." She winks.

I still feel the inclination to hug her, but I don't. "It was nice seeing you."

"And you."

"Hey," I say, "do you know what happened with his trial? I always wondered, and he never told his family about it."

"With Sunfield?"

"Yeah. From that time he was arrested."

"There was no trial," she says. "Sunfield dropped the charges in exchange for him whitewashing the one on the outside and then doing murals in each of the girls' bedrooms."

"Really?"

"Of course, the one on the side of the building came back."

"They still can't get rid of them, can they?"

She laughs. "No. Facts are stubborn things."

Her use of the word *Facts* startles me—it's something I thought only I knew. Maybe she and Mateo were closer than he let on.

"Do you think, um— Could I buy you a coffee some time or something? I'd love to hear about, you know, *him*. If you're ever in the mood to talk about him."

She's surprised, looks down at her basket and purses her lips. "Write down your phone number," she says finally. And this makes me feel stupid—it's a brush-off, I'm sure. She isn't giving me hers.

But I tell her OK and pull a corner off the circular in the seat of the cart. She's digging in her purse and hands me a pen. I hand pen and paper back with my number on it. She tucks it in her wallet, with the kind of care that makes me suddenly sure she will use it.

When I get home I

park on the street and go around to dig the groceries out of the trunk. While I'm closing the trunk with my chin Jamar pulls up in front of me, gets out, holds out his hand and I give him half of the bags.

"I accidentally went through a red light on my way home," he says. He looks good. He wears a suit to work now, suits that have to be tailored special because of his height.

"Was it because you were in such a hurry to help with the groceries?"

"Sure. Hey, how was your thing with Lou?"

"They want more fucking and they don't like the ending."

"What do you mean they don't like the ending?" We squeeze through the front door and at the bottom of the stairs I rearrange my grip on the bags. Our apartment's on the top floor.

"They don't get it. What happens to him."

"What's to get? Your Carioca surfer boy melds with his heaven wave, Tom Joad–style. Even Caleb gets it."

"But our son's a genius." I follow him up the stairs, bags scraping the scuffed green walls. The truth is, Caleb is not a genius. He seems, so far, to our huge relief, almost totally normal.

"Well I guess you have to admit," Jamar says, "we've kind of been primed to go along with that sort of thing."

"True."

"But if they don't like it, you should keep looking. Don't change anything."

"Yeah. Hey, I ran into Mateo's old landlady at the market."

"Oh," he says, "you did?" He glances down at me from

the first landing with a look of vague worry so familiar on both of our faces when Caleb was younger but which has been in hibernation a long time. The fear eased when I co-adopted Caleb and it's eased even more with the passage of years. But in the beginning, when we were still hashing things out, making our big reveals — to Cara's parents and then Mateo's — we shared a constant fear — a terror — that one of these people would present a stronger claim to Caleb than we could, and would try to take him from us. Cara's parents posed the most credible threat, at least from a legal standpoint, but they trusted Jamar and had no desire, in their middle sixties, to begin raising another child. The bigger threat came from Mateo's side, though not necessarily from his parents: If you couldn't be an astronaut, and if your son couldn't be an astronaut, then maybe your grandson can be an astronaut. No, the biggest threat is the unknown: Mateo himself was such an unknown quantity, there's no telling when someone associated with him, however loosely, might pop up and cause trouble for us. "Like, to talk to?" Jamar says.

"Don't worry, she's got nothin'," I tell him, using our old shorthand for describing threat levels. "She knew him, that's all. When he was young. When he was new here. I'm going to get together with her sometime. Hear some stories. They'll be good to know."

"OK."

"Still get a chill, huh?"

"Heh."

"Michaela home?"

"On her way," he says.

"So who's got our kid?"

"Mr. Wade. Speaking of whom, do you think he'd look at my car tonight? My rear wheel's making a worrisome noise."

We reach the top of the stairs. The door is unlocked and we enter into the living room. The TV is showing a cartoon but there's no one watching it.

"Is that how you ran the red light?"

"Probably. I was listening to it. Hey." He splays the groceries on the kitchen table and an orange rolls out of a bag.

"I need to go get my stuff."

He leaves and our apartment is quiet except for the TV.

"Where is everybody?" I say. I drop my messenger bag on a chair and my keys in a bowl on the window sill beside a picture of Cara and me. That picture was taken soon after we moved in together that year; in the photo we're cooking. I don't remember what we were cooking, and the only visible ingredients — tomatoes and a carton of oatmeal — offer confusing clues. But I do remember her smile.

"I think I just heard somebody sneeze!" I call down the hall.

There are tons of photos around and a lot of them are of Cara. Jamar wasn't sure how much Michaela would go for that, how much his new girlfriend would appreciate being surrounded by reminders of his first wife. But she didn't mind, and it wasn't too long after he found her re-hanging one that he'd taken down, that he asked her to marry him.

That's when our little foursome grew to a fivesome. We live in Jamaica Plain now, not far from where Marjorie used to live, actually. I don't know who lives in her old place; sometimes I look up at the windows that once were Mateo's and wonder who that attic bedroom belongs to now, and whether when they look up at the ceiling they see the horse with the elephant trunk. Sometimes I wonder, but not often. It's busy having a kid.

I put the blueberries in the fridge; the yellowed domestic partnership certificate signed by Jamar and me flutters on the door. Legally speaking, it was voided first by my marriage and then again by his — but still it endures.

It's grown too, to contain us all. All of the many of us. At times the apartment gets crowded. At times it gets *too* crowded. At times there are too many voices — music, video games, laughter, the robotic chirps of Caleb's toys. Some nights after he's in bed I do slip away, out into the night for a bit of quiet freedom. In the trunk of my car I keep a backpack that clinks metallic when I slip it on. I never go far; there are enough of Mateo's pieces around our neighborhood. I paint on top of his paintings, sometimes my own designs, sometimes I just trace over his lines. It feels like spending time with him. My paint holds for a little while but always by the next morning it's nothing but flakes on the ground. Maybe there's some metaphor to be found in Mateo's paint and mine never sticking, but I don't need metaphors. I know he and I wanted two different things, that we had two different heaven spots. It didn't take me long to begin thinking of Mateo not as a missed chance but as a bridge from one life to another. If that was all he could be to me, it's come to feel like everything. That year with him was the most significant relationship of my life—for without it there would not be these others. Without Mateo I may never have found this intersection of these rooms and these lives.

"There's a sneezer in this house!" I call again.

I put away the milk and ice cream and check the rooms— the little bedroom between the two larger bedrooms is occupied. I walk in and sit down on the cartoon bedspread.

"Oi Caleb," I say.

"Oi Papa." The boy is standing in front of a big splattery mural on the wall, examining it intently, squiggling his bare toes in the thick green carpet as he ponders. He turns. His hair is strawberry blond, like Cara's, but has the loops and curls of his father's side. When he was younger he'd often been mistaken for a girl, and Jamar pushed hard to shave it off, but I resisted. Now he's starting to fill into his features.

"Who picked you up from school today?" I say, though I know the answer. He can be a little aloof at times, like Cara and Mateo both, and I like to make sure he is paying attention. "Daddy?"

"Nope. Ollie."

"Ah. Where is Ollie?"

Caleb looks around the room. "He was right here."

Then we both hear a toilet flush and we giggle.

"What do you want for supper?" I say. "And don't say macaroni and cheese."

"*Don't say macaroni and cheese.*"

"Fine, but you'll have to eat some cut-up veggies too. Boys cannot live on mac and cheese alone."

"All right."

"All right." I get up and rub the boy's hair as I walk by.

"Papa," Caleb says, holding out both arms. "Watch me."

"I'm watching, filhinho."

Where I'm standing in the doorway I feel Ollie's fingers slide across the small of my back.

"Hey babe," he says.

"Ol, come watch this," I say, and he stops and stands in the doorway beside me.

"Watching?" Caleb says.

"We're watching," Ollie says.

Caleb turns away from us back to the mural and scrunches his face in concentration. His body grows tense, as though he is waiting for a whistle-blow to start a race. He holds out his hands, little hands I've spent so much time holding. His fingertips begin running with paint — green from the left hand, blue from the right. He presses his dripping fingers against the wall, and with a smile that always reminds me of Mateo, Caleb begins to paint.

AUTHOR'S NOTE

Before starting this book in 2008 I knew very little about graffiti art or São Paulo; anything I've gotten right about either of them is the result of research and (more likely) good luck. Still, I purposely went light on descriptions of the graffiti of Mateo and his SP crew because some things are too big and bright to be captured in words (at least by me). Readers interested in knowing more about what their work looks like are encouraged to check out the magnificent book, *Graffiti Brasil*, by Tristan Manco, Lost Art and Caleb Neelon.

SPECIAL THANKS

To my crew, Heather Allison, Maggie Locher and Josh Hockenberry, for their endless support and encouragement. To Tom Hardej, for always giving his honest opinion. To Ethan Brown, just because. To all of the readers who embraced *The Cranberry Hush*. And to my family, for everything.

ABOUT THE AUTHOR

Ben Monopoli lives in Boston with his husband, Chris.

CPSIA information can be obtained
at www.ICGtesting.com
Printed in the USA
LVOW11s1546211216
518286LV00004B/688/P